RED DRAGON

AN EPIC FANTASY ROMANCE

FIRE AND FANG
BOOK 2

LINDSAY BUROKER

1

WITH A GRAND FLOURISH, THE CHAMBERLAIN SWEPT OPEN THE double doors to the royal suite, revealing a spacious receiving room, office, library, and bedroom. All signs of rubble were gone, the damaged marble tiles had been replaced, and vibrant new rugs delineated seating areas. The glass in the previously shattered windows sparkled. Even the furnishings had been painstakingly plucked and swept clean, leaving nothing to indicate that two chandeliers and half the ceiling had come down during the invasion.

"Your team has done good work." Princess Syla Moonmark, her portable writing desk clutched to her chest, half-penned letters filling it, pushed her spectacles up on her nose. She lamented that she hadn't yet had time to find her optometrist to have lenses of the proper power made.

Was he even alive? So many Garden Kingdom subjects had perished when the dragon riders had sabotaged the sky shielder and attacked Castle Island.

"Thank you, Your Highness." Bald, plump, and enthusiastic

about his work, the chamberlain bowed to her, then straightened and raised his eyebrows. "Or should I say *Your Majesty*?"

"I... don't think so." Syla winced at the reminder that her mother and four older siblings were gone, not lost by chance during the attack but because they'd been targeted by the ruthless riders. Only luck—and her aversion to family dinners at the castle—had kept her from the same fate. "I understand there's a lot of... debate on the proper succession. Or rather debate on whether the proper succession will be followed. Nobody has planned a coronation or even spoken of it to me. From what I've gathered, the only ones who want a politically naive healer to assume rule over the castle and kingdom are those who long for someone else to take responsibility for cleaning up all the messes."

"That's most people in life, Your Highness. You must assert yourself. Ensure everyone knows that you've the ability to serve, the same as your father and then your mother did."

"People have rightfully pointed out my lack of experience with governing."

"As a healer, you've certainly had experience dealing with contentious and unpleasant patients. It's the same here." The chamberlain waved airily.

"My bodyguard, who's nearing retirement age and has a lot of chronic ailments that he brings up frequently, is possibly contentious." Syla smiled over her shoulder to where Sergeant Fel —shaven-headed, tall, and muscled—loomed in the hallway a few feet away, watching her back. "Definitely surly."

"Sergeant Fel, yes. We've met." The chamberlain pursed his lips.

"I'm *at* retirement age," Fel rumbled in his bass voice, "not *near* it."

"And yet here you are." Syla smiled sadly at him.

"Many *aren't* here." He shrugged.

"Yes." Syla blinked a few times to keep her emotions from flowing to the surface. Again.

"Will you go in, Your Highness?" the chamberlain asked. "See if the suite meets with your approval."

"My?" Syla touched her chest.

Why would she have to approve of how her mother's suite looked? Oh, she would like to see order restored to the entire castle, but the entire city needed cleaning and repairs. With Mother gone... Well, there was no need to prioritize this.

"Of course, Your Highness. I trust you'll want to move in as soon as possible."

"Move in?" Syla mouthed.

To her mother's suite? Her mother hadn't been dead a full two weeks. Syla couldn't *move in* to her suite. It was presumptuous. She wasn't even sure... She sighed. Yes, she was sure her mother had passed. The identities of the bodies that had been extensively burned by dragon fire had eventually been confirmed. Aside from aunts, uncles, and cousins, Syla was alone, her future daunting.

She'd succeeded in retrieving the sky shielder from nearby Harvest Island and restoring magical protection to the heavily populated capital, but now Harvest Island was in danger, with dragons hunting prey in the forests and stormers stealing crops from the fields. Ships filled with refugees were arriving in Sky Torn Harbor every day.

"Yes, Your Highness," the chamberlain said. "Moving into the suite will not only be more comfortable and proper for you, but it'll help establish in people's minds that you *are* the legitimate heir. We don't want one of your cousins—especially not that conniving gossip Relvin—or any of the military officers taking over. Did you know that they tried to install martial law while you were gone?"

"I did."

"And did you know that Relvin is having royal wine and

candies delivered to every wealthy merchant, minor lord, and landowner who might help persuade the people that *he* should be the next ruler? Why, oh, why have you invited your relatives to the castle for a meeting? It'll simply give him a chance to snoop."

"Chamberlain Julan, I do appreciate your work here, but I can't presume to take up residence in the royal suite."

"It's not a bad idea," came a new voice from the hallway.

Aunt Tibby approached, a textbook under one arm and wearing an apron so full of tools that it was a wonder she didn't clank with each step. Bespectacled and graying, she shared Syla's determination to restore full protection to the Kingdom.

"My room is fine," Syla said.

"Your Highness," the chamberlain said, "there's a giant hole that a *dragon* ripped through the roof when it kidnapped you."

"Yes, but—"

"When the workmen attempted to clear the rubble pile from in front of the door, *more* of the roof collapsed."

"With a few slight renovations and some tidying, it'll be fine," Syla said.

"It's raining on your bed as you speak," Tibby said. "I checked there for you first."

"I've been in the library writing letters to all the island lords to assure them that we're working on our mutual problem and... Well, I can't go into much detail in them in case they're intercepted. The dragon riders are *very* actively patrolling the unprotected seas between our islands and attacking our ships."

"You should have cut Captain Vorik's throat when you had a chance," Tibby said.

Hearing his name brought to mind the steamy night that Syla had spent in a cave with him, being brought to the greatest heights of ecstasy she'd ever known.

All she said was, "I didn't have a knife the last time I saw him."

"You should have given his location to *me*," Fel said. "I always have a knife, one that would delight in severing that man's arteries."

"Was its potential delight in that ability listed as a product feature when you purchased the blade?" Syla asked.

"It was implied."

Syla shook her head. "Captain Vorik isn't the problem."

Three sets of eyebrows flew up. Even the chamberlain, who'd presumably never met the powerful dragon rider, clutched his chest in disbelief.

"He's not in charge," Syla said. "He's a military man following orders."

Unfortunately. If only she could have *truly* seduced Vorik and lured him over to their side. Instead, all she'd managed was to buy a few hours of time by rendering him unconscious, thanks to the stormers' lack of knowledge about Candles of Serenity. In the end, that few hours had been enough. Her team had gotten away with the sky shielder.

Had Vorik forgiven her for that? Since he'd been ordered to seduce *her*, her actions had seemed fair, but she had no way of knowing if he held a grudge.

"He fights with the power of a dragon, if not a *god*." Fel rubbed the back of one of his sore knees, no doubt remembering Vorik kicking him there. "That he's available to take orders and work against our people is egregious."

"We need to negotiate with the tribal leaders of the stormer people, not their captains or even their generals," Syla said.

"Negotiate?" Fel asked as all three sets of eyebrows rose again.

Tibby eyed the lap desk that Syla carried. "You didn't send letters to *them*, did you?"

"To a couple of their chiefs, yes. And I also sent a messenger to try to find the leaders of the Freeborn Faction, but I have no idea where to look for them. Even the well-established stormer tribes are hard to pin down since they move from cave camp to cave camp throughout the year to hunt and forage."

"When they're not attacking our respectable, established, and *civilized* kingdom," the chamberlain murmured.

After spending time with Vorik, who'd nearly fallen over in delight at the opportunity to pick and eat blackberries, Syla had a better understanding now of what drove the stormers, that the climate across the world had grown harsher, making it difficult to find food to feed their people. The mad storm god's creations—dragons, wyverns, gargoyles, cloud strikers, and other deadly predators—had always made it challenging to survive outside of the shields, but the stormers had previously been willing to endure those threats to keep their freedom. It was the famines that motivated their choices now. A part of her could sympathize, but a bigger part of her didn't understand why they'd chosen war—to attack and *kill* her people—rather than negotiating for protection within the shields or maybe trading for food. The stormers were *choosing* to be difficult, and she doubted anything would come of the letters she'd sent.

"Any update on the sky shielder repairs?" Syla asked Tibby, both because it was of paramount importance to the kingdom and to turn the topic from Vorik—and her relationship with him. Though she hadn't told Fel or Tibby that she'd spent a very active night with Vorik in that cave, she suspected her aunt knew. Maybe they *both* knew.

"Yes." Tibby's grimace didn't suggest it would be a *good* update, but it must have had some importance because she waved at the chamberlain in a silent request for privacy.

Julan bowed and entered the suite to turn down the bed, as if he was certain Syla wouldn't be able to resist sleeping there that night.

Tibby made the same privacy-requesting motion to Fel. He crossed his arms and didn't move. Since he'd been with them on their journey and helped push and shove the two-hundred-pound Harvest Island sky shielder to the coast for transport, he was already deeply in the know.

"He's fine," Syla said. "Go ahead, please."

Tibby sent Fel a peeved look. Her objection to him probably had more to do with the magical tractor he'd destroyed—one of her creations. Apparently, she hadn't forgiven him for that.

Fel turned toward the wall and stuck a leg out to stretch one of his calves. He *did* have a lot of old injuries that vexed him, but the gesture seemed more about pointing his butt at Tibby than a genuine need for limbering his muscles at that particular moment.

Tibby lifted her chin and turned her back on him while facing Syla. "I've copied and gone over all the scrolls I brought back. Some were in the old Temple Script, so I had to spend hours and hours in the basement of the castle library—thank the moon god that wasn't completely destroyed in the attack—to translate them. I'd like to consult with your archaeology-studying cousin Teyla on the contents, but I've got the gist. I don't believe it's possible to *repair* a sky shielder, not unless you're a god yourself and can *will* magical parts into existence, especially one that was intentionally sabotaged—no, completely *obliterated*—by those stormer animals." The glare Tibby directed at Syla suggested she had Vorik in mind again, though *he* hadn't been the one responsible for the destruction. "However, one of the scrolls, one of the most wondrous and detailed and beautifully written scrolls..." Tibby clasped her hand to her chest, adoration gleaming in her eyes. "It lists all the materials necessary to rebuild—or even build from scratch—a divine core."

"And that's... a key part?"

"It's what lies deep within the orb shell and powers a shielder. We may not be able to fix the broken shell itself, but that's not crucial for its operation. It's just protection. The divine core is what creates the translucent barrier that extends for dozens of miles to shield an island."

"The shield."

Tibby nodded. "The shield."

"That's good news, then. Assuming the materials are accessible."

Tibby issued another grimace. Ah, this was going to be the sticking point.

"According to the scroll and what I've found in the texts—" Tibby lifted the heavy tome, its pages yellowed with age, "—there are three key magical components, and they *can* be found in the world, but they are either exceedingly rare or in dangerous places. Or both. A crystalline structure that's used as the main power source grows once every ten years out of a magical substrate in one of the storm god's abandoned laboratories."

Before Syla could ask for details, two men in military uniforms came around a corner in the wide hallway. General Dolok of the Royal Fleet and Colonel Mosworth of the Royal Protectors strode toward them with determination, their gazes locked on Syla. The officers had been in and out of the castle for as long as she could remember, but they'd reported to Mother and Father and rarely interacted with her.

Syla braced herself and glanced at Fel. He'd been the one to suggest she use her healing magic on General Dolok, not only because he'd received grave wounds during the invasion but because her magic had a tendency to, at least for a time, instill within the subject a desire to obey her wishes. That didn't *always* happen, with effects differing from patient to patient. Some felt nothing but the normal amount of gratitude toward one who healed their pain. Others... Well, she'd had more than one man— and two or three women—fall madly in love with her. Fortunately, the effects faded within a few weeks to a couple of months at the most. But now... she could use some loyalty from these military men. Too bad the white-haired and mustached general with intense hawk-like eyes hadn't been noticeably affected.

"Your Highness." General Dolok saluted her curtly. *He* hadn't suggested he was interested in calling her *Your Majesty.* "A stormer ship has sailed through the barrier and into the harbor. It carries stormer military officers and riders as well as two of their chiefs. They claim to be here *under invitation* for diplomatic negotiations." There went another set of eyebrows climbing a forehead.

Was it strange that Syla was prompting that facial gesture among so many people today?

"I did send a letter to several stormer tribes with known locations." Nerves assaulted Syla's belly. She hadn't expected much, if anything, to come of those letters and certainly not so soon.

Dolok and Mosworth exchanged dear-departed-gods-we're-in-trouble looks.

"You didn't think you should *tell* one of us?" Dolok flattened a hand to his chest to indicate she should have told him specifically.

Doubting it would build their confidence in her if she admitted, *I didn't think any of them would actually show up,* Syla said, "I should have, yes. That was my mistake. I apologize."

Dolok harrumphed.

The colonel lifted his blue uniform cap and scraped his fingers through his short gray hair. "Since you invited them, I assume you want us to let them off their ship?"

Dolok shook his head. "That's a bad idea."

"Just let the chiefs off—or whoever is here to negotiate. Though I suppose they'll insist on guards too since they will be entering enemy territory." Syla hesitated. "Were you able to identify the riders?" Realizing she should be more interested in the tribal leaders, she added, "Or the chiefs and which tribes they're from?"

Vorik's face formed in her mind. And his shirtless chest.

She hurried to push the imagery away. He wouldn't have been

sent on a mission like this. For all she knew, he was in trouble. When last she'd seen him, his dragon, Agrevlari, had been attacking the black dragon of his superior officer. That hadn't been Vorik's fault—the smitten Agrevlari had been protecting the wild female dragon, Wreylith—but General Jhiton had appeared to be a humorless sort who wouldn't appreciate insubordination, whether from an officer or an officer's dragon.

"Tenilor, chief of the Moonhunt Tribe," Dolok said, "and Shi, chieftess of the Wingborn Tribe."

"With a whole snarl of stormer troops and four riders in their fingerless gloves and black leathers. Their *dragons* are soaring around above the barrier." Expression sour, Mosworth pointed toward the ceiling.

"Fortunately, thanks to the hard work and dangerous mission that Princess Syla, Sergeant Fel, and I engaged in," Aunt Tibby said, "the barrier will keep those dragons out."

The officers' dour expressions didn't change. If anything, they gave her dark why-is-this-civilian-here-and-intruding-upon-our-conversation looks.

Dolok glanced at the moon-mark on the back of Tibby's hand and didn't voice such a thought, saying only, "General Jhiton and Captain Vorik are with them."

The glare that the officers pinned on Syla kept her from smiling, but her heartbeat sped up with exhilaration at the thought of seeing Vorik again. Even if it shouldn't. He was, she reminded herself firmly, the enemy.

"Why are *they* here?" Fel snarled.

Mosworth nodded at him, approving of what was the *appropriate* response to the announcement of those names.

Dolok shrugged. "They're both from the Wingborn Tribe. It's likely Shi wanted them as protection." His eyes narrowed. "But this could all be a ruse, a chance for them to enact an odious plan." He looked at Mosworth. "Our *princess* may have given them the invitation they needed to come personally to try to finish what they started two weeks ago. Killing the rest of the Moonmarks and eliminating the shield around Castle Island."

Syla shook her head bleakly. No, her healing of General Dolok had done nothing to endear her to the man.

"Show the tribal leaders to the throne room, please, General," she said. "I'll meet with them, find out if there's a way to get them to leave our people be, and then I'll send them on their way before they can enact any odious plans."

His salute was even curter than the earlier one, and he and Mosworth pivoted on their heels and strode away, boots clacking on the marble floor.

Still bleak, Syla tried not to feel like she was completely inept and incapable of ruling a kingdom, but it was hard. What if she'd made a huge mistake?

2

CAPTAIN VORIK STOOD IN THE BOW OF THE *REGAL DRAGON*, GRIPPING the railing and keeping his face neutral as the craft sailed into Sky Torn Harbor, several Garden Kingdom military vessels escorting it. Their crewmen kept glaring over while fondling their cannons. Several were aimed directly at the wooden dragon figurehead in the bow of the dragon ship; another was cheekily targeting the curving tail that extended from the tafferel in the stern. That was more an artistic feature than a tactical one, and its destruction would merely be symbolic, but the Kingdom soldiers probably wanted to humiliate as well as retaliate.

Vorik couldn't blame them for longing to open fire, not when his people had invaded their capital so recently, delivering tremendous damage. And he'd been a part of that. Never had he believed he would be sent back to this island on a diplomatic mission.

A *supposed* diplomatic mission. That was what Vorik had been told it was, but he had his doubts. It hadn't escaped his notice that a lot of talented troops from the Sixteen Talons and also the land-based Storm Guard had been brought along.

He gave his brother and superior officer, General Jhiton, a sidelong look, wondering why the two of them had been assigned to this mission. Their tribal leaders had plenty of talented troops capable of acting as bodyguards, should they worry about the locals attempting to capture or shoot them.

Griffon-fur cloak clasped back, hands gloved, face statue-hard, and short salt-and-pepper hair riffled by the sea breeze, General Jhiton stood beside Vorik, taking in everything as the ship approached a dock. When Vorik had learned they would come along on this journey, his brother had been in the middle of planning the conquest of Harvest Island. Their people had already flown in on dragons and plundered it, taking foodstuffs that could be stored in their caves for the winter, but Jhiton wanted to completely capture and hold the island, using it as a launching point for the rest of his military goals: taking over the entire Garden Kingdom.

"Mind if we stop at the market for fruits and berries on the way up to the castle?" Vorik asked lightly.

Jhiton gazed impassively at him, though the scar on his cheek made him look mean and hard even when his expression was bland.

"If we arrived with some, Princess Syla might bake a cobbler for us." Though Vorik always maintained military decorum with his older brother in public, he wasn't that worried about bringing out Jhiton's mean hardness. Yes, Jhiton could be pushed and was utterly deadly when angered, but he'd raised Vorik after their father's death, and, despite pushing ruthlessly during training, Jhiton had never truly lost his temper with Vorik. "A *delicious* cobbler. We've got nothing like their desserts back home."

"In the aftermath of our attack, I doubt *baking* is her priority."

"Maybe she has people who bake for her now that she's... Actually, I don't quite know *what* she is. Did our intelligence say?

Has it been confirmed that all her siblings were killed? Is she the queen now?"

Vorik didn't know whether to hope for that for Syla's sake or not. During their time together, she hadn't implied she wanted the position of kingdom ruler or felt qualified to take it, but she *had* been determined to help her people and fulfill her mission, and she'd done exactly that. To his detriment and even embarrassment. He smiled ruefully.

Oh, his people didn't know the details of how Vorik had let her seduce him and knock him out with those odious candles—thankfully, even Captain Lesva hadn't been there to witness that—but having his dragon turn on Jhiton's during the battle...

Technically, it hadn't been Vorik's fault, and it wasn't unheard of for dragons—who always had their own motivations, agendas, and grudges—to turn on each other, but Jhiton and Vorik were respected leaders among their people. Having *their* dragons get into a skirmish, while their fellow officers, not to mention boatloads of gardeners, looked on... had been egregious. Vorik wouldn't have blamed his brother for demoting him or putting him in shackles for a few weeks.

Apparently, his black dragon, Ozlemar, *had* demoted Agrevlari among their internal ranks.

Since that battle, Agrevlari had been composing poetry, an ode to the beauty and magnificence of Wreylith's horns, tails, and fangs. He didn't seem full of regret.

"She is not queen," Jhiton said after a long pause. He'd been observing ranks of gray-uniformed troops marching out onto the dock with swords and crossbows. "From what our spies have gathered, she is unlikely to become so."

"I wouldn't bet on that. If she wants the position, she could claim it."

Jhiton's next look wasn't condescending, but it was... knowing. Even though Vorik had made his reports as brief as he could get away with, especially in regard to Syla, his brother was no dummy. And Lesva had seen and guessed a lot more than Vorik would have wished. *Her* reports, he'd learned, had been quite extensive and vitriol-filled. Thankfully, she hadn't been assigned to this mission.

"It's her blood right," Vorik felt compelled to explain. "And she's determined. And wily."

"Clearly. She learned quickly that she could win your loyalty by baking you a fruity dessert."

"She doesn't have my *loyalty*. I just like her."

"Especially her boobs."

"Those are nice. Gardener women are..." Vorik used his hands to sketch feminine curves in the air.

"Well fed."

"The shields have permitted them less stressful lives and the ability to cultivate agriculture, but..." Vorik shrugged. He didn't want to defend the gardeners. His ancestors had originated on the same islands, but, after choosing to leave—or being forced into exile—they and their descendants had never been allowed to return. Because of that policy, the Garden Kingdom had brought these attacks on itself. "It doesn't matter. We'll *all* have the option to be well-fed soon. We've already packed away a lot of food for the winter."

"Yes." Jhiton looked toward the sky. "Does the wild dragon Wreylith always come when the princess calls?"

"I don't know." Vorik had answered variations of the question before. Since Wreylith, who'd shown up with allies as well as her sex appeal, had been pivotal in turning the tide in their battle with the Kingdom ships, Jhiton understandably wanted to know if they would have to deal with her again when around Syla.

"Is she in the area now?" Jhiton's eyes narrowed, as if Wreylith showing up today might affect something.

"You're as likely to know that as I." Vorik waved toward the dragons flying high above. Their kind could sense each other from a much farther distance than even magically enhanced humans and would be the ones to relay if any enemies approached.

"I thought your love-smitten dragon might be keeping a close eye on her."

"It doesn't sound like she wants his eyes on her."

"Odd."

"*He* thinks so."

Jhiton clasped his hands behind his back. "If you wish, speak to your princess when we arrive. Take her aside for a private talk. Or more. Whatever might allow you to draw out useful intelligence."

"Are you ordering me to seduce her again?"

That wouldn't work; Syla had never fallen for Vorik's lies, and she would be suspicious of any overture he made toward her, especially when he was with his people. That knowledge didn't keep his groin from perking at the thought of another night with her. Or even a hasty rendezvous while the diplomatic talks went on nearby. An image of pulling her into a castle closet filled him with the desire to move islands to ensure such a moment happened.

"Spend your time together however you wish." Jhiton tilted his palm toward the sky, toward Agrevlari and the other dragons flying above the translucent barrier. "Perhaps you can convince her that our chiefs are more open to negotiating for the *peace treaty* that she suggested than they'll let on. If she were to offer to give our people half the islands in the Kingdom, maybe they *would* be open to it."

"We do have the military advantage right now," Vorik said. "The Kingdom should be willing to offer *something* to get us out of their skies."

Despite failing to obtain the Harvest Island shielder, the stormers had destroyed one of the ancient artifacts and killed many of the moon-marked royals with the ability to activate them. They'd also done a great deal of damage to the capital city.

"Yes," Jhiton said. "In exchange, perhaps our chiefs would agree not to attack the other islands, to leave them for the Kingdom populace."

"*You* want them all."

Vorik watched his brother's stony face and thought of the son he'd lost. Jebrosh. Because of his hunger one winter, Jebrosh had taken a dangerous risk, and he'd fallen and died. But that wasn't all of the pain Jhiton had endured, thanks to the harsh environment they lived in. Before Jebrosh, four other babes had been stillborn or lost during the pregnancy. He'd never said he blamed the gardeners for that, or for his wife leaving him after Jebrosh's death, but Vorik had heard Jhiton curse the mad storm god and the world he'd left.

"I do, but I am in charge only of the Sixteen Talons, not our people as a whole." Jhiton tilted his head toward the tribal leaders who'd come out on deck, twelve black-clad stormer warriors flanking them.

Chieftess Shi lifted a finger toward Jhiton.

He inclined his head toward her and started that way.

"General?" Vorik asked.

Jhiton paused and looked back.

"If you don't believe Princess Syla will be made queen, then why would it matter what I can convince her of?"

Jhiton smiled cryptically. "Don't think too hard about this, Vorik."

When his brother walked away, Vorik faced the railing again. He looked forward to seeing Syla but worried he would inadvertently betray her again. More, it concerned him that Jhiton had a plan and wasn't confiding in him about it. Had Vorik lost some of his brother's trust? That bothered him a great deal, and, as much as he would like seeing Syla again, he believed it would have been better if they hadn't been sent along on this mission.

Nerves tangled in Syla's belly as she readied herself to meet the tribal leaders from the stormer delegation. The tribal leaders and *Vorik*.

What role would he play? Bodyguard? Would a high-ranking military officer have been brought along for such? And General Jhiton too? According to Sergeant Fel, he commanded the entire Sixteen Talons, working hand-in-hand with General Amalia, who led the Storm Guard. Militarily, they were equals, but she apparently deferred to him. Jhiton, especially, wouldn't be along as someone's bodyguard.

Someone knocked on the door to the room Syla had claimed —not the royal suite but a guest room down the hall, one with the roof intact. Before she reached the door, Aunt Tibby opened it and stepped in.

Looming outside, Sergeant Fel waited to escort Syla to the throne room, where she was *not* expected. While she'd been putting on an elegant dress and winding her auburn locks into an artistic bun, hoping to appear regal or at least more mature than her twenty-six years, General Dolok had sent a messenger to tell her that the military would handle the stormer delegation. He'd suggested she remain somewhere safe and out of the way. Of course, she was going to ignore that idea. Fel, who'd come to know her well these past weeks, hadn't implied he would enforce the general's suggestion.

"Here you are." Tibby yawned and laid one half of a slightly magical antique summoner on a desk.

Intended for healers to use on their patients, ensuring they didn't have medical emergencies that went untended, it was a half-moon that hooked over one's ear and looked like simple jewelry.

"Thank you," Syla said. "The linked piece is on the shielder?"

"In the tunnel outside, tucked into cracked mortar on the hidden door to its chamber. I figured you'd want to be alerted as soon as that opened. That would give you more time, before anything is done to the shielder, to get down there. Or send *troops* down there while you remain safely up here." Tibby raised frank eyebrows.

"Of course, that's the plan if anything happens." Syla smiled and hooked the antique over her left ear.

Tibby squinted suspiciously at her, then turned the squint on Fel.

He hadn't been filled in on what the magical antique did, but he squinted back at Tibby, always game to return her suspicious glowers.

"Per your request," Tibby said to Syla, "I also brought magical explosives from my workshop at the farm."

"Oh, good. And they're in the shielder chamber?" Syla had requested booby traps while envisioning trip wires and rabbit snares but wasn't surprised her engineer aunt had opted for *explosives*.

"Camouflaged and stuck to the shielder itself."

"Er, that wouldn't damage *it*, would it?"

"They'll blow outward if they're impacted. But let's hope for the sake of certainty that the shielder remains undisturbed while the stormers are here." Tibby yawned again. Day and night, she'd been studying the artifact, scrolls, and however many books she'd lugged out of the library basement. "I'm surprised your cousin Teyla isn't here yet. I'd like to consult her about the scrolls. You said she's coming, right?"

"I invited my relatives who live outside of the capital to come as soon as possible, yes. As for the threat the stormers represent... We've got the known tunnel entrances guarded and the secret harbor entrance sealed—*collapsed*, is the word Colonel Mosworth used—so I also hope the shielder won't be disturbed. It makes me nervous, however, that we haven't moved it yet. The stormers *know* where it is."

The problem was that Syla didn't know where to move the shielder *to*. They would have to come up with a new secret and safe location, and she didn't know if that should be under the castle, perhaps with new tunnels being excavated, or somewhere more distant. She objected to a location as remote as the chamber on Harvest Island, with nobody nearby to keep an eye on things. Further, the secret door, activated by a moon-mark, would also have to be moved. Was that possible? It *had* to be. Aunt Tibby would have to research how that might be done. As far as Syla knew, the doors had been created by the gods, the same as the shielders.

"Assuming you don't let Captain Vorik carry you down to that tunnel," Tibby said, "they don't have anyone with a moon-mark to open the door to its chamber. Magic, as well as brick, insulates that room. Firing a cannon at the door wouldn't open it—and our military men would notice if the delegation attempted to enter the castle with a cannon."

"I would hope so. As for the other, I'm not going to let Vorik carry me anywhere." Perhaps prompted by the words, an image of him sweeping her into his arms and taking her to a bed came to mind. Judging by Tibby's eyebrow twitch, a similar thought might have come to her. "Especially not with the rest of his delegation watching," Syla added, though maybe she shouldn't have said anything else.

"If you take him off somewhere private," Fel surprised her by saying, "you might get more information from him than you would from any of the rest of them."

"You think he'll tell me deep military secrets? Or whether his people are up to something besides *negotiating*?"

"He might avoid looking you in the eye when you ask if they are." Fel shrugged.

"Because he cares for me and would feel bad about lying?" Syla might believe that herself—Vorik had admitted as much when they'd spent the night together—but it surprised her that *Fel* would believe it. He'd made it clear that he not only believed Vorik was a loathsome enemy but that he'd been lying to and using her all along. And, pesky developments of feelings aside, Fel hadn't truly been wrong about that.

Aunt Tibby watched Fel curiously. Wondering what his response would be?

"I don't know about *feelings*," Fel said gruffly, as if such piffling things weren't worth considering, "but, of all the stormers on that boat, he's most likely to answer your questions. Or evade your probes." Fel gazed out a window that overlooked the courtyard and the castle gate. "There's their delegation now. With a ridiculously large military escort."

Syla's nerves returned with a vengeance. "They're up to something."

"Of *course* they are," Fel said.

"We'd better hurry if we're going to be a part of the negotiations that we arranged." Wearing a beige and white dress with a belt that accented the curves of her hips and breasts, Syla stepped into the hallway. The ankle-length garment didn't show much skin, but she hoped it would flatter her more than a thick blue healer's robe, the last thing Vorik had seen her in.

Even before Fel had made the suggestion, she'd been thinking she might learn more if she could draw Vorik aside. She didn't know how strong his feelings were for her after she'd tricked him and gotten away with the shielder, but he *would* be the most likely stormer to answer her questions. Besides, she wanted to speak with him again to find out... Well, it shouldn't matter what he thought, but she'd enjoyed their night together more than any other she'd spent with a man, and she longed to believe there was hope for them to be cordial with each other going forward.

"I'm going to get some rest in the room the chamberlain gave me. I'll leave the intelligence gathering and negotiating to you, but send Teyla by whenever she arrives." Tibby yawned and waved for Syla and Fel to head to the throne room on their own.

"Thank you for all the work you're doing on figuring out how to fix the broken shielder," Syla said.

"As you pointed out, we must. There's nobody else left who can."

"Yes."

3

SYLA WALKED BESIDE FEL THROUGH THE PRIVATE BACK OF THE KEEP to the more public rooms up front, including dining, meeting, and gathering halls, as well as quarters for the island lords and ladies and their entourages when they visited. She decided she wouldn't offer rooms to the stormers, though that was the traditional way to treat diplomats. Most likely, they would be more comfortable sleeping on their ship or leaving entirely after this meeting. General Dolok would *definitely* be more comfortable with them sleeping on their ship.

He and Colonel Mosworth were in the throne room when Syla arrived, along with two dozen blue-uniformed Royal Protectors with crossbows strapped across their backs and swords belted at their hips. They stood formally along the walls, backs straight and hands on the hilts of those swords as they watched the grand front entrance with hard eyes. After what the castle and city had endured at the hands of the stormers, the troops had to be seething inside.

After what *Syla* had endured, she should have been seething too, but she was too wrung out for that. For the last two weeks, she'd been living in a state of being overwhelmed, daunted, and worried. Other than a few private moments when she'd let herself weep, shout, and throw things, she'd barely had time to mourn, not when there was so much to do to secure the Kingdom and protect her people.

Judging by the cool squint that Dolok turned on her, he would prefer that she *not* take on that responsibility. Leave it to the military, he'd suggested more than once. Maybe with himself as the ruler over the Kingdom? He hadn't voiced that ambition, but he kept making it clear that he didn't believe *she* was qualified.

As Syla and Fel walked in, male and female servers approached with trays, offering snacks and drinks. She lifted a hand, not wanting to have her mouth full of anything when the tribal leaders walked in. They, too, would be judging her. Perhaps seeking to take advantage of her inexperience and naivety.

"They're in the keep," a castle page whispered from the entrance.

Syla ignored the empty throne but started toward the long blue rug that led to it from the doorway, intending to face the visitors as they entered. Her step faltered when she spotted her cousin, Relvin.

Dressed in black hose and a thigh-length green tunic with silver lace—doubtless the latest fashion—he was speaking with Colonel Mosworth while waving a slender-fingered hand with four bejeweled rings glinting in the sunlight that flowed through the windows. Just visible through his shoulder-length blond hair, a pencil perched behind one of his ears. It and a small notepad protruding from a tunic pocket reminded everyone of his job as the editor for the *Kingdom Journal*. In addition to monitoring which stories were printed, he wrote a column that covered political situations and economic concerns on the various islands.

Even though she'd sent messengers around Castle Island to gather her cousins, nephews, nieces, aunts, and uncles, Syla was surprised to see Relvin in the throne room. How had he learned so quickly about the diplomatic party? An hour ago, *she* hadn't even known the stormers would come.

"Good afternoon, Relvin," Syla said when he left the colonel and approached her. "I'm glad the messengers found you. Did Teyla come with you?" That was his sister and the cousin she liked much more than he. "Aunt Tibby is looking for her."

"She did. We came down from the estate at Lake Ferringtar together early this morning. But we stopped to have breakfast before coming to the castle, and she disappeared in the historical district near the harbor. I can't imagine *what* drew her eye, as everything is in shambles, and it's terribly dangerous in that area. *Especially* now." Relvin pulled his pencil from behind his ear and stabbed it toward the open double doors, moving shadows in the hallway promising the stormers and their escort would walk in at any moment. "But you know Teyla. Any vaguely intriguing historical find or old map of an ancient civilization in an obscure corner of the world will send her veering off to investigate."

Yes, and that was *why* she liked Teyla most among her cousins. Syla could relate, even if her interests skewed more medical than anthropological.

"Was there any trouble up at the lake?" Syla asked instead of commenting on the rest.

Relvin and Teyla had apartments in the capital but had departed, along with many others, especially those wealthy enough to have homes elsewhere, the night of the invasion. Despite Teyla's occasional fencing lessons, the two siblings weren't combatants, and Syla didn't blame them. Still, so many people had been injured and needed help in the aftermath that it would have been better if more people had stayed to assist.

"Thank the sun god, the lake estate was left alone, but it's terribly boring up there, so I was relieved to return once the sky shield was back in place. Though if I'd known *stormers* would be invited here, and so soon after they *murdered* the royal family, I might not have come so promptly to your summons."

"Maybe you'll get a story for the newspaper at least," Syla murmured, her tone distracted.

Her visitors were walking in, following an escort of Royal Protectors. The stormer entourage included a number of fit warriors in fur-trimmed Storm Guard chain mail as well as riders in black leathers with fingerless gloves that hid whether or not they had dragon tattoos on the backs of their hands. Such tattoos indicated a bond to a dragon and magical ability that included greater-than-normal strength, stamina, and agility.

Right away, Syla's gaze locked on Vorik, who walked without any signs of the many injuries he'd received during their journey. He hadn't let her use her magic to heal him, only stitching and bandaging his wounds, but it didn't matter. He'd healed fully in the past two weeks.

Even before she'd seen the bare back of his hand—and the green-dragon tattoo there—she'd known he was bonded to Agrevlari. His emerald eyes emanated power. *All* of him did, from his compact muscular frame to his angular face, his prominent cheekbones almost harsh. Most of the riders had faces like that, the leanness pronounced, a testament to the hard lives they led and the lack of abundance when it came to food. None of them looked gaunt or frail—not in the least—but they did not carry any extra fat that would have softened their visages.

Vorik also spotted Syla promptly, their gazes meeting across the long throne room. While the rest of the stormers were stone-faced, the corners of his mouth twitched, and his eyes glinted with warmth.

Even though they hadn't exchanged words, relief filled her with the certainty that he didn't hold that night against her. She started to smile at him but caught the glowers of the military men around her and also noticed the cold eyes of the rider walking beside Vorik. General Jhiton.

Syla had seen him during the sea battle where Wreylith, the red dragon, had come to her defense, but only from afar. Thanks to her old spectacles, he'd been a lean blur atop his black dragon. Now, as he approached, she could see his stone jaw, straight nose, flinty green eyes, and a scar that cut diagonally across his nose and cheek. Whether it had been delivered by sword or talon, she didn't know, but it had come close to taking his eye.

Though Jhiton shared a similar if harder look to Vorik, it took her a moment to remember they were brothers. Their green eyes were so different, ice-cold versus warm, and she'd seen Vorik grinning in delight at eating blackberry cobbler. She couldn't imagine Jhiton grinning under any circumstances.

"Chief Tenilor of the Moonhunt Tribe," the herald announced. "And Chieftess Shi of the Wingborn Tribe." He looked toward Dolok and Mosworth, then toward Syla. Shifting nervously, and probably not knowing who would speak with the tribal leaders, he didn't announce any of them.

"I am General Dolok." The officer brushed past Syla and strode forward with Mosworth at his side. Cousin Relvin had stepped back to observe from the protection of the marble throne. "Though you have established yourselves as our enemies, for this day, you are granted an abeyance and access to this room in the castle."

Syla grimaced at the undiplomatic greeting—and the fact that she'd been so busy gaping at Jhiton and Vorik that she'd barely noticed the stormer leaders. Unlike the dark clothing of their military men and women, the chieftess and chief wore colorfully dyed garments made from fur, scale, and feathers, indicative of the prey their people hunted. Bone bracelets clacked on the woman's wrists, and her male counterpart wore decorative trinkets as well, including an ivory collar. They carried swords in scabbards on their backs, the blades likely made from magical gargoyle bone. From what Syla had read, only those who succeeded in slaying their own gargoyle, and acquiring bones for the crafting, bore such weapons. Since stormers only became tribe leaders by beating others in duels, she suspected Tenilor and Shi had defeated numerous gargoyles. Likely, every stormer in the room had.

Syla walked forward to stand beside Dolok. He hadn't introduced her—or anyone else—so she would have to be assertive if she didn't want to be ignored.

"We go where we wish," Chieftess Shi said after exchanging looks with Tenilor. She focused on Dolok instead of looking at Syla. "We have come here because we received an invitation suggesting your kingdom is willing to give away some of your islands in exchange for the cessation of attacks from our people and our dragon allies."

Dolok's eyebrows flew up, and he swung a glare onto Syla. Well, at least someone was acknowledging her.

"I am Princess Syla Moonmark, and I am the one who sent a letter to you." She raised her chin and did her best to look self-confident and regal, though that had always come much more easily to her mother and sisters. She preferred a quiet room in the temple, healing people and avoiding public attention. Surprisingly, as she willed her back straight and her fortitude to show itself, a tingle of power came from the quarter-moon birthmark on the back of her hand and ran through her nerves to her entire body. "I am certain I did not in my letters offer up any of our *islands*, but I invited you to come and state what you seek to obtain from your attacks in case there is a possibility that we might be willing to barter and reach an agreement *without* further deaths. On either side."

"There have been no deaths on *our* side," one of the riders muttered with a scoff.

Jhiton looked at him, and the man snapped his mouth shut.

Vorik clasped his hands behind his back, watching Syla and his leaders while, she had no doubt, maintaining awareness of every potential enemy—and probably even chairs and vases—in the throne room.

"We've recovered from our initial surprise and are even now preparing a potent military offensive that you might find detrimental to your people." Syla lifted a finger to scratch her jaw while showing off the moon-mark. Was it glowing faintly silver? Usually, it only did that when she was healing someone and needed to draw upon a great deal of her power.

The chief's and chieftess's eyebrows arched in skepticism.

"*Very* detrimental," General Dolok said, though Syla hadn't spoken to him of military matters beyond securing the tunnels below the castle and had no idea if he had plans to do more than defend the islands.

"Will these potent offensive attacks involve your people leaving the protection of the shields the gods made for you?" Chief Tenilor asked.

"We've gathered much intelligence on where your people's cave camps are and when in the year you live in each," Mosworth said.

"Impressive," Shi said, "considering that your people never leave your islands except to scurry quickly across the sea between them, with your tails between your legs, fearing a dragon will flick a smoking nostril in your direction."

Syla lowered her hand. They'd probably noticed the glow but been underwhelmed by it and her power. They would know she was merely a healer, and they didn't seem to respect her people in the least. Unfortunately, she didn't know how to earn that respect by standing there tossing insults back and forth. Too bad none of them had arrived with venomous basilisk fangs stuck in their hands that she could have removed.

"We have all that we need here," Syla said before Dolok, who had steam wafting from his ears, could speak again. "More than we need. I understand food is scarce on the mainlands and other islands, places not protected from predators by the shields and where the climates were not magically modulated by the gods before they left."

"There is enough out there to sustain people strong enough to obtain it and protect it," Shi said.

From what Vorik had said, that wasn't as true as it had once been.

"Then why are you stealing our crops from Harvest Island as we speak?" Syla asked.

"We are *stealing* nothing," Chief Tenilor said. "The dragons are hunting there because they enjoy the prey that lives there."

"You're taking fruit, grains, and vegetables from the cultivated fields, orchards, and bog lands that our people work hard on throughout the year to ensure we have plentiful harvests."

"Work *hard*." Tenilor scoffed. "You gardeners haven't the faintest idea what it is like to work while you forever watch the sky for predators who'll kill you in seconds if you let your guard down. When those predators strike, you must drop what you're doing and grab your weapons to defend yourself against foes with all the power the mad god could infuse into them because it amused him to do so."

"Our people work very hard, I assure you." Syla groped for something else to bring up, something that might intrigue them and get past their desire to throw insults, but the chiefs' choice to do so made her believe they hadn't come because they wanted to negotiate. What *did* they want? She looked at Vorik, but he was keeping his face neutral now and didn't signal her in any way. As Fel had suggested, she would have to get him away from his people before he might reveal something. "As I said, we often have a food surplus. In the past, the Kingdom has decreed that trade with stormers is forbidden and illegal for our people, so it's existed only when skirting the law. Since the world is changing, we must be willing to change. We would be open to trading some of our food to you in exchange for the goods you make, the pelts you procure, and the valuable medicinal plants you forage from around the world and that are useful to our people."

"We're not giving them *food*," Dolok snapped without bothering to add *Your Highness* or any sign that he respected Syla. "Like godder zealots leaving out offerings on their knees in the hope that the deities will return one day."

Syla gritted her teeth, more annoyed with him than with the stormers. Why couldn't he make a show of being on her side, at least in front of them? Even if he didn't support her, they needed to put up a united front.

"We have food that we could spare." Syla smiled and reached out to pat Dolok on the shoulder, letting her hand linger and hoping that if she treated him like an ally—perhaps one she was disagreeing with at the moment—the stormers wouldn't believe them divided. "Were we to receive something in return, such as the cessation of hostilities you mentioned, we might also be talked into sharing some of our recipes or sending a few pies and cobblers along with the more practical staples."

When she glanced at Vorik, she caught a wistful expression on his face.

"What's a cobbler?" one of the younger Storm Guard troops whispered.

"A dessert," Vorik murmured over his shoulder to the man. "Sugary and sweet with juices that run down your chin."

General Jhiton looked at him with a quelling glare, the same as he'd given the other rider. Vorik grinned back at him, licked his lips, and rolled his eyes skyward. The glare hardened. Vorik sighed slightly and returned a neutral expression to his face, though he slipped in a wink toward Syla.

Warmth spread through her, and for some reason, it pleased her that Vorik's cold general couldn't quash his personality.

"*Cobbler?*" Dolok whispered harshly. Incredulously? "This isn't a negotiation. It's a farce. Princess." He reached up to push her wrist away. "You lack experience. Let *me* handle this."

Not wanting to be shoved away, Syla tightened her grip on his shoulder to keep it in place and looked him in the eye, willing her power to influence him. Even if her magic hadn't bound him in any way, wasn't it possible he felt some shred of loyalty or gratefulness to her for healing him? He'd had so many broken bones, it had looked like he'd fallen off a cliff.

"General, please be open to this discussion." A zing of power flowed from her hand, down her arm, and into him. His eyes widened with surprise. It surprised her as well. She hadn't hurt him—she was sure of that—but merely shared magical energy. And maybe a touch of a warning? "It is our current relationship with the stormers that has prompted them to attack. Something must change. We must be open to bartering."

"Bartering an *island*, not a dessert," Chieftess Shi said.

"Multiple islands," Chief Tenilor added.

Seething, General Dolok lifted a hand, as if he would shove Syla away, but he must have thought better of that. Instead, he stepped back, which prompted her hand to fall. She let it, wondering if she'd imagined the zing she'd believed she'd shared with him. Though she could feel her magic tingling within her, she'd never learned to do more than heal with it.

No, that wasn't true. In the past weeks, she'd managed to use it to hold on to a dragon, and she'd wrapped it around a captor's heart, making him feel pain, enough that he'd released her. She could do more than heal, but she didn't want to threaten or harm her own military officers, especially not with stormers watching on.

But maybe she'd affected him in a small way because Dolok

frowned and looked at her hand, the moon-mark still glowing a slight silver. A disturbed furrow creased his brow.

"We will not give up any *islands*," Mosworth snapped when Dolok didn't. "If that is what you came here to demand, you might as well leave now."

Syla expected the stormers to agree and walk out, but the chieftess and chief glanced at each other, then looked at General Jhiton.

"Chief, Chieftess," Jhiton said, his voice similar to Vorik's baritone but cooler and clipped, "we might gain ground if I could speak with General Dolok and the other military leaders and properly convey the wisdom of working with us instead of against us. And Chieftess Shi might have a similar discussion with their female leader." Jhiton tilted his head toward Syla without looking at her.

"Because we will naturally bond by discussing *female* matters?" Shi asked dryly. "Should I inquire about cycle lengths for gardeners and their methods of managing their menses?"

Syla's jaw drooped in surprise, but she did think she would get further by speaking to one of their leaders in private. So many of their responses, vitriol included, seemed for show. Maybe the chiefs felt they had to remain strong in front of their troops. Syla would, however, prefer to speak with *Vorik*. And not about menses management.

"If that would facilitate the acquisition of several islands for our people," Jhiton said, deadpan, "it might be a worthwhile topic."

"I have no interest in discussing that or other topics with a gardener female," Shi said. "Send your brother to apply his tongue to her."

If Syla had been shocked by the woman's comments before, she almost fell over at that one. Belatedly, she realized Shi had to mean the tongue application would refer to *words*, not anything... physical.

"Hasn't he a reputation for charming women?" Shi added.

"He does," Jhiton said.

Vorik's eyebrows had drifted up. Had he not been told they would send him off with Syla? She certainly hadn't expected it. She'd *longed* for it, but she hadn't known how she might make it happen without rousing suspicion, both among her people and his.

"General Jhiton. The colonel and I will speak with you." Dolok extended a hand toward a table along one side of the room while flicking his other hand in dismissal toward Syla and then Vorik. "Woo her if you wish, Captain, but she doesn't have the authority to give away islands. *Or* cobblers."

"There will be no wooing. There may be cobblers." Syla looked defiantly at Dolok, but he'd already turned his back on her, waving for Mosworth and Jhiton to follow him.

Vorik smiled slightly, but he masked his face again when Jhiton looked at him before strolling after Dolok. Was there some significance in that look they exchanged?

As Syla watched them, she couldn't tell for certain, but her instincts told her this had been premeditated. For some reason, the stormers *wanted* Vorik to speak with Syla.

That worried her but not so much that she didn't wave for him to follow her toward a private window in the back of the throne room. She would have preferred to take him to another room, but that would make tongues wag. They could speak quietly at the window.

Fel walked at her side, a reminder that she might not be able to arrange an *entirely* private meeting.

Her cousin watched as Syla and Vorik passed, and took out his pencil again. To write down notes that would be turned into a newspaper column the next day?

Before settling at the table with the other officers, General Dolok glowered darkly at Syla and Vorik. His eyes suspicious, he looked like he wanted to put an end to their conversation before it started. Then his gaze shifted toward the portraits of the royal family high on the wall opposite the windows, lingering on the one of Syla's older sister, Venia.

With a flash of insight that rocked her, Syla realized why Dolok hadn't wanted her here or involved with anything important. He had to have figured out that Venia had been the one responsible for the original Castle Island shielder being destroyed and the protective barrier dropping. As Syla had herself learned, her sister had been romantically involved with a stormer spy, one who'd used her to get to the shielder chamber and destroy the precious artifact inside. Venia had paid for that mistake with her life, but as Dolok watched Syla with Vorik, he had to worry that she would also allow herself to be seduced and beguiled, to inadvertently betray her people.

No, Syla would not do that, but she now understood the general's concern. She would do her best to ensure he and the other officers who knew of Venia's betrayal wouldn't have a reason to think Syla was a liability, but she feared that she had a lot to prove if she wanted them to trust her.

4

THE WINDOW IN THE BACK OF THE THRONE ROOM OVERLOOKED A fountain in the courtyard, a past king raising a hoe and a sword as he stood upon a sphere depicting the full moon. Two weeks earlier, as much blood as water had filled the pool surrounding that marble moon, and bodies ravaged by scavenging wyverns had been draped around the fountain. Syla couldn't let herself forget what the stormers had done—how many they'd killed. And she couldn't forget that the man who stood beside her, his hands clasped behind his back, had been a part of that invasion.

Vorik hadn't yet spoken, merely stopping to gaze out the window with her, but his face softened when she looked at him, her eyes doubtless full of questions.

Before speaking, Vorik glanced back at Fel, the only protector who'd followed Syla across the throne room, though numerous soldiers remained along the walls, and a server wandered nearby with a tray of beverages. Was he someone's spy? Maybe so.

"I shall find it difficult to woo you with so many ill-tempered generals lurking in the area." Vorik tilted his head toward the table where Dolok and Mosworth had settled on one side and Jhiton opposite. Numerous of their soldiers stood behind them as the two parties faced each other.

"*Generals*?" Syla asked to emphasize the plural. "Is your brother ill-tempered?"

"Usually, quite." Vorik smiled, his back to the room as he faced her, the expression for her alone.

Fel stood far enough back to give them a modicum of privacy. He had been the one, after all, to suggest this plan.

"If you can't woo me, you've no hope of getting islands out of me," she said.

"You know I'm here for the cobbler."

"I know you'd *like* a cobbler. I doubt that's why you're here." Syla gazed into his eyes, inviting an explanation.

Why *had* the dragon riders been brought along? And what did the tribal leaders truly want? Since they'd barely acknowledged her, she doubted they'd come because she'd invited them to negotiate. If anything, they were using her invitation as an opportunity, but to do what?

Vorik spread his arms, as if he didn't know why he was there. Syla doubted that, but she wasn't surprised he wouldn't tell her. Since she'd learned without a doubt that he had nothing to do with the Freeborn Faction, he'd stopped trying to pretend he was anything but a loyal stormer, his older brother's dutiful soldier. She couldn't fault him for that, but she wished things could be different.

Syla lifted a finger to wave the server to them. He'd been around the castle for years, and she managed to dredge his name from memory.

"Rodderen, isn't it?"

He blinked in surprise. "Yes, Your Highness."

"Please go to the kitchen, and see what's in the pantry. If there are fresh baked goods, have them wrapped up so that we may send them along with the stormers. As a sign of goodwill and a desire to foster something besides hostility." Syla needn't have explained her reasoning to the server, but she wasn't accustomed to giving orders and expecting to be obeyed. At the temple, she'd been treated as an equal among her colleagues. Further, she was reluctant to test her power in the castle and find out that the staff wouldn't obey.

"Ah." The server looked at Vorik, then bowed and backed away. "Yes, Your Highness."

"Do you think the rest of my people will be as easily won over as I was by a cobbler?" Vorik rested a hand on his chest.

"That would be nice—it's fortunate that the castle baker survived the massacre because she makes *excellent* desserts."

Vorik grimaced at the word *massacre* but didn't try to absolve himself of having been involved, nor did he suggest that it was a melodramatic word for what his people had done. It wasn't.

"I also wanted to send the server away. I think he's someone's spy." Syla looked toward Relvin, but there were, as she'd already gotten the gist, many people with their eyes on the throne. With a chill, she recalled the now dead Sergeant Tunnok from Harvest Island proposing to her on behalf of his eighty-year-old father and suggesting that if the old man couldn't get her with child, he would gladly step in.

"Your position here is tenuous," Vorik said, more of a statement than a question.

She needed to get intelligence from him, not the other way around, but it sounded like he could already tell that. "For now. I wasn't in anyone's plans."

"Are you intending to insert yourself into their plans?" Vorik looked at the back of her hand, though the birthmark had stopped glowing.

"Is that your way of asking if I'm going to attempt to arrange my coronation?"

"More or less." Vorik looked her up and down. Assessing her

physical fitness and presentation to determine if it was suitable for a monarch?

Maybe not. His gaze lingered briefly on her chest. He might simply have their past liaison in mind.

Syla had a thousand things besides *sex* to worry about, but her body heated under his gaze, a tingle that had nothing to do with magical power flowing through her.

"I haven't decided," she said. "I would have to gather allies and probably win the support of the populace. Since I've *healed* a number of our local people, the latter might not be that hard, but most of my allies are fellow healers. We're not an overly martial sort."

"You'd have the power to acquit yourself against formidable enemies if you wished." Vorik smiled, gazing into her eyes now.

Oh, that was nice. Not only the smile but the encouragement and belief behind it. What she'd done to earn it, she didn't know, but she wished she could lean on him—*trust* him—because she dearly needed someone supportive. Right now, beyond those healer colleagues that had survived the destruction of Moon Watch Temple, she had Sergeant Fel and Aunt Tibby and not many more.

"Captain Lesva was vehemently irked that you didn't give up your secrets to her when she attempted to extract them from you," Vorik added.

"You mean when she tortured me?" By the eyes of the moon, that had been an excruciatingly painful hour that had seemed like an entire night. The only good part had been that the interrogation had been delivered through magic that hadn't maimed and disfigured her the way physical torture would have, and it had been within her ability to heal the damage that it *had* done. Mostly. More than once, she'd woken from nightmares, that woman's hard face inches from hers. Mental traumas were never as easy to heal.

"Yes," Vorik said quietly, all humor gone from his face. "I regret that I didn't find you in time to keep that from passing."

"I'm happy that you came at all when you had... another mission. Your captain was frustrated. I think she might have killed me eventually."

"She would have passed out from your odious candles before then, I'm certain." His eyebrows twitched, the only indication that he might resent the tiniest bit that she'd caused *him* to pass out.

"Candles of Serenity aren't odious. They're magnificent."

Vorik snorted. "How did *you* refrain from losing consciousness as well?"

"We use them in the temples often to sedate patients undergoing surgery. Most healers build up an immunity to the vapors over time."

"Ah. It was clever of you, then, to bring them."

Syla didn't think her impulsive decision to stuff them in her backpack had been brilliant, but she didn't wave away the compliment. If he thought her clever, maybe he would be less inclined to try to trick her again. Though it was likely he was doing that right now. He must have been sent over here by his people to extract information from her.

"How did you convince Wreylith to come to your aid for a third time?" Vorik asked. "She couldn't have needed more healing salve."

Speaking of extracting information...

"I'll answer that question for you if you tell me why your chiefs accepted my invitation when they have no plans to negotiate." Syla crossed her arms over her chest and waited to see if he would deny that.

Vorik's face turned wry. "I wasn't told."

That wasn't the answer she'd expected. "You weren't told why you were coming?"

"General Jhiton ordered me and the others along to guard our leaders."

"I thought... Well, you're reputed to be your general's trusted right-hand man."

"I hope that's still true. You may have noticed that our plan to get the Harvest Island shielder didn't turn out that well, and my dragon had something to do with that."

"Because of his love for Wreylith?"

"It moved him to make an inappropriate choice."

"Love can do that."

"Indeed." His eyebrows twitched again. Why was that expression so appealing?

Syla had the urge to step closer to him, to rest a hand on his chest, to gaze up into his eyes, and to part her lips for a kiss. But even if they had been alone in the throne room, she couldn't have. He was the enemy.

"For my curiosity only, you'll not tell me how you lured Wreylith into helping you?" Vorik asked. "She was pivotal."

"If I answer, will you tell your people?"

He started to shake his head.

She added, "What if your brother asks?"

Vorik paused and looked out the window thoughtfully. Then he sighed. "If he asked, I would tell him. And he *did* ask after the battle. He wanted to know why, by all the cursed minions of the storm god, the wild red dragon involved herself. Not only that, but she called *other* dragons to help."

"Yes, she did. It was glorious."

"For *you*."

"Yes. It was even more glorious when your dragon bit your general's dragon in the ass."

"It was the left flank, and I should glower at you for delighting in what was quite embarrassing to me."

"Glower all you wish. I'm having a painting commissioned."

Vorik laughed softly and stepped closer, lifting a hand, as if he would take her in an embrace. Her body wanted that, even if her mind was wary of him, and she leaned toward him. But he looked over his shoulder toward the rest of the throne room and kept his place, dropping his arm.

The chief and chieftess and numerous of their entourage had disappeared, but many of the military men remained, the officers still negotiating, or whatever they were doing, at the table. Dolok's face was red. Things probably weren't going his way. Jhiton was impassive, impossible to read. He didn't glance over when Vorik looked back, but it didn't matter. Jhiton had already arranged for Vorik to speak with Syla.

To what end? To find out if Wreylith would come again to aid Syla if the stormers attacked? Or something more?

"We'll cede no ground to you." Dolok pushed his chair back, the legs screeching on the floor. His words were, for the first time, loud enough for Syla to hear from across the room. "No islands. And you'd better get your people off Harvest Island. We've almost got that shielder repaired, and those people will be protected again soon."

If only that were true. Syla needed to speak with Tibby to get more details on those components she'd mentioned.

Whatever Jhiton's response was to the outburst, it was too quiet for Syla to hear, but he remained calm, seated with his fingers threaded and unperturbed that Dolok loomed from across the table.

"If you've no better offers than that to make," Dolok said, "you can get in your ship and leave. The next time it appears in our harbor, we'll fill it with cannonballs."

"As long as you are aware that we'll have a similar stance toward the ships that *leave* your harbor," Jhiton said. "Any of your harbors. It would behoove you to negotiate."

"It would behoove you not to be bullies."

"I wonder if Wreylith will appear to guard your ships," Vorik mused, gazing thoughtfully at Syla instead of watching the officers at the table.

Though the red dragon had returned the figurine that could be used to communicate with her, Syla had no delusions about Wreylith coming to her assistance again. She wouldn't randomly defend Garden Kingdom ships, regardless, nor would she want the Harvest Island shielder to be repaired. Wreylith and the other wild dragons were *enjoying* hunting the apparently delicious elioks that lived there. Since they were wild and elusive, Syla had never had the meat, so couldn't speak to their taste.

Aware of Vorik watching her and waiting for a response, she said, "I believe she adores me now and can't wait to drive enemies away from our ships."

A laughable notion, but Syla would be smart to feed Vorik false information instead of truthfully answering all his questions. She should be the one getting information from him. That was how spying worked, wasn't it?

"That seems unlikely, given her stance on humans in general," Vorik mused. "I do wonder if she might drive enemies away from whatever ship you were on."

"Are you and your people planning to target my ship if I go on a journey?"

"If it involves you taking a repaired shielder to the unprotected island, they might."

"Because your goals are still to destroy all of the shielders and leave every island unprotected? Captain Lesva suggested that." The woman who'd tortured her probably wasn't a reliable source, but, given the circumstances, Syla had deemed her more likely to be telling the truth than Vorik.

"Plans are in flux."

A vague answer that she could have guessed. She didn't have experience interrogating people and didn't know how to fish information from his depths. He was as wary with her as she with him —maybe more so.

Syla sighed and leaned on the windowsill, gazing out at the fountain. The sun had disappeared behind clouds as it sank toward the horizon, evening creeping over the island.

"I don't suppose you'd like to spend this time with me talking about inane and unimportant things?" Syla asked.

Vorik smiled sadly, looking like he understood the reason for her request. Maybe he even regretted trying to finagle information from her.

"I *would* like that actually. Do you... How are you doing? I know this will sound hypocritical, given who I am and what my people are doing, but I regret that you've lost so much. I've lost family myself and understand how hard it is, but I can't fathom what it would be like to lose everyone at once."

His words and sympathetic tone brought her emotions to the surface, tears threatening as her throat tightened. She shook her head, realizing she should have kept the talk political rather than personal. This was more dangerous. She'd cried in front of Vorik before—and he'd held and comforted her—but she couldn't do that here. She dared not let Dolok see her being friendly toward him in any way, and she also didn't want to break down in front of the general or anyone else in the room.

Blinking to keep the tears from falling, Syla stiffened her spine, tightened her grip on the sill. "It is difficult, yes."

Vorik, perhaps realizing that he was making things *more* difficult rather than less, lifted an apologetic hand.

"Who have you lost?" she asked, not trusting her voice—her emotions—if he asked more questions. Better and safer to ask them of him.

"My mother when I was little, and my father when I was slightly less little. When I was about twenty, I lost a brother who was between Jhiton and me in age. He was also training to be a dragon rider, but neither of us had mounts of our own yet. We sought to prove ourselves in a sea hunt that would bring in a great deal of meat for the tribe's winter stores. We risked seeking the great tusked seals in the Strait of Tempest's Torment. The name isn't melodramatic. It's a deadly area when a storm comes up. And, as we learned, cloud strikers also like to hunt the seals there. That day, they hunted us. We defeated them, but they put us off our course, and when a storm came up, it hurled our craft against the rocks and destroyed it. I lost my brother and almost my own life as well. Jhiton came on his dragon and found me. We searched all over for our brother, but he must have drowned. It's been ten years, so if he'd survived, he would have found a way home by now."

"I'm sorry." Syla had heard of the strait and the seals, but, other than a few brave explorers and hunters who went out more for sport than necessity, her people didn't seek out such creatures, not when they could hunt and fish from their safe islands. Since the shields did not deflect rain and wind, the islands weren't immune to storms, but the weather was less dangerous than at sea.

"You needn't be, but thank you."

"Have you lost, uhm. Were you ever married?" Syla blinked when she realized he could be married now, and she wouldn't know it. The stormers didn't wear rings or outward symbols to indicate they were wed. "Or *are* you married?"

"I'm not, no. My brother wouldn't ask me to seduce a woman on a mission if that would require me being unfaithful to a wife. Our people aren't always monogamous, but that's something couples figure out, and he's always been, or, ah, *was* a believer of that." Vorik waved, as if to dismiss a topic he hadn't meant to bring up.

It occurred to Syla that getting information about General

Jhiton and what motivated him might be more useful than asking Vorik about himself.

"Did *he* lose a wife?" she asked.

Vorik grimaced and glanced back. Not comfortable sharing anything about his brother without permission?

The officers had left the table, however, and Syla didn't see Jhiton. Actually, she didn't see *anyone* in that area and looked around in surprise. Sergeant Fel remained, watching her back as always, but the officers and all their military men had departed. A couple of castle staff and a single soldier in a Royal Protector uniform stood near a door, keeping an eye on Vorik. As if *that* would be a sufficient enough force to handle a dragon rider if he attacked her. Did General Dolok *hope* that would happen and that he could be rid of the last Moonmark child? And what were his men doing? Were all the stormers being escorted back to their ship? The negotiations, such as they'd been, considered complete?

Syla looked at Fel, wondering if he thought it odd that they'd essentially been left alone. He widened his eyes toward Vorik.

What, did he want her to ask more prying questions—more militarily *pertinent* questions? She thought inquiring about what motivated the general in charge of the Sixteen Talons was pertinent.

"His wife lives." Vorik's tone was a little puzzled. As attentive as he was, he must have noticed his people leaving, but maybe he hadn't expected to find so few of *hers* remaining. His gaze was curious when he looked thoughtfully back to her, but he continued to answer her question. "They are no longer together, however."

"They divorced?"

"Perhaps not formally, as that's not a common practice among our people. For that matter, we don't have marriages that are as elaborate and full of ceremony as yours. A couple merely bonds in their own way and then informs the tribe. But they... after their only living son passed, it was difficult for both of them. His wife returned to the tribe into which she was born, and Jhiton threw himself into his duties."

"Like planning a war?"

Vorik spread his hand, as if to say that was information he couldn't divulge. Of course not.

"What can we talk about that's safe?" Syla whispered, not wanting him to go but wondering if he would stay if there was no chance of gaining intelligence.

She removed her spectacles and rubbed at her temple, a headache creeping into her. Her neck and shoulder muscles were tense, as well, but she could hardly complain if those were the worst of her maladies, not when so many had lost so much more. Some had lost everything.

She swallowed and looked away, wishing she weren't always on the verge of tears, but in the aftermath of all the atrocities, it had to be normal.

"You could give me the ingredients for making one of your cobblers," Vorik offered. "Or is that a matter of kingdom security?"

"I don't know. Would having that information encourage your people to attack more of our islands to gain greater access to berries?" She wished it were a joke.

A troubled expression in Vorik's eyes suggested he did too. "You look like you could use a neck rub."

"Are you offering?"

"I would, but..." He gazed at the castle staff, any of whom might spread gossip if they touched.

Normally, *gossip* wouldn't trouble Syla, but these were different times. Everyone from generals to relatives to lords and ladies she'd never met were scrutinizing her.

"Your people might object," Vorik finished.

"Yes."

He cocked his head. "Would *you* object?"

"I should." But she wouldn't. She was relieved he was speaking with her after she'd tricked him. Many men, she believed, would not want to spend time with a woman who'd gotten the best of them. Had their situations been reversed, she didn't know if she could have forgiven him. "But I'm so often tense that I'd be foolish to reject neck rubs from anyone. If a cane with a capable bent offered one, I would have to take it."

"That's an interesting image."

As she lifted her spectacles to return them to her face, Vorik raised a hand.

"May I hold those for a moment?"

Though puzzled, she handed them to him. Maybe he wanted to look through the lenses and see what it was like? She was on the verge of explaining how the corrective power would hurt his keen-sighted eyes, but he merely lowered them to his side and nodded to her. Thanks to her blurry eyesight, she almost missed the gesture.

"If you focus on your peripheral vision rather than what's straight ahead, it may help you relax. Especially if you make it a regular practice."

"You mean the vague blurry stuff to the left and right?" Syla waved to suggest what she saw.

"And up and down. If it helps, it's a little blurry for everyone. Or at least less sharp. Especially out here." He snapped his fingers near his ear. "But if you're able to be aware of what's to the left and right and above and below, instead of being focused on what you're looking at, it means your body is in a calmer state. By shifting your awareness to the periphery, you may be able to *guide* your body into a calmer state."

Syla eyed him—or rather, his blurry form—skeptically. "I'm a healer, and I've read hundreds, if not thousands of books on all aspects of the body, and I've not encountered anything about that."

"Do your people know everything there is to know about the body?"

Syla resisted the urge to say they knew more than *his* people. Her instinct was to look down upon the stormers because most didn't read or write—and because they'd savagely attacked and killed so many of her people. But she admitted that having an oral tradition didn't mean they were less intelligent, just that they had less stored knowledge in the form of books.

"Not necessarily." Syla attempted to smooth the skeptical expression from her face and focus on the blurry curtain to one side and the even blurrier Sergeant Fel looming a dozen paces away.

"Have you tried to heal your eyes? Is that possible?"

"I looked into it and read everything we have on the subject of optometry, but myopia, which is what I have, isn't an injury or disease, so you can't cure it the way you might stitch a wound or help the body fight off a flu. It's usually a result of an elongation over time of the eyeball, which causes light to focus in front of the retina instead of directly on it, and that makes the vision blurry."

Vorik considered that with a thoughtful expression. What a strange thing to be discussing with one's enemy. But it was safe, she admitted. They weren't divulging any secrets, unless the axial length of the eyeballs of kingdom subjects might determine their capabilities at firing cannons. Fortunately, most of the men who went into the military weren't that prone to myopia.

"That ailment is rare among my people," Vorik said. "Even our elders don't usually have much trouble."

"You're clearly a genetically superior people." Syla shifted slightly to move what was visible in her peripheral vision. She couldn't tell if it was doing anything to calm her down. Maybe one had to be able to see more than blurs.

"We are not that many generations removed from being the *same* people."

"I know. I was being sarcastic. I don't think you're superior."

"No?" Vorik raised his eyebrows and touched his chest.

"*You* with your dragon magic might be."

"Yes," he said agreeably. "What causes the elongation of the eyeball?"

"There's some debate, since not everyone who seems like they would be a candidate becomes myopic, but we think those most at risk are the people who spend a lot of time reading or focused for hours at a time on other near work. I've read voraciously since I was three, and I got my first spectacles at seven or eight."

"At three, I was running around, looking into the sky for dragons and dreaming of flying on them."

"The eyes are supposedly most relaxed when looking into the distance. You'll probably never develop myopia."

"I also challenged my older brothers to duels with sticks."

"That sounds like a way to *lose* an eye."

"It is. That's a more common injury among our people." Vorik offered her the spectacles back. "Perhaps, in addition to spending time relaxing your eyes and being aware of your periphery, you should focus more on the distance."

It amused her that he seemed to take it for granted that she would take his advice on the peripheral viewing. Maybe she *would* try it now and then, when she wasn't busy helping defend her kingdom from invaders—or defending herself from plotters.

"I bet you get all kinds of practice looking into the distance," Syla said. "I should be like you and spend time riding a dragon."

"*Yes*. Agrevlari would be happy to carry you on his back."

"If you're also there?" She put her spectacles back on. "With your arms around me?"

"Yes." His eyelids drooped. Now that he was no longer blurry, she had no trouble interpreting that look and recalled discussing riding dragons together in a rather aroused and somewhat frenetic manner when they'd been about to have sex.

Her body heated at the memory.

"It might be better for me to ride Wreylith," she murmured.

"Is that likely to happen again?"

"Ah, we've left the safe topic and turned back to discussing advantages and disadvantages."

Vorik inclined his head, his mouth quirking with sad acknowledgment. "You could try juggling."

"Pardon?"

"That wouldn't help distance vision, but it's good for the periphery. You can't focus on all the balls at once, but you can *see* them all if you are calm and aware of what's around you." He tapped the side of his eye.

"I can barely catch one ball that someone warns me they're going to throw," Syla said, an automatic protest, though she appreciated that he'd been willing to veer back to the safe topic.

"All the more reason to learn a skill that improves your ability to throw and catch. Would you be open to learning?"

"Would I have a charming and handsome instructor with gifted hands?"

His eyelids drooped again. "*Very* gifted hands."

Syla opened her mouth, but a boom came from the direction of the harbor.

"Was that a cannon?" Syla leaned as close to the window as she could, her spectacles clunking against the glass as she tried to peer in that direction. The courtyard walls were being rebuilt, however, and there were no gaps through which she might see toward the ocean. The harbor was below the bluff on which the castle perched, regardless.

Fel rushed forward, reaching for her as he came shoulder to shoulder with them.

"I'm not planning to jump out the window," she told him.

"It wouldn't be the first time you escaped that way." Fel didn't grip her arm, but he *did* loom close.

"If you're referring to when Wreylith absconded with me, it was more of a kidnapping than an escape, and it was through the roof, not the window."

He gave her a dour look.

"Fireworks." Vorik had leaned close to the window from her other side and pointed at a narrow red blaze that streaked into view against the darkening sky.

"We don't have any celebrations planned," Syla said. The solstice festival had taken place well before the invasion, and there was certainly nothing to celebrate now.

"It's Night of the Hatchling," Vorik said. "A celebration time for our people."

"Night of the Hatchling?" Syla eyed him.

What kind of holiday was that?

"Dragon eggs take a long time to mature enough for the babies to come forth. They lay them in the spring, but this is the time of year when they'll hatch. Since they've been bonding with us, we've started to celebrate their birth, the potential for future allies to join our people."

Fel also squinted suspiciously at him. "Are you saying *your* people are lighting fireworks off from their ship?"

Several additional booms sounded, strong enough to make the floor thrum underneath them, and two more flares streaked into view over the harbor, one red and one orange. The unsettling colors reminded Syla of dragon fire.

"I wasn't aware that they planned to do so," Vorik said, "but it's possible one of the chiefs ordered it as... Well, I wouldn't say it's part of their negotiating strategy, but they may want to signal that they're not cowed by your forces surrounding their ship."

"How would they be cowed when your *dragons* are surrounding our island?" Syla shook her head, finding it hard to believe either of those chiefs had thought loosing fireworks in an enemy harbor was a good idea.

Shouts came from men on the courtyard walls, several pointing toward the edge of the bluff. From their elevated positions, they would have a good view and a better idea of what was going on.

More fireworks streaked across the sky, this time from a more distant origination point.

"Those had to have been lit from beyond the barrier and out to sea." Syla looked at Vorik again.

"We do have more ships out there. There were concerns about letting our leaders enter when our dragons can't fly in to help if there's a problem."

Another boom, which seemed closer and stronger, coursed through the bluff.

"What are your people up to, Vorik?" Syla peered into his eyes, certain he knew something. He was a high-ranking military officer, not a first-year soldier who wasn't told anything.

"I'm not certain, but..."

"They're plotting *something*," she said with certainty.

"Likely so."

"There were no fireworks to accompany that last boom." Fel was watching the sky.

Syla backed from the window. "It's a distraction." She pointed at Vorik. "And so are you."

Everything had been, she decided, realization thunking into place like a key turning in a lock. That farce of a negotiations party... The stormers had never intended to negotiate.

Vorik gazed back at her without playing ignorant or denying it. Maybe he didn't know exactly what his people were up to, but he wasn't surprised by her statement.

"That did cross my mind," he admitted. "I almost shared the thought with you, but... my loyalty is to my people. You are... complicated."

"You're complicated too."

"No, I'm simple. Feed me berry cobblers, and I'll faithfully entertain you in bed."

"But not shift your loyalties."

"That's more difficult."

"It takes more cobblers."

"Many more, yes. I'm afraid more than you have." Vorik shook his head sadly.

Another boom sounded, a faint tremble going through the floor. The floor or the entire bluff?

"Private," Syla called to the lone Royal Protector in the room. "Find Colonel Mosworth or General Dolok. Tell them to get men into the tunnels under the castle." Eyeing Vorik, she added, "I think there are stormers down there."

"Yes, Your Highness." The man jogged out.

A buzz came from the summoner on Syla's earlobe, and she cursed. "There are *definitely* stormers down there. And they're after the shielder."

Both shielders were down there, the working one they'd brought from Harvest Island and the original, broken but awaiting repair. Damn it, if the stormers got back into the chamber and destroyed everything, that would leave *two* islands undefended.

"You ordered the tunnels sealed," Fel reminded her.

"I know, but they found a way in. They're down there with explosives using their *fireworks* to try to cover up the noise." Syla gave Vorik an exasperated look, then started for the exit.

Since the summoner had buzzed, that meant the door was already being disturbed, maybe *opened* with stormers scant feet from the shielders. The castle troops wouldn't know where to look. She had to go down there herself.

Fel lifted a hand to stop her.

She darted to go around him. "Come with me, Sergeant. We'll go together. I need to—"

Vorik glided close and caught her by the arm. "Don't go down there."

In an instant, her exasperation turned to anger. "You want me to let your people destroy another shielder? I can't do that, Vorik."

"Let go of her." Fel jerked his mace free and moved around Syla to give himself space to swing at Vorik.

"It is for your safety that I tell you not to go, Syla." Vorik raised a hand to defend against Fel if he needed but didn't yet draw a weapon. "If my people *are* down there and that's their intent, they'll need you to get into that chamber. If you walk down there, you'll give yourself to them. Let your troops handle this, and stay safe in your castle."

Though his mace was poised to swing, Fel didn't strike. Maybe he agreed with Vorik's argument.

But the summoner told Syla that the chamber had already been disturbed. Maybe the stormers had found someone else with a moon-mark to drag down there to open the door. She looked around, realizing it had been some time since she'd seen her cousin Relvin.

"They're already in," she said grimly.

Outside, fireworks continued to boom and blaze in the sky. Syla nodded to Fel that she wanted to join the troops in the tunnels. They had to. They had to stop the stormers before they destroyed another shielder.

When she stepped away from Vorik, he tightened his grip.

"Let me go!" Syla roared at him and almost ordered Fel to take his swing. But she'd witnessed Vorik disarming her bodyguard and driving him to his knees not once but twice. Fel wasn't a match for Vorik, and she didn't want him to be hurt. Or worse.

Vorik hesitated, his eyes grave. Maybe he genuinely wanted to protect her—if he didn't, he would let her go—but he ultimately released her and stepped back.

She raced for the door, aware of how far into the tunnels she had to run and how close the shielder was to the hidden chamber door. She might already be too late.

As Syla ran into the castle hallways, she glanced up frequently, as if she might see or sense the shield dropping and dragons once more coming to invade. She half-expected to spot Vorik following them, but he was either still in the throne room or he'd gone to reunite with his people.

The loyal Sergeant Fel chased after her, following Syla through the halls to the theater, the closest access point to the tunnels, the one they'd used two weeks earlier when they'd been too late to stop the sabotage.

She couldn't be too late this time. Her people were depending on her.

5

VORIK WATCHED SYLA AND HER BODYGUARD RACE OUT OF THE throne room, then trotted after them before he'd fully decided that he should follow her. No, that he *would* follow her. He doubted he *should*. Jhiton would have told him about the plan if he'd wanted Vorik involved. That he didn't... disturbed Vorik. It spoke of a lack of trust, at least when it came to something involving Syla. He *hoped* he hadn't lost his brother's trust in general.

There weren't too many uniformed guards in the halls, men who would object to a dragon rider in black leather jogging through the castle, but there *were* staff. Numerous men and women with cleaning implements or carrying laundry spotted Vorik and skittered back in alarm or ran, shouting for guards. Vorik gave them cheerful waves and kept going, not wanting to lose Syla. Intelligence reports promised the way he'd gotten into the tunnels below the castle before had been blocked and that the lagoon was no longer accessible. He needed to enter by the same means as Syla.

Rounding a corner, he almost ran into the server that she'd

sent for desserts. The man was returning with cylindrical boxes that smelled of sweets, their tantalizing aromas wafting in the air. Frosting? Berries? Both?

Vorik darted around the man and directed his nose back into a forward position, telling himself that desserts weren't the priority. Making sure Syla didn't walk into a trap was.

As he knew from his previous incursion into the tunnels, it would take someone with a magical moon-mark on his or her hand to open the doorway to the shielder chamber. Vorik had spotted a blond man about his age in the throne room who'd had such a mark—some relative of Syla's—but doubted Jhiton had been aware of the person ahead of time to include him in the plan. More likely, laying a trap was exactly what Jhiton, or whoever he'd put in charge of the mission, was doing. Luring Syla down so that she could be forced to open the door. With a dagger to her throat?

Vorik shook his head, irritation and exasperation creeping into him. That the generals and chiefs were scheming to bring down more shields and expose more islands didn't surprise him, but he didn't know why their plans kept involving *attacking* the royal family. Jhiton had better not be planning to put an end to Syla. It worried Vorik that his brother might be considering it and that was why he hadn't said anything to him.

"You, stormer!" A guard that had been standing duty down a stub of a hallway spotted Vorik as he jogged past.

Ahead of him, two more men in blue uniforms rushed toward him from the direction Syla had gone. Had she sent them to deter Vorik? He'd been staying far enough back that he'd believed she wouldn't see him, but she might have anyway.

Though he didn't want to fight, both because it would delay him and he didn't desire to cause trouble when he hadn't been ordered to do so, Vorik had little choice. Before the invasion, he'd memorized a map of the castle put together by stormer spies, but that would do no good when he didn't know Syla's destination.

Grim but determined, he rushed straight at the men. They drew swords.

Vorik didn't pull his own out, instead angling left, toward the man who appeared less lithe and formidable, and leaped for what was likely his weaker side since he carried his blade in his right hand. The guard lunged at him, sword leading, as his comrade tried to flank Vorik.

Though the men appeared competent, they weren't as fast as the riders that Vorik trained with. He ducked and dodged slashes, shifting so that one man blocked the other's attacks, then knocked his foe's sword arm to the side, following with a heel strike to the jaw.

The guard's head snapped back. His comrade grabbed him and tried to push him aside, but Vorik had the power of dragon magic surging through his veins, giving him greater speed than they had. He kicked the man, knocking him back into the wall, then punched the first guard as he struggled to recover. With three more kicks and a head butt, he'd driven them both against the wall, one's knees buckling. Vorik grabbed their wrists, twisted hard enough to make them gasp and open their fingers, and took their swords. After delivering two more blows that would ideally daze them for a few moments, he continued on.

Though he'd escaped the guards, shouts elsewhere in the castle promised more would show up. Worse, the delay had allowed Syla and Fel to escape his sight.

Vorik hurried in the direction they'd been going. He tossed the guards' swords into an open room that he passed, then ran down a carpeted hall toward an intersection ahead. There, he would have to guess which way Syla had gone. Or so he thought. When he reached an open door to his right, a sign labeling the cavernous room inside as a theater, he spotted movement.

Fel crouched atop a stage at the far end, a trapdoor open, and a lantern in his hand. Syla had already disappeared through the door—or so Vorik assumed—and Fel descended after her.

As Vorik ran down an aisle between rows of seats, the trapdoor thudded shut. He leaped lightly onto the stage and opened it as another door, this one set into the flagstone floor underneath, also shut. He dropped down and pulled an iron ring, debating how he would convince Syla to let him remain with her, but the ring didn't budge. A tingle of forbidding magic buzzed against his palm, and he released it. Did this door also require someone with a moon-mark to open it? Might another type of magic do? Or break the seal defending the door? He knew, since his people had tried before, that only a moon-mark would allow one into the shielder chamber, but he sensed this was a simpler magic.

Vorik drew his gargoyle-blade sword from his scabbard.

I sense Wreylith, Agrevlari spoke into Vorik's mind from beyond the Castle Island barrier. *I believe she has been hunting on the Island of Eliok, but she is flying in this direction.*

Vorik slid his sword into the gap between the trapdoor and its frame, the magical gargoyle blade as slender and fine as any crafted from steel. *Have you lured her with poetry? Or perhaps your masculine magnificence?*

I do hope that latter is having an effect, and she's realized what a loyal, wonderful, and devoted mate I could be. I have not attempted to recite poetry to her, but I've little skill with languages. You have written ballads about dragons. Perhaps you could help me compose something.

We can try later, but she'd probably be more touched by something that came from you.

She is coming directly this way. Perhaps my allure is drawing her.

Vorik doubted that. Thus far, the red dragon hadn't been interested in Agrevlari's attempts to woo her. Was it possible that Syla had once again called Wreylith? And the dragon was *coming*? As long as the shield was up, Wreylith wouldn't be a threat to whatever Jhiton was doing under the castle, but if the general succeeded in *dropping* the shield...

Well, his black dragon as well as those of the other riders who'd come along were out there. As strong a fighter as Wreylith was, she wouldn't be a match for so many. Unless she'd brought allies again. And unless Agrevlari defended her against his *own* allies again.

Vorik growled at the situation, fearing his people had underestimated Syla. Worse, the trapdoor didn't budge as he tried to find a way through it with his sword. Frustrated, he jammed it all around the frame, trying to find and break a lock or the hinges.

Something snapped under his strength and the power of his sword, but its defensive magic flashed like lightning, and a startling shock blasted up his blade. It struck him, knocking him back, and he hit his head on the low wooden stage above. He managed to twist and land in a crouch instead of flat on his back, but he felt chagrined that such a minor defense was thwarting him. He was a dragon rider, damn it. Strong, powerful, and with magic gifted to him through his bond with the even stronger and more powerful Agrevlari.

What rhymes with love? his dragon asked.

Vorik grabbed his sword and patted around the trapdoor, aware of shouts in the castle, maybe in the theater. Did the guards know about this access point to the tunnels? Syla had ordered troops into the underground passageways before, so the entrances couldn't be that secret.

Ah, he'd broken one of the hinges. Risking more magical ire from the trapdoor, Vorik jammed his sword into a second one.

Vorik? Agrevlari prompted.

Yes, I'm still here. The second hinge snapped without putting up a fuss. Maybe Vorik had broken the magical defense.

Love?

I'm a little busy right now. Vorik hefted the heavy stone trapdoor and moved it aside, then ran down dark stairs. *Glove,* he offered.

Syla and Fel hadn't lit any of the lanterns mounted along the way, but that suited Vorik. He could see in all but pitch darkness, and even then, he navigated decently, thanks to his magical senses.

Really, Vorik. As you might imagine, gloves are of little interest to dragons.

There aren't that many words that rhyme with love. Vorik reached the bottom and heard voices down the tunnel he entered. And in the distance, a *lot* more voices sounded. Stormers? Castle troops? Both?

Fel and Syla were already out of sight. Vorik hurried forward, senses outstretched so that he wouldn't run obliviously into someone else skulking around without a light.

Dove, Vorik offered as he ran.

I did consider that, but those birds are so tiny as to be insignificant to a dragon. Too small to make even a bite-sized snack. You'd need a whole flock to comprise an appetizer.

Most poems about love don't involve eating *doves.* Vorik passed an intersection lit with a lantern and sensed that he wasn't alone. Syla? No, there was someone else nearby. Someone quiet and deadly and dangerous. One of his people? A more talented Royal Protector than he'd run into so far?

Those are poems written by humans for humans, Agrevlari said.

Try shove. Or above. Do you know where Jhiton is? Or Temur or Frandal? Vorik added, naming the other riders who'd come along on the dragon ship, though it was possible the stormers who'd sneaked into the tunnels to set explosives and try to reach the shielder had arrived in another vessel or swum in unnoticed from beyond the barrier.

I may be able to work with above. You would have to speak with Ozlemar about your brother's location.

You can't check with him? Vorik passed quickly through the lantern light at the intersection, not wanting whoever lurked nearby to spot him. *I don't have any way to reach out telepathically.*

Ozlemar is currently irked with me. The approach of Wreylith will remind him of that.

Moving slowly since he heard troops in the tunnel now, in addition to the other threat he'd sensed, Vorik turned toward the shielder chamber. His toe brushed against rubble on the floor. A lot of rubble. He caught the scent of spent black powder in the air. The gardeners may have sealed this tunnel, but his people had blown it open.

Lanterns came into view ahead, several castle troops heading straight toward him. He eased near the wall so that his silhouette wouldn't be visible in front of the light of the lantern of the intersection behind him.

"They're down here," one man snarled. "We'll find them."

How had Syla and Fel evaded the troops? Or had Syla seen them but commanded them to let her continue on her own? Vorik hadn't yet figured out how in charge she was. The general hadn't bowed to her, but the staff had. And, of course, her bodyguard remained faithful.

Vorik started to back away, but two stormers stepped into the lit intersection behind him. The soldiers spotted them, one barking an order to charge.

Caught in the middle, Vorik would have to reveal himself, joining his side. Or...

He glanced up at the arched ceiling, then sprang, twisting in the air as he thrust his legs and hands out. His boots caught one side of the wall as his fingers pressed into the other. He spider-walked himself up into the shadows as the soldiers ran past underneath him.

Clangs sounded as they engaged with the stormers. Vorik's people were outnumbered, and he debated dropping down to join them, evening the odds by attacking the soldiers from behind, but a feminine gasp sounded in the distance. More clangs followed it, originating in the same place. The shielder chamber lay in that direction.

Vorik scooted farther along the ceiling to get away from the skirmish, then dropped and ran toward where the gasp had come from. He rounded a bend, where a couple of lanterns on the walls had been lit, and glimpsed a chamber at the far end of the tunnel. From his previous trip, he knew that it was one of several below the castle that held sarcophagi and that the hidden passageway opened from a side wall before the tunnel reached the chamber.

That passageway stood open, silver light similar to moonlight flowing out. The sounds of a fight, metal striking metal—or maybe gargoyle-bone blade—came from beyond the secret door, but someone already lay crumpled on the ground. Sandaled feet and the hem of a dress stuck out of the passageway. The person wasn't moving.

"Syla?" Vorik whispered, fear and concern surging through him.

What had she been wearing on her feet? He didn't remember. He'd looked her up and down but had been distracted by the curves of her body and hadn't paid attention to her footwear. She *had* been wearing a dress.

Forgetting to be quiet and wary, that other threats were in the tunnels, Vorik sprinted toward the fallen woman. He doubted Jhiton would have killed her, not while they needed her moonmark, but one of his subordinates, not realizing her value, might have made that mistake.

He'd almost reached the hidden passageway when someone in black leather strode out of the burial chamber at the end of the tunnel. Jhiton. Two riders walked behind him, all three men with swords drawn as they strode with determination toward the hidden doorway.

Vorik slowed, confused about where they'd come from. That burial chamber was a dead-end, wasn't it?

Only when shadows moved behind Jhiton and the other two men—Lieutenants Garblon and Hix—did Vorik spot a hole that had been blown into the wall between two tombs. That was how his people had gotten into the tunnel system this time.

Though Vorik was still confused, because his sense of direction promised they weren't anywhere near the bluff, he didn't have time to ask about the excavation. Face set with determination, Jhiton didn't hesitate when he spotted Vorik. With his twin swords in hand, he strode straight into the tunnel and toward the shielder chamber.

6

SYLA DUCKED OUT OF THE WAY AS FEL BATTLED ONE OF THE TWO stormers they'd found when they rushed past her crumpled cousin, Teyla, and into the shielder chamber. There hadn't been time to check if Teyla was dead or simply unconscious. How the stormers had found her and dragged her down to use her moon-mark to open the door, Syla had no idea, but she couldn't worry about that now.

Fel swung his mace, doing his best to battle an agile young stormer with a fresh burn on half his face. Syla hoped one of her aunt's booby traps had been responsible and that it hurt. A *lot*.

"You'll not attack the princess," Fel snarled as their weapons clanged together.

But the stormer wasn't trying to get to Syla. Neither was the second man. This time, when she and Fel had rushed in, the two invaders had been in the process of shoving the broken shielder toward the door and examining the mounted and operating one. Probably trying to detect and remove the camouflaged traps.

One stormer had turned to defend against Fel's attack, but the other was only glancing at Syla as he pulled scrolls out of a nook in the stone wall. Were those the same scrolls that Aunt Tibby had brought from Harvest Island and had been studying?

Syla wouldn't let him get away with them—with *anything*. Though she had no weapon, she dodged the fight and rushed toward the stormer. "Release those scrolls, you thief."

He started to reach for a dagger sheathed on his belt, but then looked dismissively at her and didn't draw the weapon. In her dress and with her hair swept up to greet the diplomatic party, she couldn't look like a threat. Let him believe that.

Syla gripped his arm and summoned her power, the power she'd trained from an early age to use for healing. But twice before, she'd used it to attack, and, as the back of her hand tingled and the moon-mark flared silver, she willed its energy to flow into the intruder.

"Back off, princess," the stormer said, "if you want to live another day."

"Tie her up," the man battling Fel said. "The general will want her for a prisoner. They'll negotiate a lot more if we've got their heir."

"You'll not touch her," Fel snarled and increased the speed of his attacks. His mace almost took off his foe's head as the half-distracted stormer barely ducked in time.

Syla did not *back off*. As the stormer reached for her with his free hand, she sent her magic toward his trachea, the airway that allowed precious air to flow into his body. At the same time, she tightened her power around his heart, clenching the beating muscle.

He froze, his expression at first stunned and then... afraid. His face grew ashen.

"Get off me," he rasped, his constricted throat tightening the words so they were almost unintelligible.

Using his body, he shoved at Syla, then spun her about to press her back against the wall. She hit it hard, but she kept her grip on his arm and sent even more magic into him.

His heart fluttered, beats turning erratic. With her power wrapped around it, she felt it, and his face had turned from ashen to red as he wheezed, trying to get air past her constriction. She could have killed him, but she shied away from the thought. He was an enemy and wanted her people to die, but her gods-gift was for healing. She'd always believed that.

Afraid he would gain the advantage if she lessened the constriction, she kept it in place, but she didn't apply more pressure. She didn't squeeze his heart so much that it stopped altogether.

A sword clattered to the stone floor, and the stormer that Fel had been battling flew across the chamber. He struck the wall between two sarcophagi and crumpled, blood leaking from his nose and his eyes rolling back into his head.

Fel spun toward Syla, taking a step toward her to help, but her stormer dropped to his knees, his face turning from red to purple. Fel gaped, not at him but at Syla. He had his mace up, ready to fight, to come to her defense, but as he watched the oxygen-deprived man tip over onto his side, Fel touched two fingers to his chest to indicate the eyes of the moon and drew a circle around them. The superstitious gesture was meant to request protection from the gods.

Seeing the bodyguard who'd defended her and stood by her side these past weeks look at her like she was a terrifying gargoyle or griffin made Syla jerk her power back. She hadn't killed the stormer, but he didn't move.

"What are your orders, General?" came a clear and familiar voice from the tunnel outside.

Vorik. And... was he speaking to General Jhiton?

"Close the hidden door," Syla whispered to Fel.

There wasn't anywhere to run. Vorik sounded like he was right outside the door.

Fel reacted instantly, rushing toward it, and Syla ran after, realizing she would have to use her moon-mark to close it.

"Get the shielders," came General Jhiton's cool reply, his voice farther away but not nearly far enough.

Syla slapped her hand to a copper plate on the wall that emanated magic. It flashed silver when she touched it, and the door started to shut, but Teyla's body lay in the passageway, an obstacle. Her spectacles lay near her face, surprisingly not broken.

"Get her," Syla whispered to Fel.

Fel hesitated, spotting Vorik standing at attention in the tunnel outside, not yet moving other than to look at them. Fel hefted his mace. Syla awkwardly grabbed her cousin, but she wasn't strong enough to pull her out of the way without help.

The door caught on Teyla's hip. Syla had been worried her cousin would be crushed, but its magic prompted it to halt.

"*Fel*," Syla whispered as she tugged under Teyla's armpits, glad to notice heat in her body. And did she groan slightly? At least she was alive.

Fel looked like he would spring at Vorik, but he spotted a second man coming from the side. General Jhiton. And there were two more stormers—two powerful *riders*—right behind him.

Not taking his eyes from them, Fel crouched, wincing as his knee or another joint in his leg pained him, and grabbed Teyla. Together, Fel and Syla pulled her back. She managed to snatch up her cousin's spectacles, knowing she would be blind without them.

The door resumed shutting, but when it was inches from closing completely, a hand thrust through, halting it.

Fel swore. He and Syla pulled Teyla into the chamber, barely moving her out of the way before the door ground back open. As Syla set her cousin's spectacles atop a sarcophagus, and Fel tucked her out of the way near the wall, General Jhiton strode into the doorway with his swords in his hands and death in his eyes.

Syla glimpsed Vorik in the passageway behind the general but knew he wouldn't attack his own brother to help her. He couldn't.

She lifted her hand, thinking she might use her power on Jhiton, but she would have to touch him. And even that might not be enough.

No, she decided, recalling her attempt to stop Captain Lesva's interrogation by using her power. It definitely wouldn't be, not if he was bonded to his dragon and magically enhanced. Though he wore the fingerless gloves that so many of the riders favored, he radiated power and she knew without a doubt that he was also bonded.

And the two riders striding in after him? They probably were too.

Fel sprang in front of Syla, stepping into the passageway to block the stormers from entering the chamber. But he wouldn't have the power to beat Jhiton either.

Syla glanced at the shielder, wishing she hadn't had Aunt Tibby do such a good job of camouflaging the explosives. They blended in so well that she couldn't pick them out any better than the intruders had. And she would have to be careful searching. More than a slight impact, and the booby traps would explode.

"The stormers!" came a shout from the tunnel beyond the hidden entrance. "There they are. Get them, men!"

Jhiton and his riders paused at the arrival of Kingdom troops, keeping an eye on the dangerous Fel but also glancing back.

Searching for the booby traps, Syla gingerly patted around the orb, its power tingling against her palms. She willed Jhiton and his men to run out to face her soldiers. That might be a death sentence for the Kingdom men, but she had to be willing to sacrifice people to keep the shielders safe. Just as she was willing to sacrifice herself to do so.

Unfortunately, Jhiton and one of his riders rushed *into* the chamber. With a few swift sword slashes, they drove Fel back. His mace clanked as he managed to parry the blows, but, pressed by superior numbers, he had to give ground. Soon, his back was to the ancient sarcophagus in the center of the chamber, a few feet in front of the shielder.

As footsteps thundered in the tunnel outside, Syla's fingers brushed over one of the camouflaged traps. She tugged it away from the curving surface of the orb and lifted it to throw, but Fel blocked her view as he tried to keep Jhiton from reaching her. Syla stepped to the side, hoping to line up a safe throw.

Vorik ran into the chamber.

"Let the door close," he said to one of the riders who'd paused to put his back against it to keep it open.

The stormer released it and ran inside with Vorik, but the Kingdom troops, a mix of Royal Protectors from the castle and black-uniformed Royal Fleet men, reached the passageway and charged inside before the door ground to a close.

Jhiton knocked Fel's mace out of his hand and hurled him into a wall, but he then had to turn to face the new threat. Syla's heart lifted as her troops rushed in. A dozen of them? *Two* dozen?

"Yes," she cried, feeling they might be enough to defeat even the enhanced riders. "Protect the shielder. And get the general!"

As the cacophonous clamor of swords clashing against swords rang out, Syla realized her men would target *everyone* in black leathers, Vorik included, but she couldn't bring herself to yell at them to leave him be. Not when he'd moved to stand side-by-side with his brother, their backs to the wall as they faced the greater numbers. Vorik was fighting her people. He was an enemy. She couldn't let herself forget that.

Vorik's and Jhiton's faces remained calm as they defended against soldiers swarming into the chamber—so many that Syla worried her people would strike each other in the confined space.

But they switched their styles from swinging slashes to thrusts, trying to slip in side-by-side to reach the riders. All four of the stormers drew opponents, but the greatest concentration of soldiers targeted Vorik and Jhiton. That was fortunate because Jhiton kept glancing at the active shielder nestled within its mount.

Fel and Syla stood in front of it, so he would have to go through them to reach it, but she had no doubt that the general would do that. Jhiton's face was a cool mask as he breathed through his nose, as if whipping his swords about, defending against so many, took no effort, but Syla could read the determination in his eyes. It was almost like the religious zeal of the godders prostrating themselves at their temples and making offerings, certain their actions would result in the return of the deities.

A man cried out. One of the soldiers. He tumbled back, dropping his sword and clutching his chest, blood from a stab wound washing his fingers.

Healer's instincts calling her, Syla stepped in that direction. But Fel gripped her arm to keep her back. She couldn't have reached the soldier even if she'd believed it wise. Another had replaced him as a comrade pulled him back so he wouldn't be trampled by all the boots. It didn't look like a mortal wound, and she could attend to him later, but as another man cursed, stumbling back at a blow to his hip, she was reminded that the riders might very well overcome the greater numbers. Especially in the confining chamber where only so many soldiers could attack them at once.

"Get out of here if you spot an opportunity." Fel released Syla without looking away from the fighting. "You can heal the survivors afterward. From the safety of the castle."

As strange as it seemed with more than twenty men fighting in the chamber, nobody was attacking them at the moment. The riders were too busy defending against superior numbers.

"Of course," Syla said, but she wouldn't leave while the shielders were in danger. It was bad enough that fighting went on all around the broken one—the invaders had succeeded in pushing it halfway to the exit.

And what of Teyla? Syla couldn't abandon her cousin. Though they had tried to tuck her against the wall behind a sarcophagus, she was in danger of being trampled.

Syla tightened her grip around the explosive. She had to do something.

Vorik lunged to the side, away from the general as he cut off two soldiers trying to slip in by the wall to get behind them.

Syla took that moment to throw the device at Jhiton's opposite shoulder. She *wanted* to throw it square at his chest—or maybe between his eyes—but she didn't want to hurt Vorik. Enemy or not, he meant something to her. Too much.

Despite defending against eight attacks simultaneously, Jhiton saw the flat square explosive sailing toward him. It had blended in with the silver of the orb but stood out as it arched through the air. The faintest hint of confusion made one of his eyebrows twitch, but his sword came up, batting it aside.

Upon impact, it exploded scant feet from Jhiton's head. The force of the shockwave hurled him against the wall.

Even from halfway across the chamber, Syla felt it, her hair blown back, sooty smoke and intense heat blasting over her. It was as if she'd opened the oven door of the gods. Soldiers who had been near Jhiton stumbled, two falling to the ground.

The flash and smoke hid Syla's view of Vorik, and she held her breath, afraid she'd hurt him as well as the general.

She'd *better* have hurt the general. Somehow, Jhiton remained on his feet and hadn't dropped his weapon. Neither had Vorik. And, as the smoke cleared, she could see them again, faces blackened, clothes torn, and burns blistering their skin, especially Jhiton's. But they remained in the battle. If anything, their faces grew more determined, their sword strikes faster, deadlier.

Another soldier went down. All around the chamber, people coughed, the smoke distracting them. It made Syla's eyes water and her throat itch as well. She couldn't *believe* she hadn't taken down the general.

Fel looked at her in exasperation, and Syla expected him to berate her for not following his instructions.

"Next time you do that," he said, "at least use the opportunity to escape."

"We can't abandon the shielder." Syla glanced toward the passageway where a soldier held the door open.

"*We* won't." Fel thumped his chest. "But you need to get out of here. You never should have come down." His expression turned aggrieved as he no doubt regretted not forcibly keeping her in the castle.

Syla shook her head. She had to protect the shielder. She belonged down here.

The soldier in the doorway spun around, then bent in half. Another black-clad stormer had arrived. Two more. They shoved the dispatched soldier aside and stepped into the passageway.

"We're here, General," one yelled.

Vorik was the one to answer. "Good! We've got them surrounded!"

Jhiton gave him a sidelong look, one hard to interpret. With the soldiers still outnumbering the stormers by far, Syla didn't know how much the odds had changed, but she would never bet against Vorik, and Jhiton was just as capable. Those two alone might have held off an entire army.

Syla turned and patted the orb, forcing herself to keep her touch slow and methodical, not frantic. The last thing she wanted was to accidentally blow up Fel and herself.

How many explosives had Aunt Tibby placed? Syla wished she

had come down to help. Then she would have known where they were.

"There," she whispered, brushing one.

She carefully unstuck it and was tempted to whirl and throw it, but if she could find two, that would be better. The general might see one coming and knock it away again, but if she could throw a second right after, before the smoke cleared and Jhiton recovered, she might defeat him this time.

Fel grunted and jerked his arm up, defending against someone who'd decided to try to get to the shielder. Or maybe to Syla. Trusting Fel's ability, she kept patting, shifting around the orb, needing to find one more of Tibby's devices.

A strangled cry of pain announced another man going down. One of her soldiers, she feared.

Tears of frustration welled in her eyes. She should have moved the shielder already, not merely boobytrapped it. It could have sat in a hay wagon under a tarp in the courtyard, and the night would have turned out better than this.

There. She found another explosive.

Fel grunted, dropping to one knee, but he kept his mace up. A sword pressed against it, one of the riders trying to force his way past Fel's defenses.

"Move the princess, and expose the shielder," came Jhiton's voice from the wall.

Syla spun, a trap in each hand, ready to throw them. The stormer who'd driven Fel to one knee glanced toward his general and backed up a few steps.

"She's got explosives," the man warned.

"Don't let her touch you," another man rasped from the other side of the chamber. "She's not a healer. Someone lied about that."

It was the would-be scroll thief. He'd recovered enough to rise to his feet, but he rubbed his throat and leaned on a sarcophagus for support.

Fel swore as he pushed himself back to both feet. Whether it was because of his injuries or the situation, Syla didn't know. The chamber had grown quiet, and bleakness washed over her as she looked around. Almost all of the soldiers who'd run in to help were on the ground, dead or too severely wounded to continue fighting. It looked like others had fled. She hoped they were getting reinforcements because only one of the riders was down—hopefully the bastard was dead. Vorik and another rider remained on their feet, armed and not far from the shielder. Further, Jhiton and the two stormers who'd charged in to help crouched near the passageway—blocking escape. They were all injured, Jhiton worse than the others, but they were on their feet and retained their weapons.

Syla swallowed and raised her arms higher, making sure they all saw the explosives she held. "I'll let you leave if you go now, but if you try to take the shielder, I'll blow us all up."

One of the riders snorted. "Including yourself?"

"By the storm god's cursed minions, yes. You're *not* getting our shielder." Syla was answering the rider but looked at Jhiton.

He was in charge. He was the one she needed to convince. Unfortunately, he'd already survived one explosion and probably realized the devices weren't powerful enough to blow up everyone in the room. But with two, she might get her target. She shifted to make it clear that *he* would be her target.

Jhiton gazed at her, not noticeably alarmed by her obvious intent. He lifted his swords as if to say he'd knocked one aside and could handle two more. With his face blackened and burned and his clothes shredded, blood visible from numerous wounds, he didn't *look* like he could handle a pair of explosives being thrown at him, but she wasn't positive. The riders were freaks of nature—freaks of their dragon magic.

Syla could see Vorik to her side but didn't look at him. She couldn't let him influence her decision one way or another.

Shouts came from the tunnels. A lot of them.

"Find the princess!" someone yelled in the distance.

"Seal the tunnels, and kill the invaders!" came another cry.

Reinforcements. But would they arrive in time?

A distant boom filtered through the layers of rock and earth. Had that come from the harbor? Syla hoped the fleet was firing on the stormers' ship, but she had a feeling they had moved it out from under the barrier before sending their incursion team in. Still, her people's ships might have gone out after it.

"Orders, sir?" Vorik watched Jhiton warily.

Jhiton looked up at the stone ceiling. Was his dragon up there? Flying over the barrier and warning him of something? He also looked at the man Syla had attacked earlier. The stormer straightened and lowered his hand from his throat, tapping a hip pouch. Jhiton's gaze shifted to the shielder. He would have to go through Syla and Fel to reach it, but he was surely capable of that.

Tense, she moved her arms enough to remind him of the explosives. He already knew she *would* throw them.

But if she did, and Jhiton and his men leaped away, something they would more easily do now that they weren't distracted by defending themselves, she wouldn't have any other way to attack, to defend the shielder.

Maybe Jhiton believed exactly that because, despite more shouts—*closer* shouts—in the tunnels, he raised his swords and strode toward Syla.

Fel lifted his mace, bracing himself to defend her. She lofted one of the explosives over his head toward Jhiton. As she'd predicted, he sprang to the side, not touching it with his sword this time. She tracked him and threw the other, hoping it would glance off him as he landed. But he anticipated her attack and threw one of his swords. It struck the closer explosive, keeping it from reaching him. It blew at the same time as the first hit the ground.

The shockwaves blasted through the chamber, the lids on the

sarcophagi rattling. Fel stumbled back, bumping into Syla and knocking her to the ground. A shard of something sharp slammed into her thigh, and she gasped at the agonizing pain.

Rocks banged down in the tunnel. Only the magic imbued in the chamber kept it intact as everything shook and smoke flooded the air.

"That way!" soldiers yelled, closer now.

"Was that the shielder?"

Inside the chamber, the smoke cleared enough that Syla could see General Jhiton still on his feet. He'd already retrieved his sword. She tried to stand, but a sharp piece of rock embedded in her thigh made her grunt in pain as soon as she moved her leg. Fel groaned, also injured, and struggled to push himself to his knees.

His mace was on the ground between them. Syla grabbed it. Not worried in the least about her ability to hurt him with it, Jhiton strode toward her—her and the shielder. From the ground, she couldn't protect it. She had to—

Movement to the side made her jerk the mace that way, fearing another threat.

Vorik strode out of the smoke. At first, she thought he would grab her and heft her to her feet, maybe pull her away from the shielder so his general could destroy it. Instead...

Vorik stepped in front of her and blocked Jhiton from reaching her.

"Get out of the way, Vorik," Jhiton said, his voice icy.

"We have to leave now if we're to have any hope of escaping." Without stepping from in front of Syla, Vorik pointed toward the passageway.

Judging by the shouts, more soldiers than before were coming. And the stormers were injured. Would Vorik be able to reason with his general?

Jhiton halted and looked at him. From the ground behind

Vorik, Syla couldn't see their expressions, but she did catch Vorik lifting his chin. Determined? Defiant?

Facing each other, Jhiton and Vorik stood still, holding gazes for what seemed minutes or hours but could only have been a couple of seconds.

More shouts from the tunnels spurred them to movement.

"Retreat," Jhiton said quietly, then turned on his heel and led his men out.

Vorik went last, looking over his shoulder at Syla as he did. His expression was worried, but she didn't know if it was for her or for his future among his people—with his brother—after defending her. Either way, he managed a quick half-smile and saluted her, the same as he had after the dragon battle over the whaling ship, before disappearing into the tunnel with his comrades.

With the rock shard stabbing her with pain, Syla let herself slump onto her back. The shielder remained in place, its power protecting the island, but soldiers lay dead all around them. She couldn't feel like she'd won a battle.

7

WITH SOLDIERS POUNDING DOWN THE TUNNEL TOWARD THE shielder chamber, Vorik raced out after Jhiton and the others, his wounds making each step painful. He half-expected his brother to snap at him that he ought to stay and deal with the wrath of the gardeners since he was so fond of their princess. But Jhiton didn't look back at him at all, merely leading his men down the tunnel and into the burial chamber with the freshly blown hole in the far wall.

A tunnel lay beyond that hole. When had his people carved it? And did it lead all the way to the bluff and the sea?

There wasn't time for sightseeing, but Vorik couldn't help but glance around, trying to figure how the stormers could have managed an excavation with a castle full of people above, people who would have heard explosions. Even if the hard rock had been chiseled, that would have made noise. And when could his people have done it? In the days after the invasion when the island hadn't been protected and the castle dwellers had been distracted by repairs and funerals? It scarcely seemed enough time.

The tunnel didn't go far before widening into a natural cave.

Two Storm Guard soldiers rose from crouches to either side of the transition area, torches in their hands and kegs placed along both sides of the passageway.

"Blow them," Jhiton said, running past the men without slowing.

Shouts behind them promised the soldiers had found the hole in the burial chamber. Some of them had likely found their princess and Syla's relative or whoever that other woman had been—the person Vorik had originally believed to be Syla—but others ran after the intruders.

"Yes, sir," one man said.

"A big explosion right there might bring down the castle," someone pointed out.

"Darn," Jhiton said.

He rarely shared a lot of emotion, but he sounded annoyed, and he didn't hide the exasperation in his expression as he glanced back at Vorik.

Vorik spread his arms but didn't apologize for defending Syla. And the rest? It wasn't his fault the rest of his brother's plan hadn't worked, that someone had booby-trapped the shielder.

The soldiers lit fuses that led to the stacked kegs, then ran, catching up with the group.

The cave grew broader and higher, something that Vorik sensed more than saw in the dark. Had this place existed *before* his brother had planned his invasion? It must have. Maybe it had existed centuries earlier, before the castle had even been built. Had the gardeners known about it?

As the kegs exploded, their booms thunderous in the enclosed space, light flashed upon walls that held statues in large alcoves, and Vorik gaped. They were statues of dragons. And there was a griffin. And a wyvern. A gargoyle. A cloud striker? Were these *all* of the storm god's winged creations?

Rocks tumbled down in the aftermath of the explosion, most

behind them, where the kegs had been set, but one of the statues also toppled. A wyvern. It pitched forward, and a wing broke off. What was that set against the rock wall behind it? Vorik thought of the stone sarcophagi in the chambers they'd just left. But who would have built a tomb for a wyvern?

Before the light faded, Vorik also spotted nooks carved into the walls in an area with an ancient stone table thick with dust. A few beakers and flasks remained, coated with so many spiderwebs that they might have been there since the beginning of time. Was this some kind of workshop?

A hint of a sea breeze brushed Vorik's cheeks, mingling with the scent of spent powder. Jhiton looked back. The soldiers who'd lit the explosives were catching up, their torches now the only source of light.

"The way is blocked?" Jhiton asked.

"Yes, sir. But the gardeners will get through eventually."

"We'll be long gone by then."

"Yes, sir, but we won't be able to gain entrance this way again. I'm sure they'll seal the area once they discover it."

"I can't believe they didn't know about this place before," another man said.

"It's from before the gods moved all of humanity to these islands and placed their protection around them," Jhiton said. "I only know of it because of Ozlemar. Even he isn't old enough to have visited it, but the elder dragons remember the stories that their mothers and fathers passed down. This was one of the storm god's workshops, its existence long forgotten by humans, even those living right above it."

"We won't be able to try again to destroy the shielders. Not going in this way."

"We may have something almost as good." Jhiton looked toward Devron, the soldier who'd warned them about Syla's power.

"Yes, sir. I've got the scrolls. I'm not the best reader, and I didn't get a chance to take a good look anyway, but I'm sure they'll hold something of worth."

"A map to the locations of all the shielders, if we're fortunate," Jhiton said.

Vorik looked sharply at him. He didn't think that was likely—every Kingdom subject he'd spoken to on the matter believed that only the royal Moonmarks knew the locations and that the knowledge was passed down but never *written* down.

"We'll have Lieutenant Wise study them," Jhiton added.

They reached the end of the cave and entered a short tunnel with a hint of dim light at the end, the faint glow provided by the night sky. Rock shards littered the floor. This had been excavated recently.

The tunnel led to a jagged vertical slit overlooking the ocean rather than the harbor. They'd come out around the point from where the dragon ship had been shooting off fireworks. Vorik trusted it had sailed away before the Kingdom military vessels descended upon it.

Several men groaned at the prospect of the climb. Aside from the two troops who'd waited to light the explosives, everyone in the party had been wounded. Most of Vorik's body ached or outright sent stabs of agony through him, but pain was an old friend, and he didn't allow himself to groan, not with his brother right there. Jhiton had taken the brunt of that explosive and had to hurt as much as or more than Vorik, but he said nothing as he started down in the dark without a rope.

None of the stormers had them, but most of the tribes lived in caves—the only types of domiciles that could be properly defended from dragons, wyverns, and other threats—so shimmying up and down cliffs was second-nature to their people.

As one, the group descended toward kayaks tied to the rocks far below. There was no beach or landing spot, merely waves crashing against the cliff, threatening to destroy the tiny vessels. A single stormer perched on a ledge, keeping an eye on the craft.

As the group climbed down, experienced fingers finding holds in the vertical rock, even in the dark, Vorik found himself shoulder to shoulder with Jhiton again.

He groped for something to say. An apology? An explanation? Something that would convince his brother that he could still be trusted.

Was that entirely true? Where Syla was concerned, Vorik couldn't stand back and watch her be killed. She didn't deserve that. She hadn't deserved any of what befell her.

Jhiton was the one to speak first. "I can't believe you stopped me from killing the woman who tried to *blow us up*."

"She tried to blow *you* up. I was foolishly standing nearby."

"She tried to blow me up *twice*." Jhiton still sounded exasperated, but the fact that he was speaking suggested he wasn't as angry as Vorik had feared.

"Yeah." He dared grin a little.

After a few more seconds of descending, Jhiton looked over. "I see why you like her."

Vorik's grin widened. "Yeah."

Any update on Wreylith? Vorik asked Agrevlari. During the chaos, he'd forgotten about the red dragon and to wonder what had brought her. Could Syla have called her? Though he could understand why she hadn't wanted to give him any intelligence, he was curious for his own sake how she'd won the dragon's assistance again. *Where she is and what she's up to,* Vorik added, sensing smugness through their telepathic link. *Not anything about her beauty or the poem you're composing.*

She called Ozlemar cowardly for attacking a healer and wanted to know if our presence here means the shield protecting this island will soon drop again.

Why would she care about that? Vorik asked.

She did not say.

Again, Vorik wondered if Syla had somehow reached out to the dragon. Surely, Wreylith wouldn't be out here gathering intelligence for a lowly human, even one who'd done a favor or two for her. That had to be beneath a wild dragon who called those of her kind who bonded with humans *domesticated* or *pets.*

She did, however, mention that she took note of my actions during the skirmish over the whaling ship.

Your actions? Vorik asked. *Like when you bit Ozzy in the flank?*

I believe she approved of that, yes. There was the reason for Agrevlari's smugness. That was the first time that Wreylith had said anything kindly toward him.

Syla liked it too.

A wave washed against the cliff below Vorik and Jhiton, cold ocean spray reaching them. The men angled toward the kayaks. Lights burned on two ships that had rounded the point and come into view. Kingdom ships? Yes, they had to be. They had to know stormers remained behind and hadn't left with the dragon ship, and they were looking for them.

Your princess? Agrevlari asked.

The sole remaining princess of the Garden Kingdom. She is not mine.

Wistfulness filled Vorik at the statement. Maybe he should have wanted nothing to do with Syla after she'd gotten the best of him on Harvest Island, but he'd been far more annoyed with himself than with her over that. She'd been doing her duty for her people, the same as he'd been doing his. He couldn't resent her for that. No, he respected her. And tonight... Vorik smiled at the memory of her holding those two explosive devices aloft, ready to throw them at Jhiton. He wagered she'd been instrumental in placing them. She'd *known* his people would try again, that their shielder wouldn't be safe.

"Shall we leave you there, Captain?" Jhiton called up from one of the kayaks.

The rest of the team had found seats in the lightweight craft, two already heading out toward sea.

"No, I'd like to come along." Vorik slithered off the cliff and into a two-seater kayak with his brother.

"I'm pleased that's still the case."

"Had I had an opportunity to taste the baked desserts the princess offered, I might have felt differently." Vorik grew even *more* wistful as he remembered the cylindrical boxes of cobblers and who knew what other treats. How lamentable that he hadn't been able to bring them along. It would have been difficult to steer a kayak with a cake perched between his legs though.

Once settled, Vorik grabbed a paddle and helped Jhiton push away from the cliff. It wasn't easy with the waves and currents churning everything toward the rocks, but his people were almost as practiced with kayaks as with climbing.

"If only the gardeners knew how easily your loyalties might be won," Jhiton said.

"All soldiers are ruled by their stomachs. Perhaps we should take up Syla's offer of trade. Then you could get cobblers for your troops to ensure their undying devotion to you."

Busy steering through the waves, Jhiton didn't respond. Maybe he didn't think the comment *worth* a response.

The Kingdom ships lurking out there between them and the barrier were concerning, but all the stormers had to do was paddle far enough out that their dragons could pick them up.

"What scrolls did Devron take from the chamber?" Vorik asked. "You don't really expect to find the locations of the other shielders written down on parchment, do you?"

"We'll find out once we return to our headquarters."

Vorik didn't recall seeing scrolls the last time he'd been in that chamber. What were the odds that Devron had grabbed a shopping list that someone had left down there?

A wave sprayed Vorik with water, and the splash brought realization as well as moisture. Of course. Syla had spoken to her aunt about seeking out schematics as well as the Harvest Island shielder. She or Tibby must have located them and brought them back to study. Essentially instructions on how to repair the broken shielder. If that was what the party had gotten away with, Vorik's people might have left the gardeners in a bind again.

And Syla, despite Vorik stepping in and trying to help her, might resent him for being a part of that.

As he paddled, he gazed bleakly toward the starry sky. He'd hoped that they would one day find a chance to relive the night in the cave, this time without him being drugged in the end. But the odds of that seemed poorer than ever.

8

Syla's entire body ached, but she endured the discomfort and remained to direct the soldiers to clean out the shielder chamber so she could close the hidden passageway again. She also asked them to carry her cousin, who'd remained unconscious throughout the event, to one of the infirmary rooms in the back of the castle.

As soon as one of the higher-ranking officers arrived and could take over, she would go up to help Teyla. How her cousin had ended up down here, Syla didn't know. All she could guess was that the stormers had found her in the city and kidnapped her. Where the higher-ranking officers were at the moment, she also didn't know, but she assumed they'd been out in the harbor, overseeing attempts to take down the dragon ship. Even if that vessel had held the two tribal leaders, it hadn't been the problem. It and its fireworks display had been a distraction, the same as Vorik.

Thinking of him made Syla grimace, a conflicted mishmash of feelings tangling inside her. In the throne room, he'd cheerfully served his purpose, keeping her busy while trying to extract information from her, but in the tunnel outside the shielder chamber, he'd delayed his own side and deliberately given her a heads-up that Jhiton was coming. And then he'd stood in front of the general to keep him from killing her or capturing her or whatever the man had planned.

"My death probably." She well remembered Jhiton's icy tone and the granite set of his jaw.

Fel, who'd been helping the soldiers drag out bodies, despite his own injuries, looked over at her.

"I'm just thinking about how we're lucky to have survived that." Syla touched her thigh. She'd removed the shard of rock and stopped the bleeding but hadn't yet healed the wound fully. Later.

"Yes."

"While acknowledging that you would have preferred it if I'd stayed in the castle." She smiled apologetically at him, though she would make the same decision again.

She looked around the shielder chamber to see if the stormers had managed to sabotage anything before she'd arrived. Reminded of the man who'd been plucking up scrolls, she headed for the nook that had held them.

"I would have preferred that, yes." Fel straightened, winced, and rubbed his lower back. "But I think the stormers might have gotten the shielder if you *hadn't* been here."

"I think so too. I had no idea they had Teyla. Her brother didn't seem to know she'd been kidnapped."

"I also think the stormers would have gotten *me* if you hadn't been here." Fel gazed thoughtfully at her. "And your... suborned captain."

"He's not that."

If only he were. Not for the first time, Syla wished Vorik were on her side, that he could be an ally.

"He defied his general to keep you alive," Fel said.

"It's complicated." She smiled and wished she'd been able to get some baked goods into Vorik's hands. Mostly for him, but maybe he would have shared a cobbler with General Jhiton and the sweet would have prompted the man to become less villainous for a time.

Syla swept her hand through the nook. It was partially hidden by a sarcophagus so she checked it twice. The tools her aunt had brought back were still there, appearing innocuous and plain to one who couldn't sense their magic. The scrolls, however, were gone. She slumped.

"I think they got the schematics and that list of components Aunt Tibby was talking about," Syla admitted.

"For the shielders?"

"Yes, everything Aunt Tibby has been studying."

"The scrolls she began studying while we were all supposed to be pushing the Harvest Island shielder miles to that cove."

"Yes, those are they. She found them fascinating."

"I recall." Fel rubbed his back again, probably remembering that he'd done the majority of pushing on that trek.

Syla bent forward and gripped her knees. "I hope Aunt Tibby made copies of the scrolls."

A soldier peeked into the chamber and looked around for more bodies, but the last of the dead had been removed. Only one stormer had fallen while many Kingdom soldiers would not see another dawn. Syla regretted sacrificing them. Or rather being the reason they'd sacrificed themselves. She and the shielder.

"Corporal, thank you for your help." She straightened and faced him. "Will you have someone get Aunt—uhm, Lady Tibaytha and bring her to the infirmary?"

Hopefully, Tibby was staying in the room she'd taken in the castle and hadn't gone all the way back to the farm. As soon as possible, Syla needed to know if she had copies of the scrolls. If not...

What? She would stage an infiltration of whatever cave the

Sixteen Talons were headquartered in and steal them back? She would politely ask Vorik if *he* would steal them back? She knew he wouldn't. Instead, he would talk to her about peripheral vision and juggling.

"Yes, Your Highness."

"Thank you." Syla waved for Fel to leave the chamber with her, then closed the hidden door before they headed through the tunnels. Later, she would have to find a new resting place for the shielder or booby-trap this one again. "Both," she murmured, thinking of all the relatives she'd invited to meet her in the castle. Were any more missing? She would have to check on that too. "I want a vacation, Fel."

"*I* was supposed to retire this week," he said.

"The ultimate vacation."

"It was supposed to be."

"What were you going to do?"

"Visit my mother and cousins in Promontory Peak. Fish. Lie in the sun. Walk nude on the beach. Well. *Hobble* nude on the beach. I don't know if I'll ever recover from all my injuries, but I had plans to try."

Syla didn't remark on the imagery that popped into her mind of her nearly six-and-a-half-foot-tall scarred bodyguard limping naked as he collected agates and sand coins. "I believe you would be bored after two weeks of that. Think how much more exciting your life protecting me is."

"I've nearly been killed half a dozen times this month. Maybe a dozen."

"*Exciting*," she assured him as they climbed the stairs toward the theater.

The domesticated dragons are again attacking healers, a female voice boomed into Syla's mind. Wreylith.

Syla blinked in surprise and looked up, though she of course couldn't see the sky through the multiple ceilings above her head.

She sensed, however, from the telepathic origins of the voice that the dragon was close. Perhaps directly overhead, skimming above the sky shield.

They vex you and this island instead of taking the opportunity to hunt on the now-exposed Island of Eliok. Were they wild dragons, they would know to enjoy such activities instead of servilely obeying the mandates of puny humans.

I think they're idiots too, Syla replied.

Yes. I have brought you meat.

Uhm, meat?

A haunch of sumptuous eliok. As a powerful dragon who has seen many centuries, I neither need nor want the advice of humans on where to seek game, but I did find many delicious prey in the trees near the mushrooms that you described.

So you're appreciative.

I have brought you meat. Since the haunch is neither a dragon nor other winged predator, it may fall through your sky shield, but I do not wish for it to land in the dirt and be sullied.

You want me to run outside and... catch it? Syla imagined a huge bloody, furry eliok leg plummeting from the sky and smashing her to the ground.

Prepare a proper receptacle, and I will release the haunch onto it.

Now, Syla imagined herself holding out a platter and trying to catch the meat as it landed, spattering gristle and blood onto her dress. How did one politely refuse a gift from a dragon? Maybe she would ask Vorik later, but she had a feeling it was unwise to turn down presents from beings capable of breathing fire.

I've family that I need to heal, but let me see if I can send someone from the kitchen staff to lay out a tarp in the courtyard. Will that suffice?

If you trust your underlings with something as valuable as eliok meat. I would not.

I have excellent underlings. Syla thought of General Dolok and almost laughed. Though the castle staff had humored her so far when she made requests, she doubted she had even the cooks' and maids' loyalty.

At some point, she needed to decide if she wanted to attempt to claim the throne and, if so, make serious plans to thwart the competition. She would happily have stepped aside for another capable family member, but if her cousin Relvin was who sprang forward and wanted to rule... He wasn't who came to mind when she envisioned someone capable. Ambitious, maybe. She also wouldn't step aside and hand the Kingdom over to a Royal Fleet or Royal Protector officer to impose a military dictatorship or junta. Her people were mostly fishers and farmers; they didn't want to be ordered around by troops marching through the streets.

"Your Highness?" Fel stopped at the theater entrance and looked back at her.

Musing and conversing, Syla had fallen behind and hurried to clamber off the stage and catch up.

"Sorry. I'm thinking." She thought about mentioning Wreylith and seeing if Fel wanted to head to the courtyard with an empty tray, but he doubtless believed his duty was at her side, wielding a mace, not a meat platter.

"Not about Captain Vorik, I hope."

"Only in that I might ask him for advice on dragons the next time I see him."

"Are you planning to do that? See him again?" Fel squinted at her.

By now, he had to trust that she wouldn't betray the Kingdom because of her feelings for Vorik, but he also had no reason to love the rider captain. Every time they'd tangled, Vorik had disarmed him and forced him to his knees or against a wall.

"I'm not, no, but he keeps appearing."

"I've noticed." Fel bared his teeth.

No, there was no love lost between those two.

In the back of the castle keep lay narrower hallways with sleeping quarters for the staff, storage areas, and a small infirmary. Syla entered one of the rooms and bared her own teeth when she found not only Teyla, lying in a bed and holding a compress to the side of her head, but Cousin Relvin.

Speaking of the competition that Syla needed to thwart...

Relvin's focus was on Teyla as he alternated frowning and pursing his lips at her. "I can't believe you wandered off and let yourself be captured by stormers."

"I didn't *let* myself be captured." Teyla lowered the compress and tucked her shoulder-length brown hair behind her ear, revealing a cut along her jaw to go with what had to be a contusion on her head.

Syla set her spectacles on a table beside her bed.

"Lieutenant Vanbarik said they must have toted you over their shoulders down into the tunnels and ordered you to apply your moon-mark to open the secret passage to the hidden shielder chamber." Relvin raised his eyebrows toward Syla. Wanting verification?

Syla had no idea how the stormers had found and apprehended her cousin.

"Lieutenant Vanbarik wasn't there," Teyla snapped, lowering the compress with a pained grimace. She needed a healer, not a lecture. "*I* wasn't even there for most of it. Not with awareness."

Teyla shifted into a sitting position and grimaced again, though the second gesture might have been less due to physical discomfort and more the awareness that she'd been used against the Kingdom.

"Two men in black leathers leaped out at me in plain sight," Teyla said. "It was so unexpected. I did yell for help and try to fight them off, but they were so fast that I barely blurted a word before they dragged me into an alley, flattened me against a wall, and put a damp cloth against my face until whatever was in it caused me to lose consciousness. I didn't expect— I mean, I wouldn't have thought— The sky shield is back up, right? I didn't think there would be danger in the capital."

"Unfortunately," Syla said, "the sky shield only keeps out aerial predators, not humans."

Teyla slumped back against her pillow. "I know, but the military... I'd thought they'd reestablished order, especially in the core of the capital. I was near Moon Watch Museum—I'd heard that it and the temple and everything else on that block had been destroyed and wanted to see if there's any hope for rebuilding. I always loved that museum. Do you remember when we used to play there as children?"

Syla, a couple of years older than Teyla, said, "I remember that I was training to become a healer, and you sneaked into the temple to steal antiques from the collection I'd recently started, thanks to a few foundational gift pieces from Uncle Savarik. As I recall, you claimed that such wondrous items should be on display in a museum instead of tucked away in my room."

"I wasn't wrong. Curator Landol praised me for being a conscientious contributor to the museum at such a young age."

"You stole my tonsil guillotine."

"You had it stuffed in a drawer and barely knew it existed. I *framed* it and hung it in a room full of ancient torture implements."

"It's a medical instrument."

"It *looked* like a torture device. My tonsils agreed."

"Vocal, are they?"

"When need be. And delightfully still intact." Teyla opened her mouth to show them off.

Relvin cleared his throat. "We've wandered away from the topic about how my sister, however inadvertently, allowed stormers to gain access to the shielder."

"It could just as easily have happened to you." Teyla's frowning blue eyes said she *wished* it had happened to him.

Syla would have preferred it that way too, if only so Relvin would have no reason to look smug and superior as he made accusations about his sister instead of defending her. It wasn't as if any of this had been Teyla's fault.

"The stormers, especially the dragon riders," Syla said, moving to sit beside her cousin to examine her injuries, "are talented fighters and probably didn't have much trouble avoiding the enforcers patrolling the streets."

"I've been talking to people and gathering information for a newspaper article," Relvin said. "It sounds like you've spent time with stormers lately and have learned quite a bit about them, Syla. Especially that one who singled you out in the throne room and wanted to chat."

"His people chose for him to chat with me."

"Because you two have some kind of weird *relationship*."

It wasn't weird. It was wondrous.

"Please step outside, Relvin," Syla said. "I appreciate you coming to the capital at my behest, but I want to heal Teyla and wait for the rest of our kin to arrive before we discuss our plans for the future."

"Teyla is fine. It's not like you get wounded by having a rag pressed to your mouth."

"I hit my head trying to escape those men. Hard." Teyla left the compress in her lap but probed gingerly at the side of her head.

"Let me take a look." Syla made a shooing motion to Relvin. She had plenty of experience healing people with an audience, but she would prefer him to go away.

"Gladly," Teyla said.

Lips pursed again, Relvin remained where he was. Syla looked toward Fel.

He stepped close, looming effectively, almost a foot taller than Relvin. "You will exit the room, Lord Relvin."

"Now that most of my cousins are gone, I'm a potential heir to the throne," he told Fel. "Some might even believe me a better choice to rule than Syla. Thanks to my years of speaking with various wealthy and influential individuals for newspaper articles, I have more connections than she does. I certainly am more likely to get backing from the military."

"You will exit the room or I will carry you," Fel said.

Relvin's eyes narrowed to slits. "If I *do* gain the power of the throne, my first action will be to fire you."

"Promise?" Fel's expression grew wistful.

The response puzzled Relvin, but Syla laughed.

Despite the fantasies of fishing and nude beach-walking that surely popped into Fel's mind, he rested a heavy hand on Relvin's shoulder, his intent clear.

Relvin lifted his chin, glared, and pushed the hand away, but he did walk out of the room. He slammed the door on the way out, as if leaving were his idea.

"He has the maturity of my cousin's hounds," Fel remarked.

"Goofy puppies, are they?" Syla asked.

"One runs, jumps, and barks its head off if a raven lands in a tree. It seems to think it can *bark* the birds into falling from the branches."

"My cousin does bark a lot."

"I've noticed." Fel opened the door, stepped into the hall, and looked both ways, probably to make sure Relvin wasn't spying with his ear pressed to the wood, then took up a position out there.

"Let my aunt in if she comes, please," Syla asked as Fel reached to close the door.

"She *also* barks a lot."

"Mostly at you because you destroyed her tractor."

"It was trying to *kill* me at the time." Fel closed the door.

"It was a magical tractor," Syla explained at Teyla's confused expression.

"Does that make it more or less alarming that it was trying to kill your bodyguard?"

"I'm not sure. Is the lump on your head your only major wound?" Syla waved to indicate the cut, but it wasn't deep.

"I think it's the only big one. I suppose I should be grateful, but I'm mostly chagrined that they knocked me out so easily. You may recall that I've had combat training."

"I remember bandaging your arm after a fencing incident involving antique cutlasses in the museum."

"I was just a kid then. I'm a lot better now. Usually, I cause the *other* person to need bandaging. But the stormers... Well, I think those were *riders*. Maybe bonded." Teyla looked hopeful, like it would be embarrassing to have been outfought by lesser combatants.

"Two against one is difficult to deal with under any circumstances." Syla lifted her fingers toward Teyla's head but hesitated, remembering how she'd used her power to attack the stormer, to cut off his air and render him unconscious. Her gods-gift had come so easily for that. It would have let her *kill* the man; she was certain.

She'd never heard of anyone in her family with the ability to use his or her gift to kill. Usually, the power lent itself most easily to assisting with one's passions. Like engineering, for Aunt Tibby, and deciphering puzzles and forgotten languages for Teyla, who adored history and archaeology. Another cousin was a woodworker and made beautiful furniture. An uncle was a shipwright and embedded magic in the vessels he crafted.

Syla had always used her gift for healing. How dreadful to

think that defending herself against enemies—killing people—might have become her *passion*.

No, she hadn't killed anyone yet, and she didn't intend to. Though... she admitted that the scrolls might not have been stolen if she'd finished off the stormer. Would she come to regret that she hadn't?

"It's right here." Teyla pointed a couple of inches above her ear. "Go ahead. I give you permission to heal me."

"Thank you," Syla said with a smile, though that wasn't why she'd hesitated.

Reminded that her cousin was in pain, she pushed aside her self-doubts and rested her hand on the side of Teyla's head. Her healing magic came readily to her, the moon-mark on her hand warming almost cheerfully as she sent a trickle of her power into the contusion to repair blood vessels and lower the inflammation. Teyla closed her eyes, slumping back with a sigh as Syla healed the damage, and the swelling went down.

"I practice my sword work with a couple of the guards an hour in the evenings several times a week," Teyla said. "I'm *not* inept."

Was that something Relvin had said? Probably.

"I'm certain you're not," Syla said.

"When that odious Lord Verrinmark came to court me and couldn't accept that I wasn't interested, I practiced on *him*."

"Were bandages involved?"

"I believe so. I feel no guilt. Relvin set that up, saying a woman not married and birthing babies by twenty-five is a waste on society. As if *that's* the only way one might contribute. I've had papers published in the leading scholarly journals on archaeology and had a theology publisher recruit me for a well-researched article on what prompted the storm god to go mad and think creating *dragons* was a good idea."

"What was your conclusion on that?" Syla finished healing the contusion and leaned back, thinking of Wreylith flying about, looking for someplace to drop her haunch of meat.

"There's evidence that when he spent time in the mortal world, he ate mukroog root for its supposed brain-boosting effects."

"Mukroog root is a hallucinogenic and, at higher quantities, a poison."

"Exactly. Slow-acting. It makes you sharp before it gives you kooky visions, but it also builds up in the brain and ends up being deleterious. The records show that he either voluntarily took it, because he liked the visions, or some human underling who sought to get rid of him was putting it in his food. This was more than a thousand years ago, so it's hard to find *real* evidence. There are supposedly paintings on ancient ruins in the rainforests of Froha." Teyla looked wistfully toward the room's high window. "I'd love to visit the continents one day, but Mom... never came back. I've always been hesitant."

"It's dangerous out there."

"Danger is everywhere these days. Even in the streets of our capital."

"Unfortunately true. You'd better increase your sword-fighting practices to two hours a night."

"Tell me about it." Teyla smoothed her hair where the wound had been.

"While I wouldn't normally discourage you from your studies and adventures—maybe from wanting to travel to a continent full of gargoyles and wyverns—I need you here in the capital, Teyla."

"You're not going to try to put me down as an heir to the throne, are you? After you, it should be your father's brother, though his brain is going early, speaking of kookiness, but what about his nieces and nephews?"

"None of them are moon-marked." Syla waved her hand,

reminding her cousin that the gods-gift only sporadically appeared on offspring born to relatives who weren't directly in line for the throne. Beyond that, it was less predictable, usually requiring only that one parent had a mark, but it had been known to skip a generation too.

Scientists had studied the phenomenon, inasmuch as the royal family had allowed, but results hadn't been definitive. Those who believed the gods hadn't abandoned mankind, as so many thought, attributed the appearance of the gifts to their ongoing intervention.

"I still can't believe Relvin got a moon-mark," Teyla said. "And me, for that matter. Mother had one but not Father. Relvin is a brat and doesn't deserve one." Teyla looked frankly at Syla. "You need to watch out for him."

"Relvin?"

"Yes. He craves... I wouldn't say power, exactly, but to be important. To matter. He's been snubbed a lot for his work with the newspaper, as if that's terribly pedestrian and only for those who want to read Garden Kingdom gossip, and it galls him. He wants to rule over all those who wouldn't talk to him for a story or suggested he wasn't doing noble work. He's hoping you'll name *him* as your heir, though he's also campaigning, I guess you'd call it. Working with all those he's managed to make friends with, usually those who share his vices, and hoping he can convince enough of the right people to insist that you're not qualified to run the Kingdom—and *he* is."

"I did get that gist."

"I don't know if you're qualified, Syla, but he surely isn't. And he wants it too much. He wouldn't be good for our people."

"I agree. And I will watch out for him, though I'm more concerned about those lurking out there who are less vocal and will enact their schemes in silence."

"I'd worry about that too." Teyla met her eyes again. "*Do* you want the throne? I never thought you had any interest in that."

"I didn't, and no. I'd prefer to continue to work in the temple and do what comes naturally to me, but I worry about stepping aside and losing all say in who does end up in charge and how the Kingdom is run. We have external threats we need to worry about right now. Chaos and in-fighting wouldn't be good for us."

"Agreed. The stormers have been scheming for generations, but now..." Teyla again touched the spot where her wound had been. "They're serious now."

Syla thought of Vorik's statements about how the climate had changed and how hard it was getting for his people to survive out there. "Yes."

A knock sounded but was cut off, and the door banged open.

In the hallway, Fel glowered as the white-haired General Dolok strode in. His dark eyes burned with accusation as his gaze landed on Syla.

She stood and mentally braced herself. Earlier, she'd been annoyed that he and so many of his troops had allowed themselves to be lured off, chasing the dragon ship and its fireworks display, but she could tell he was annoyed with *her* as well.

"Are you in need of healing, General?" she asked, partially to be polite, in case he *was* interested, but mostly in the hope of derailing what looked to be a tirade poised to erupt.

"I've more than a dozen men dead and another dozen injured," Dolok said.

"Please bring the wounded here, and I will tend them."

"You'd better tend them. And what about the dead? How will you heal *them*? This is your fault. You *invited* those people here." Dolok thrust a finger in the direction of the harbor.

Syla exhaled, willing her body to remain calm at the accusation. But there was an unsettling truth in it that put her on edge. He wasn't wrong.

"I invited them to bring diplomats in the hope of negotiating for peace, yes."

"There can be no peace with the people who *just* invaded our capital—our entire island—and killed *thousands* while destroying centuries of history, our buildings, our culture, our *city*. And they're still in the Kingdom, stealing all the crops from Harvest Island while their *dragons* denude the wilds of animals. And they're angling to get the rest of our islands. You *heard* them. That's the *negotiating* they were interested in. I can't believe you brought them and gave them the opportunity to try again for our shielder... I relieve you from serving in any capacity to make decisions for the Kingdom."

"I'm not an officer, General. You can't relieve me of duty."

"I can have you forcibly removed and thrown in the dungeon."

From the doorway, Fel growled like a guard dog.

"Your *single* bodyguard isn't going to stop me." Dolok didn't even bother glancing at Fel.

Syla took a moment to collect her thoughts before responding. Dolok might already have gathered troops and be able to call people in to grab her and restrict her freedom. She couldn't let herself be chained. There was too much to do.

"General Dolok, I agree that the night did not go well, but we still have the shielders, both the existing one and the one my aunt has been researching how to repair." Syla didn't mention the stolen scrolls. "She needs my help to return a working shielder to Harvest Island. The *Kingdom* needs my help."

"*You're* not the engineer. What can *you* do to help the Kingdom? Except send letters through which our enemies will exploit us?"

"I can help in many ways. By healing your troops, to start with. Bring all who are injured to me." Doubt creeping into Syla kept her retort from being as strong and certain as she wished. "As to the stormers, that may have been a mistake. I agree. But I felt I had to reach out to them because... I've seen them in action, General. Our troops aren't a match for their riders."

"Only because they command *dragons*."

No, not only that. But Syla, not wanting to further offend the general, didn't argue that the stormers were better—faster and more agile and deadly—warriors even without the dragons. "I need you and the military to focus on defending the islands."

"We can't do that when you're *inviting* our enemies inside the barrier."

"I won't do so again."

"I would *hope* not." Dolok shoved a hand through his short hair. "What Venia did has nearly destroyed us, and you— you want to help things along by letting that Captain Vorik into your bed, or whatever under the moon you have in mind there."

"Not that. Focus on defending the Kingdom, General, and I'll find a way to repair the Harvest Island shielder and get it back into place."

"It's not a kid with a bruise. You can't *heal* it."

"No, but we are researching what can be done."

"*We*." Dolok scoffed. "Your aunt is an *agricultural* engineer. And your only use is here, using your magic to heal people who *do* have the power to keep the Kingdom safe. If not for that, I would have already had you thrown in the dungeon. I may yet."

Dolok spun to storm out the door, but a boy of thirteen or fourteen wearing the whites of the kitchen staff had arrived. He clutched a silver platter with a haunch of meat resting on it.

"Uhm, Your Highness?" He peered past the general to look at Syla. "I stood in the courtyard, as directed, and a huge red dragon dropped this from the sky. What... should I do with it?"

"A *dragon*?" Dolok stared at the meat.

"I heard... I mean, we think it's eliok, Your Highness." The kid looked reverently at the meat. "It's supposed to be really good when it's all seasoned and prepared properly."

"Cook it for dinner," Syla said. "The meat is indeed eliok, and it's... a gift."

"From a dragon?" Dolok demanded. "It must be poisoned. You should throw it in the ocean."

"The military is not to be consulted on kitchen matters," Syla told the boy. "Season it as you deem proper, and cook it up."

The kid eyed the fuming general, the red tint to his face reminding Syla uncomfortably of the stormer whose airway she'd temporarily cut off. Next, the kid considered the meat, eyeing it with more pleasure than Dolok.

"I'll give your order to the kitchen staff, Your Highness," the boy said, then darted away. "Eliok," he could be heard calling. "We're going to have eliok for dinner. A gift from a *dragon!*"

"You may be too stupid to even be allowed to walk freely to heal people," Dolok told Syla and fondled the sword hilt at his belt.

Fel watched his movement through slitted eyes.

"Just handle the military, General," Syla said. "Let me get the shielder repaired and back up on Harvest Island. After that... if you want to stage a coup and lock me up, we can discuss it. With shackles around my wrists if you want."

Teyla's eyebrows flew up. Maybe Syla shouldn't have gone that far.

"*After* I ensure the shielder is repaired," Syla said again.

Dolok growled and stalked out, deliberately knocking his shoulder against Fel's as he left. A testament to his size and fitness, the big bodyguard didn't budge.

"I may have been mistaken when I told you to heal him," Fel said to Syla. "I'd hoped he would feel magically bound to you."

"That doesn't always happen."

Fel grunted, saying, "Too bad," as he returned to standing guard in the hallway.

Syla tried to exhale some of her tension. At least Fel was still on her side. She didn't entirely know *why* he was, as the bond he'd felt after she'd healed him should have faded by now, and, as much as she hated to admit it, Dolok was right. She'd invited the stormers here. This disaster had been of her making. More than ever, she felt the need to see the other shielder repaired and returned to Harvest Island. She had to fix the damage she'd done.

9

SYLA SAT WITH FEL AND TEYLA IN THE DINING HALL, KEENLY AWARE of how few allies she had and also wishing she'd chosen a place to eat that hadn't hosted so many family gatherings. The empty chairs, along with the stress of the day, threatened to bring tears. Syla thought of Vorik, wishing for the dozenth time that he could somehow be an ally. She had Fel, at least. And Aunt Tibby. And maybe Teyla. None of them would be a match for the entire military if General Dolok followed through on his threat to stage a coup, but... Syla had to be grateful for the help she had.

"This is delicious," Teyla said, carving off tender pieces of the meat that the kitchen staff had prepared. "What did you say it is?"

Apparently, some of the gift had been reserved, along with the bone, for a stew for the next day, but there'd been enough to fry for a late dinner. The chaos of the stormer incursion had delayed meal preparations, and it was creeping toward midnight.

"Eliok, I'm told," Syla said.

"I had no idea they're so tasty. They're elusive though, aren't they? And found in only a few spots in the world?"

"Only on Harvest Island, I'm told. In the rest of the world, they were hunted to extinction, no doubt because of their great deliciousness."

"Who's been doing all this telling?" Fel, who'd deigned to join them around the table instead of looming by the door, gave her a squint eye.

"It wasn't Vorik, if that's who your eye-skewer of disapproval is for."

"My..." He touched the side of his left eye.

"Wreylith was the one who shared the information. A couple of weeks ago. Today, she just brought that." Syla pointed to the slices of meat resting on a tray in a wine-based gravy.

"Wreylith?" Teyla asked.

"A red dragon who's linked to a little magical figurine that my father left me. I haven't quite figured out how that came to be, as in why he had it and who linked it to the dragon or why she bothered to come, but she helped us get the Harvest Island shielder."

Teyla stared at her. "I thought the kitchen boy was joking when he said a dragon dropped the meat from the sky."

Fel forked a piece of eliok and chewed it thoughtfully. "The information given by a wild dragon may or may not be more reliable than that offered by a stormer."

"I think when the topic is hunting, it's probably reliable." Syla looked out a window toward the night sky, wishing she could call the dragon down to flambé General Dolok. And Relvin while she was in the neighborhood. As a healer, it wasn't appropriate to wish all her enemies to be horribly killed in dragon-crafted infernos, but only the gods could condemn her for her fantasies. "Maybe I should have waited a few more days before activating the borrowed shielder," she murmured.

"What?" Teyla asked.

"I hope Aunt Tibby gets here soon. I regret that she's barely gotten any rest, but... I need her."

"I'll brace myself for her incendiary wit," Fel said.

"I'll give her some eliok meat," Syla said. "That'll make her happy."

"Unlikely."

As the meal neared its end, Syla started to worry that Aunt Tibby had not returned to the farm but gone off somewhere else in the city and couldn't be found. It was also possible the military was keeping her from entering the castle. But even if Dolok had decided to fight Syla, he would want the shielder repaired as much as she did. And Tibby, agricultural engineer or not, had been the one studying it and the scrolls.

Finally, Tibby walked in, rumpled and looking like she'd been woken from a deep sleep. The exasperated frown she slanted toward Syla also suggested it.

"What is this about stormers getting into the tunnels and threatening the shielders again?" Tibby asked her without preamble, though she lifted a hand toward Teyla and gave her a warmer I-need-to-consult-you look.

"We got a chance to use both the medical antique—" Syla touched the summoner still looped over her ear, "—and the explosives."

"I'd hoped that neither would be necessary. What happened? Did the explosives blow without damaging the shielder?"

"Yes." Syla described the evening's events, resisting the urge to leave out all mention of Vorik. He'd been too integral at too many points not to bring up, but she did gloss over his contribution— and hindrance. The scrolls were the important part. "Please tell me you made copies of them," she said after admitting they'd been taken.

"Of *course* I made copies. In triplicate. I've got a set at the farm and put the other set in the basement library here."

"Eyes of the moon, bless you," Syla said.

"Don't thank me yet. It could be disastrous that the stormers have that information."

Syla grimaced. "How so?"

"For starters, the schematics will give them a much better idea of how to quickly *destroy* the shielders if they gain access to more of them."

"They managed that fine without instructions," Fel said. "Destroying things is easier than creating them."

"So you acknowledge that you *easily* committed a heinous crime when you tore the engine of my tractor to pieces."

Fel clenched his jaw.

"Eliok meat, Aunt Tibby?" Syla lifted the tray in offering, a few pieces lingering in the gravy.

Tibby started to lift a hand but paused to look curiously at the meat. "Did you say *eliok*?"

"Yes, it's a dragon favorite."

"It's my new favorite too," Teyla said, still chewing heartily.

"Hm." Tibby selected a piece to sample. "You're correct that none of the scrolls held maps or information describing where the other shielders are located, but with the schematics and that list of components, including roughly where in the world they can be found—Teyla, I'd like to consult you on my translation of that —one might figure out how to make a shielder from scratch. It takes magic in addition to know-how." Tibby showed them the moon-mark on the back of her hand. "But if their dragons helped the stormers, it might be enough. Or *more* than enough. Reputedly, dragons have power that can rival that of the gods themselves."

"I don't know if there's historical evidence to support that hypothesis," Teyla said. "There was only a very short window of time where the gods and dragons existed in the world at the same time."

Tibby adjusted her spectacles, then lowered a bag slung over her shoulder to delve inside. "I concede that we don't have any way in the modern era to compare the magic that current-day dragons have and the gods had. Even when both existed, there wasn't a *scale* by which to measure their power."

"That's true," Teyla said. "The texts do offer accountings that may be helpful but certainly aren't scientific and might have been hyperbole. Did the gods truly, as legend suggests, render volcanos extinct, alter the air and water currents, and travel from this world to another when they departed?"

"A thousand years and more after the fact, it's difficult to say. We *do* have recent accountings of dragons altering land masses and shifting the flow of rivers by making changes near the sources."

Syla lifted a finger, intending to steer the increasingly academic conversation back to the important matter at hand, but a voice sounded in her mind.

You've found the meat of the eliok sufficiently succulent, I presume, Wreylith said.

Less booming, her voice came from farther away than before. Maybe she was flying out at sea now instead of over the castle.

It's extremely tasty. Thank you for sharing it with me. Perhaps belatedly, it occurred to Syla that Wreylith might *want* something. After all, dragons weren't known for giving gifts or displaying gratitude toward humans. From what she'd learned of the stormers and their relationship with dragons, both parties found it mutually beneficial. Dragons certainly didn't serve humans. *You must be a mighty hunter to have found enough eliok to satisfy your needs and have some left over.*

Of course I'm a mighty hunter, Wreylith said as if it were the most obvious statement in the universe. *Were I able to fly down to your island, I could show you by hunting the horn hogs that amble through the valleys in the core of that land. Or I could fish for venomous sword iglets in your eastern lagoons. Like the eliok, those species are difficult to find in the rest of the world. Only here where they've been protected by the sky shields do they remain abundant.*

Unfortunately, due to the distraction that you inflicted upon me, I was not able to hunt on your island before you returned the shielder to duty.

I apologize for inconveniencing you.

As you should. Are you aware that dragons have bonded with your kind in the past?

Uhm, my kind? Syla heard Teyla and Tibby continuing to debate on whether dragon magic could rival the magic of the gods, citing sources to back up their beliefs, but she barely registered the conversation. A new idea was percolating in her mind. Might she convince Wreylith to help her again? It almost seemed like the dragon, in returning to the area, wanted to do so. Wreylith wanted *something* anyway. Venomous sword iglets, perhaps. *You mean stormers who train to become riders?*

No.

Tibby lay papers filled with notes on the table, and her discussion with Teyla turned to her translations.

Those humans with a moon-mark on their hand, Wreylith added. *The lingering power of the gods.*

Someone with a moon-mark bonded with a dragon? In the way that the stormer riders do? Receiving magical power from the dragons in addition to that gifted to them by the gods?

It has happened, but only when humans from your kingdom were wise enough to realize the greatness of having a dragon ally.

I'd think a lot of humans from any nation could see the benefit of that. But why would a dragon—

Through a bond with such an individual, Wreylith interrupted, *my ancestors discovered that a dragon is granted access to the islands protected by sky shields. That is only true for the specific island that the bonded human is on or flying to, but it was a way for those dragons to hunt in waters and on lands otherwise denied to their kind.*

That's fascinating. I hadn't heard... I've read a lot of our history books and haven't encountered that.

Your people have short memories and inadequate accountings of the past.

That's... possible.

Your own Queen Erasbella, for a time, wielded both her gods-gift and the power of a dragon, through such a bond.

That wasn't that long ago, even for us short-lived humans, Syla said. *I'm shocked that I haven't read about that, especially since Erasbella was my great-great grandmother. I'm a direct descendant.*

I'm aware. As is the krendala.

The... That's the figurine, right? Syla remembered Vorik using that term.

It is. Of course, it is a monumental choice to bond with another being, especially a decidedly lesser being, so it is not to be undertaken lightly.

Even for access to iglets.

Even so. Delicious though they are. I admit to feeling some distaste for the idea of even considering it with one who cannot see without eye tools and who is so feeble as to have no defensive or offensive abilities and barely the ken to stay on a dragon's back.

"Syla?" Tibby touched her shoulder. "Are you listening?"

"Sorry, I'm being insulted by a dragon."

Tibby, Teyla, and Fel looked around, as if said dragon might be lurking in a corner or perhaps up among the ceiling rafters.

"Wreylith is in the area." Syla pointed out toward the harbor and beyond. "She finds me feeble."

And that was far from the only deficiency in the dragon's list. Syla touched the frame of her spectacles.

"She came here to tell you that?" Tibby asked.

"There must not be a lot going on in the world of dragons," Teyla said.

"They're hunting the prey on Harvest Island to extinction," Fel grumbled.

There is some truth to that, Wreylith said, somehow hearing the conversation from afar. Or could she experience it through her link with Syla? *With so many dragons scouring the forests there now, the hunting has grown poorer.*

Maybe that was what had prompted Wreylith to recall a way that only *certain* dragons were allowed to hunt on the protected islands.

"Did you hear me say that it would behoove us to gather the components promptly, in case the stormers are able to translate the scrolls and decide to do the same?" Tibby asked. "Even if they don't want a shielder of their own, surely, they will want to keep us from repairing ours."

"I didn't hear that, no, but I understand and agree." Syla wished that stormer hadn't gotten the scrolls and fantasized again about sneaking into their headquarters and stealing them back, but they had camps all over the world. Even if General Dolok had intelligence on the Sixteen Talons' current headquarters, he wouldn't give it to her. "What *are* the components? And how hard are they to get?"

Tibby and Teyla exchanged long looks.

Before either spoke, Syla knew the answer would be, *Not easy*.

"The magical moss bulbs grow in the rainforests around the world," Teyla said, pointing to an item on the list, "but since this requires them in an ancient version of desiccated powder—"

"I thought you said petrified," Tibby interrupted.

"I'm not sure of that translation. Finding something petrified would be even harder."

"We know the magical teal ore is in the Everfrost Mountains on Droha though," Tibby said. "It's rare and hard to extricate, but it's findable."

"I would think so." Teyla nodded. "But the last... This doesn't even have a name beyond *crystal orb*, some magical growth that the storm god created to assist in crafting his creatures."

"I've seen the crystal orb in the broken shielder," Tibby said.

"It's like a miniature of the outer shell, but it's at the core of every-thing, according to the schematic, and both the brains and brawn of the artifact."

"The only one in the world—that hasn't already been harvested and put to use, that is—can supposedly be found in what was the storm god's main laboratory in the Dire Desert of Droha. Only one at a time grows out of a special substrate that he created, and it takes ten years to form. Another doesn't start forming until the last is removed."

"So we can only ever make one shielder every ten years?" Syla asked.

"*If* the crystal orb is there at all after all these centuries. With the gods gone..." Teyla spread her hands.

"Had our ancestors been wise, they would have gone to that laboratory every ten years and stockpiled the orbs." Tibby pinched her lips in disapproval.

"Well, it doesn't sound easy to get into." Teyla waved at a para-graph of text, presumably part of the translation from the scrolls. "Or like a place one would want to wander around in. It was made by a god who hated humans, after all. Or didn't care that his creations liked to eat our people."

"True," Tibby said. "And there was a mention of security defenses for the laboratory."

"Can you imagine how fun it would be to try to break through security created by a *god*?" Teyla grimaced. "Even the Dire Desert itself can kill a person easily. We haven't sent many archaeological teams there over the centuries."

Syla sat back in her chair. "If we can only get one of those particular components every ten years... we can't let the stormers reach it first."

"Agreed, though it does sound like a moon-mark is required to gain entrance to the laboratory," Tibby said.

"One of our moon-marks gets a person into the storm god's

laboratory?" Syla arched skeptical eyebrows. "That doesn't make sense."

"Well, the shielders were made after the storm god was driven away, remember," Teyla said. "Another god may have added that element to allow one of our relatives access in case they ever needed a replacement component."

"But the same god didn't deactivate the security defenses?" Syla asked.

"The gods can only do so much to help us," Tibby said.

"That's the truth," Fel muttered, half-listening as he rotated and massaged one of his stiff hips.

Syla waved at the notes. "It sounds like we need to pack for a quest."

Fel frowned at her. "*We?*"

"I will, of course, bring you along, Sergeant Fel, if you're willing to continue working with me." Syla smiled at him, certain that hadn't been his objection.

"*You* should stay here," Fel said. "As we've discussed before, it's important to keep you alive, not put you at risk."

"You don't think I'd be more at risk here?" Syla smiled sadly, silently acknowledging that if she left, a new monarch or government system might have been put in place by the time she returned. Of course, Dolok might already be scheming to do that. If she *didn't* leave, she could end up stuck in a dungeon cell.

Fel opened his mouth, as if to deny that, but he'd been there for the general's threats.

"You'll need me to help you navigate the world out there and find these ancient components." Teyla nodded firmly. "I have some books and ideas on where in the desert that laboratory might be located."

"You're talking about a journey of weeks if not months," Tibby pointed out. "If a moon-mark weren't required, I'd suggest you send a team out to look for these things. Do you even have a ship that would carry you to the mainland, if you choose to go? The queen's *Swift Darter* was destroyed in the invasion."

"Maybe Captain Radmarik would transport us again." Syla had no idea if he remained on Castle Island or how to get in touch with him if he'd returned to Harvest Island or sailed elsewhere to avoid the chaos.

"I heard his last adventure with you was daunting," Tibby said.

"We survived it."

"His ship took damage."

"Yes, but the escorting guard ships were destroyed completely."

"Something that might not entice him to want to take you on another journey," Tibby said.

After the discussion Syla had engaged in with the captain, she was less certain. He was married, in heart if not legally, to a stormer woman who'd left her people and was high up in the Freeborn Faction. Apparently, *she* had been the one who'd suggested Radmarik assist Syla. Too bad Syla had been too concerned about installing and activating the shielder to speak with the captain again after they'd arrived. She'd arranged payment for him, but he and his whaling ship had disappeared before she could thank him again personally.

"Even if he would," Tibby added, "you'd be very vulnerable out there unless you could command a lot of cannonball-filled guard ships to escort you."

Syla noticed that her aunt kept saying *you* instead of *we* or *us*. It didn't sound like she intended to go on another adventure with Syla and Fel. Perhaps understandable. She was resourceful, but it might be a good idea to have an ally back here, keeping an eye on the political situation. Inasmuch as an engineer would pay attention to that.

"Right now," Syla said, "I think it would be easier for me to get the help of a dragon anyway."

Tibby laughed, but Fel looked upward, as if Wreylith might land atop the castle.

"I believe that," he said.

Tibby looked at him.

"You weren't there when she waved the red dragon and her allies down to drive off the stormer riders and *their* dragons," Fel told her.

"I did hear about it," Tibby said.

"You also weren't there when General Dolok threatened to throw her in the dungeon," he added.

"Was that recently?" Tibby's gaze shifted to Syla.

"Before dinner."

"That's recent."

"Yes. He blames me for everything that happened with the stormers."

"And gives her no credit for dealing with them and keeping the working and broken shielder out of their hands," Fel said.

Syla appreciated that he was supporting her—the moon god knew she needed supporters—but she shrugged. "I lost the scrolls."

"If you could arrange a dragon to transport a group, that *would* make collecting components from around the world easier." Tibby pressed her lips together. "Assuming the dragon could keep from dumping you into the ocean a mile from shore."

"That was as close as Wreylith could get because of the barrier." Syla wondered if she should tell her aunt that it would be the same dragon that would help again. It wasn't as if Syla knew others to call upon. She wasn't even positive Wreylith would do it. It sounded like she wanted to hunt on the shielded islands, not search for magical engineering components on a continent that she could always access.

Tibby shuddered again. "Regardless, if you had a dragon, you'd have a chance of beating the stormers to the components.

Going by ship and walking inland... It could be a journey of *months* to gather those components. If not *years*. And the stormers could fly to them within days."

"They may not go after them," Syla pointed out.

"Right." Teyla brightened. "What are the odds that they even have someone who can translate the temple language? Most of their people don't learn to read."

"Let's hope," Syla said.

"Even if they aren't involved, gathering the components as quickly as possible would be ideal," Tibby said. "Harvest Island can't withstand years peeled open to the elements—and predators."

"I agree," Syla said.

"With the assistance of a dragon... *Can* you get it?"

"I'll try, though she may only be able to carry two, if she's willing at all." Syla looked at Teyla and admitted that having an archeologist along could be helpful, but, if she had to choose, she needed her bodyguard.

"Darn," Tibby said, clearly not desiring to ride on a dragon's back again.

Was it crazy that Syla did? Even the back of a dragon who had insulted her and described all the ways she was puny and inferior?

"We can go together. I'll defend you." Teyla rose from the table and made fencing motions over her empty plate.

"She needs a *bodyguard*," Fel said, "not a historian with delusions of combat experience."

Syla feared that not even her bodyguard would be sufficient to deal with whatever security the storm god had set up to protect his laboratory from intruders. Again, she wished Vorik were an ally she could call upon.

"Actually," Tibby said, raising a finger, "if Syla has a dragon to protect her, someone with archaeological and especially cartographical experience may be an ideal companion."

"These two *girls* aren't going off into the world alone. And a *dragon* isn't a proper bodyguard." Fel looked appalled at the notion.

"A dragon could eat a proper bodyguard." The way Tibby smiled at him suggested she might like to see that.

Fel glared at her.

"I don't think Wreylith would be quite as reliable as Fel in keeping me alive," Syla admitted, remembering how the red dragon had tossed her to the ground near the lighthouse. It would have been to her *death* via a broken neck if Vorik hadn't run over to catch her. "Wreylith doesn't quite understand human frailty. Especially *my* frailty."

Fel folded his arms over his chest in an I-told-you-so stance.

"Let me see if she's even willing to do this," Syla said. "I may be making assumptions."

10

IN THE DARK OF NIGHT, THE DRAGONS AND THEIR RIDERS FLEW across the Sea of Storms. As the squadron neared Dark Dagger Point and the cave overlooking the water that the Sixteen Talons were currently sharing with the Moonhunt Tribe, Vorik and Jhiton requested that their dragons fly ahead to drive away wyverns circling above the cliff.

Male and female archers on the ledge of the cave were firing at them, but the fast aerial predators could evade arrows by flying inland or spinning and darting about in the air. Wyverns often followed human foraging parties in the wilds, hoping to capture a lone person who wandered too far from the group, but to appear over a cave full of strong warriors—not to mention their dragon allies—was unusual.

They've grown too brazen, Jhiton said telepathically.

Hunger drives them, Agrevlari replied.

Perhaps, but fury filled Vorik at the presumptuousness of the scavengers. Though his people were always careful—they had to be to survive—more than one wyvern had successfully stolen away a baby or small child in the past. The idea of one snatching up a toddler that came near the ledge made him lift his bow and start firing before they were in range.

Despite the distance, one of his arrows clipped a wyvern on the wing. It screeched, warning others of the approaching threat.

Agrevlari's powerful wings beat rapidly as he closed the distance between the squadron and the scavengers. At his side, Ozlemar matched his pace, their past grievances forgotten, or at least set aside as they focused on the threat. Jhiton joined Vorik in firing, the wood-shafted arrows they commonly used for hunting doing little good on the magical creatures but the more precious and harder-to-come-by gargoyle-bone arrows driving through scale and into flesh.

More screeches filled the sky, and the wyverns flew inland, over the cliff to try to escape. Neither Jhiton nor Vorik relented, and the rest of the squadron shouted from behind, hurrying to catch up.

Perhaps bolstered by the sound of the dragons returning and driving away enemies, more men and women with bows stepped out onto the ledge of the cave. One loosed an arrow at a wyvern that had made the mistake of flying parallel to the coast instead of inland. The projectile took it in the shoulder, and the creature careened off the rock face.

Meanwhile, the dragons, with their larger wings and greater musculature, caught up with the retreating wyverns. Vorik slung his bow over his back and drew his sword for close-range fighting.

Agrevlari caught up with a yellow-scaled beast that dove and flew low over the ground, darting between rock formations in an attempt to elude the larger dragon. It didn't work. For all his grousing and griping, Agrevlari was agile and powerful. He caught up and bit the wyvern on the back above its tail. Vorik leaned over as the creature reared in the air, snapping its jaws defensively at the dragon. Vorik drove his blade into the wyvern's long neck. With a much greater snap, Agrevlari caught it on the spine and crushed vertebrae. The beast clipped a rock formation and tumbled to the ground, its back broken.

Vorik and Agrevlari flew higher to seek more enemies, but the rest of the squadron had killed the remaining wyverns. Though disappointed that the battle hadn't been longer and he hadn't been able to vanquish more enemies, Vorik was relieved when Agrevlari banked and turned toward the cave. After the long day, Vorik looked forward to a night's rest.

A lone female warrior with a bow and a sword stood atop the cliff, having climbed up from the cave. Even in the dark, Vorik recognized Captain Lesva and grimaced.

After their battle on Harvest Island, during which he and a precisely timed lightning bolt had sent her plummeting a hundred feet into the ocean, she'd returned injured and, with the help of her dragon magic, had spent days in a healing trance, a gift she had that many envied. Because of that, they hadn't spoken since that night. Vorik would prefer not to talk to her this night either, but she watched him and Jhiton as they flew toward the cave. Something told him he wouldn't avoid a conversation with her.

Their dragons flew over the ledge, dove, and twisted to enter the wide mouth of the cave, alighting near the front. Cheers went up, especially from the women and children, many of whom waved apples or other treats the riders had been bringing back from their foraging on Harvest Island.

No, not foraging, Vorik corrected. His people were taking crops that the gardeners had planted and tended through the year. As happy as it made him to see previously hungry people smiling with food in their hands, this war didn't sit well with him. Maybe because he'd gotten to know a certain gardener woman...

Vorik sighed as Agrevlari landed, then slid off and started toward Jhiton, hoping to be dismissed for the night so that he could rest, but Devron had already jumped down and was showing the general something. The scrolls he'd taken.

"Good evening, Captain Vorik." Geahi, a slender woman in her twenties, smiled and stepped into his path. She had warm gray eyes and always greeted him when he returned from a hunt. "Do you have a moment? Leonodor and I would love to thank you for your work of late." A few minutes ago, she'd been on the ledge with a bow, but now she carried a toddler, who appeared more interested in sleeping and drooling than displaying gratitude.

Vorik looked wistfully at the kid, wanting to sleep and drool a little himself. Behind him, the dragons left the cave to find perches in the rocks above. Their kind didn't usually live with humans but, if they knew another mission was coming, would stay close.

"The fruit and vegetables from the gardener island are so wonderful," Geahi said. "We're enjoying them immensely."

"I'm glad, but I'm not the one bringing them back. You don't need to thank *me*." Vorik touched his chest and smiled when the toddler yawned and dug his fingers into his mother's hair. "In fact, Hohan is on the gathering team, isn't he?"

That was the brother of the husband that she'd lost. The man had been trying to nobly step in to wed her, and everyone thought it would be a good match for a mother with a son to care for. Of course, Geahi didn't feel that way, and she eased forward, shifting the boy so she could rest a hand on Vorik's chest.

"From the stories that are being told, *you* were paramount in the sky shield dropping so that our people can forage there."

Vorik shook his head. He hadn't been paramount in much of anything except losing that shielder during the battle over the whaling ship, and he didn't deserve credit for the harvest his people were now enjoying.

"The general wants you, I see." Geahi tilted her head toward Jhiton, who was holding the scrolls open but also looking at Vorik. *Thoughtfully* at Vorik? Wrath of the storm god, what was he planning now? "Come to my furs later if you wish, and I'll show you my gratitude completely. A full stomach is an aphrodisiac, you

know, and Leonodor sleeps the whole night through these days."
She winked at Vorik.

"Thank you for the invitation, Geahi," Vorik said. "I think my
brother is scheming his next mission for me, but I appreciate your
offer and will keep it in mind."

Disappointment entered her eyes as she interpreted his words
as a rejection. Vorik bowed apologetically toward her but walked
away without looking back. Whether it was wise or not, he'd, of
late, had another woman on his mind. The memory of Syla
looking suspiciously at him as he suggested how she might relax
her eyes—and her body—flitted through his thoughts. She'd been
understandably suspicious throughout their entire chat, but he
hadn't minded. He'd enjoyed spending even that brief time with
her. His only regret was that he hadn't gotten to leave with the
cylindrical boxes of sugary desserts. He imagined sharing a
cobbler or other sweet with Syla, the taste of sugar on their lips as
they kissed.

Jhiton looked up at his approach, his face grim.

Vorik wiped away whatever goofy—or lusty—expression had
been on his face. Jhiton and Devron weren't looking at the scrolls,
though Vorik knew his brother had no trouble reading the
Kingdom language. He'd always been a far better student than
Vorik, who'd preferred hunting and playing outside to squinting at
letters and numbers that his people never used in their lives.

"I'm telling you, sir," Devron said, "she's a lot more than a
healer."

Vorik's ears perked as he realized they were discussing Syla.
Since Devron had been in the chamber before he and Jhiton
arrived, he may have interacted with her. Judging by the way he
rubbed his throat, that interaction hadn't been pleasurable.

Vorik raised his eyebrows. He had a hard time imagining Syla
getting the best of a trained stormer in a battle. She didn't even
carry a weapon.

"*What* more?" Jhiton asked the man, though his gaze remained on Vorik, as if he expected *him* to know.

"She almost... I mean, I'm sure my strength and stamina would have protected me from..." Devron also looked at Vorik. "She couldn't have killed me with her magic, could she?"

Vorik shook his head. "She's a healer, not a killer. How would you even kill someone with magic?"

The power he derived from his bond with Agrevlari enhanced his physical attributes, which made him more effective at defeating foes—sometimes *permanently* defeating foes—but it wasn't as if he could wave his hand and end a person's life. Of course, some riders with dragons more predatory and merciless than Agrevlari received power that might be able to let them do something like that. He'd heard stories of riders lashing out with less tangible weapons than swords and bows, but didn't that usually require close contact?

"It was like an invisible garrote wrapping around my neck." Again, Devron touched his throat. "It kept me from breathing. At the same time, I felt like this snake of power was winding through my body. It wrapped around my heart. For a moment, I thought she was going to... I don't know. *Kill* me. The way she looked into my eyes with the certainty that she could was, uhm." Devron glanced at Jhiton and didn't say something like *terrifying* or *soul-shriveling*, instead opting to save face with, "Concerning."

"That's the reason you were unconscious when we entered the chamber?" Jhiton asked as Vorik shook his head, having a hard time believing Syla had used her power to knock someone out. She'd never suggested she could do that. She'd emphasized that she used her magic for healing.

"Yes, sir. I couldn't breathe, and then I blacked out. I didn't think... I wasn't sure I would wake up."

"What *exactly* can she do with her magic?" Jhiton directed the question at Vorik.

"I don't know. I thought only healing."

"Over the years, our spies have reported that the moon-marks give those with them power that they can direct in different ways, depending on their natural talents and interests," Jhiton said, "but I haven't heard of any of them becoming assassins."

"Syla isn't an *assassin*." Vorik couldn't keep the exasperation out of his voice. "She's a healer. She wears their robes. She bakes *cobblers*."

Devron's brow scrunched in puzzlement. The poor man had probably never had a cobbler. Admittedly, Vorik hadn't until Syla had given him one, but now that he knew they existed, he wanted more of them.

"Well, if she wears a *robe*," Jhiton said, "she can't possibly be an assassin. Everyone knows they have different sartorial preferences."

"That's right. They dress more like this." Vorik plucked at his brother's black sleeve and waved at the equally dark cloak.

"Funny."

"I aim to entertain." Vorik pointed at the scrolls, hoping to change the subject, but he sensed the approach of someone new.

"She can do more than heal," Captain Lesva said coolly.

She came to stand at Jhiton's side while leveling a cold look at Vorik.

He sighed, deciding he should have gone to her when she'd been recovering from her injuries, but he hadn't wanted to deal with her snark. And he couldn't have brought himself to apologize for being responsible for her falling off that cliff. She'd brought that upon herself by disobeying Jhiton's orders and capturing— capturing and *torturing*—Syla.

"What more?" Jhiton eyed her without warmth, but he didn't step away from her either.

"When I was questioning her—"

"*Torturing* her," Vorik interrupted.

Lesva shot him the cold look again. "When I was attempting to learn that which Vorik had failed to learn, the location of the Harvest Island shielder, I used my magic to try to lower her defenses and convince her to speak the answers you sought." Lesva pointed at Jhiton as she said that *you*, as if everything she did was for him and the good of the stormers and the Sixteen Talons.

Yeah, right. Vorik knew she craved a promotion and power. If she got her way, she would lead her tribe one day, and she would do anything necessary to reach her goal.

"I believe I told you," Jhiton said mildly, "that would prove ineffective. Moonmarks are notoriously resistant to mental attacks and interrogation. We've attempted to forcibly question members of the royal family before."

Vorik also wanted to correct his brother, swapping in *torture* for *forcibly question*, but one didn't correct one's superior officer, especially not in front of witnesses.

"You did, sir," Lesva said.

"And I told you not to attempt to capture and interrogate the princess," Jhiton continued, his tone still mild, but his green eyes were hard. He'd stripped people of their rank before when they'd disobeyed his orders. When they'd disobeyed in a way that put the Talons at risk, he'd even killed them. With his own hands.

Vorik didn't wish that fate on Lesva, but if she were demoted, he wouldn't object. After the pain she'd inflicted on Syla, *some* punishment should be in order. Unfortunately, Jhiton probably didn't care much about Syla. She was a royal from the Garden Kingdom, after all, an obstacle in the flight path to achieving *his* goal.

"You did, sir," Lesva repeated, and bowed her head, though such a gesture had to be difficult for one with such a stiff neck. "I thought you would forgive me my choice if I could destroy the shielder. But my choice resulted in the death of my lieutenant, and

I regret it. Honestly, I thought the gardener girl looked so soft that there was no way that she could fight off my magic." Lesva glanced at Vorik again.

He clenched his jaw, remembering Lesva's unflattering description of Syla. She wasn't rangy, lean, and muscular, like stormer women, but she wasn't *soft*. She had grit and determination. And power. More, if Devron's accounting was correct, than any of them had realized.

Was it possible the dragon *Wreylith* had realized it? Maybe that was why she'd come when Syla touched the krendala.

Even though Vorik hadn't intended to trick Syla into giving up information, he did wish he'd managed to find out how she'd finagled Wreylith's help during that battle. That had been unexpected and almost disastrous.

"I believe the loss of your lieutenant is punishment enough," Jhiton said, "so I will not demote you, but you will *not* disobey my orders again."

Vorik told himself that he shouldn't be disappointed that Lesva wasn't being demoted, but he disagreed with the loss of one of her squadron as being sufficient punishment. Lesva, despite her aspirations to lead her tribe, didn't have a lot of warmth and compassion for others, not that he'd noticed. He doubted she'd lost much sleep over her lieutenant's death.

"I understand, General. But what is the mission going forward? Simply continue to demolish Harvest Island and take their food? Or do you have plans to gain access to more of the islands?" Lesva's mouth twisted as she lifted her head and met Jhiton's gaze. "And get rid of that girl?"

That girl? Syla?

Vorik clenched his fist. Lesva had been the one to torture Syla. What grudge could *Lesva* hold?

"You know what my plans are," Jhiton said quietly. "We will not only have *access* to the other islands, but we will *have* them."

"Excellent, sir. Is there anything I can do? I've recovered enough for duty." Lesva leaned forward, eager for a mission.

Not wanting to appear anything but a loyal officer desiring the same, Vorik attempted to look alert, though he was far more eager for a night's sleep.

"I want you to take two squadrons to Harvest Island to establish rule over the capital city while Captain Vorik makes sure a shielder is never returned to its shores to reinstate the sky shield. Not unless *we* choose to put one in place."

Vorik raised his eyebrows and looked at the scrolls, guessing they tied in with his portion of the mission.

Lesva frowned, as if she wanted to object to such a simple task, and she also looked at the scrolls. Certain some great secrets that were key to their plans lay within? And that she should be involved?

"You'll leave in the morning," Jhiton told her, pointing toward the cave exit and out to sea in the direction of the Garden Kingdom islands.

"Yes, sir," Lesva said but hesitated. "What about the girl? If Devron is right, she's even more dangerous than I believed. And if she commands Wreylith—"

"I am certain she doesn't *command* Wreylith," Jhiton said, dry again.

"No, sir, that's probably true, but I think we need to get rid of her."

"That's not necessary," Vorik caught himself saying, though maybe he should have kept his mouth shut. Jhiton hadn't indicated he would send Lesva off on an assassination mission. Further, if Vorik kept defending Syla to his people... they would grow suspicious about his loyalties.

The squint that Lesva sent him promised that she was *already* suspicious, at least when it came to his feelings for Syla.

Vorik folded his arms over his chest, refusing to take back his words. "She's not a threat."

"She threw explosives at us," Jhiton reminded him.

"At *you*."

"Thus making the behavior acceptable."

"She was trying to defend her people's shielders," Vorik said.

"The shielders that *we* must destroy so that our people have a better future." Jhiton gestured around the cave at the fires burning, families happily eating their fill for the first time in a long time.

"I know." Vorik lowered his arms. "I don't oppose that, and you know I'll do whatever you ask, General. I just don't think we need to worry about Princess Syla."

Long seconds passed as Jhiton regarded him. Vorik willed him to send the lurking Devron and Lesva away so they could speak privately. Jhiton would be annoyed by him questioning him in front of others, but alone, he would be more reasonable. Or so Vorik hoped.

"She's more than a healer," Lesva said.

Devron nodded vigorously.

"Getting rid of her would be wise," Lesva added. "Sir, if you want, while I'm on Harvest Island, it would be a simple matter to have my dragon fly me close to Castle Island. I could swim through the barrier with my weapons and end the princess as a threat to our conquest."

"Just focus on securing Harvest Island," Jhiton told her. "Send a report back to me when their capital is ours."

Lesva looked like she wanted to object further, but she managed a respectful, "Yes, sir," and bowed and walked away.

"You're also dismissed, Devron," Jhiton said.

"Yes, sir." Rubbing his throat again, Devron headed for the fire where his wife and children camped.

"What mission do you have for me involving the scrolls,

General?" Vorik pointed at them, hoping Jhiton would explain their significance—and forget all about this new determination that Syla was some kind of threat.

"You're going to gather the components that are apparently necessary for repairing a sky shielder." Jhiton opened a scroll filled with writing. "This is in an older tongue, and Devron and I can't translate everything, but the first component is believed to be found in the rainforests of Froha and Droha, the second in the mountains of Droha, and the third in its great Dire Desert. Lieutenant Wise might be able to ascertain more details. He can take a look while you're flying down the coast to the rainforest on Droha."

"I... All right. Will you humor me and tell me *why* you want to repair a shielder? We don't even have a broken one."

"No, but the gardeners do."

"I'm assuming you don't want me to gather the components and give them to the Kingdom."

"I do not. From what this says, the components are rare, one specifically appearing only once every ten years. If *we* collect the items, they won't be available for the gardeners." Jhiton handed the scroll to Vorik. "Take Wise, find the components, and bring them to me."

"Yes, sir."

"I trust you'll know what to do if you cross paths with Princess Syla."

Vorik started to say that was unlikely—it wasn't as if *she* would be sent to collect components from around the world—but hadn't she been the one to go to Harvest Island? With only her aged bodyguard for protection? What if she went on this quest too?

"Invite her to my furs in the hope that she'll divulge kingdom secrets while in the throes of passion?" Vorik didn't grin, though the idea pleased him. More the part where they would share his furs than the divulging of secrets. He thought they'd both enjoyed themselves more when they'd been discussing *safe* topics.

"Do you think it likely that will work at this point?" Jhiton raised a skeptical eyebrow.

Vorik wanted to say *absolutely* and that he would do his best. A stirring in his groin suggested his penis wanted that too, and he almost rolled his eyes at himself. Letting his lower extremities in on decision making was never a good plan.

"Probably not," he admitted. "I don't think I ever fooled her by claiming to be a part of the Freeborn Faction."

"I'm also skeptical of that."

"I *did* try."

"I have no doubt." Jhiton glanced down.

Heat seared Vorik's cheeks before he realized the general was eyeing the scroll, not giving a significant look to Vorik's crotch. Jhiton, after all, was never one to be crude.

"If you encounter people she's sent for the components," Jhiton said, "kill them. If you encounter her..."

"I'm not killing her."

"I assumed not." Jhiton looked in the direction that Captain Lesva had gone. He wasn't reconsidering her assassination offer, was he?

"But I'll deter her," Vorik hurried to promise. "I'll make sure she doesn't get the components back to her people."

He hated the idea of sabotaging Syla, but it was better than the general deciding she was too dangerous and sending someone to kill her.

Jhiton's gaze grew thoughtful again. Bloody daggers, what was he scheming now? Vorik didn't think Jhiton was looking at Lesva but out the cave into the dark of night.

"You care about her," Jhiton stated.

"I... Yes." Vorik doubted he should admit that, but it was probably clear to everyone concerned by now anyway.

"Does she care about *you*?"

"What woman *wouldn't* care about me? I'm delightful and charming, not to mention sexy, with the devastating smile we discussed previously." Vorik offered that smile as he touched his chest, but this line of questioning worried him. Jhiton was scheming up something new, something that wouldn't be in Syla's best interest.

Jhiton gave him a can't-you-give-me-a-serious-answer look.

"She could have killed me the night we, uh." Vorik waved vaguely. He hadn't explained to his brother what exactly had happened in that cave, but he *had* mentioned those candles. More because he'd been certain Lesva would talk about them than that he'd wanted to admit Syla had gotten the best of him. "Another time, she could have let me drown in the sea when I was unconscious. I believe she's quite fond of me."

"Or she has the heart of a healer and doesn't wantonly kill people, even enemies."

"I don't know if Devron would agree with that," Vorik said though *he* believed it to be true.

"No." Jhiton's eyelids drooped.

Maybe Vorik shouldn't have reminded him of Devron's encounter with Syla.

"What I'm asking is if she would come back here with you." Jhiton pointed at the cave floor.

"Like... for negotiations or something?"

"To be your mate."

Vorik rocked back. "You think she'd give up being a princess—no, a *queen*—to the entire Garden Kingdom where she lives in a luxurious castle and has servants to bring her food and clean up after her? So she could come live in a cave with me?"

"That castle isn't luxurious anymore."

"They're rebuilding it."

"As to the rest," Jhiton said, "women do such things for men they love, don't they?"

"I don't think women who feel a duty to protect their people do."

"Will they even allow her to be coronated and rule the Kingdom?" Jhiton asked. "I would have expected it to happen by now if she wished it—and *they* wished it. That general thought he was in charge."

"That general was a gargoyle's cock. As to the rest, she didn't mention her status as queen-to-be or queen-not-to-be when we spoke."

"What *did* she mention? Did you get anything useful out of her. Like how she convinced Wreylith to show up?"

"No. I did ask. She was oddly reticent to divulge important information to me."

"You're not a very good spy, Vorik."

"Tell me about it. I do think that if she *wants* to be queen, she will be."

Maybe she would then invite him to live with *her*? Would he ever consider that? A life of ease and comfort in a castle where the sky was protected from predators and men didn't have to constantly carry their weapons around? It was hard to imagine such an existence. But there would be fruit aplenty. Desserts. And... Syla.

But they hadn't known each other that long, and half the things they'd spoken to each other had been lies. Jumping to the notion of being *mates* and living together was ludicrous. He'd enjoyed their interactions—*especially* their interaction in the cave—but all that he truly wanted was for her to be safe and for them to be...

Oh, he didn't know. For them to be able to spend time together without it being part of a spy mission.

"Here. Leave in the morning, and bring back the components."

Jhiton, probably tired of watching Vorik's face as he fantasized about Syla, handed him the scrolls. "If you see her and she's willing to become your mate—one of our people—I wouldn't object to it, and I can speak with our Chieftess Shi about inviting her into the tribe. A healer with a gods-gift and the power to do more than bandage and prescribe tinctures... I don't have to tell you that our people could use that."

"Ah," was all Vorik said as he realized why Jhiton was entertaining this idea. He wanted Syla's *power*.

Meanwhile, all Vorik wanted was...

The memory of his night with Syla sprang into his mind, of her standing between those two candles and removing her robe to show him all her beautiful curves, her full lips parted and her eyes hot with passion as she invited him to take her. His groin tightened again, and he envisioned bringing her back here to join with her every night. But she would never agree to that. She was as devoted to her people as he was to his. And they were so different.

Still... if he saw her again, he might *mention* Jhiton's offer. Just to see if she had any interest in escaping her responsibilities—no, the machinations and assassins of those who wanted to take the throne for themselves—and living a simpler life. One where they could spend time together. And regularly have sex. And feed each other desserts. Hell, maybe he *did* want a mate. Unfortunately, he doubted Princess Syla would be interested in the position.

11

From her room in the castle, the roof now covered so rain wouldn't fall through, but the ceiling in need of patching, Syla wrapped her fingers around Wreylith's figurine. The krendala. Its magic warmed her palm, sending a pleasant tingle up her arm.

Are you out there and able to hear me, Lady Wreylith?

I'm nesting on the Island of Eliok. Her telepathic voice sounded distant and less booming than usual. It was amazing that they could converse at all from so many miles away. *Since the sky shield has returned to your Castle Island, there is nowhere there to sleep, unless one wants to perch on a distant rock formation that's been shit all over by seagulls.* An accusation lurked in the words, as if Syla were to blame for the unpleasant situation.

She supposed she was and chewed on her lip, debating how to suggest that a dragon somewhat peeved with her agree to take her and however many allies Wreylith could carry on a journey around the world. Well, technically the locations of the components ought to all be on the continent of Droha, but they might be hundreds or even thousands of miles apart. Like the other great landmass in the world, Froha, Droha framed the great Sea of Storms and claimed countless climate zones and topographical features. Her people often referred to it as the desert continent, since so much of its interior received little rainfall, but there were rainforests and temperate forests along the coast. Syla hoped the first component, the petrified moss-bulb powder, could be found in such an area.

Seagull droppings are unpleasant, she agreed.

Especially to sleep upon.

I imagine so. Earlier, you spoke about dragons bonding with humans. If we were bonded in the way you mentioned, you said you would be able to fly through the sky shield and sleep here?

I'd be able to hunt *there.* Images of horn hogs, sheep, and goats accompanied the words. *The delicious soft prey of your islands, unstressed animals that haven't needed to grow as tough and stringy to survive against a barrage of deadly predators.*

Can you come if I simply invite you? The impression I got from your, ah, description of me is that you believe I have a few flaws and wouldn't consider bonding with me.

You are not Queen Erasbella.

I expect not. I am, however, determined, teachable, and well-read in addition to being experienced in the art of healing.

Which of those traits will help you ride on the back *of a dragon?*

Why did Syla have the feeling her temporary dragon ally had been affronted, or maybe embarrassed, by having a human dangling from her tail during their battle?

During our first journey, I was starting to figure out how to use my magic to stay on your back. I might merely need more practice. Is it possible you'll give me a chance for that practice?

I cannot come through the sky shield because you invite me, Wreylith said, opting to answer the earlier question.

That is unfortunate, because I would invite you to hunt here. I owe you that after you helped me.

Yes.

I admit I'm also hoping you'll help me again.

I assumed. As puny as you are, you need the assistance of a dragon. Perhaps many *dragons.*

If only Syla could object to that, but she and the whaling ship wouldn't have survived the stormer attack if Wreylith hadn't come and talked other wild dragons into assisting.

I am puny, but I have potential.

That might have been an arrogant thing to say, but dragons seemed to like confidence. Maybe even bravado.

That must *be true,* Wreylith said. *The krendala would not respond to you if you did not.*

Syla looked down at the figurine. When she'd first contacted Wreylith through it, she'd wondered why her father had never said anything about its powers, but was it possible it hadn't done anything in his hands?

She shied away from the thought. It was hard to believe that he, a supremely capable leader who'd been an excellent fighter and athlete in all kinds of endeavors, wouldn't have had the potential to bestir the magic. Maybe Wreylith hadn't been flying around the Garden Kingdom during his lifetime or he'd never happened to pick it up when she'd been nearby, so he hadn't felt the warmth of it emanating power.

Learn if you have the potential that Queen Erasbella had, Wreylith said, *and then I might deign to carry you again. As much as I would enjoy hunting on those islands, I do not know if I could ever bond with someone so...*

Brave as to pull a venomous fang from the foot of a dragon?

Humph.

Would you consider giving me an opportunity to prove myself? As Queen Erasbella must once have to you? Syla vowed to search in the library for information on her great-great grandmother. She couldn't believe she'd never heard family stories about her

bonding with—or at least having a relationship of some kind with
—a dragon.

In what way do you desire to prove yourself?

*I must hunt down the components of a shielder so that my engineer
aunt may rebuild our damaged one.*

That concerns a dragon not in the least. Your shields, in fact, vex *us.*

*If they were not there, protecting these islands and those animals
that graze here, would your kind not have hunted some completely to
extinction? Perhaps you should be grateful that the gods placed the
shielders here.*

*Grateful that the delicious animals we desire to eat are forever kept
from us.*

*They're not extinct at least. Listen, if you give me a ride to three
places on the continent of Droha where I can seek these components, I'll
do my best to prove myself along the journey. There'll likely be combat
and adventure.* Syla would prefer to find the components *without*
either of those things, but all that she'd heard and read about the
dangers on the mainlands promised a high likelihood of adversity
along the way. In particular, the idea of breaking into a laboratory
that had been used—and secured—by a god was daunting.

*During which you will impress me with your improving martial
prowess? And ability to climb up a dragon's tail to her back?*

*I'll definitely work on that. As to the rest, I'll use my magic to keep
us safe, and I'll attempt to be crafty to thwart whatever vicious predators we encounter.* Did craftiness matter to a dragon? Syla didn't
know. *And when we return, even if you're not willing to bond with me,
I'll send hunters to wrangle whatever prey from our islands you wish
and deliver them to you.*

A feast is much more delicious after a vigorous hunt.

*Are you saying you wouldn't accept offerings of sheep or horn hog
meat?*

Those are tantalizing. Wreylith shared the telepathic equivalent
of a sigh. *Come to me on the Island of Eliok, and I'll consider taking you*

on your quest. But I expect many *horn hogs when we return. And darn-yar. And, yes, definitely sheep.*

I agree to finding those animals for you. Syla hoped she could locate a hunter willing to take on the task. She would need to dig into the castle coffers again. Assuming General Dolok or another hadn't staged a successful coup by then and usurped the throne. She had best go about her quest as quickly as possible and return before anyone missed her. *Any chance you'll come to Castle Island to get me and... I need to take a couple of allies along. Can you carry more than two? Or bring a friend?*

Bring a friend! Dragons do not have friends.

You have many admirers.

I have not agreed to carry more than you, much less talk another wild dragon into humiliating himself by accepting a human rider. It is bad enough that I'm considering such an undignified task. I would not be nearly as appealing to males if they saw me so demeaned.

I appreciate your willingness to endure that. I'll throw in goats and a lukbar as well as the aforementioned offerings. Syla imagined a shepherd guiding an entire herd of animals through town and onto a cargo ship so they could be floated out beyond the barrier for a dragon.

There was teasing *after the tail incident.*

Two lukbar? Our people quite enjoy their meat. We slow-roast them over a spit, brushing them with blueberry glaze each hour so they're sweet as well as savory.

Wreylith either considered that for a moment or was busy scratching an itch. Finally, she said, *You will come to me on the Island of Eliok if you wish my assistance. There is no barrier here to keep me from plucking you up.*

For now, Syla thought, determined to change that. What she said to Wreylith was, *I'll be there as soon as I can.*

The books in the library on Queen Erasbella said nothing about dragons.

Instead of sleeping, Syla had spent the remainder of the night packing for the journey, telling Fel and Teyla to do the same, and was yawning her way through a shelf filled with books on her lineage and notable ancestors. Queen Erasbella *did* have tomes dedicated to her, as she'd ruled for more than twenty years before a ship carrying her to a meeting had disappeared at sea during a storm. She'd been a great beauty, accomplished at diplomacy and politics as well as needlepoint, sewing, knitting, and swordsman-ship—apparently, she'd enjoyed all hobbies that included thrusting and stabbing with pointy objects.

As Syla skimmed through the books, seeking mentions of Wreylith or dragons in any capacity, the hair on the back of her neck rose. Had someone else entered the library? Someone who was more than a bibliophile eager to read before first light?

Syla peered up and down the shadowy aisle she stood in, bookcases looming to either side. At the end, on a table next to a lamp, her pack lay stuffed—Fel would say *over*stuffed—with food, water, clothes, maps, and a first-aid kit that included all the neces-sities, as well a few antique medical tools she'd taken from her room. Because they might be useful, she'd told herself, not because she worried her *room*, as well as the rest of the castle, might be inaccessible to her when she returned. The antique venom extractor had come in handy on her first trip. It *wasn't* a superfluous piece of nostalgia. The reflex hammer and metacarpal saw wouldn't likely be needed, but she'd tucked them into her surgical kit in case she once again found herself needing a weapon to help in a fight. She could wield medical tools far more comfort-ably than swords.

Beyond the high, narrow windows on one wall, predawn light was brightening the courtyard, but the shadows inside the keep lay deep. Syla didn't hear anyone but couldn't shake the sense that she was no longer alone.

When Fel had finished packing, she'd sent him to the harbor to try to find passage to Harvest Island for them. She had few whom she could trust and figured he had more experience doing such things than Teyla, but maybe sending him away had been a mistake.

A *snick* sounded. A door closing?

Syla started toward her pack, thinking to grab it before someone noticed it.

"Are you sure she's in here?" a low male voice asked from the front of the library.

Syla froze.

"Yes," another male speaker said. "There's her pack."

"Where does she think she's going?"

Syla didn't recognize the voices. She retreated farther down the aisle from the table and the revealing lamp. At the end, she eased behind a bookcase but peeked back toward the light. Two uniformed men came into view, looking down at her belongings.

"A dungeon cell is what I heard. I'd pack a bag too. She might be there a long time."

"You really think that's the general's plan? If he wants to take power, or he's helping someone else take power... it would be better if, you know." The soldier made a throat-slitting motion.

"Well, I'm not assassinating a princess, so he'd better not ask. I don't even want to... She's a healer. She fixed up my arm a couple of years ago."

"I don't want to kill her either, but we have to be realistic. *She's* not going to take and hold the throne. The military is going to belong to whoever does, so we have to follow orders." The soldier lifted the pack, as if Syla might be hiding underneath it, then looked into the aisles to either side of the table.

Syla didn't move or even breathe. The shadows wrapping

about her *should* keep the men from spotting her, unless they had eyes like Vorik's. But it was getting lighter outside, so she might not be as fully hidden as she wished.

"Not orders to assassinate her."

"The general didn't say anything about that. We're just supposed to lock her up."

Since Syla didn't want to suffer either of those fates, she backed away. After turning down another shadowy aisle, she debated on circling past the bookcases and trying to slip out through the front door. But they had her pack. In addition to the practical—and nostalgic—items she'd tucked into it, Wreylith's figurine was inside. She couldn't leave that behind. It was the only way she could communicate with the dragon from afar.

Syla spotted the stairs in the back of the library that led to the basement. Aunt Tibby had found much of her research material down there, and Syla knew it held tomes that weren't accessible to the castle staff or visitors who wandered through. In her youth, before she'd moved to the temple and become a less frequent visitor here, she'd enjoyed reading the offerings down there. There was even a small room that took a moon-mark to open. Tibby might have found her books in there.

The soldiers' boots thumped softly on the thin carpet. It sounded like they were also heading toward the back of the library. They would likely think to check the basement. Or would they? There were no lamps lit on the stairs or anywhere around them. Still, if she descended and they followed, they might trap her.

Unless...

An idea popped into her mind. Unless she trapped them.

Impulsively, Syla dug a kerchief out of her pocket, a mono-grammed M on it. She dropped it at the top of the stairs, then hurried down and patted her way to and through the door at the bottom. There were lamps on the walls, and she groped in the tray under one for a dragonspark match. Ah, there was one.

Footsteps neared the top of the steps as she lit the lamp. She hurried away, passing a couple of tables and entering aisles not as long as those upstairs. Down here, no windows let light inside, so it was dark as soon as she left the influence of the lamp. The bookcases, shelves bowed with age, held ancient tomes written by hand before the printing press had been invented. There were numerous scrolls as well, and there... There was the special chamber.

She rested the back of her hand against a silver plate by the door. It opened, revealing more bookcases and scroll repositories inside a single room.

Murmurs came from the top of the stairs. The soldiers had found her kerchief.

She wished the special room were larger. With only a small table with chairs and a couple of bookcases in the center that one might hide behind, it wouldn't take long to search.

Syla thought about tossing something else inside, like a hound trainer leading animals by putting down a trail of treats, but she didn't want to be too obvious about setting her trap. The open door ought to be enough to convince the men to check inside. Besides, what treats did she have? A blackberry cobbler might have lured Vorik in, but she didn't keep those in her pockets.

As she backed away from the door, the moon-mark on her hand tingled and glowed a slight silver.

Syla stared at it. When that happened, it was typically because she was drawing upon her power, but she wasn't trying to do that now. If anything, with the men walking into the basement, she didn't want to risk the glow giving her away.

She started to clamp her other hand over it, but as the mark tilted slightly, the silver glow illuminated a few books on a case near the door. The filigreed title on the spine of a tome bound in leather reflected the light.

The Secret Life of Queen Erasbella.

Goosebumps rose all over Syla's body. She wasn't shocked that such a book existed but wondered by what whim of the gods her moon-mark had guided her to it.

"Check over there," came a whispered voice from the bottom of the stairs. "She wouldn't have left a lamp on if she'd departed."

Syla grabbed the book off the shelf, a cloud of dust that accompanied it wreathing her face. She backed out of the room, her nostrils tickling, and looked for a nearby place to hide while the men searched inside. But the aisles were such that they would be able to see down them.

A sneeze surprised her, and she barely kept from swearing.

"Princess Syla?" one of the men called, footsteps heading straight for the room. "Is that you? General Dolok sent us to deliver a message."

The other man snorted.

A message. Right.

Syla took several steps down an aisle, leaned the book on a shelf, then started climbing. The wood groaned, threatening to give, and she wished she were athletic and lean instead of curvy and plump. If the entire bookcase collapsed... the men would find her easily.

Worse, her nostrils were quivering as badly as the shelves. She worried she would sneeze again.

"She must be in there," one of the men said, lantern light bobbing on the walls as he approached the special room.

Of course they'd brought a form of illumination.

Syla reached the top of the bookcase and eased her body onto it, lying parallel to the ceiling.

"Is that a secret room? I didn't know it existed."

"What if there's a hidden door back there, and she disappeared into the tunnels? I don't want to go down there again. Roxin and a bunch of others got killed under the castle by stormers."

"They've been cleared out."

"We *think*. The stormers never should have been able to get in there to start with. If she's down there, she's on her own."

Syla kept her body hidden and didn't dare peek down, instead listening to their voices and footsteps, trying to gauge by their sounds when they went into the room.

"There might not be a secret door," one said.

He was inside. Syla risked peeking over the edge. Neither man was visible from her perch. Had they both gone in?

"They're all over the castle," the other said. Yes, he was inside too.

Willing her descent and her nostrils to be silent, Syla eased off the bookcase. A faint creak made her wince.

"Did you hear something?"

She reached the floor, heard something bump in the room, and gave up on silence. She lunged and pressed the back of her hand to the plate by the open door.

Both men turned to look at her. They were toward the back of the room, and one had been peeking behind a bookcase.

"Princess Syla," the other blurted, lunging around it and jogging toward her.

The door swung to close, but would it do so quickly enough?

"Thank you for not wanting to assassinate me," she said to the nearer man, his face vaguely familiar. He must have been the one whose arm she'd healed in the past.

He hesitated.

"Shit, get her." The other man vaulted over a bookcase.

The door thudded solidly shut before they reached it, and a moon-mark glowed on the plate to indicate it was secured.

Not certain how sturdy the door was, especially from that side —it had been designed to keep people out, not in—Syla didn't hesitate to snatch up the book on her great-great grandmother and run for the stairs.

Thumps and muffled shouts followed her. She apologized to the precious books housed within the chamber and hoped the soldiers wouldn't grow so irate as to destroy them. Someone would be along to rescue the men eventually.

Still running, she reached the table upstairs and barely slowed as she grabbed her pack. She spun to hurry out of the library and almost crashed into another uniformed man. Swearing, she came up short. What would she say?

But it was Sergeant Fel who gazed blandly down at her. "I've arranged transportation."

"Oh, good."

He looked behind her, his hand lowering to the mace belted at his hip. Expecting enemies on her trail?

"Nothing I couldn't handle," she assured him, spotting Teyla leaning through the door, a pack of her own over her shoulders, several book-shaped objects bulging against the seams. Syla almost laughed. Every woman in the family packed in a similar manner.

"Who's after you?" Fel asked, not yet moving to follow.

"General Dolok sent minions."

His eyes narrowed. "To do what?"

"There was chatter of assassinations, but I believe their current orders are to throw me in the dungeon."

Fel scowled, though he had been present for her last interaction with Dolok and couldn't be surprised. "This may not be an advisable time for you to leave the castle."

"It actually struck me as an extremely *good* time to leave."

"If you don't return for weeks—"

Syla lifted her hand. "I know. Dolok may have seized power by then. Or someone else may have." She thought of her ambitious cousin, Relvin. "I'm hoping those who think themselves the next rulers of the Garden Kingdom will end up squabbling amongst themselves and won't have solidified power by the time I return. If we can get the shielder repaired, Harvest Island back under protection, then..." She tilted her palm toward the ceiling. "That's as far as I've gotten with my plans."

"You will gather allies and assert your right to be queen."

The way he said it, Syla couldn't tell if it was a question or an order.

"If you don't," Fel added softly, "yours won't be the only life at stake."

Syla gazed bleakly at him, then also toward Teyla. Surely, her friends and relatives wouldn't be targets, would they? Hadn't all those associated with her suffered enough?

No, Fel was right. They might all be targeted if there was a military coup. Anyone with a moon-mark, with royal blood and a link to the throne, would especially be considered a threat to a usurper's right to rule. The Moonmarks had been placed in power by the gods themselves before the divinities had departed. For many people, those with the birthmark were inextricably linked to the throne. And might not a bodyguard for one of the Moonmarks be in danger too? Fel's grim face suggested he believed that.

"I'll keep that in mind. I promise." Syla nodded to the door, wanting to escape the castle before more soldiers showed up.

Fel grunted, grabbed his pack off the floor, and followed her, waving for Teyla to follow *him*.

As they slipped out through the gatehouse in the back of the castle, where Fel exchanged a few words with the guard on duty, thanking him for saying nothing of their departure, Syla tried not to feel like she was abandoning the capital, if not the entire Kingdom, to chaos, anarchy, and the ambition of power-hungry men.

12

VORIK ONLY SLEPT A FEW HOURS, THEN ROSE BEFORE DAWN TO PACK for his trip by the glowing orange embers of the campfires in the cave. He picked his way between sleeping forms, not looking too long at a couple who'd woken early for amorous activities, and angled to where Lieutenant Wise camped with a few of the other younger riders. But a lone figure standing in the mouth of the cave, his back to the wall, caught Vorik's eye. With stars still dotting the sky outside, he wouldn't have known who it was, but Jhiton usually wore the cloak that indicated his military status.

Someone was approaching him. A woman?

More aloof than inviting, Jhiton rarely responded to invitations from the opposite sex. Before his wife had left, he'd been monogamous with her, despite their difficulty in having children. Only the loss of Jebrosh had driven them apart. Since then, Vorik didn't think his brother had taken a lover. But, yes, that was a woman approaching him, long hair down, a blanket wrapped around her form. Maybe *only* a blanket.

Well, good luck to her. To both of them. Jhiton could use a release and happiness, though Vorik doubted sleeping with a woman could provide that for him. He was too wrapped up in his plans for the future.

Vorik reached Wise and shook him awake.

"Ready to go on a mission?" he whispered, trusting the general had told him about it and the scrolls the night before.

"Yes, sir. Let me pee and grab a few things. Did you know there are *pears*?" Wise spoke with the same longing that Vorik felt for sweet, delicious fruit.

"I heard Leonli is going to slice them and dehydrate them so we can have them in the winter," Vorik said.

"That sounds wonderful. We're not going with the squadrons to the island we've conquered, are we?"

"Harvest Island?" Vorik doubted Syla would appreciate hearing his people refer to it as *conquered*. "No. We've another quest."

"To the mainland, the general said. The wyvern-, griffin-, gargoyle-, and rock vulture-filled mainland. There aren't any pears there, sir."

"Sorry, but this is part of Jhiton's plot to get and keep some more islands for our people."

"Brilliant."

Agrevlari? Vorik spoke telepathically as Wise finished packing a bag. He sensed his dragon and a few others perched above the cave. *Are you awake?*

Certainly. A dragon never rests.

What do you call it when you lie in the grass with your limbs in the air and your tail twitching as you sigh contentedly?

Luring enemies into believing they can take advantage of me. It's a battle tactic.

Vorik looked toward the front of the cave, thinking to tease Agrevlari further, but he happened to catch the woman speaking and recognized the voice. That was Captain Lesva, and was she *leaning* against Jhiton?

Vorik curled a lip. It wasn't as if he could disapprove of them getting together since *he'd* gotten together with Lesva numerous times and enjoyed the athletic vigor of their pairing, but knowing her as well as he did, he couldn't help but feel protective of Jhiton. He had enough to deal with. He didn't need her sharp tongue.

Not that his older brother and superior officer needed protecting, or even to be warned, but Vorik caught himself bristling anyway. If he thought Lesva genuinely wanted the stoic Jhiton's company, he wouldn't think anything of it, but she probably thought to use him to further her goals. Vorik, who'd made captain before she and even—he winced to remember it—put in a good word for her when she'd been hoping to be promoted, was almost sure of it.

Vorik headed toward the cave entrance, though he had no idea what he would say. Nothing, he decided. It wasn't his place to speak. But if he happened to decide to wait for Agrevlari, and Wise and his dragon, five feet away from Lesva and Jhiton, there wasn't anything wrong with that.

His keen ears caught a few words as he approached, the sea breeze blowing them back into the cave.

"You can't trust him the way you can me," Lesva said softly, her chest against Jhiton's side as she looked toward the sea while keeping his face in her side view. Watching for his reaction?

Vorik hadn't meant to sneak up on them, but he paused, a hand on the cave wall, to listen. Though he hadn't heard his name, his instincts itched all the way up and down his spine, and he knew she was talking about him.

"He's always had a soft spot for gardener women," Lesva added. "Or a hard cock for them, I suppose. Though I can't understand why. It's a wonder they can even take care of themselves. If any of them stepped their plump bodies outside of the shields, they'd be snatched up and devoured instantly. Hardly any of them know how to use a sword, bow, or even a dagger. Maybe Vorik likes that they're helpless."

His jaw clenched, his fingers tightening on the cool rock of the cave wall. Didn't Lesva have anything better to do than gossip about him?

If Jhiton responded, Vorik couldn't hear it. He would gather intelligence on enemies in a heartbeat, but he'd never been one to ask an officer to share gossip on another officer. Still, he didn't push Lesva away. Vorik wished he would.

"No respectable stormer man should want a helpless woman," Lesva added.

Syla was hardly that. She'd resisted Lesva's attempt to interrogate her, and Lesva, thanks to her dragon bond, was much stronger than the average woman. Than just about *any* woman.

"With luck, she'll disappear," Lesva said. "But your brother isn't what brought me over here."

"What *did* bring you, Captain?"

Vorik nodded in approval at Jhiton using her rank, putting a wall of professionalism between them. Or so it sounded. Lesva wasn't leaning professionally against him. Was she indeed naked under that blanket?

"Loneliness," Lesva said.

Oh, please. Her ambition kept her company.

"Excuse my presumption, but I think I sense that in you too, General." Lesva rested her hand on his chest. "Do you want company?"

"I do not." Jhiton shifted to the side and stepped away from her.

Vorik silently cheered until Jhiton walked into the cave. The shadows might have hidden Vorik, especially since he stood by the wall, but too many embers burned orange in fires. Or maybe Jhiton simply sensed him with his magic, for he gave Vorik a long look as he walked past. He didn't *say* anything, but he wouldn't have appreciated being spied upon.

When Vorik looked toward the cave entrance, Lesva was also regarding him. Wonderful.

You can fly down here any time, Agrevlari. Wise is almost ready. And I'm... more than ready.

I will arrive shortly. There are semiloni eggs in nests up here.

Those can't be a sufficient meal for a dragon.

They taste wondrous though. Far better than the fruits you spoke of with your lieutenant.

I'm sure. Shall I ask Syla to bake a cobbler using them?

Dragons do not crave sweets.

Maybe gardeners can make savory cobblers.

It's possible I'm intrigued.

Though he didn't want to speak with Lesva, Vorik resisted the urge to pretend he'd forgotten something and retreat into the cave. Instead, he continued to the entrance ledge. He was, after all, a grown-up and an officer in the Sixteen Talons.

"He's a challenging one, isn't he?" Lesva asked, as if they were still on friendly terms. "So aloof. Doesn't he have any needs?"

Since Lesva was from another tribe, she might not know all the details of Jhiton's ex-mate and lost son, but Vorik had no interest in filling her in.

"He's busy doing what's best for our people." Once on the ledge, Vorik faced outward instead of looking at Lesva.

"Is that still *your* primary concern?"

"Despite what you think of me and my cock, of course." Vorik hadn't intended to let her know he'd heard that, but irritation made his tongue unwise.

Lesva chuckled and adjusted the blanket draped around her body—her *naked* body. Instead of more fully covering herself up, she let it shift aside, the starlight gleaming on the slight swell of her breasts and taut abdomen. "It's a shame *it* has little loyalty to our people. I quite enjoyed my time with it."

"But not the rest of my body?" Vorik looked over his shoulder, hoping Wise was on the way.

"It has some appealing features, and you *know* I enjoyed your agility and athleticism under the furs. On that rock. In that tree. And, oh, halfway up a cliff. We're lucky a wyvern didn't come along and pluck us up that time since we didn't appoint a sky watcher."

Vorik eyed her, suspicious of what was, for her, good-natured ribbing. Considering the battle they'd engaged in before, he had a hard time believing she wasn't holding a grudge.

"I do enjoy new partners," Lesva said, "new experiences, if you will, but if you want me to remind you how much a stormer woman can make you holler, do let me know."

"The last time we hollered, it was because we were in battle."

"I found it stimulating."

"Even when lightning struck the cliff, and you fell?"

"That was terrifying but exhilarating. And I survived. Few would have."

"I agree. You've always been impressive, Lesva."

She tilted her head as she regarded him. Looking for the insult in his compliment? Once, she'd baited him, drawing out snark from him, but he didn't care to insult her anymore. He was done with that part of his life.

"Would you have killed me? If the lightning hadn't struck? You weren't that fully engaged at first, but then... Then you were determined."

"You disobeyed your orders."

Lesva chuckled. "And *that's* why you came to the girl's defense."

"The defense of the woman, Princess Syla, yes."

"Was she so grateful that she dropped to her knees and sucked your cock afterward?"

Agrevlari? I'll help you gather dozens of eggs if you come now.

"There must be a reason you crave the company of gardener women," Lesva said. "Do they fawn over you? Tell you how magnificent you are while making you come?"

"One moment you proposition me, and the next you insult me. You've an interesting way with men."

Thank the moon, Wise was picking his way toward the front of the cave.

"*Is* it an insult? Or simply the truth?"

Vorik shook his head and waved toward Wise, hoping to divert Lesva's attention.

But she stepped closer to Vorik, putting a hand on his chest, the same way she had to Jhiton scant minutes before.

"You're *not* bringing your gardener wench back here to become one of us," Lesva whispered.

Vorik's heart thumped noticeably at the admission that she'd spied on his conversation with Jhiton the night before.

"I don't care what the general thinks, but she'd dilute the tribe with her weak blood. Any children you had would be soft and probably half-blind. Wyvern bait. You don't deserve that any more than the tribe does. *You're* not weak, Vorik. If you were, I wouldn't bother with you." She slid her hand down his chest toward his groin.

He caught her wrist to stop her.

Undaunted, she said, "You owe it to the tribe to have strong children who will ensure our survival."

"You needn't concern yourself about what children I may or may not have." Vorik should have stopped speaking then, pushed her away, and turned his back, but he unwisely went on, moved to defend Syla. "But her offspring wouldn't be weak. You saw for yourself that she has power."

"I would have killed her easily if I hadn't been trying to extract information from her."

"Fighting prowess isn't the only kind of power a person can have. Jhiton saw her in the shielder chamber. He knows."

Lesva squinted at him. "Don't tell me *he's* into soft gardener women too."

"Is sex all you think about?"

"It's most of what you *men* think about. I've learned that well. Trust me." Face cold, she looked back into the cave, past the approaching lieutenant and toward the fire where Jhiton had settled to rest.

Vorik pushed a hand through his hair. He hoped he hadn't just implied that his brother was also interested in Syla. Vorik highly doubted *that* was true. "Just because he doesn't want you doesn't mean—"

"I know exactly what it means." Lesva pulled her wrist from Vorik's grip and stepped back.

Wise had come close enough to hear their words, but he slowed his pace, looking out to sea instead of at them.

"Wish me luck on my mission, Vorik," Lesva said. "With the gods behind my back, perhaps I'll get an opportunity to end the threat to our tribe."

"What threat? Syla?"

Lesva smiled cryptically at him, then swept her blanket around herself and strode into the cave.

Making his voice as cold as he could, Vorik said, "Stay away from her, Captain. Or next time, you'll find out exactly if I would have finished you off or not."

Lesva brushed past Wise, deliberately bumping his shoulder and giving him a pat on the ass, before continuing into the cave.

Wise came to stand beside Vorik. "I hear she eats men after mating with them."

"I know some haven't survived her attention," Vorik said, but his heart was numb. He hadn't meant to remind Lesva of her hatred for Syla and now worried that he'd done the princess a disservice. Jhiton was sending Lesva to the island next to Syla's and Vorik off on a quest who knew where. Lesva might get an opportunity to attack Syla while Vorik would be far away and helpless to assist.

Many minutes later than Vorik wished, Agrevlari finally alighted on the ledge, stretching his wings and his tail out with a yawn that was almost a roar. Wise's dark-gray dragon, Tonasketal, came after, taking up less room on the ledge when he landed.

"You have egg in your fangs," Vorik told Agrevlari.

Smoke wafted from the green dragon's nostrils, and the next yawn brought fire roiling from the depths of his throat. Fortunately for those camped near the front of the cave, he didn't send a gout of flames into the interior. He *did* sear whatever remained of his breakfast off his teeth.

Better? Agrevlari asked.

"Much. Let's go and get this mission over with." Vorik hurried to climb on, vainly hoping that he could find the components and bring them back before Lesva had an opportunity to bother any gardeners. Especially the one he cared about.

Clouds hid the sunrise, but the day grew brighter as Fel led Syla and Teyla down from the bluff and through the streets toward the harbor. Once, Syla would have given friendly nods to the gray-uniformed enforcers on patrol, but she avoided their gazes and hurried past them now, afraid General Dolok might have given orders for her arrest. Though the Royal Protectors, Royal Fleet, and Kingdom Enforcers were all different arms of the military, they often worked together, and Dolok had been around a long time. He had a lot of influence.

Fel didn't say anything, but he must have been thinking similar thoughts because he also skirted the enforcers, taking a longer route than usual to reach the harbor. They passed through a seedier section of town near the docks that her bodyguard usually would have avoided while she was with him.

"That's Princess Syla," a freckle-faced girl blurted from a corner where she and her equally freckled brother were selling small brown bags of cookies and biscuits from a box.

"It can't be." The boy looked to be about eight, a couple of years older than the girl. "The princess is royal and important. She would have an entourage and a huge gilded carriage with eight horses."

"Why eight?" The girl squinted at them. She was barefoot and wore a sleeveless dress that might have been made from a grain sack.

Fel touched Syla's arm, trying to hurry her past, as if small children should be avoided as assiduously as the enforcers.

"Important people have *at least* eight horses," the boy said. "And bodyguards."

"She has *him*." The girl pointed at Fel. "He's *huge*. And look at his muscles."

Fel lifted his chin.

"He's old," the boy said.

Fel shot the kid a glare and picked up his pace.

"Princess Syla." The girl grabbed three bags of cookies and ran to intercept them. "Is it you? You're a healer, aren't you? My aunt worked at Moon Watch Temple before the attack."

Syla slowed down, worried the girl would say she'd lost her aunt, and feeling she should, at the least, buy some of the cookies and give her a hug.

Fel lifted a hand, as if he might stop the girl from getting close, but he must have decided a six-year-old wasn't a threat. He *did* give the eight-year-old boy an ominous look though, perhaps contemplating thumping him to show how *not* old he was.

"I'm a healer, yes. Is your aunt?"

"No. She washed the dishes in the kitchen and sometimes fetched vegetables for the stock pots. She got away before the attack and is all right."

"I'm relieved to hear it."

"We don't have much time," Fel murmured, looking at Teyla, as if she might hurry Syla along.

Teyla, this part of town perhaps reminding her of her kidnapping, had been touching the sword strapped to her pack while peering nervously into the alleys, and she missed his look.

"Can you heal diseases of the private parts?" the girl asked.

Syla blinked. "Er, yes, usually."

"My mom is very uncomfortable and can't work a lot right now." The girl held up the bags. "I'll give you all these cookies if you can heal her."

"We're supposed to *sell* those," the boy whispered.

"If mom can work again, we won't need the money from them. You can go back to *eating* what we make."

The boy opened his mouth, like he might object, but maybe the logic suited him.

Syla smiled faintly, recognizing a fellow schemer in the girl. "I can take a look at her if she's near?"

"Your Highness," Fel objected. "We've got a captain to meet. And you can't go to a *brothel*."

Until that comment, Syla hadn't fully put the pieces together about what the girl's mother did, but she realized his guess was probably correct.

"It's very close." The girl thrust the bags at Syla.

"You don't have to give me your cookies," Syla said, though the scents of cinnamon and sugar reached her nose, and she wondered if dragons liked sweets. Probably not, but... "Well, maybe one bag. They smell delicious."

"Here. Take them. Please. My mother is just down that alley."

"Alley," Fel grumbled distastefully.

Syla followed the girl, who left her brother to man the sale of their baked goods. After his sister's back was turned, the boy slid a cookie out of a bag and chomped on it. Syla had a feeling she was the more responsible kid in the family.

"This isn't a good idea." Fel squinted at a pair of enforcers a block away.

On patrol, they didn't turn up this street, instead continuing through the intersection along the waterfront. Even so, Syla noted their presence. Normally, she would be glad that order had been restored to the city, but as the day grew brighter, she worried about escaping. If a street urchin had recognized her, the enforcers would too. A carriage with eight horses might have been a good idea, though that also would have drawn attention.

"Next time you're going to sneak out of the city," Teyla said, walking at her side, "you should grab a cloak with a big hood that can hide your whole head. That's what adventurers in the Kingsman's Tales always wear."

"It's the end of summer. You don't think cloaks and hoods would be conspicuous?"

The girl led them down an alley so narrow that Fel's shoulders brushed the sides, then through a side door for a building that had been marked as Sailor Services out front.

"Not as conspicuous as you with your auburn locks, regal air, and hand glowing moon-silver." Teyla eyed Syla's birthmark instead of her locks or regalness. "Mine doesn't glow. Is that *normal*?"

"Usually only when I use my magic." Syla glanced at her hand, surprised it hadn't stopped glowing since the library.

"Odd."

"I do seem to be, yes."

They stepped into a narrow hall, thin rugs on wooden floors and the air smelling of perfume and incense. Thumps and groans came from behind a door they passed.

Fel quickened his pace, trying to hurry the girl along while glancing back at Syla, as if her sensibilities would be mortally offended by being in such a place. She thought about mentioning that she'd traveled to brothels before to heal people—not everyone could make it to the temple—but the girl opened another door off the hall.

Gripping his mace, Fel strode in after her and looked around, lifting a hand to keep Syla back as he checked the space.

"I doubt there are enemies lurking in here," Syla murmured to him, then jumped when a man buckling blue uniform trousers hurried out past them. "I could be wrong," she added.

Apparently, the girl's mom wasn't taking off completely from work.

Head down, the soldier didn't look at them and hopefully didn't recognize Syla.

"Hylina," came a woman's startled voice from the bed. "You're supposed to be selling cookies, not bringing me clients. Or, uhm, are you..." She'd been looking at Fel, but her gaze shifted to Syla, and her mouth dangled open in shock.

"See, she recognizes you," Teyla whispered from the doorway. "You need a cloak."

"I brought a healer, Mom," the girl said.

"That's... You're..." The mother stared at Syla.

"Yes." Syla knelt beside her bed, aware of time trickling past. By now, someone might have found those soldiers in the library. By now, Dolok might have put orders out to the entire military to grab her if they saw her. "Your daughter offered me cookies in exchange for healing."

"That's... My sister worked at the temple. I know healing costs more than *cookies*."

"Perhaps, but I'm collecting offerings for a dragon, so I need cookies right now."

"I don't know what to say to that. Is it a joke?"

"Probably. Dragons seem to prefer meat. Sergeant Fel, wait outside, please."

"Don't take long," Fel warned. "If the captain thinks there's trouble, our ship won't wait."

"I know." Syla made a shooing motion to imply *he* was delaying her more than the healing.

He harrumphed and closed the door, taking Teyla out with him.

The woman seemed embarrassed to explain her concerns, but Syla assured her that she'd healed all manner of injuries and illnesses, and that little fazed her. "It'll be more effective if I use magic on you, but the power might linger and make you feel loyal to me for a time. Let me know if you're all right with that." Syla had packed a few medications but didn't have access to the entire pharmacy that existed in a temple, so she didn't know how effective she could be if the woman *didn't* want to be bound. Syla had brought a contraceptive powder and yerathma root for the trip—just in case—but those didn't help with sexual diseases.

"Yes, magic is fine. I've... never been touched by magic." The woman looked curiously—and maybe with awe—at Syla's glowing hand. She used her finger to draw a moon with two eyes over her chest, but then took a deep breath and nodded firmly for Syla to go ahead.

"It's not too bad. Better than being touched by overly handsy men." As soon as the words came out, Syla wished she could take them back. She didn't want to insult the woman's profession or career choice.

But she laughed. "*Most* things are, Your Highness. I'm getting long in the tooth for it, truth be told." She waved to the hallway. To indicate her daughter? "I'm Celena, by the way. It's real good of you to come in. I'm not one to take handouts though. I'd like to pay you."

"Your daughter has already arranged that." Syla smiled and took the woman's hand. The power in her moon-mark flared with tingling heat, as if it couldn't wait to be unleashed.

"*Cookies* don't seem a fair trade for medical attention."

"Of course they are. Lots of healers, especially out in the country, barter for their services. I've a pen pal at Earth First Temple who goes around to farms to heal people, horses, cattle, and dogs, and she's often received payment in meat, eggs, and, last winter, she got a lovely wool scarf and mittens."

Syla was about to ask Celena to disrobe and let her do an examination, but as her magic surged into the woman, she almost instantly received through their link an overview of her ailments. Everything came to her much more clearly than it usually did, and Syla wondered what had changed. Her learning to use her magic for more than just healing? Or maybe the proximity she'd had of late to shielders and their great power? Or dragons and *their* magic? No, that wouldn't rub off. Stormers had to do a ceremony to bond with dragons. Wreylith didn't think Syla was worthy, so she wouldn't be sharing any magic with her.

Syla didn't know the reason, but she easily discerned not only a sexually transmitted disease, as the daughter had said, but an abscessed tooth that would have needed pulling soon. Celena also had a toenail infection that contributed lesser pain. In addition, Syla could see that several of her ribs had been broken in the past and healed poorly, and faded bruises lingered on her jaw. Poor woman. She wasn't much older than Syla, but this couldn't be an easy life.

As Syla started healing her patient's ailments, old and new,

Celena relaxed back onto her bed with a groan of relief. "*Much* better than handsy men."

"I'm glad," Syla said, and she was, though she could hear creaks on the floorboards in the hallway.

Fel shifting his weight from foot to foot? Worried they were taking too long?

"Come by, and I'll make you cookies *any* time." Celena gazed through lowered lashes with a look Syla had received from patients before, though more often from men than women. Not just gratitude but adoration.

Syla made herself smile, but gazes like that never failed to make her uncomfortable. Thank the gods that the feelings prompted by her magic usually faded before long. Once she was gone, she wouldn't likely cross paths with Celena again, so the fondness wouldn't come into play, even if it lingered.

"It's my dream," Celena added. "Baking. Not just for spare change, but I want to open a place in a better part of town. I'm saving for it."

"That's a good goal."

"Yes." Celena smiled sleepily. She'd probably been up all night, and healing was draining for the patient as well as the healer.

A soft knock sounded at the door, and Fel stepped in with a newspaper tucked under one arm. Teyla slipped in right after him. They averted their eyes, probably expecting Celena to be in the middle of a revealing exam.

"I need a minute more." Syla glanced at the paper, wondering if Fel had absently picked it up to read on their voyage or if he'd spotted a concerning headline. Probably the latter, unfortunately. Fel didn't strike her as someone who got the newspaper for the Divine Divinings section.

"Take your minute." Fel turned, cracking the door slightly so he could watch the hallway. "We'll want to wait until he's gotten on his horse and is gone."

"He?"

"Colonel Mosworth. He just came downstairs from another room." Fel pointed toward the ceiling. "I recognized his voice, and we came in to avoid him spotting us."

"We've a lot of high-ranking military regulars," Celena said around a yawn. "Some minor lords too. Important people. The girls here— Well, we're not proud or full of ourselves. We can't afford to be. We'll do things that the expensive ladies of the night servicing the high-powered won't."

"General Dolok ever come?" Fel asked.

"I'm not sure about him, but some other generals. Fleet captains. Especially fleet officers. And Minor Lord Dallingswok comes regularly for Yeera. She's a real looker. Draws a lot of men and commands a high price. Brings in the Vollard brothers too. They're rough. I'm glad they've not looked my way." Celena touched her jaw, maybe noticing that the bruises didn't hurt anymore—or remembering someone who'd hit her.

Fel looked thoughtfully at Syla.

She'd finished the healing and stood up. "What does that expression mean?"

"Someone contending for the throne and with many enemies could use informants in places where powerful people visit."

"I didn't heal Celena so she would spy for me," Syla said.

Celena surprised her by sitting up and grasping her hand. "I would *love* to share the things I see here with someone. Especially if... Dear departed gods, some of those powerful ones think they're so special. Above the law. They hurt the girls because they know we can't do anything about it, that the enforcers would blame *us*. If you could change that... I mean, even if you couldn't, I owe you." Her grasp tightened on Syla's hand, the adoration in her gaze again—the magically induced adoration.

Syla wanted to flee that look. "You don't owe me anything, Celena, but if I can, I'll help. I'll..." Storm god's wrath, she didn't even know if she would be able to take the crown. More likely, she would end up in Dolok's dungeon cell. How was she supposed to help this woman or anyone else?

"Come back regularly, Your Highness, and I'll tell you everything I see and hear that might be important. Like I said, all kinds of powerful people come here. I'd *love* to help you do something to stop them from hurting others." Celena released Syla and clasped a hand over her own chest, though she didn't add *stop them from hurting me.*

"I'm off on a mission, but I'll try to come by again." Syla patted Celena on the shoulder and made herself walk out, though she wanted to flee from the adoring gaze that followed her.

Once in the hallway with the door closed, she slumped against it.

Fel looked at her, less adoring but still contemplative. "I thought this would be a waste of time."

"You've changed your mind?" Syla waved toward the door to the alley exit.

"Now, I think maybe you should visit every brothel in town."

"Let's... fix the shielder first."

Teyla brightened. "Yes. Our quest awaits."

Syla hoped *Wreylith* awaited. It was taking longer than she'd hoped to get out of the city, and they still had to sail to Harvest Island.

13

Syla expected Fel to lead her and Teyla to a Royal Fleet ship with a captain loyal to her family. She *didn't* expect him to hurry her down the pier to the most remote dock where an unassuming whaling ship was moored, burn marks and gouges from dragon claws visible on its hull.

"Captain Radmarik is taking us?" A briny breeze swept through the harbor, and Syla gripped the hood of the cloak Fel had found for her in the brothel, leaving a coin for its purchase. He'd apparently thought a disguise, or at least covering, was a good idea for a traveling princess. "I thought he left after receiving payment," Syla added.

As her aunt had pointed out, after the *last* sailing Syla had gone on with Radmarik, he shouldn't have wanted to take her aboard again. His vessel had survived—barely—but several of the accompanying guard ships had been sunk—or torched by dragon fire. This time, there weren't any guard ships nearby.

Syla bit her lip. If Wreylith didn't agree to take her to the various places where the components could be gathered, this would have to be the vessel that transported her all over the Sea of

Storms and waited for her while she trekked inland. Would a hired captain be willing to do that? Since Radmarik had a link to the Freeborn Faction, a band of stormers who'd left their people to pursue peaceful relations with the Kingdom, that might bode well for her, but Syla had never met any of them. She questioned how much assistance they and their allies would offer.

"He did leave," Fel said, "but he returned while I was attempting to arrange transport. After talking to officers in the Royal Fleet and finding their loyalties had been more to the queen—or the years-dead king—rather than to you, I worried about telling them of your plans. One of them didn't even know *which child* you were."

"Maybe I should have been more of a public figure over the years." Syla had always preferred her duties in the temple as a healer and her books and collections to anything *public* and couldn't help but wince at the notion.

"There was one captain whom you'd healed about a decade earlier. I almost confided in him and asked for transport, but his first officer is someone I've seen in the castle before, chatting with General Dolok, so I had doubts. It was as I stood on the deck of that vessel that the whaling ship sailed into the harbor."

The *Striking Falcon* read white-painted letters across the wooden hull, claw marks gouged through the G and F. Syla didn't know if she'd caught the whaling ship's name before, but if she was to sail on it again, she would make a note of it.

"The captain and I fought side-by-side on the deck against the dragons trying to uncover the decoy." Fel's voice had a fondness to it. For the battle? Or for finding someone worthy of engaging in battle alongside? Maybe the latter. "When my knee tried to buckle —" he scowled down at the offending limb, a stiffness to his gait suggesting it was wrapped under his trousers, "—he covered my back and kept a wicked set of talons from taking my head off."

"In other words, you two bonded."

"That's right."

Captain Radmarik stood on the deck, his half-chewed hunk of sugar cane in the corner of his mouth like a pipe, and he lifted a hand when he saw them. He didn't appear perturbed by their approach.

"That is a less, ah, stately vessel than I imagined a princess sailing on," Teyla observed, her gaze snagging on a harpoon loaded in a rear launcher. The tip hadn't been cleaned, and what looked like dried blubber and possibly a piece of intestines dangled from it.

"A princess or the archaeologist cousin of a princess?" Syla asked.

"I do usually get slightly more refined transportation when I travel. I don't mind roughing it though. It's mostly because so many of my trips have been with Relvin, and *he* insists on a degree of opulence, that I'm used to it."

"Traveling with him must be a joy."

"I read and ignore his frequent pompous utterances."

"Wise."

"When you immerse yourself in a quality book, you can ignore almost everything."

"I've found that to be true. Do you prefer a fictional story? Or a historical tome?" For recreational reading, Syla usually chose biographies and real historical accountings, but she'd been known to enjoy a mystery or collection of myths and legends. She itched to find time to read the book she'd snagged from the library basement on her great-great grandmother, certain from the title that it would offer a more fascinating interpretation of the queen's past than she'd found in other texts.

"Historical *and* fiction," Teyla said. "Ideally with romance, though the more torrid the love story, the less likely the history included is to be accurate. I enjoy borrowing books from the library, taking notes to mark all the inaccuracies, and then leaving my additions between the pages for future readers."

"You don't think other people are reading for pleasure and don't care about the inaccuracies?"

"*Don't care?*" Teyla gave her a scandalized look. "Everyone should care. Even if they don't, they should be educated."

"You don't send letters of corrections to the authors, do you?"

"Only the authors who are still alive."

"Well, that's good. It would be awkward for the sexton to try to deliver the others."

"That's my belief too."

Fel gave them a long look over his shoulder—what, was this a strange conversation?—before leading them up the gangplank onto the *Striking Falcon*.

"This is how women bond," Syla informed him. "Not by fighting dragons but by discussing books they've read."

She again noticed the newspaper he was carrying. He hadn't yet shown her an article, so maybe he had picked it up for his reading pleasure. Either that, or the articles were so awful that he was waiting until they had time to discuss them in depth.

"If this adventure proves as challenging as I suspect from the little you've told me," Fel said as they walked onto the deck, "you might get to bond *both* ways."

"Won't that be a delight?" Syla murmured.

"I brought my sword." Teyla patted the scabbard tied to her back, a perkiness to her eyes suggesting she found the notion much more appealing than Syla did. Her first real battle might cure her of that perk.

"Welcome back, Your Highness." Captain Radmarik removed his sugar cane and offered it to her, the moist, macerated end not any more appealing than it had been the first time he'd tried to entice her to chew on it. Syla trusted this was a new piece, but she couldn't be certain. The cane appeared immensely fibrous.

Syla lifted a hand to decline the offering. "Thank you for agreeing to let us sail with you again."

"I'd say it was my pleasure, but it was more my wife's insistence."

"Is she here?" Syla peered about, curious to meet someone from the Freeborn Faction. A *real* member.

Vorik had claimed to be a part of the faction when he'd first been trying to gain her trust, but that had been a lie. Was it strange that she still wanted to spend time with him?

"Nah, we had a brief encounter—brief but *wondrous*—" Radmarik's eyes rolled back in his head, but, thankfully, he didn't go into detail, "—when I returned to Harvest Island. But, after the fall of the sky shield there, she left to attend a meeting with her people. *I* left because stormers were showing up on ships in the harbor as well as on dragons. The Freeborn Faction are meeting to decide whether to give assistance to your people or not. You clearly need it. But... even though my wife's allies oppose the tactics of the rest of the stormers, they've never yet raised weapons toward the tribes, preferring peaceful interactions not only with the Kingdom but with their own kind. Aside from a touch of spying, of course. I don't get filled in on everything going on with the faction, but I gathered from my wife's comments after the battle that she was pleased that I'd survived and wanted to know who's going to end up in charge of the Kingdom." Radmarik looked frankly at Syla. "I relayed that *you* said you might be interested in establishing peaceful interactions with them and allowing those willing to follow Kingdom laws to come to the islands, but she pointed out that you becoming the ruler is anything but assured."

"That's... unfortunately accurate."

The look Fel slanted toward Syla suggested she shouldn't have admitted that, not if they wanted Radmarik to sail them around.

"My priority right now is to repair the Harvest Island shielder," Syla added. "It requires a journey."

"That starts on Harvest Island?" Radmarik pointed his sugar cane at Fel. "That's what your bodyguard said."

Fel's gaze had shifted to the pier. Two squadrons of Royal Fleet in black uniforms were jogging toward a military vessel. Several of the men glanced in the whaling ship's direction.

Syla adjusted her hood, making sure they couldn't see her face, but was that another military vessel getting ready to set sail from the other side of the harbor?

"Yes," Syla replied. "I'm hoping to meet someone there." Did a dragon count as a *someone*? "If they're not able to help, I may need to charter your ship for a longer journey." A *much* longer journey. "If you're available."

"We'd have to see about that. This *someone* isn't one of the non-faction stormers, is it?" Radmarik squinted at her. "Like Captain Vorik?"

Syla wondered what kind of gossip had gotten out to the general public about her relationship with Vorik. Nothing, she hoped, but when she considered all the people at Lavaperch Temple on Harvest Island who might have said something about her disappearing for a night into their tower with her *prisoner*, she feared gossip might be spreading throughout the Kingdom.

"I'm not expecting Vorik, no," Syla said.

"He and his dragon sank two of the guard ships that were with us."

"But he *didn't* sink your whaling ship."

Radmarik's squint deepened. Yes, arguing that Vorik had been anything but an enemy to them during that battle would be hard for anyone to believe.

"His dragon ripped the roof off my wheelhouse," Radmarik said.

"He was trying to get to me."

Radmarik gazed at her as if she were an idiot. She thought about changing *get to me* to *rescue me*, but it was probably more *kidnapping* than *rescuing* when one stole a princess off her own ship. While one's allies were attacking it.

"Captain Vorik shouldn't know that I'm going anywhere," was what Syla decided to say. "It's actually the red dragon, Wreylith, that I hope to, uhm, connect with."

For the first time, Radmarik's face brightened. "The dragon who *saved* us? With her glorious crimson scales gleaming in the morning light as she drove away the stormer dragons?"

"That's Wreylith, yes."

"Will she help us again if we run into trouble?" Radmarik looked toward a couple of guard ships adjacent to the closest military vessel. The crewmen were readying cannons while continuing to glance at the *Striking Falcon*.

That was concerning.

"I'm not sure," Syla said, compelled to honesty, though it might have been better to assure Radmarik that Wreylith was on their side and would be available in a bind. If he thought military vessels were going to follow them out of the harbor, he would be less inclined to help, especially if his wife was hedging bets and waiting to see who ended up in charge of the Kingdom. "I may have to prove myself first."

"Set sail now," Fel told Radmarik, nodding toward the preparations on the military vessels.

"Yes. That may be wise." Radmarik glanced at Syla but didn't give the order she'd feared, for her to get off his ship.

Instead, Radmarik trotted around the deck, quietly instructing his men to take his vessel out of dock—and out of the harbor—as quickly as possible.

"You two ladies had better go belowdecks," one of the officers said as he strode past. "There are a few empty cabins down there."

"Thank you," Syla told him but didn't move.

If they were followed out of the harbor, she wanted to know about it. What she could do about it, she didn't know, but she wouldn't hide in a cabin.

"Delaying at the brothel may not have been a good idea," Fel said when he was alone with Syla and Teyla.

"I thought you approved of me fostering a spy for future intelligence-gathering purposes," Syla said though they both knew she hadn't been doing anything so premeditated.

"I'd *approve* of us not being killed before we escape the harbor." Fel scowled, not at Syla but at the two military vessels also making ready to set sail.

Teyla lowered her pack from her shoulders and untied her sword scabbard.

"I'm going to have a hard time keeping you two in a cabin, aren't I?" Fel asked.

"Sorry, Sergeant. Maybe we should have brought another bodyguard." Syla didn't mention that she hadn't yet figured out how she would bring *him* along if Wreylith agreed to fly her about.

"You should have brought an *army*."

"I suppose I should do my best to convince everyone that I should be queen so that I'll be able to acquire one." Syla said it as a joke.

But Fel nodded firmly. "*Yes.*"

If only that were an easy task...

"This isn't the way down the coast to the rainforests," Vorik said dryly as Agrevlari flew across the sea. "We're to start our search on Droha, not one of the Kingdom islands."

I heard Wreylith is still spending time on the Island of Eliok and pines for companionship, Agrevlari said. *It's on the way to the rainforest.*

"It's not remotely on the way, and I don't think Wreylith is capable of *pining*."

I'll be a better dragon ally if I can hunt and eat my fill of elioks before we start this search.

And share the poem you've composed with Wreylith?

If she'll allow me to, yes. Though I'm still refining it. Lieutenant Wise informed me that mangrove doesn't rhyme with love.

No, it does not. Vorik looked to the side at Wise flying astraddle Tonasketal. He was studying a scroll as the wind tugged at his short prematurely white hair. No doubt, his ability to read the modern and ancient tongues made him a likely human with whom to discuss poetry—and rhyming.

Perhaps I'll just screech a dragon song at her, Agrevlari said.

Females do enjoy being screeched at.

Dragon females prefer it as a vocalization method. The reverberations we can feel against our eardrums please our senses.

You're a quirky kind, aren't you?

Silence, Vorik. I have called to the beauteous Wreylith, and she has answered me.

Telepathically, I assume. You didn't screech.

Further, they were miles yet from the closest of the Kingdom islands.

Interesting, Agrevlari said after a time, the gray sky starting to spit rain as they flew high above the sea, waves undulating below. *She is not hunting but waiting to take your princess somewhere.*

Vorik leaned forward, flattening his hands to Agrevlari's scales. Was it as he'd considered? That Syla herself was undertaking a mission to find the components for the shielder?

Assuming she proves herself worthy of riding on a dragon again, Agrevlari added.

How does Wreylith want her to do that? It hadn't occurred to Vorik that he might gain information about Syla through dragon gossip. *She's not a combatant.*

As soon as the words came out, Vorik remembered Devron's assertions. He wished he'd stepped into the chamber in time to see and sense exactly what Syla had done to him.

Wreylith wants her to demonstrate her potential and also that she can ride on a dragon's back *rather than cling ignobly to her tail.*

Vorik bit his lip, remembering that. At some point during that battle, Syla had gotten ahold of Wreylith's tail and hung on. Since he'd been having a dragon disaster of his own at the time, he hadn't seen all of it, but it had been an amusing sight.

Wreylith is, however, currently wondering if the princess will arrive on the Island of Eliok since her sailing vessel is being set upon.

Set upon? Vorik straightened, thinking of Captain Lesva and her threats.

When he and Wise had left, she hadn't yet departed, but she *had* implied she might attempt to eliminate Syla while she was engaged in her mission on Harvest Island. Was it possible her dragon had flown at top speed and gotten to the area before Agrevlari?

Vorik looked over at Wise again, but he continued to examine the scrolls that Jhiton had sent along. If he even realized they were flying over the sea instead of down the coast, Vorik would be surprised.

Yes, Agrevlari said after a pause—he'd probably been waiting for clarification from Wreylith. *By other humans.*

Not dragons?

Wreylith did not mention dragons, only that she is waiting to see if the princess can handle her predicament herself without intervention. Also, Wreylith is enjoying a freshly caught eliok, so she understandably does not wish to leave her meal prematurely.

Well, we'll be premature. Vorik patted Agrevlari's back. *Pick up the pace, will you? Let's find Syla's ship.*

Vorik hoped they wouldn't be too late.

A moment ago, you did not approve of me flying in this direction, Agrevlari said.

That was before I knew Syla was in this direction. Go, go. I know you can flap those wings faster when you're properly motivated.

Do you believe if you rescue the princess, she will engage in coitus with you again?

No, I just want to make sure she doesn't die. Vorik hesitated. *After that's assured, I wouldn't turn down the other thing.*

I thought not.

Don't sound smug. You're hoping for coitus with Wreylith too.

Agrevlari picked up his pace, probably more at *that* thought than because Syla was in danger. *Indeed, I am. Perhaps we shall both employ poetry to woo our females.*

I'm not screeching at Syla about mangroves.

Perhaps you can sing a ballad. You've a decent knack for that.

Despite my lack of screeching?

Quite. It is because you appropriately note a dragon's majesty in the lyrics you compose.

Something that's sure to get a human woman in the mood.

I would think so.

Wise looked up, startled by Agrevlari surging ahead of his dragon. Maybe he was paying attention, after all.

Vorik waved for him to keep up. If only human enemies were attacking Syla, Vorik and Agrevlari might be able to deter them without much trouble, but if Lesva and her squadron were *also* in the area... Vorik would need help.

On the horizon, the dark green-and-brown outlines of two of the Kingdom islands came into view. Castle and Harvest. Far in the distance, a shadow on the horizon, lay the third island in the area—Bogberry Island. The others in the chain were much farther apart and to the south.

As Agrevlari continued closer and Vorik scanned the surface of the sea with his keen eyes, he spotted numerous ships navigating the waters between Castle and Harvest Islands. Several were military craft, and was that the boom of a cannon that floated to him over the whistling wind?

At first, Vorik thought the military fleet was escorting the ship slightly in the lead, but that was a whaling vessel rather than a transport ship. With a start, he recognized it. It was the same whaling vessel that had carried Syla weeks earlier, with what, at the time, he'd believed was a shielder on board. And was it carrying her again now?

Those ships harry the vessel with your princess aboard, Agrevlari said, perhaps plucking the question out of Vorik's thoughts.

Another cannon boomed. Vorik was close enough now to see the puff of gray smoke as the weapon fired.

"They're doing more than *harrying* it. Why are her own people firing upon her?" The answer came to him as soon as he spoke the words. "It's a coup. Or at least, that fleet was sent by the people who *intend* a coup. The bastards." Vorik drew his sword.

A few weeks ago, he never would have believed he could have cared one way or another about who sat on the throne of the Garden Kingdom, but now he knew Princess Syla, and he'd met the stiff-necked General Dolok. He didn't know who else might be involved in trying to kill Syla, but he had no trouble labeling them as *bastards* as well.

"Are we going to attack those ships, sir?" came Lieutenant Wise's call on the wind, his dragon flying behind and to the side of Agrevlari.

"Yes!"

"That's a whaling ship, not a cargo ship." Wise sounded confused.

Of course. With the exception of a couple of tribes, who acted more like pirates preying upon Kingdom ships, the stormers and especially the Sixteen Talons didn't wantonly attack vessels unless there was a logical reason. Food to be acquired or a notorious enemy to be vanquished. They didn't harass fishing or whaling vessels.

"Princess Syla is aboard," Vorik called, though, as Wise's superior officer, he didn't need to explain his actions.

"Are we... kidnapping her, sir?"

Vorik almost said they were *rescuing* her, but Wise gathered intelligence, and Jhiton might very well have chosen him as much for his ability to read scrolls and advise Vorik as his willingness to spy upon him. Jhiton might want to make sure Vorik didn't make any foolish decisions when it came to the Kingdom and especially Syla. And since Vorik wasn't even supposed to be coming to these islands right now...

"I want to question her again about the shielders, especially these components."

Wise shook his head, but it might have been because he hadn't caught all the words on the wind. He wasn't the type to argue with his superior officers. Spy upon, maybe. Argue, no.

The dragons drew closer to the battle, more cannons firing and a boarding party readying itself to leap from one of the military vessels to the whaling ship. Vorik shook his head, at that moment not caring what his lieutenant thought. As he had once before, he spotted Syla.

She had her back to the wheelhouse—the roof Agrevlari had ripped off had been replaced—and she was staying out of the way, but not far *enough* out of the way. Why didn't that oversized limping bodyguard of hers hoist her over his shoulder and carry her belowdecks?

The harpoons on the whaling ship launched, and crewmen with bows and crossbows loosed their weapons at the surrounding vessels, but they were outnumbered. *Greatly* outnumbered.

Though the military vessels took hits, two soldiers appeared for every one that fell. A harpoon crunched into the hull of the ship with the boarding party, but it didn't start taking on water quickly enough to keep it from drawing even with the whaling vessel.

Once close enough, the boarding party leaped over the railing. Swords clanged as the attackers crushed into defenders that swarmed forward, attempting to stop them. As the boarders surged forward, cannons from their ship fired to assist them. The projectiles blasted into the whaling ship's defenders. A ball striking one man in the chest killed him immediately. The boarders succeeded in spreading out across the deck, ten men clad in black instead of wearing uniforms, with masks pulled down to hide their faces. Several angled toward the wheelhouse.

Grim, Vorik urged Agrevlari to descend rapidly. Those men could only mean to assassinate Princess Syla.

14

A BATTLE RAGED ON THE DECK OF THE WHALING SHIP. SYLA AND Teyla had retreated into the wheelhouse, though they doubted that would provide safety for long.

Eyes wide, Teyla crouched with her sword in hand, ready to attack anyone who got past Sergeant Fel. He stood in front of the door, firing his crossbow at men in black who'd leaped over the railing. They fought the crew of the whaling ship, but, with archers and cannons from their ship assisting, they steadily encroached upon the wheelhouse.

Syla gripped the reflex hammer from her medical kit in one hand and the red dragon figurine in the other. Warm against her palm, the latter was more likely to be of help, but when she attempted to call out telepathically with an urgent, *Wreylith?* she didn't get an answer. Was it because Wreylith wanted Syla to prove herself?

"As if *battle* is how I would ever do that," she whispered.

Teyla glanced at her. "Do you want to get behind me?"

"I'm already behind Fel."

"Yeah, but he's being set upon." Teyla pointed her sword

toward Fel, his crossbow firing with one final *twang* before he was forced to switch to his mace for close-quarters fighting.

"We're *all* being set upon." Syla hated hunkering inside the wheelhouse while others were wounded—or worse—but she feared Fel would soon be overwhelmed and the battle would come to them.

Two men in black and wearing masks attempted to flank Fel so they could attack him from both sides. The wheelhouse and doorway guarded his back, but he had to sweep his mace back and forth rapidly to keep them at bay.

When a second telepathic call didn't bring a response, Syla pocketed the krendala. She wished she had a crossbow instead of the small hammer. Then she might have fired around Fel. Even more black-clad men were trying to get at him. No, they were trying to get *past* him and to her.

One of the masked men pointed a hand-cannon at Fel's head.

"Look out," Fel called over his shoulder as he ducked.

Syla had been about to yell the same to him but realized that when he lowered himself, the weapon pointed through the doorway at *her*. She leaped to the side an instant before it fired. The projectile slammed into the wooden wheel behind her, knocking off one of the handles.

Snarling, Fel deflected a sword slash, then sprang for the man with the firearm.

Though he tried not to let anyone past him, one of the black-clad figures slipped through the doorway, blue eyes bright and eager behind his mask. After glancing dismissively at Teyla, he charged at Syla with a spiked mace in his hand.

Teyla stabbed him in the shoulder on his way past. Startled, he howled in pain and spun on her, raising his mace. Syla jumped forward and struck him on the back of the head. Unfortunately, the small hammer didn't deliver a crippling blow. He stumbled but didn't drop his weapon. Syla lifted the hammer to strike again, but a second man slipped into the wheelhouse.

"Need help guarding the princess!" Fel yelled amid clangs and thuds.

He was doing his best to block the way, and had downed one of the would-be assassins, but others were keeping him too busy to stop more.

Clangs sounded as the mace-wielder attacked Teyla, now determined to get her out of the way. The second masked assassin leaped for Syla with a dagger in his hand.

Though terrified, she swung the hammer at his arm, hoping to knock the blade away. With fast, easy speed, he dodged her swipe and leaped toward her, catching her wrist to halt further attacks. She jerked back, trying to escape his grasp, but he was too strong. Without effort, he pushed her against a wooden wall, knocking the breath out of her. Fear surged through Syla's veins, and she kicked out, but her foot glanced off his leg and did nothing to stop him.

"Sorry, princess." The man sounded sincere, but that didn't keep him from raising his dagger. "Orders."

Terrified for her life, Syla reacted on instinct, summoning her power faster than she ever had before. The back of her hand flared silver, bright enough that the man paused, glancing at it. Through his grip, she hurled tendrils of magic from her body and into his. One tendril shot toward his heart and another toward his brain, and she directed great pressure into crucial blood vessels. Instead of healing them, as she'd done a thousand times, she willed them to burst, to hurt him enough to drop him to the ground, anything to keep that dagger from slitting her throat.

"Fire!" someone outside cried.

"Dragons!" another man yelled.

A roar and a splitting of wood came from above, but Syla's attacker didn't glance up. He swept his dagger with unerring accuracy toward her throat.

But he didn't finish the stroke. Abruptly, fear widened his eyes, the only part of his face visible behind the mask. Fear and confusion. His focus turned inward, the dagger hanging in the air between them. Then his grip softened, and he released Syla. He staggered back, dropped his dagger, and reached for his head. With an inarticulate noise, his face twisting in a rictus, he pitched to the deck.

Syla slumped back against the wall, drained by using so much power so rapidly, but she also stared at the man, scarcely able to believe she'd stopped him so quickly. No, she'd done *more* than stop him. His eyes were frozen open. Dear moon god, had she... killed him? With her magic?

All she'd wanted was to stop him, to do something dramatic to keep him from finishing that blade stroke.

Teyla grunted in pain, and Syla jerked her gaze up, reminding herself that the battle wasn't over. The other assassin had driven Teyla back to the opposite wall and disarmed her, her sword clattering to the deck.

Syla tried to step forward, but her legs nearly gave out, her muscles rubbery and weak. She'd used so much power in that handful of seconds that she almost pitched to the deck beside the assassin's body.

But Teyla needed help. Gritting her teeth, Syla supported herself on a console beside the wheel and willed energy into her leg muscles, hoping to spring on the man's back to stop him.

Before she could, someone leaped down from the roof— through a newly formed *hole* in the roof—and twisted in the air to land behind the attacker. The man wore dark riding leathers, with windswept black hair framing his familiar face, and a travel pack and sword strapped to his back.

"Vorik!" Syla glimpsed green scales through the hole in the roof.

Agrevlari breathed fire at the nearby military ship that had sent the boarding party.

After making sure Syla wasn't in immediate danger, Vorik gripped Teyla's attacker from behind and hurled the man through the doorway with far more power than most people possessed. The assassin shouted in alarm as he flew into another black-clad man who'd been about to rush inside. They tumbled over two assassins unconscious or dead on the deck. Beyond them, Fel was climbing to his feet, recovering from a blow—or had he been shot?

Pain contorted his face, but he'd kept his weapons and stepped over one of the downed men to club those discombobulated by tripping over their comrades.

Vorik rushed to Syla's side, his sword in hand, though he hadn't yet bloodied it on an enemy. He must have flown straight to the wheelhouse. As he looked her up and down, checking for wounds, fire blasted across the huge windows behind the wheel.

Another military ship had been approaching, but the navigator must have spotted the dragon, because it was already turning. Or were there two dragons? Syla glimpsed a gray-scaled tail as another flew past outside.

Relieved for the help, Syla gripped Vorik with both hands. She might have hugged him, but the chaos continued outside the wheelhouse. Further, Teyla remained inside, a witness alternately gaping at Vorik and through the rooftop at Agrevlari's belly. The dragon roared and breathed more fire, targeting another military vessel within range.

"Good morning, Syla," Vorik said calmly, though he eyed the dead man on the floor. Wondering what had felled him when there was no blood?

Even though the assassin had been trying to kill her, Syla couldn't feel triumph over the way she'd stopped him. No, she felt horror. She was a healer, and she'd used her power to kill. She hadn't *meant* to, though in hindsight she realized she'd chosen vital targets and couldn't be surprised by the outcome. At the time, with that dagger swinging toward her throat, she'd been too scared to opt for subtlety.

Though he kept his sword pointed toward the doorway, Vorik wrapped his free arm around her. "I've been pining for you and thought I would come for a visit."

"I'm glad you did," she whispered, tearing her gaze from the fallen man and leaning against Vorik's side, glad for the support. She looked at Teyla to make sure she was all right.

Her sleeve was ripped and blood dampened her tunic, but she picked up her sword and nodded that she could handle more if needed. Her wound must not have been too grievous.

"They're pulling away!" someone outside yelled.

"Do we shoot the dragons?"

"No." That was Captain Radmarik. "Continue to Harvest Island."

"There's a dragon on the wheelhouse, sir!"

"He can come too."

Fel staggered into the doorway, a bloody gash on his sweaty face but his mace in his hand. He spotted Vorik promptly, and anger rather than relief boiled in his eyes.

"You!" He pointed the mace at Vorik, then curled his lip at Vorik's arm around Syla and her leaning on him.

"He came to our assistance." Syla thought about pulling away from Vorik, lest they look like lovers, but her legs were still weak. Besides, she didn't *want* to pull away. Still stunned and distressed by having killed the man at her feet, she needed support.

Fel didn't spring at Vorik, but he growled and flexed his hand on the grip of his mace.

"I've missed you as well, Sergeant," Vorik said. "Though my pining is for the princess alone, my back is ever bored and bereft without the need to stay alert to the possibility of you swinging a weapon at it."

"Bored and bereft?" Fel curled his lip again.

"Do you not care for alliteration? We enjoy it immensely in our ballads and chants. It helps with the memorization too."

"Are the ladies all right, Sergeant?" Radmarik looked through the doorway.

Fel turned partially toward him but didn't seem to want to take his gaze fully from Vorik.

Vorik was unconcerned about him, only keeping his arm around Syla and nudging the dead man with the toe of his boot. "Did you handle this one, Your Highness? You may not have been as in need of saving as I believed."

"I need..." Syla didn't know how to explain her distress. She should have been ebullient to have survived, but the dead man would haunt her, especially since these were her own people. That was almost as distressing as everything else, that soldiers who'd faithfully served the royal family her entire life had abandoned their loyalty in a heartbeat with her mother's passing. "I don't know what I need," she whispered, then let herself fall fully against Vorik and removed her spectacles so she could bury her face in his shoulder.

Maybe she shouldn't have displayed her feelings for him openly in front of others, but, as strange as it was, she could trust him more than any of the soldiers in the Kingdom military. And even the crewmen of the whaling ship were in question. Might they not have taken coin from General Dolok or whomever was behind the assassination attempt? Fel and Teyla were the only people here she could fully trust. Captain Radmarik might help her, but he'd already admitted his wife was waiting to see what happened, not throwing her weight behind Syla.

Tears leaked from her eyes, but she hid them in Vorik's shoulder. In a minute, she would gather herself and be strong.

"Is *that* dragon getting a ride too?" a crewman outside asked.

Syla remembered that she'd seen different-colored scales.

"If a dragon wants a ride, it's best to give him a ride," Radmarik said.

"A wise policy," Vorik said while sheathing his sword and wrapping his other arm around Syla. "You're not injured, are you?" he asked softly, the words for her alone. "Just... distressed?"

"Yes." She turned her head enough to wipe her eyes.

Vorik rested the side of his face against her forehead and stroked her hair. A tingle of warmth swept into her. Ah, that was nice. She hadn't realized how much she longed to be comforted.

"Sir?" A stormer in black rider leathers stepped over one of the bodies and into the doorway, blurry in Syla's peripheral vision. Was that a sword in his hand? He kept it at his side. "Do you need help questioning the princess?"

Fel, standing inside the door now, growled at the man and raised his mace.

The newcomer eyed him and halted but soon looked to Vorik and Syla. "Er, is she crying, sir?"

"Yes, it's how I question women," Vorik said. "They're more likely to burble secret Kingdom intelligence when they're weeping and distraught."

"Oh. I see, sir." Did the bastard sound *approving*? Maybe he just appreciated his captain's wit.

Syla wiped her face again, put her spectacles on, and looked Vorik in the eyes. "Questioning the princess?"

"That's not in my orders," he said quietly, holding a finger up toward the stormer. To keep him back so that he wouldn't overhear?

Fel hadn't lowered his mace and was making it clear that *he* would keep another stormer from entering. Likely by braining him. Judging by the occasional growls that wafted from him, like a dog protecting the bone it was working on, Fel still wanted to brain Vorik too.

Maybe that was the correct way to feel toward him, and Syla was being foolish for granting him any degree of trust.

"What *are* your orders?" She wondered if he would answer.

Vorik looked from her to those in the wheelhouse watching. "May I have a private moment alone with you?"

"No," Fel stated.

Sensing Vorik would admit more if they were alone, Syla opened her mouth to ask the others to leave but noticed the green belly through the hole again. "Won't privacy be hard to achieve with a dragon on the roof above a giant hole?"

"Agrevlari can read my thoughts, so our interlude wouldn't have been entirely private regardless."

"I'll keep that in mind. Especially if..." Syla thought of the night they'd spent in the cave and hoped the dragon, kept a mile away by the barrier at the time, hadn't been reading Vorik's thoughts then.

"I succeed in expressing my relief at finding you alive and unharmed?" he finished for her.

"Yes."

Nobody had moved, so Syla waved for Teyla, Fel, and the stormer whose name she didn't know to leave the wheelhouse. Teyla hesitated but did so, giving curious backward looks to Vorik as she did. When Vorik nodded at his man, the stormer walked out, but he also sent a few curious looks over his shoulder on the way. Further, his gaze lingered on the body near Syla before he departed.

She told herself that they couldn't possibly know how the man had died. Just because he wasn't bloody didn't meant mean anything. Sergeant Fel might have broken his neck.

Thoughts of neck-breaking likely on his mind now, Fel hung his mace on his belt but folded his muscled arms over his chest as if to say he wouldn't go anywhere.

Syla made a shooing motion toward the doorway. "You can stand right outside, if you wish, Sergeant."

Vorik's eyebrow twitched, but he didn't object.

"I'm going to ask our rider guest a few questions," she added, hoping that might sway Fel. "I think he'll be more likely to open up without you glowering at him."

"Interrogations aren't done by pressing your chest up against a man," Fel stated, but he grabbed one of the bodies to haul outside.

"I rather think she could get a lot of information out of me by maneuvering so," Vorik said.

Fel growled at him. And glowered.

"Is there something that's irritating your throat, Sergeant?" Vorik asked. "Your vocalizations sound strained. Perhaps you should see a healer and acquire an herbal tea."

"I want to club him with my mace," Fel told Syla.

"A lot of people do, but go outside anyway, please. And close the door."

Fel scowled but pulled the second and last of the bodies out with him as he left the wheelhouse. Maybe he didn't think Syla should be surrounded by death. After all she'd endured, she ought to be used to it, but she would be glad not to have the frozen eyes of the deceased staring accusingly at her while she spoke with Vorik.

Fel made a point of standing immediately beside the doorway, his shoulder visible. Without releasing Syla, Vorik unsheathed his sword and used the tip to push the door shut. Save for a porthole in it, the walls to either side were solid, giving them a modicum of privacy, at least from the direction of the deck.

"That's better," Vorik said cheerfully.

"I agree."

He returned his sword to its scabbard, then dropped it and his pack to the deck before sliding both arms around Syla and kissing her. Though she hadn't expected it, her arms lifted to wrap around his shoulders of their own accord, and she melted into his touch.

Passion filled his kiss, but there was more than that. Relief? Vorik must have been able to see the battle unfolding as his dragon flew in, the boarding party arriving and men breaching the wheelhouse. Maybe he'd worried he would be too late.

The implication that he cared touched Syla, and she struggled to remember that she wanted to ask him a few questions—to learn what his orders were. What had brought him here? She highly doubted he'd simply been in the area.

But as his lips stroked hers, and his hands started roaming, they woke up her numb body. His strong fingers slid over her shoulders, stirring sensations as they trailed down her arms, shifted to her waist, and finally cupped her backside. Pleasure replaced her distress, pleasure and *desire*.

Her thoughts grew fuzzy as she caught herself returning his kiss while pushing one hand up to brush through his hair to rub his scalp. He groaned with pleasure of his own, tightening his grip on her, and she felt his own longing through his trousers. Knowing she could inspire such desire in a man like him—a man who could have had any woman—excited her, just as it had the night they'd joined. She wanted to let a hand drift lower, to touch him and feel—

No. Sergeant Fel was outside, and Agrevlari perched above. Syla made herself stop her explorations, grip Vorik's shoulders, and lean back from his kiss.

The heated expression in his emerald eyes promised Vorik didn't want to stop their reunion, but she had to know why he was here. What if he'd been sent to interfere with her mission again? And was using the appeal of his body and his charm—and those expertly talented lips—to distract her from thinking about that?

"What are your orders, Vorik?" Syla forced herself to look away from his lips and into his eyes, though they were just as dangerous.

Surely, the desire and heat in them couldn't be faked? He'd been moved to kiss her because he wanted to, not because his general had told him to.

Could she believe that? She wished she could be certain.

"They weren't to question you." Vorik's gaze lowered to *her* lips.

He licked his, as if he longed to return to their kiss, and a tingle went through her, tightening her core. She longed for that too. But voices drifted in from the deck, the captain ordering his men to restore order to the ship and get them to Hazel Harbor on Harvest Island as soon as possible.

"What *are* they?" Syla had a feeling he wouldn't answer. "Why are you here?"

And why couldn't she step fully away from him? She'd broken the kiss, but her body remained molded to his, her soft curves pleased to be pressed against his hard length. Anticipation filled her lower region, as if, independent of her mind, it was certain of where this would go.

"Believe it or not, it's happenstance. Well, not exactly. I have orders that will take me elsewhere, but my dragon—you may remember that Agrevlari is also pining—brought me here to check on Wreylith. Apparently, she's hunting elioks on Harvest Island?" Vorik arched his eyebrows, silently asking if Syla knew what Wreylith was up to.

Wariness crept anew into Syla as she recalled his questions back at the castle. He remained curious about her relationship with Wreylith. His *general* probably did too.

"I understand dragons find them irresistible," was all Syla said.

Vorik smiled, probably recognizing her evasion. Since he was being evasive too, she refused to feel guilty about it.

"For once, I'm relieved that my dragon has a crush even if you didn't truly need my help." Vorik glanced at the spot where the body of the man she'd killed had been.

They *had* needed help. Syla might have kept one man from assassinating her, but there'd been too many enemy ships. No, Royal Fleet ships that *shouldn't* have been enemies. Eventually, her allies would have been overwhelmed. It had been the dragons showing up that had convinced the military ships to depart.

She decided to keep those thoughts to herself. Vorik was probably aware of all that, but she didn't think she should admit that she owed him a favor. Not when she still knew nothing about his orders.

"I can't speak of my mission," Vorik admitted, "but I do want to warn you... You're aware that Captain Lesva survived, right?"

Syla grimaced. "You implied that, yes. I'd rather hoped she hadn't. Sorry. I know she's your..." She thought about saying lover, since Lesva herself had said that, but it had sounded like a relationship from the past. Syla *hoped* it was all in the past. Even if she couldn't have any kind of relationship with Vorik, she hated the idea of him being close to such a vile woman. "Colleague," she finished.

"Yes." Something in Vorik's eyes suggested he knew what she'd almost said. "We have a contentious relationship, so I won't be affronted on her behalf if you wish her ill. It would, in fact, be wise if you are extremely alert going forward and keep an eye out for her."

Syla's stomach sank. "Is she after me?"

"I'm sorry." Vorik lifted a hand to the side of her face, stroking her cheek with his thumb. "It's not an order from General Jhiton or any of our superiors. It's... personal."

Syla didn't want to tear up again, but it was hard not to feel overwhelmed. This was the last person she should confide in, but she couldn't keep from whispering, "*Everyone* is after me, Vorik."

"I'm not," he offered with a smile.

"No, but I think that makes you more dangerous than all the others."

His smile grew sad. "Does that mean you won't kiss me again?"

"A part of me is tempted to do that and more and hope you'll let me know what you're up to while in the throes of passion. Inspired by my mouth around... a certain body part of yours." Syla tried to make her tone teasing, but was it even a joke? If they'd truly been alone instead of with people—and *dragons*—around to overhear, might she have attempted to seduce him and extract information? She admitted she would love to have sex with him without any other motivation beyond their shared pleasure. Besides, she was such an improperly trained seductress that she would probably forget to ask him anything. As she recalled, *he'd* been more in charge than she last time. She'd been lucky he hadn't questioned *her.*

"A certain body part of mine would like me to be less than honorable by suggesting you might indeed extract truths from me in that manner," Vorik said, "but I don't think my lips are that loose."

"No. All of you is taut." Syla squeezed his shoulder, enjoying its hard roundness under her grip.

Humor sparked in his eyes, mingling with passion and desire. "A certain body part *especially* is."

Agrevlari shifted his weight, and a few pieces of the wooden ceiling clunked to the floor behind them. A reminder of all the potential eavesdroppers.

Sighing, Syla leaned back. Disappointment flashed in Vorik's eyes. She held up a finger, recalling that she'd brought something for him. Maybe that would make her choice feel like less of a rejection.

She slipped away long enough to grab her pack from the corner of the wheelhouse. Fortunately, it hadn't been disturbed during the battle. She fished out the paper bags of cookies she'd gotten from the children, then returned to stand close, facing him.

"A small gift for you," she said.

His eyebrows rose as he accepted the bags and peered inside, nostrils twitching. "Baked goods?"

"Yes. I received them as barter in exchange for healing someone this morning. I've not tried them, but I hope they'll be delicious and that you'll enjoy them."

"Excellent." Vorik turned toward his own pack, as if he might tuck them away for later, but he paused to delve into one of the bags and break off a piece of a cookie. Without hesitation, he popped it into his mouth and chewed.

Though Aunt Tibby had tried to talk Syla into poisoning a blackberry cobbler that she'd made for Vorik, and she was positive he'd heard at least some of that discussion, he never hesitated to consume anything she handed him. That he trusted her that much was surprising. And it touched her. He *shouldn't* have trusted her, but maybe... Well, considering how little time they'd actually spent together, he seemed to know her well. He didn't assume she wasn't dangerous—surprisingly—but he knew she wasn't dangerous to him.

The broad smile that sprawled across his face as he chewed, his eyes rolling, was achingly handsome. *He* was achingly hand-some, and she longed to reach out and run her fingers along his jaw.

"It's delicious. Blissful. So sweet but also the chunks of... what is this called? These pieces are sweet but rich with the fat of... not an animal."

"Those are chocolate chunks, I believe. They're made using milk from cows and roasted cacao beans that come from our southernmost island, the same place we get our bananas, coconuts, and coffee beans."

"So amazing. There's nothing like this out there that I've foraged."

"Well, we process it to turn it into a sweet. The natural beans themselves aren't very... uhm." She'd grown distracted by Vorik licking his fingers. Memories of how he'd used that tongue to lick *her* sprang to mind, and her cheeks heated. Her entire body threatened to heat.

Oblivious, he raised his eyebrows and lowered his hand.

"I wish I had a gift for you." He gazed contemplatively at her.

For some reason, the heat intensified. Was it possible he was thinking of *intimate* gifts he might give?

The mission, she reminded herself, was more important than gifts, intimate or otherwise. Besides, this wasn't a very private spot.

"You could give me the gift of telling me what your general has ordered you to do." Syla looked into his eyes, willing him to feel enough for her that he would share his people's secrets, at least those that endangered *her* people. But that wouldn't be any more honorable than what they'd just spoken about, and she wasn't surprised when he shook his head. The sadness that lingered in his smile suggested he did regret that he couldn't accede to her wishes.

"I can't do that," Vorik said, "unless you'd like to come with me? I know you're not exaggerating when you speak of all those who want you dead. As unfair as it is, your existence must be interfering with the plans of many."

"I healed General Dolok of a plethora of injuries, and he's *still* against me."

Syla didn't want to whine, but, as she'd told him, everyone *was* after her, and it was frustrating. She'd healed a man, and her reward was assassins on her trail.

His eyes narrowed contemplatively, as if he might visit the general with a dagger. If only Syla *could* send Vorik to deal with her enemies.

"Is he the one who was behind this?" Vorik waved toward where the body had been.

"I don't know. There are others, as well, who aspire to rule the Garden Kingdom."

Many others. Syla shook her head bleakly.

Vorik brushed her cheek with his knuckles. "If you come with me, I can keep you safe."

Was that a genuine offer? She couldn't go, of course, but she wished she could.

"Your people want me dead too," Syla said. "Especially Captain Lesva, apparently. Since I had the gall to *not* spew my secrets when she tortured me."

"You did have gall." The brush turned into a caress that sent tingles to her core. "You were magnificent."

Her nerves sang from his touch, his words, and the warmth of his smile and approval in his eyes. He leaned back enough to look her up and down, longing in his gaze, and it heated her as much as his touch. By the molten core of the earth god, she wanted to work *with* him, not against him. She wanted—

With a faint growl, Vorik picked her up. Startled, Syla tightened her grip on his shoulders, but her legs wrapped around him of their own volition. He set her on the console next to the wheel, pushing aside a map of the islands, and settled against her, his hard shaft pressing into her through their clothing.

"Vorik," she whispered as he leaned in for a kiss that she eagerly returned, her legs tightening around his hips, tightening him against her. "The whole ship would hear us."

"Agrevlari will keep them from intruding."

"*Intruding* isn't what I'm worried about."

He kissed her with such passion that she couldn't keep from responding, from gripping and kneading his shoulders, then running her fingers over the powerful muscles of his arms and chest. Her heart pounded, or maybe that was his. He slid a hand down her leg, shifting her dress up so he could stroke her bare thigh, his thumb brushing close to her underwear—to her *heat*. Maybe her body's earlier anticipation of sex hadn't been without merit.

"Come with me," Vorik said, an order this time. A command her body wanted to obey.

"Where?" she whispered. "Where are you going?"

His lips parted, as if he would answer, but his eyebrows drew together. Indecision marked his handsome face, and she sensed that he wanted to answer, to give her at least something.

Instead of replying, he kissed her again, hard and impassioned. Passion of her own flared, and she rocked into him as she ran her hand down his chest, groping for the ties in his tunic. She wanted to tear it off him, to slide her fingers over his bare muscles, to lick and kiss and nip at his taut flesh, and then shift lower, bringing her lips to his—

But he was the one to lower his head, dropping to one knee as he pushed her dress up farther. His thumb stroked the sensitive flesh of her inner thighs, and she spread her legs, inviting his touch, inviting *him*.

Reminded of the pleasure he'd given her in the temple, she leaned back, breathless, eager, hardly caring that he hadn't divulged his secrets. She wanted him to give her pleasure like she'd known then, the memory so intense that she still woke up nights with it in her dreams, her lurid dreams that left her aching with need. She arched toward him, throbbing with desire, hoping he intended to...

Yes, he lifted her enough to slide off her underwear, then, as if he couldn't hold back, brought his mouth to her throbbing core. She gasped, barely able to keep from crying out, from alerting the entire ship of his intensely exquisite touch.

His hands gripped her ass, pulling her close so he could lick and stroke her with his skilled tongue.

She couldn't keep from calling, "Vorik!" and begging, "*Please.*"

She tried to make it a whisper instead of a cry, but such ecstasy came with his every stimulating stroke that she struggled to remember why she cared that people were about. What did it matter? This brilliant warrior was bowing his head to her and sucking her such that tremendous throbbing pleasure swept through her body. Tremors made the console creak as she arched toward him, so close to her climax, needing just a little...

"More," she whispered. "More."

"Come with me," he said again.

"Where?" she panted, gripping his head, digging her fingers into his scalp as he teased her with her tongue. He *knew* she was close to the edge, but he looked up, eyes intent.

"I'll protect you and keep you safe."

If only she *could* go with him. She could leave the convoluted mess of the Kingdom, the assassins now stalking her, and she could just be a woman. A woman who could have sex every night with this magnificent beast of a warrior with the most talented tongue.

"I can't," she whispered, though she feared he would stop, that he would leave her without satisfaction.

But, if anything, the fiery passion in his eyes grew stronger. Maybe he respected her decision?

He slid his tongue into her with a growl, and she arched up again, so close, so full of need for him. He sucked her deep and hard, and she came with such intense satisfaction that she would have tumbled off the console if he hadn't held her. Waves and waves of pleasure made her eyes roll back in her head, and she longed to take back her words and agree that she *would* go with him. If only they could be together.

With another primitive growl, Vorik shifted up her body, his mouth returning to hers. His fingers remained lower, to rekindle her need, to ready her for *his* need, and the thought of giving *him* pleasure made her wrap her arms around him again. She could be ready again soon. For him, she could *always* be ready.

A dragon tail flapped against the window of the wheelhouse, and glass shattered. Syla jumped, pulling her mouth from Vorik as she turned to gape.

"Agrevlari," Vorik snarled in exasperation.

Wreylith comes! the green dragon announced, sharing the words with them both.

15

VORIK DID *NOT* WANT TO LEAVE SYLA, NOT *NOW*. WHY DID THE minions of the gods always show up when they were in the middle of—

"I need my underwear," Syla whispered, grabbing her spectacles and donning them to peer around.

"I need *you*," Vorik said in frustration.

"I know. Later?" She gripped his shoulders and gave him a hopeful smile.

"Are you coming with me?" Vorik doubted she'd changed her mind, unless her adoration for him and utter delight in his lovemaking abilities had swayed her.

If only...

"No," Syla said. "You should stay with *me*."

Vorik sighed. He couldn't abandon his mission and his people any more than she could. Although, if not for Wise, he might have been tempted to *delay* his mission for a couple of days. Especially since Captain Lesva would be in the area and a threat to Syla.

Even if it would put them at odds, Vorik hoped Syla *was*

leaving on a quest to find the shielder components. Anything to keep her away from Lesva.

A shout came from outside, someone announcing the appearance of a *third* dragon.

Wreylith seems dangerous and determined, Agrevlari noted.

Doesn't she always? Reluctantly, Vorik stepped back, plucked Syla's underwear off the deck, and handed them to her.

Yes, but I've yet to succeed in winning her favor after facing her in battle as an opponent. I suggest you fasten your lower-limb garments and prepare to leave swiftly if this doesn't melt her heart.

If what doesn't?

A horrific screeching croon came from the roof of the wheelhouse. Vorik winced.

Syla flung her hands over her ears. "What is your dragon *doing?*"

"I believe he's singing to Wreylith, possibly about love and mangroves."

Syla's jaw dropped in an incredulous expression as another round of screeching caterwauls came from the roof.

"What is that?" someone yelled, voice pained. "Will that one attack?"

"Will the *red one* attack?"

Per Agrevlari's advice, Vorik fastened his trousers, then grabbed his pack and sword scabbard, returning them to his back. Syla slipped her underwear on and straightened her dress a second before Lieutenant Wise flung open the door.

"Sir, I think we should go." Wise had to shout to be heard over the serenade from above. "Wreylith is coming, and your dragon..." His gaze drifted upward. Visible through the hole, Agrevlari's scaled torso flexed as he took a deep breath to issue what had to be the next verse.

"Is pissing her off?" Vorik gripped Syla's hands, wishing he could stay, but he realized that if Wreylith was coming, he might not *need* to stay. If the red dragon intended to protect Syla, Lesva wouldn't be as keen to attack.

Leave the vessel of the human princess, you odious fool! Wreylith boomed into their minds.

"Uh, is she talking to you, sir?" Wise asked. "Or Agrevlari?"

"*I'm* not the one singing to her." Vorik kissed Syla, then released her. "Be careful, Your Highness."

He turned to leap through the hole but not before catching her mouth the word, "Singing?" as if she couldn't believe even a dragon would classify those horrible noises thusly.

"Goodbye, Vorik," Syla called softly as he pulled himself onto the rooftop and climbed onto Agrevlari's back. "Thank you for coming."

Vorik almost called back that he cared for her and would *always* come, but he was now in view of dozens of men, and, thanks to Agrevlari's screeches, most of them were looking toward him. They were also glancing with worry toward the red dragon approaching the vessel from the direction of Harvest Island, but they wouldn't miss Vorik blurting something cheesy. And Wise wouldn't either. He had run out on deck, looking for *his* dragon, but Tonasketal had taken to the air already. The gray dragon remained in the area but was eyeing Wreylith's approach—yes, she *did* look determined—and staying out of her flightpath.

"Up here, Wise," Vorik called.

Instead of shouting words of adoration down to Syla, he dug into his pack and pulled out three of the squishy juggling balls he toted around to entertain himself while on missions. Thinking of their last conversation on the hobby, he smiled and tossed them through the hole to land at her feet. Syla blinked at him but picked them up.

Wise grunted as he pulled himself onto the roof of the wheelhouse. Not bonded to his dragon, he lacked the magical strength and agility that some riders had, so his climb wasn't that agile, but he managed and scrambled up behind Vorik. He even retained the scrolls, the bent parchment stuffed through his belt.

Agrevlari drew in a deep breath, but Vorik placed a hand on his scales and implored him, "Give it a rest, please. She's not here for you."

Wreylith was close enough now that they could see her golden eyes were focused on the wheelhouse. Vorik didn't know when Syla had called the dragon—when the battle had first started and before he'd arrived?—but he had no doubt Wreylith had come because of her, not the pining Agrevlari. Indeed, when Wreylith, red scales gleaming in the morning sun, glanced at the green dragon, her eyes flared with inner light, as if to warn him to get his ass off the princess's vessel, as she'd called it, before she lit him on fire.

Agrevlari must have interpreted her expression similarly, because his big inhalation turned into a sigh rather than another round of the screeching chorus. With his tail drooping a little, he sprang into the air. Vorik lifted a hand to wave to Syla, in case she was watching, as Agrevlari flew off to join Tonasketal.

Seconds after they departed, Wreylith landed on top of the wheelhouse. Yes, she'd come for Syla. No doubt.

Vorik watched to make sure Syla hadn't inadvertently irked the red dragon, and wouldn't be plucked up in her jaws, but Wreylith gazed down through the hole. Starting a conversation? This time, whatever telepathic words she shared were for Syla alone.

Oh, Agrevlari, Vorik said to his dragon, speaking silently so that Wise wouldn't overhear. *I've got to work on my timing.*

You have experienced an interruption in mating again.

Yeah.

At least you were invited to start the mating process.

I'm not sure I was invited so much as accepted when I showed up and started the, uh, process, he said, using Agrevlari's word.

Coitus.

We didn't get that far, unfortunately. Something his *certain body part* was unhappy about and would be for some time. Still, Vorik couldn't begrudge the red dragon's arrival. With Lesva's threat fresh in his mind, he was glad Wreylith would be around Syla— even if it would have been better for General Jhiton's ambitions if a powerful dragon *weren't* seemingly allying herself with the last member of the royal family in the kingdom they were trying to take over.

I fear Wreylith would not accept anything from me, should I attempt to start the mating process.

No, I think she'd rip your tail off.

I've heard she's slain potential suitors in the past. Even ones she mated with before *the slaying.*

That wouldn't surprise me. If I were you, I'd wait for her to give a clear invitation. Vorik had no idea how that worked for dragons but envisioned Wreylith in a nest on a high rocky perch, flicking her tail in the dragon version of a come-hither wave. *Or stick to females who haven't the power to slay you afterward.*

Vorik smiled, the next image to enter his mind of sweet Syla gazing at him through her spectacles.

But she was far from helpless, wasn't she? Vorik thought of that unexplained body with nary a wound visible.

He hadn't killed the man, and the cousin awkwardly wielding a sword hadn't run him through. The bodyguard *might* have clubbed him in the head with his mace, but, when Vorik had arrived, Fel had been so busy outside the wheelhouse, trying to keep assassins from gaining entrance, that Vorik didn't know if that was likely. The memory of Devron explaining how Syla had used magic to cut off his airway and render him unconscious lurked in his mind. Was it possible that his sweet healer princess was far deadlier than he could have imagined?

Females without great power are not as stimulating, Agrevlari remarked as he and Tonasketal flew east, toward the mainland, to start the mission they should have departed on that morning.

You think so?

I know *so.*

Vorik looked thoughtfully back over his shoulder, past Wise and toward the whaling ship now floating alone in the ocean, the vessels that had attacked it all having fled. He decided it would be good if he and his lieutenant could reach the shielder components before Syla.

He didn't worry about her using deadly magic on him, but he wanted to be her lover, not her enemy. It would be bad enough when she realized they were on the same mission. He didn't want to have to fight her openly to do his duty.

After Syla tucked away the juggling balls that Vorik had left—did he truly think she could master such a sport?—she stood under the hole in the wheelhouse ceiling, looking up at the now *red* scales of a dragon's belly. Outside, Captain Radmarik and what seemed like every crewman aboard stared, alternately through the doorway at Syla and up at the red dragon.

Wreylith had been watching Vorik and his man—or more likely the two dragons carrying them—depart, but she shifted so that her long neck could lower her substantial head into the wheelhouse. Syla wondered if Radmarik was furious that the same hole had been made twice in less than a month by the same dragon. At the moment, his chunk of sugar cane drooped from the corner of his mouth as he observed whatever was about to unfold.

One of Wreylith's horns clipped the side of the hole, knocking pieces of wood free. Her great head seemed to fill the entire wheel-house, and Syla tried not to feel trapped with her back to the console. She also tried not to feel embarrassed that she was going to converse with a mighty dragon from the same position where she'd moments earlier been brought to ecstasy by Vorik. Well, not the *exact* same position. Her cheeks heated as she remembered dropping back and throwing her legs wide for him, utterly unashamed about the crew outside, close enough to hear. No, not *unashamed*, precisely. Just... too distracted to remember or care that people had been nearby.

As Wreylith gazed at her with her golden eyes, reptilian slits for pupils, Syla tried to push the memories from her thoughts. Dragons, she reminded herself, could read minds.

"Greetings, Lady Wreylith." Syla stepped around her head, glad the dragon's maw wasn't open to reveal her long, pointed fangs, and shut the door after holding up a wait-please finger toward Radmarik. "Thank you for coming. Dare I hope you've decided that you're willing to carry me to collect the shielder components? I would be surprised if it was Agrevlari's allure—his *screeching* allure—that drew you."

Wreylith exhaled a warm breath that stirred Syla's hair. Was that how dragons snorted?

I am certain that no female ever has been drawn by that male's allure. Also, his screeches are off-key.

To say the least. Syla doubted, however, that she would recognize *on-key* dragon screeches if she heard them.

"You don't think he's handsome when he keeps his mouth closed?" Syla didn't know why she asked, other than that she cared about Vorik, and his dragon ally seemed earnest. Agrevlari had been aiding Vorik, who'd also aided her, so she felt an obligation to put in a good word for him. "He did help us during our battle."

I did not need *the help of an inferior domesticated dragon!*

"Of course you didn't. *I* didn't mind it." Maybe Syla shouldn't have admitted that. She was, after all, supposed to be proving herself worthy to Wreylith, who had yet to say she'd come to offer a ride. Maybe she was still deciding?

It wasn't entirely unamusing when he turned on his own superior to end the battle. Wreylith's lips parted, revealing the fangs Syla had been appreciating *not* seeing. Fortunately, it seemed more a smile than a threatening gesture. Like a content dog lolling its tongue out after a run.

Wreylith's jaws snapped shut, and her lids came down to narrow her eyes. Syla reminded herself about the mind-reading possibility. No, the *likelihood*.

"It was amusing, yes," she said. "And very helpful since I longed not only to live and complete my mission but keep this whaling vessel from being destroyed by dragon fire."

Poor Captain Radmarik. His ship had been set upon and damaged twice now because of her. She would have to arrange payment again so he could finance a second round of repairs. How she would manage that, she didn't know, since General Dolok might *already* have taken over the castle—and its coffers—in her absence.

We await another, and then we may begin your journey.

"Oh? You're willing to take me? Us? Will the other carry one of my allies?" Syla waved toward the doorway to indicate Fel and Teyla outside.

I will carry you. The inferior domesticated dragon has agreed to port the others. Unlike superior wild dragons, she was born to weak dragons who kowtow to puny humans, so she is accustomed to the idea. No wild dragon that I tangentially broached the subject with showed interest.

"I would be delighted and honored to have the assistance of another dragon, no matter what her origins."

After the words came out, Syla questioned them. What Wreylith called *domesticated dragons* were dragons allied with the stormers, those who let riders on their backs and battled *her* people. Even though they retained their independence and were only allies—not at the beck and call of the stormers—would it be safe for Fel and Teyla to get on the back of one? What if this new dragon was coming along so that she could spy and report back to the stormers?

Of course you are honored. Dragons are vastly superior to your kind.

"You're right. I should have brought you an offering." Syla thought of the cookies she'd given to Vorik but doubted the carnivorous dragon would have enjoyed them.

That would have been appropriate, but you've promised me numerous delicious animals in exchange for my help. In particular, I look forward to the horn hogs.

"After we get back, I'll get those animals, yes. It'll just take me some time to arrange for hunters to acquire everything on the agreed-upon list." Syla didn't mention that it might be as hard for her to arrange that as to get money out of the castle coffers. If Wreylith helped her, she would find a way to make good on her promise. Even if she had to wander the countryside herself, bartering healing for meat.

You might have brought a preliminary morsel, thus to ensure my willingness to stick with you throughout what might be a tedious journey of many days. An image of a sheep standing in a pasture accompanied the words.

"You're right. I should have thought of that." Syla also didn't mention that she'd had to flee Castle Island and that carrying a sheep draped over her shoulders would have made that more challenging than it already had been.

Wreylith's warm breath filled the room. Another snort? *The domesticated dragon will arrive soon.*

"So we can go? Let me tell Captain Radmarik that we'll depart." Syla lifted a hand for the door latch but paused, making sure Wreylith truly did intend to take them.

We can go, yes.

"What made you decide that I'm... worthy of helping?"

Maybe Syla didn't want to know. She wasn't proud of having

killed that man and worried that was what had swayed the dragon. Had Wreylith been able to see or sense that all the way from Harvest Island? Syla didn't berate herself for defending her own life, but she wished she'd been able to incapacitate the man instead of killing him. If there'd been more time and she hadn't been reacting on instinct—on sheer terror—maybe it could have gone differently.

You successfully defended yourself from an assassin, Wreylith said.

Syla nodded grimly and unfastened the door latch. It was what she'd expected the dragon to say.

And you lured what humans would consider a powerful individual to kneel before you and satisfy your sexual needs.

Syla almost fell through the door. That *wasn't* what she'd expected the dragon to say. How could Wreylith have known what was going on in the wheelhouse from so far away? From *any* distance. The door had been shut, Agrevlari's belly had blocked the hole, and there was nothing but sea beyond the front windows.

Wreylith's jaws parted, again bringing the thought of contented dog-tongue-lolling to mind. And did those golden eyes glint with *humor?*

Riders are, of course, still puny humans, but those who've convinced dragons to lend them power are less puny than most.

"Er, yes." Syla imagined telling Vorik that Wreylith had described him as *less puny than most.*

To have won such a mate for yourself speaks to your prowess as a female, Wreylith added. *Whether you'd ever be worthy enough for a dragon to desire to bond with you, I do not know, but I believe you are correct. As you said, you have potential.*

"Because Vorik, uhm, satisfied me."

From his knees!

Syla bit her lip, barely keeping from saying that it hadn't signi-fied anything like Wreylith seemed to believe, and that she would have happily knelt before Vorik to satisfy *him* in a similar manner. Maybe one day, she would correct Wreylith, but for now... she needed a ride. With the stormers threatening Harvest Island, and continuing to plot against the Kingdom as a whole, her *people* needed her to have a ride.

Perhaps one day, Wreylith added, not commenting on her thoughts, *you will be like Queen Erasbella.*

"She sounded like a capable ruler." Syla looked forward to reading about whatever secret side of her great-great grandmother was in the book she'd found. "I would be proud to be like her."

Only belatedly did Syla think to wonder if the dragon was implying her great-great grandmother had led a... lurid life. The other books hadn't mentioned sexual escapades, so that would indeed be a *secret side.*

Yes. Now climb up here and get onto my back. Not my tail. Igliana has arrived.

Syla grimaced, knowing that she would not only have a hard time pulling herself onto Wreylith's back but that even clambering onto the roof of the wheelhouse—what remained of the roof— would challenge her athleticism. Oh, to have even a tenth of the ability that Vorik possessed.

Curious about who Igliana was, Syla affixed her pack over her shoulders and walked outside. Some of the crew had started on repairs that could be done while at sea, but many continued staring at Wreylith and also at a smaller dragon that had arrived. A vibrant orange dragon, it—*she*, Syla reminded herself—perched on one of the harpoon launchers, balancing easily considering how small it was compared to a dragon. The newcomer might not be as large as Wreylith, but she was still capable of carrying two riders.

And, Syla thought, her earlier concerns returning, capable of flying back to the stormers and reporting the group's activities.

Greetings, humans! The orange dragon sprang into the air, flew vertically dozens of yards, then turned and tucked her wings in close to dive.

She plummeted into the sea ten feet to the port side of the whaling ship. Scant seconds later, she came up on the starboard side, then arched over the deck like a leaping dolphin. Droplets of water spattered down as she barrel-rolled through the air before finishing with an acrobatic maneuver that Syla, after a moment's consideration, labeled as a pirouette.

The captain's jaw dropped. *Most* of the crewmen's jaws dropped.

Wreylith sighed into Syla's mind. *There were few options available.*

"Is she... young?" Syla guessed.

Very young.

Once again, the dragon—Igliana—alighted on the harpoon launcher. *Climb aboard, humans who will ride me. I will take you aloft for a glorious flight.*

Teyla stood near the railing of the ship, and her eyes brightened, then turned hopefully toward Syla. Did she *want* to ride with Igliana? Hadn't her sword fight taught her that she wasn't quite as prepared for the world as she'd imagined? And, surely, no Kingdom woman was prepared for *dragons.*

Fel, still standing by the door to the wheelhouse, hadn't missed any of this. Older and wiser than Teyla, he gave Syla a baleful look. No doubt, he already anticipated that he would have to ride that dragon—and figure out how to stay on her back. What if she barrel-rolled and pirouetted while a thousand feet in the air?

Syla spread her arms apologetically, but that didn't keep her from saying, "I'll go with Wreylith, Sergeant. I need you and Teyla to ride that one. Her name is Igliana."

Fel grumbled under his breath as he retrieved his pack. The newspaper he'd picked up in town was tucked under one of the straps, and he offered it to Syla while looking with dread toward the orange dragon. Meanwhile, Teyla danced across the deck toward Igliana. She might even have pirouetted. If she could stay on, she and that dragon might be perfect for each other.

"I didn't want to stop to make you read while we had soldiers stalking us," Fel said, "but you should probably know about that."

"I like reading, Sergeant. You never have to *make* me do it." A true statement, but Syla and Teyla had been busy discussing how to find the various shielder components since leaving the harbor, so she hadn't had time for reading. Now, she grimaced as she accepted the newspaper.

"For that, *making* might have been required." Fel shouldered his pack, a resolute expression on his face, and strode toward the orange dragon.

The headline on the front read: *Invaluable Shielder Scrolls Lost; Harvest Island Lost; Princess Syla to Blame.*

"Wonderful." Syla correctly anticipated her cousin Relvin's name on the byline, but she was surprised he'd chosen to so blatantly defame her. Shouldn't one use a fake name when one was secretly angling for the throne? "How did he even find out about the scrolls?" she muttered and started reading.

A shadow fell over her before she'd absorbed more than a paragraph—Wreylith's head blotting out the sun.

Syla jumped, almost dropping the newspaper.

"Look out!" someone barked.

Before Syla could look *anywhere*, Wreylith wrapped her maw around her, fangs tightening with terrifying power. As she'd done in the past, the red dragon hefted Syla from her feet. Her fangs didn't puncture clothing or skin as the jaws lifted her into the air, but the alarming pressure made Syla gasp and clasp her hand over her spectacles. Being flung almost made her scream, especially when her trajectory took her in an arc *past* the wheelhouse. She would land in the sea. Or on the railing. Keeping one hand to her spectacles, she flailed the other arm, twisting in the air to try to get her feet under her.

Wreylith sprang from the wheelhouse, angling so that Syla would land on her. Even with the dragon's precise timing, Syla almost bounced off. She *did* lose the newspaper, pages fluttering in the breeze. Only by desperate scrambling did she manage to spread her arms to land with a painful thump on the dragon's back. Her spectacles slid down her nose, and when she reached up to catch them, *she* started sliding. Alarmed, she flattened her hand to Wreylith's scales and willed healing power into the dragon, trying to use it as a way to anchor herself, as she'd done before. This time, Wreylith didn't have any injuries in need of repair, but Syla's tendrils of magic spread into the muscled back and did as she wished, creating a connection with the power to keep Syla in place.

She peered over the dragon's side, distressed to see the newspaper pages flying away. "I need those. Please."

Wreylith turned her head, breathed fire, and incinerated them. *Lesson Number One of riding a dragon: When instructed to do so, promptly climb onto her back. Lesson Two: Do not irritate the dragon by dallying.*

Wreylith flapped her wings and flew away from the whaling ship, her powerful form radiating magical energy, and Syla decided not to argue. Later, she would ask Fel for the details of the article. He'd likely read it while she'd been healing Celena.

"All right. Noted." Syla wouldn't be meek, having always heard dragons respected bravery, but Wreylith was doing her a huge favor. Syla would do her best to abide by those lessons.

Worried that Fel and Teyla might have suffered similar fates—and not managed to stay on their dragon's back—she peered in their direction. Igliana had also taken off, following after Wreylith. Unlike the determined and straightforward red dragon, the orange had a distinct sashay to her flight, swaying and tilting left and right, emanating enjoyment at being in the air. Or simply being alive? Maybe she was excited to have been asked to join Wreylith.

Fel, his face green as he hung on, didn't appear to appreciate Igliana's joy. If anything, he looked like he might throw up. Teyla was flattened to the dragon's back, much as Syla and Aunt Tibby had been for their first ride, but she wore a grin as she gazed down at the sea.

"At least someone's having a good time," Syla murmured.

What is the first destination? Wreylith asked.

"We need to find a rainforest, ideally on Droha since the other components should be there too."

Wreylith banked to adjust her flightpath. *This route will take us in the same direction that the domesticated dragons are going. I sense them some miles ahead of us.*

"The domesticated dragons? Agrevlari and... the one with him?" Syla hadn't caught the name of the other stormer or his dragon.

Correct. Do they fly to the same destination?

Syla shook her head and started to say *no* but paused, remembering her last conversation with Tibby. Vorik hadn't told her his mission, but if her aunt was right and the stormers wanted to find the components to keep the Kingdom from having them, General Jhiton could have assigned him that task.

Syla closed her eyes as distress crept into her. "I can't *believe* I gave him cookies."

They will be rivals in this quest?

"Unless you can catch up and kick their asses."

Wreylith considered that for a moment, one of her eyelids flickering as she glanced toward the sashaying orange dragon. *As you may have deduced, I recruited Igliana from those dragons allied with stormers. She is not in any of their combat squadrons, but I would be uncertain of her allegiance were we to engage with them. Further, while I could certainly best either of those pet dragons in a one-on-one battle, I might be challenged to fight both of them, especially when they would be assisted by experienced warriors, one enhanced by dragon magic, and I...*

"Just have me. I get it." A powerful warrior, Syla was not.

How did you kill the assassin?

Syla kept herself from saying it had been by accident. "With my healing power except... not in the typical manner." She winced. "I think I have to be touching someone to use my magic on them, and I couldn't..." She groped for a way to say that she couldn't use deadly power on Vorik. Even if he was to be pitted against her—*again*—she couldn't change that she cared for him.

Should you need to slay that one, you could attract another mate who would satisfy you, Wreylith said. *You have proven this ability.*

"Maybe," Syla said, "but I like the way *he* satisfies me." She rolled her eyes at herself, hardly believing she was discussing this with a dragon. Wreylith would be anything but sympathetic.

It is useful to find a mate good at satisfying one's needs, Wreylith surprised her by saying.

"Very useful, yes."

But if he impedes your quest...

"I'll think of a way to stop him. One way or another."

16

Not long into the flight, Wreylith banked to lead Igliana on a new trajectory. Busy reading from *The Secret Life of Queen Eras-bella,* Syla almost missed noticing. At first, she assumed Wreylith was changing her route because of the wind or to fly more directly, but then she spotted other dragons to the north. More than a dozen of them were heading west, toward the Kingdom. Toward Harvest Island, Syla feared, when she picked out riders on their backs.

She shifted uneasily, spotting a blue dragon. Captain Lesva had ridden a blue dragon.

Though they were too far away for Syla to identify any of the riders, Vorik's warning came to mind, and she imagined the flinty woman gazing across the distance, debating an attack. If Lesva *was* with those dragons, was she leading them? Would she be able to detour from her mission?

"Are you communicating with those dragons, Wreylith?"

I informed them that if they pestered me, I would bite their heads off.

"Did that work? There are a lot of them."

More than half the wing is male.

"So... they're in love with you and won't fight you?"

Not all seek to mate with me, but one has already made flirtatious remarks. The others are aware of what happened during my last battle with stormer dragons, and they do not seek to endure a repeat of the event.

"Like the flirtatious male turning on one of his own kind?"

To impress or defend me, yes. That was deemed chaotic by many.

"I liked it."

Yes. Wreylith sounded smug.

Syla couldn't blame her and was relieved when the dragons didn't change course to try to intercept them. Her relief was short-lived though as she remembered they were heading toward the Kingdom. Syla needed to find the components as soon as possible so Aunt Tibby could repair the shielder and return it to Harvest Island. She couldn't do anything until she reached the mainland, however, and returned to reading.

"The other books all said my great-great grandmother knew from an early age that she would rule the Kingdom and trained and studied hard, learning to use her gods-gift to become a talented diplomat and leader. Supposedly, she was always a responsible girl, prepared to do her duty. But this says she ran away *three* times because the pressure was onerous and she wanted to have adventures. Once, she bribed a merchant captain to take her away from the Garden Kingdom to see the world. Out there, she was chased by wyverns, almost lost at sea, and kidnapped by stormers. Once, she was kidnapped by *pirates*. She escaped from her predicaments and, in the process, met a dragon —a *red* dragon—and somehow talked *her* into taking her by air to see the world. Wreylith, is that right? Was that *you*?"

You are skimming. The story was much more involved.

"I'm only in the introduction so far. Did she pull a venomous fang out of your foot?"

She was not a healer. That is not how she proved herself worthy of a dragon's consideration.

"This doesn't say anything about enticing a powerful mate to satisfy her sexual needs."

We all prove ourselves in different ways, came Wreylith's dry reply.

Doubting she would get the story from the dragon, Syla turned to the first chapter.

As she read and hours passed, the air grew warmer and more humid, with Wreylith and Igliana flying south as much as east. The magic inherent in dragons gave them the power to soar faster than ships could have sailed, and they were able to skirt roiling gray clouds, a storm that covered miles, if not hundreds of miles, and return again to clear weather as the sun sank toward the horizon. Though they had flown all day, it was far sooner than Syla could have imagined that the continent of Droha came into view.

At this point along its coastline, a dense tangle of lush green foliage stretched. Faintly visible many miles inland, the snowy peaks of mountains rose above the verdant rainforest.

Syla was glad they would reach land soon. Many hours had passed since the dragons had stopped on an island to drink water from a pond—and the humans had attended to their own biological needs—and she needed another opportunity to relieve herself. She also looked forward to seeing one of the continents for the first time in her life. Since the islands of the Garden Kingdom provided all the food that its subjects needed, few ever left them. The only ones who did were intrepid explorers, brave archaeologists, and capitalistic foragers, fishers, and hunters who risked their lives to find and sell rare plants, sea life, and animals that had value.

Where in this land do you need to go? Wreylith asked as they flew lower and closer, the outlines of trees more distinct. From those trees came the sounds of animals hooting to welcome the sunset, the varied calls audible over the roar of waves crashing to the shore.

Syla closed the book and pulled out her copy of Aunt Tibby's translations.

"The component that comes from the rainforest is a cylindrical bulb shape that forms out of a kind of moss that carpets the side of a certain species of tree that grows in this climate." Too bad the scroll hadn't said *which* species. "The bulbs eventually wither, detach, and fall to the ground. Usually, they decompose quickly, but if they are taken somewhere to dry for preservation, they eventually become magical. That takes years and years though. The indigenous peoples only discovered it because they found some that had landed in such a way that they eventually became petrified. Once magical, the moss-bulb powder apparently had a lot of uses."

You will trade with these indigenous people for powder?

"I wish, since that would make things easy. While it's *possible* there are still people living in the area, Teyla said archaeologists have looked for the ancient mainland tribes before and found nothing but ruins left behind from their abandoned settlements. Back when the storm god was unleashing his creations on the world, the humans who didn't obey the other gods and come to the Garden Kingdom for protection didn't have a high rate of survival." As far as Syla knew from the history books she'd read, it had mostly been those who'd allied with dragons and become known as the stormers who'd managed to survive in the changed world.

You have spoken much but did not tell me where you wish to be taken.

"Can you fly around and look for evidence of past human

settlements?" Perhaps it was a vain hope, but Syla thought they might find preserved specimens in those ancient ruins. If nothing else, maybe clues left by early man could lead them in the right direction.

Look for evidence through all the trees? They are very dense with their canopies impenetrable to even keen dragon sight. Also, in this area, the closeness of the growth would make it difficult for us to fly through the branches to land.

"If you can detect magic from afar, maybe that could guide us? The preserved moss bulbs, as I said, would have power that you might be able to sense, though I admit it wouldn't be nearly as noticeable as the shielders created from them." Even the shielders weren't that noticeable when they weren't activated, so Syla might have been making an impossible request.

Where will we take our humans? Igliana asked, flying closer so that she was almost wingtip to wingtip with Wreylith.

Fel sat behind Teyla on the orange dragon's back, his face less green now, but he looked wistfully toward land. Even if it was filled with deadly predators, he would probably prefer standing and dealing with them to flying.

The human astride me has no idea, Wreylith replied.

They do not know where they desire to go?

"We're looking for something." Cheeks warm, Syla pointed toward her cousin's pack, which balanced between her legs. She'd brought even more books along than Syla. "Teyla, do you know of any old human settlements in the area?"

"I don't even know what *area* we're in."

"That should be the Lokdoran Rainforest."

"The *rainforest* sprawls a thousand miles along the Yanasazi Coast."

"Well, pick a likely spot, and we'll ask these wonderfully patient and magnificent dragons to fly us there." Normally, Syla wouldn't have opted for flattery, especially since the dragons didn't seem to think much of obsequiousness, but she wanted them to know she appreciated their willingness to fly a few humans around. And they *were* magnificent. To have arrived here in hours when it would have taken many days aboard ship... It was brilliant. She almost envied the stormers. "I think the moss grows throughout the area, and it sounds like it's useful enough that any humans living in the rainforest would have collected and preserved it."

"There weren't that many civilizations here," Teyla said. "Even before the storm god unleashed his killer insects, sea monsters, and animals, this wasn't that hospitable of an area. The vegetation grows so densely and quickly that trails you try to carve out are overgrown within days. People navigated somewhat via waterways, where they existed, but the snow that melted from the mountains tended to flood the rivers." She leaned forward peering left and right as the dragons banked and flew along the shoreline. "I can't wait to explore it."

"Let's hope it's not the flood season."

"If we can find the Ingris River, I know there were settlements along there. Oh, look." Teyla pointed toward treetops as green-and-blue furred flying creatures the size of wyverns flew into view, long whips of tails swishing as their leathery wings carried them away from the dragons. The creatures had thick manes that whipped about in the wind, and maws that revealed fangs when they parted. *Long* fangs. Beady eyes looked toward the approaching group. "Those are cloud strikers, right?" Teyla asked.

"Yes." Not sure how much her archaeology education had included on flora and fauna—especially ill-tempered mutated-by-magic fauna—Syla added, "The storm god supposedly bred them from bats, ostriches, parrots, lions, and a bunch of other things. Seeing where they fly sometimes lets you predict when a storm is coming in. Unlike most animals, they go *toward* dense black clouds because they're hoping to be struck by lightning. They'll fly up in them, tails swishing so that it looks from below like they're hitting them, though clouds, of course, aren't dense enough to hit. The lightning strikes energize them, making them glow yellow for a bit, and then they're twice as deadly when they attack prey."

"Prey or humans." Fel sounded more grim than curious. He might have encountered cloud strikers before when he'd been in the Fleet. The sky shields kept them away from the islands, the same as dragons and wyverns, but the Sea of Storms was understandably a favorite place for them.

They fear dragons, Wreylith announced. *As all creatures that aren't rabid or otherwise deranged do. They will not attack while you remain with us.*

"We're lucky to have you with us," Syla said.

You are. I am occasionally salivating as I remind myself of all the delicious livestock you have promised to give to me in exchange for my assistance here.

"We'll finish as quickly as possible so I can get that for you." Syla didn't need the reminder to remember that Wreylith wasn't helping out of the goodness of her heart. "Did you promise to share with Igliana?"

Or would Syla have to come up with a separate reward for the orange dragon's assistance?

She is young and unwise in the ways of the world, so she is honored to fly with me to learn about wild dragons and how we are superior to the domesticated creatures she has been raised by.

"So, she's not getting even one horn hog?"

Igliana looked over, her eyes curious and hopeful.

Perhaps a small one.

Igliana sashayed, her back tilting enough that Syla was surprised Fel and Teyla didn't have to flatten themselves and clench everything to stay on. They *did* lean forward, hands splayed on the dragon's scales, but they didn't appear too alarmed. It was possible Teyla, who was moon-marked herself, had figured out how to use her magical gift to stay on, but Fel... Fel had only his balance and muscles to rely upon.

I believe what you call the Ingris River is perhaps fifty of your miles to the south. Wreylith was already soaring in that direction. *We will take you there.*

"Thank you," Syla said.

Large birds flew up from trees along a white-sand beach. A type of vulture, Syla thought, awed by their size. One standing on its feet before her would have been level with her chest, at least. There didn't seem to be any *small* creatures here. With huge, sharp beaks clacking, the birds didn't look much less dangerous than the cloud strikers.

As the dragons skimmed over the trees, an insect the size of Syla's fist buzzed past her head, making her flinch. She glimpsed a stinger as long as her pinky finger and was glad it hadn't struck her. The first-aid kit she'd packed held numerous tinctures and ointments, but she would prefer not to test their efficacy against the insects, snakes, basilisks, and other venomous things known to live in the area.

I've sensed the other two dragons a number of times. One of Wreylith's eyes rotated inland toward some spot between the coast and the distant mountains. *And twice seen them miles away.*

With far less keen eyes, Syla hadn't seen them. "I'm surprised we haven't *heard* them. Agrevlari, anyway."

Wreylith growled.

Igliana was close enough to listen in and swished her tail and made a clucking noise. Dragon laughter?

"Didn't you enjoy his singing?" Syla asked.

I told him that if he made such caterwauling noises in my presence again, I would tie his tongue in a knot so that he wouldn't be able to breathe fire ever again. Or breathe at all.

"He's trying hard to earn your regard."

A male must prove himself worthy to stir the libido of a powerful female dragon. Not by caterwauling.

Syla didn't point out that a *lot* of people—and other beings—had to prove themselves worthy to Wreylith. "Like in battle? He did nobly leap in and keep that big black dragon from attacking you."

I could have handled Ozlemar. We've fought before and mated long ago, before he grew so sour and grumpy. No female wants a dragon with such a disposition in her nest.

Syla blinked. "You mated with General Jhiton's dragon?"

Long ago. He was more appealing in his youth.

Syla didn't know what to say to the new information. She supposed it wouldn't affect her and her mission. It didn't sound like Wreylith had *feelings* for the dragon, such that she might be tempted to turn Syla over to the stormers if he asked.

Back then, he wasn't lowering himself to let humans ride him, Wreylith said with her usual disdain for the idea, not acknowledging that she, at that very moment, had a human on her back.

Not wanting to risk irking her and being abandoned on this wild continent, Syla didn't point that out.

For all of his life, he was a wild dragon, distrusting of humans and far more inclined to destroy their settlements than work with them.

Wreylith didn't sound *approving* of the idea, not exactly, but Syla got the impression she was more likely to respect a dragon like that than one who allied with humans.

"What made him decide to align with the stormers? General Jhiton specifically? Do you know?" It hadn't occurred to Syla that Wreylith might be a resource on the stormers, or at least the stormer *dragons*. How the information might be helpful, she didn't yet know, but once she completed this quest, she had little doubt that her people would have to battle the stormers to drive them off Harvest Island and reclaim it. Every tidbit of intelligence that she could gather might later be useful.

I do not know. The stormer officer must have proven himself worthy.
Syla snorted. Of course.

Maybe he drew a basilisk fang from Ozlemar's foot, Wreylith added dryly.

"I know that's what's endeared you to me and made you eager to assist me."

It didn't unendear *me.*

"I'll bet the salve delighted you too."

It tingled pleasantly while soothing the ache. Of course, dragons are extremely stoic and do not need *soothing. Especially not by humans. They can endure any pain and grow stronger for it.*

"Oh, I assumed so."

That earned her a baleful eye rotating back in her direction.

"I brought some of that salve along. Just in case we run into basilisks foolish enough to bite dragons."

Good. Wreylith's eyes turned back forward, a wide waterway emptying into the sea visible ahead. *Igliana may need it. The young are never stoic.*

When they reached the mouth of the river, sandbars visible where it flowed into the sea, the dragons turned inland to follow it upstream. Unlike smaller streams they'd passed, the waterway was wide enough that the branches of the trees couldn't stretch across it, so they could easily trace its route. The branches *did* obscure everything along its banks from above, and as they soared inland, Syla realized they would never spot the remains of human civilizations from the air. They wouldn't spot *anything*. Hoots, screeches, chirps, and roars promised a great deal of wildlife inhabited the area near the riverbanks, but unless something flew out of the trees and over the water, they couldn't see any of it. Further, it had to be the season for flooding, because the river stretched far beyond its banks and into trees that grew densely together, vines and foliage making it impossible to see far.

"Can you fly lower so that we can look into the trees on either side? Or even swim up the river with us on your backs?" Syla had no idea if dragons were like horses that could ford a waterway with their riders still astride. She knew their kind fished, capturing everything from octopi to walruses to nosh on, but hadn't heard of them cruising for miles in the water. Their bodies didn't seem designed for that.

Wreylith growled. *Dragons are not* boats *for humans to float upon.*

"Sorry." Syla didn't know what the rules were—was flying with a rider on one's back less ignoble than swimming in a similar vein?

Wreylith angled lower so that she skimmed closer above the water but added, *Dragons are also not porpoises that would swim around with humans clinging to their backs, nor do we, other than for fishing purposes, flit around in the water.*

Perhaps oblivious to the words, Igliana dove into the water with a splash and swam about like an otter, looking quite pleased to cool off in the river. Teyla wrapped her arms around her pack, trying to keep it dry from the water droplets flying up.

Wreylith growled again. It might have been a grumble, accompanied by thoughts of the immaturity of youth. *Fish in those waters have fangs sharp enough to pierce dragon scales, and they are dumb enough to attack our kind. Giant piranhas, hurricane eels, and freshwater megalodons are especially tedious.*

Syla thought the comment for her but Igliana replied. *I am not so young and poorly traveled that I am not aware of the dangers of the great rainforest rivers. I am merely cooling my belly after a long flight. I have also been expending my magic to keep my riders from falling off.*

Riders should be capable of holding on of their own accord without needing you to magically strap them on, as if you were one of their beasts of burden.

Syla hadn't known a dragon *could* magically strap a human rider onto its back. Since she'd figured out her own method, she wouldn't ask Wreylith about doing that in the future. She could already guess how warm the response would be.

Igliana screeched and flew abruptly out of the water.

Fel and Teyla lurched, and Teyla almost lost her pack. Before Syla could ask what had happened, Igliana contorted, twisting in the air so that she could fly upward and breathe flames onto the river. The water rippled, and shadows stirred under the surface as something retreated.

I warned you, Wreylith said blandly, continuing to fly upstream, keeping at least a few feet between her and the surface.

Igliana huffed and flew after her, perhaps reapplying the magical straps for her riders, because Fel and Teyla settled back, their faces less alarmed.

Glad for Wreylith's assistance, Syla didn't allow herself to feel wishful, even if the power she had to continually use to stay on was taxing her and making her wonder what would happen if she fell asleep while riding the dragon. She imagined splashing into the middle of the river and being devoured by whatever type of fish or shark had thought Igliana a tasty treat on which to nibble.

As they flew farther upriver, numerous aerial creatures departed from the branches, either to hunt or due to their alarm at dragons passing nearby. Syla peered as far into the trees as she could on either side, but she couldn't see anything to suggest humans had ever lived in the area. With the floods, it seemed impossible, though they did spot a few high banks where the water didn't flow inland. Still, the trees were as dense as anywhere else and kept them from seeing far.

"I don't suppose you have any maps that mark old civilizations?" Syla waved toward her cousin's pack.

"Yes, but the one I was consulting earlier is very old. This area hasn't been explored much by our people since the storm god's work changed everything."

The stormers hunt in these areas, Igliana said. *They may know where the ruins you seek lie.*

"Uhm." Syla hadn't entirely forgotten that she was a stormer-allied dragon, but it had slipped her mind, and she hoped she hadn't spoken openly about anything that she didn't want to get back to her enemies. "We're competing with them in this."

As it was, she hoped Vorik and his colleague—had that other rider been their equivalent of an archaeologist or other research specialist?—didn't know that people had once cultivated the moss bulbs.

You do not believe they would give you information? Wreylith asked. *The rider who knelt before you and stimulated your sex orifice must feel compelled to please you.*

Teyla and Fel both looked over, and Syla's cheeks turned molten.

"He's not— He didn't. I mean, humans don't talk about such things." Flustered, Syla took her spectacles off and wiped her sleeve over her face. The humidity was making her sweat. The moltenness of her cheeks didn't help.

"If you were wondering," Teyla said, "we could kind of guess what was going on."

"I was choosing *not* to guess." Fel shook his head and looked toward the trees. Hell, were *his* cheeks red? Maybe there were things about his princess that he preferred not to know. After all, Syla was young enough to be his daughter.

"There were noises," Teyla added.

Syla groaned and dropped her face against Wreylith's scales. She wondered if Vorik's dragon embarrassed *him* in front of other people.

Because he is compelled to please you, Wreylith said, unperturbed by the discussion, *he may answer your questions related to your quest.*

"I can't ask him without possibly giving him clues. When it comes to the moss bulbs, they're not only rare, but it'll be hard to find preserved samples that have survived in this climate. And the other shielder components are just as rare. Or more so. The last one on the list requires us to enter one of the storm god's laboratories and use a moon-mark to access it. We can't share clues with the stormers."

"There's a promising bank." Teyla pointed. "It looks like it's above water year around, and I don't see any vipers hanging from the branches." A shudder suggested she might have spotted a couple of those already.

Since Syla wore an older and weaker pair of spectacles than she needed, she might have mistaken snakes for vines. She didn't know whether to lament that she hadn't had an opportunity to visit her optometrist or be glad.

"Did you see anything to suggest humans might have had a civilization inland there?" Syla asked, following her cousin's pointing finger with her gaze.

The back of her hand warmed slightly, drawing her attention. Huh. Her moon-mark was glowing a faint silver.

"I suppose that's possible," Teyla said, "but I meant... Well, I meant promising for, er, I was just telling Igliana that I need to pee."

"Oh."

I will attempt to perch there so that you can get off. Igliana angled for the bank. *It is tight though. The growth is too dense here for dragons to penetrate easily. You may have to seek the civilization while we wait elsewhere.*

Or hunt. Wreylith looked at large birds taking flight farther upstream. *The journey has made me hungry.*

I am very *hungry. I have carried two.* Igliana landed on a clump of roots sticking out of a vertical bank, her back almost even with the top.

As Syla watched Fel and Teyla clamber off her and onto land, a roar sounding not far in the distance, she worried about something new—surviving in this dangerous place without the dragons nearby. It hadn't occurred to her that their allies wouldn't be able to stay close. Syla was glad Igliana had come along so they'd been able to bring Fel.

Wreylith flew back and forth, pacing in the air while she waited, and Syla was about to say that she also needed to relieve herself, and mention that her moon-mark liked this area, but Wreylith glanced upward and said, *They approach.*

"Who?" Syla asked.

Then two dragons flew into view, one green and one gray. From their backs, Vorik and his man peered down toward the river. No, Vorik was peering straight toward Syla. He waved cheerfully at her.

Syla glowered up at him and considered making a rude gesture with her hand. Wreylith roared at them. Agrevlari sped up, flying fast to escape her ire.

Too bad Syla couldn't shoot magical beams of power out of her moon-mark to light enemies on fire. Or at least toast parts of their anatomy. Alas, her moon-mark wasn't even glowing anymore. Maybe that had been a fluke or her eyes playing tricks on her.

"Syla?" Teyla called. "We've found something."

Syla waved and held a finger to her lips, tilting her head toward the other dragons. A *normal* human would have been out of earshot, but Vorik's ears were much keener than typical. And who knew what those dragons could hear?

Teyla, standing ten yards inland and looking up at a tree, didn't seem to notice, but she didn't call out anything else. She only pointed upward. Was that a cylindrical green *moss bulb* growing high up on the bark?

Syla touched Wreylith's scales. "Will you land, too, please?"

As she'd told the others, the still-living specimens wouldn't do, but if they grew in the area, that was promising.

Agrevlari says there are indeed ruins from human settlements up and down this waterway. Wreylith turned toward the bank.

"You asked him?" Syla groaned. "I told you we're competing with them, not *working* with them."

Should they acquire that which you seek before us, I will take it from them.

"Earlier, you didn't want to fight them."

Earlier, I did not have a compelling reason.

Reason or not, Syla didn't think such a battle would go well for them. "Let's just find the component before they do."

17

AGREVLARI CONTINUED FLYING UP THE RIVER, NOT SLOWING DOWN until they'd gone around a bend and Wreylith's roars had faded. Wise's dragon barely kept up.

"I don't think your wooing song, or whatever you would call it, worked on Wreylith." Vorik looked back as they flew, wondering if Syla's group had found something or if they'd stopped for biological necessities. As he well knew, even though dragons flew fast, their magic and raw power making them speedier than any bird, flights across the sea were long.

My wooing song was magnificent, but she has, for strange reasons, aligned herself with the enemy. Were she not conflicted, she would have likely succumbed to my mating call, and we would even now be engaged in amorous activities.

"When she roared, she didn't come across as *conflicted* to me. And Syla isn't the enemy. She's..."

I understand you enjoy sexual encounters with her, but she is indeed a part of the nation that we seek to overthrow, and have not Garden Kingdom humans and your stormer tribes been antagonistic with each other for many centuries? I've flown you down to attack their cargo ships and abscond with their food.

"Yes, yes, but she's..." Vorik groped in the air. "Garden Kingdom troops *attacked* her. She can't feel that kindly toward them right now."

They attacked her because rule of the Kingdom is being contested, and she's one of the contestants, not because she does not still consider herself one of them.

"Will you stop being so logical?"

I am not incorrect, am I?

"No, and it's very annoying. Do you know that other dragon that's with them? I didn't recognize her. She looks young."

I do not know her. It is possible Wreylith summoned wild dragon allies from the far side of the world. There are many of our kind who live and hunt on the continent of Froha whom I've never met.

"They don't attend the dragon tribal meetings, huh?"

Dragons, as you know, are usually solitary outside of mating season. We who work with your people make exceptions to band together into wings for military purposes. Being forced to work and serve together can create tensions, however.

Vorik remembered Agrevlari barreling into Ozlemar to protect Wreylith, who probably hadn't *needed* protecting.

That was not a tension. That was a typical way for a dragon to begin the courting flight.

"By getting rid of the competition?"

By ensuring other males do not harm the female one desires.

"Sir?" Wise called, lifting one of the parchment scrolls, the breeze tugging at the corners. He swatted away an insect large enough that it was visible from ten yards away. "I've figured something out, and I think... We may need to discuss it."

Vorik waved an acknowledgment. "Can you find a place to land, Agrevlari?"

There are few in the area. The rainforest lacks clearings, the water is unsafe, and the tops of these trees would not support our combined weight.

"Well, look for something, please. We don't want to get that far from Syla. We're keeping an eye on them."

As one does with one's enemies.

Vorik sighed. "We need to make sure to get that moss thing first. I'd prefer that to trying to *take* the components from Syla later."

It was bad enough that his orders pitted him against her. He didn't want to be a bully too.

Vorik swatted an insect pestering *him*, well aware of the diseases they carried and that their travel first-aid kits weren't the most complete. It would be distressing if he had to go to his adversary for healing because he'd developed the Shriveling Sickness or Fatal Fengulu.

I see a perch. Agrevlari flew away from the river to a rare rocky outcropping that rose above the canopy.

Several wyverns that probably called it—or maybe a cave in its side—home squawked a warning at him. Agrevlari roared, and Tonasketal flew after him, ready to lend his might.

The roar, perhaps conveying extra irritation due to Agrevlari's failures with Wreylith, convinced the wyverns of his threat, and they took flight, flapping off at top speed in the other direction.

There was barely room for two dragons atop the rocky perch, so Vorik didn't dismount. It was a long fall to the ground. Tonasketal landed beside Agrevlari, their wings folded in to make room for each other.

If only the beauteous Wreylith were the one perched so close to me.

Trust me, Vorik replied. *I'd rather be shoulder to shoulder with someone sexier than Wise too.*

Despite the comment, which he made only for Agrevlari, Vorik waved for his lieutenant to show him what he'd learned.

"You've figured out where we get the moss thing?" Vorik asked.

"Oh, no. Nothing about that. But I *was* considering earlier, when we first got here, that in this humidity, finding a desiccated specimen would be difficult. Things must decompose quickly here rather than drying out."

"Well, Syla's team is looking for something they expect to find here."

"Yes." At her name, Wise looked pensively at him.

"What?"

"There are what I've been thinking of as hieroglyphs along the bottom of this scroll, sir, under the passage about the storm god's laboratory and all the dangers waiting inside of it. I realized... Well, I immediately thought that the quarter-moon symbol might refer to the moon-marked humans of the Garden Kingdom, and now I'm thinking... For this third component, it may only be accessible by someone with a moon-mark. It's some kind of magical crystal the storm god long ago propagated in his laboratory, and only one grows at a time, so it's rare. Very rare. If the gods who created the shielders wanted to make sure humans from the Garden Kingdom could get a replacement crystal if they needed one, it makes sense that they would have locked it up somehow so only one of their chosen could reach it."

"I guess we'll have to arrive at the same time as Syla and sneak in after her."

"And steal the component from her afterward?"

"I suppose we'll have to. Or try to slip past and get to it first." Vorik looked back over the canopy, wondering if Syla was even now acquiring the first component. The dragons and humans had disappeared for too long to account for biological needs.

"Or..." Wise hesitated, considering him.

"Or?"

"Well, if we kidnap her, sir, or another moon-marked person, and get there first, we can ensure things go our way."

"Or another moon-marked person? I think Syla is the only

option unless that other girl is a relative." Vorik tried to remember if the woman had been marked, but he'd barely glanced at her. When they'd torn their way into the wheelhouse, he'd been focused on saving Syla—not that she'd needed saving. He smiled at the memory.

"The other woman had a moon-mark, sir." Wise looked in puzzlement at him.

Because Vorik *usually* noticed everything around him? Yes, but he'd been concerned about Syla. The other woman might have had eight boobs and he would have missed it.

Agreed, Agrevlari stated. *She had the power of one of the gods-gifted humans.*

I also sensed it, Tonasketal added.

Of course. None of Vorik's allies had been distracted by romantic feelings.

She is not as powerful as Princess Syla, Agrevlari added, *but more akin to the aunt who rode with the princess to Harvest Island. She can likely open doors attuned to the moon-mark though.*

"I'm not kidnapping Syla *or* anyone in her party," Vorik said.

Wise tilted his head. "You don't think it would make sense, sir? To ensure we fulfill our mission? Before I left, General Jhiton said..."

"What?" Vorik remembered his earlier thought that Wise, despite being an easygoing and affable fellow, was dedicated to his duty and might partially have been sent to keep an eye on Vorik.

"I'm to report in to him along the way if anything is going to prove difficult." That didn't sound like a full truth.

"Who are you going to report to down here? Nobody but the Freeborn Faction have a headquarters within hundreds of miles, and we don't even know more than the general area that they might be in." Vorik waved toward the peaks that rose so high that they had snow and glaciers on them year around, even this far south, but, as far as he knew, there were only rumors suggesting the faction was camped in the mountains this summer. Their leaders always worried, somewhat amusingly so, that the tribes would raid them, so they moved frequently. Vorik's leaders, however, didn't care to annihilate their own people, deserters or not. Of course, that might change if the faction did more than occasional spying and truly declared the stormers enemies.

"You don't think they would enjoy my reports, sir?" Wise smiled, though there was a troubled look in his eyes. Maybe he'd figured out that his captain's feelings were conflicted on this matter.

"They'd probably love to hear about everything we're doing."

"I expect that's true. Did you know they've a link to that whaling ship the princess has been traveling on?"

"I didn't, no."

"The captain is allied with them."

"So, they want Syla to end up in charge of the Kingdom? Is that why he's been helping her?"

"I don't know, sir. We just know of the link."

Vorik scratched his jaw. He believed that Syla could take her rightful spot as queen of the Garden Kingdom if she wished, but he didn't know if he should hope for her to do that or not. When he'd implored her to come with him, he'd mostly been thinking about protecting her from Lesva, but Jhiton's offer might have been in the back of his mind too. If Syla were forced into exile, or had to flee because she had assassins after her, she might more seriously consider an invitation to join the stormers. He couldn't wish for her to be endangered, but...

He sighed again and murmured, "Conflicted."

The Swordhawk Tribe wing is flying up the coast, Agrevlari said.

Tonasketal had turned his long neck to gaze out toward the sea. They'd flown far enough up the river that it was barely visible, but Vorik didn't doubt that the dragons sensed others in the area.

"The general mentioned summoning more people to solidify

our holding on Harvest Island," Vorik said. "They might be flying up the coast to report to him before heading out over the sea."

"General Amalia was also talking with General Jhiton yesterday," Wise said, "about a plan to attack Bogberry Island to split the Kingdom forces. They seemed to think they might be able to learn the location of the shielder there and disable it, but I haven't heard any new intelligence about that."

"Neither have I, though I know Jhiton would like that island. He wants to claim the three northernmost because they'd be easier to defend. Oh, he wants the whole Kingdom, but I think his back-up plan is to acquire those three. They'd be enough to feed our people if we wanted to settle down and farm." Vorik wondered how many of his foraging, hunting, and nomad-life-loving kin would be willing to do that. If it meant a more stable existence, at least some would, but maybe not all.

"Settle down? That's not what General Amalia and Chief Tenilor were talking about."

Vorik frowned, wondering why he hadn't been invited to whatever meeting this had been. At the least, Jhiton usually filled him in on things. The uneasy thought that his allegiance might be in question right now bothered him.

"What *were* they talking about?"

"Ruling over the gardeners and keeping our existing life while they farm for us." Wise shrugged. "It sounded a little tyrannical and despotic to me, and I don't think that's what all our leaders want, but... it was being discussed."

"Enslaving them."

"Essentially. Some people like Captain Lesva have grudges, family members who tried to go back and were turned away. Others who hoped for healing or refuge for a time have also been turned away. That is a common theme."

"I'm aware, but we're not *enslaving* an entire nation. I know that's not Jhiton's plan." Vorik squinted at Wise, hoping that was the truth, that his brother's plans hadn't changed without Vorik being informed.

"No, I don't think that's what he wants, sir. But he's only the leader of the Sixteen Talons."

"*Only.*"

"I didn't mean he's not important and doesn't have a lot of sway, but the tribal chiefs are in charge of the military." Wise shrugged again, then looked toward the sea.

A dragon with a female rider was approaching. She lifted a hand toward them.

That's Balinskil, Tonasketal said, naming the dragon rather than the rider.

"And Lieutenant Savlin." Vorik recognized the woman's broad face and short wiry black hair as he remembered the dragon she rode. "There's not room on this perch for anyone else."

Wise laughed. "No, sir. We'll move."

Tonasketal took off, the breeze from his wings riffling through Vorik's hair. In a few moments, Savlin and her dragon landed beside Agrevlari.

"Good evening, sir," she said, smiling. "It's always a pleasure to run into you, but what brings you way down south?"

"A mission for the general. The usual."

"Of course. We're heading to check in with General Jhiton now, and I'm eager to sample the pears we heard proliferate on the Kingdom island we took."

"They're delicious."

"When we sensed you, I decided to check in to see if you need anything." Savlin raised her eyebrows.

"Just a moon-marked gardener, apparently."

Savlin blinked. "Sir?"

"Never mind. We'll acquire that ourselves." Vorik only said the latter because Tonasketal was lazily circling the area, close enough for Wise to listen in. He thought about shooing them away but didn't plan to discuss anything clandestine during a chance meeting with a Swordhawk Tribe lieutenant. Further, he didn't want Wise to think he had anything to hide.

"Yes, sir." Savlin tilted her head. "Do you need any supplies? Or do you have any messages that I can take to the general? We're going to fly through the night and arrive before dawn."

Wise's chin came up. "Will you tell him that I deciphered what he requested, and we need..." He glanced at Vorik.

Vorik knew what his lieutenant intended to share and was too far away to clamp a hand over his mouth.

"A moon-marked gardener?" Savlin guessed.

Vorik sighed. "Yes, you can tell the general that. And that we know where to find one."

"I hear there are a lot of them in the Garden Kingdom," Savlin said dryly. "Though fewer than there used to be."

"Yes," Vorik said, far more grim than amused. Now that he knew Syla personally and was aware that his people had assassinated her entire family, it was impossible to be anything but grim. Still, aware that his fellow riders wouldn't understand, he forced a smile. "There are pears at the headquarters camp. Make sure to get some before you leave. They're magnificent."

"I look forward to it, sir. And I'll deliver your message, Wise." Savlin waved to them, and her dragon sprang off the perch, flying off to catch up with the rest of her wing.

"Was it... all right that I said that, sir?" Wise asked.

No, Vorik thought.

"Yes, of course," he said. "Especially if Jhiton asked you to decipher the scrolls, and that's what they said."

"Yes, sir. He did."

Vorik closed his eyes and tilted his head toward the darkening sky. He didn't want to kidnap Syla and force her to do anything, but with General Jhiton soon to learn that it would be necessary... how could he do anything else? If he didn't acquire someone with a moon-mark, Jhiton would send someone else to complete this mission. Someone who wouldn't care about Syla and might hurt her in the process. Or worse.

"Should I climb up and pull it down?" Fel's voice promised he did not want to do that. Even as he asked, he was leaning against a tree, alternately stretching his calf and flexing his ankle and knee. His muscles and joints must have stiffened up on the long ride. His mace hung from his belt, but he'd leaned his crossbow against the tree, the weapon never more than a few inches from his grip.

"Thank you, but that won't be necessary." Syla pulled her gaze from the cylindrical green bulb twenty or thirty feet up in the thick tree, its details barely visible as twilight deepened. She shifted her weight, trying to find a place to stand where leaves, thorns, and vines didn't threaten to stab or entangle her. The air was warm and close, myriad scents of growth and decay dense around them. "We need a version that's died and naturally petrified or was preserved by people long enough ago that it's completely dried out and has gained magic."

"We can't get one and dry it?" Fel asked.

"It sounds like it takes a long time before magic permeates it and that more was involved than slicing pieces off and dehydrating them in the sun." Syla spread a hand. Despite her extensive knowledge of medicinal plants, she'd only known a little about the moss bulbs before Aunt Tibby had shared the information on the scrolls. "The people who used the bulbs had to replicate the petrification process, essentially."

Teyla jumped as a winged bug buzzed past her ear, half-swinging her sword at it before stopping herself. Countless unfamiliar animal, bird, and insect noises came from the trees and the river, most ominous and threatening to their inexperienced ears. A stormer would probably know which indicated danger and which did not. Though, from what Vorik had said about his world, including that they had a dedicated term—sky watcher—for someone who kept an eye out for approaching threats, maybe *everything* could be dangerous.

For the moment, the dragons remained nearby, hanging from root perches below the bank, but the position did not look comfortable. Among the dense trees and tangled undergrowth, there wasn't room for them to stand on the ground, even with their wings folded in, and Syla suspected they would soon leave to find a more comfortable place to wait. For now, they appeared to be communicating telepathically with each other, heads tilting and wings occasionally twitching in response to each other's comments.

Syla pulled a compact lantern out of her pack and dug out dragonspark matches. "The reason I want to find ruins is in the hope that we might chance upon already-preserved specimens inside. As I was saying earlier, the bulbs were commonly collected by the indigenous peoples in the area, back before the gods relocated humanity to our islands."

"You may not want to light that." Fel stepped away from the tree and took his crossbow in his arms again. "It'll bring animals and insects to you."

As if to affirm the statement, Teyla jumped again, swatting at something that must have brushed her neck.

Growling, Fel eyed a winged insect that whizzed past his face. It was the size of a bluebird back home.

"We need to be able to see." Reminded of the huge insect that had buzzed past with a stinger like a sword, Syla pulled out her first-aid kit and withdrew a pungent salve. "This keeps mosquitoes on the islands away."

"That wasn't a *mosquito*," Fel said.

Something landed on Syla's hand, instantly stinging or maybe biting her, and she shook her arm with a grunt. Her moon-mark surprised her by glowing a slight silver. A warning of danger? Or was it offering the same message as it had on the river? That this area held something important?

Mindful of Fel's warning that light would attract *more* insects, Syla pulled her sleeve over the glowing birthmark, then uncapped the salve. Its strong citrus and banebark scents joined the earthy odors of the rainforest, and she smeared her exposed skin with the stuff.

"Here." She handed the salve to Fel and Teyla with instructions to do the same. "It can't hurt, and maybe it'll help."

The other dragons have passed, Wreylith said, sharing her words with all. *We will depart to hunt.*

"Other dragons?" Syla had been reaching for her lantern but paused.

A wing of domesticated stormer dragons flew along the coast, heading north. One came up the river and stopped to speak with Agrevlari.

"They had riders?"

Yes, the rider likely also spoke to the stormer captain.

"Vorik."

Someone sent by his general with an update to his orders? Had the passing dragons said anything to Igliana? Were they kin of hers? Allies?

The dragons are all gone from our senses now, Wreylith said.

"Agrevlari and the other one too?" Syla jumped as something scurried through the undergrowth near her foot, brushing her trouser leg. Another insect buzzed past, stirring her hair.

Yes.

"Maybe they went with the others," Teyla said.

"Leaving us alone to search for the component?" Syla should have found that heartening, but if the rainforest was half as dangerous as described, she would have preferred Vorik to be in the area. Even though he was undoubtedly at cross-purposes with her, she also didn't doubt that he would come to help if he heard her scream.

"Let's hope," Fel grumbled.

We can sense other dragons from afar since they are so strongly magical, Igliana said. *We sense most humans not at all, except by scent and sight and sound, since few have any magical signature.*

We can sense the princess and the rider captain, Wreylith said, *simply not from as far away as dragons.*

Yes.

Syla took the commentary to mean that Vorik and his officer might be in the area but undetectable by her allies. She lit a drag-onspark match. Fel stepped close to return the salve container, but he also held a hand up toward her lantern again.

"I wouldn't. We can camp and wait until morning to search for your ruins."

Syla hesitated. As the princess and heir apparent to the throne, *she* was in charge of this expedition, but Fel had a lot more experience out in the world. Maybe he'd even traveled to the mainland before as a soldier. Or maybe he just had more of an idea what was out there.

An insect the size of a bat flew out of the darkness and toward the lit match. Syla gasped and dropped it.

In an instant, Fel had his mace out and swung toward the thing. Even with the fluctuating light as the match fell, he managed to strike the huge insect. Blood spattered Syla's face, mingling unpleasantly with the mosquito deterrent she'd applied, and the bat-bug fell to the ground beside the smoldering match. She glimpsed a long stinger before Fel stepped on the match and extinguished it.

"We should move farther inland—away from the water—to camp." Fel waved in that direction. "There might be fewer insects and animals there." Something roared from the direction he'd pointed, the noise sounding more feline than dragon, and he lowered his arm. "Fewer insects anyway."

"Are you sure?" Syla asked.

"No."

She gazed up toward the tree with the moss bulb. Even though her eyes were gritty from fatigue, she was reluctant to huddle in the dark and attempt to sleep when Vorik might be out there, hunting for exactly what they sought. And *he* had that extra keen night vision.

We depart. Wreylith sprang from her perch and flapped her wings. *Be wary. Many creatures that can threaten those without fangs, fire, and talons live in these wilds.*

"Yes. Thank you." Syla rubbed the bite mark on her hand, the skin already warm and swollen. "Wait. Can you light a fire before you go?"

In the darkness, she could only *sense* Fel's glower, not see it, but his objection had been to her carrying a lantern with her, hadn't it?

A fire?

"So we can see the area better." Syla attempted to share an image of a cheerful campfire, though it wasn't as if a dragon would gather logs and kindling. More likely, Wreylith would—

The dragon angled toward the bank and opened her maw. Fire roiled in the back of her throat.

"Get back!" Fel grabbed Teyla and Syla to pull them farther from the bank.

Wreylith wouldn't have struck them, but when she poured a gout of fire into a thick tree growing near the edge, the flames *did* flow inland alarmingly far beyond her target. Even from thirty feet away, Syla could feel the heat against her cheeks.

Branches caught fire, leaves incinerating, and Wreylith banked, her red belly gleaming in the orange light before her wings carried her upriver and out of view.

"Thank you!" Syla called after her.

The tree didn't burn as spectacularly as one bathed in dragon fire in a drier climate would have, and Syla could already tell the flames wouldn't spread, but they did provide some light. She picked her way back to the moss bulb, peering up at it, then all around. Instead of the signs of a past civilization that she sought, she spotted a knee-high red-capped mushroom at the base of a nearby tree.

"Oh, is that a tendric toadstool? A tea made of dried powder from the cap treats digestive ailments and intestinal parasites."

"Delightful," Fel rumbled, eyeing the burning tree.

Insects were indeed being drawn by the flames, but fewer of them were molesting Syla, so she considered that a boon.

"Does anyone see—" she started to ask but glimpsed vibrant moss dangling from another tree. "Oh, a blue bryophyte. They're known to lower inflammation when added to a poultice." Had the ground been less uneven, she would have skipped happily to the branch to pluck off a few clumps. Maybe she would add it to a poultice for her fresh bug bite later. She *could* repair such wounds, but if many were acquired, it was more taxing to treat each one with magic than simply let them heal on their own. "This place is wondrous."

Teyla whirled, swinging her sword at something that flew past, hissing as it went.

Another roar floated out of the rainforest.

Fel slapped at the back of his neck. "*Wondrous.* Right."

"I see a Frandle fern." Syla clambered over a log, picking her way to huge gray-green fronds. "They're named for the herbalist who penned a book on edible and medicinal ferns before the Gods War. I think his people lived on the coast not far from here and traveled inland up the rivers to collect and study plants. I can't wait to see what we can find in the morning when there's more light."

The roar sounded again, closer.

"We may not be here in the morning." Fel still held his mace, and he eyed the darkness in the direction of whatever great cat was prowling closer. "Is she always so easily distracted?"

The question was for Teyla, but Syla answered, barely noticing another bug brushing her, though she reflexively swatted at it.

"You've seen me in the antiques shop, Sergeant. You should know that items related to certain passions of mine can capture my attention."

"At least there aren't artificial-leech contraptions out here," Fel grumbled.

"No, but I bet there are *real* leeches. Numerous varieties."

"You shouldn't say that with such excitement, Syla," Teyla said. "Not when we have to sleep out here tonight."

"Well, stay out of the water." Though Syla would happily have hunted every square inch within the influence of the firelight, she reluctantly admitted that foraging for medicinal plants wasn't her mission. Maybe one day, if she could talk Wreylith into giving her another ride, she could return with an expedition to seek useful plants, fungi, and mosses. Weren't razorcoons, known for their hollow quills full of the protein-repairing asaka liquid, native to this area? Maybe she could even find *new* useful substances that humans hadn't yet learned had value. In the meantime... "Does anyone see any ruins?"

"The likelihood," Teyla said, "of us stumbling upon the remains of an ancient civilization within fifty feet of the place we happened to come ashore is slim."

"We wouldn't be *stumbling*." Syla stepped onto the log, moss and soggy bark squishing under her feet, and gazed into the depths of the rainforest. "We chose this spot because it was a rare section of high ground that appears to escape the floods. Local people would have valued such a locale. And there's a richness of medicinal plants here. Oh, and the fiddleheads of the Frandle ferns are edible. And, I've read, tasty. People would have naturally been drawn to a place like this. They may even have cultivated some of these plants if they lived in the area." She brightened at the thought. "In fact, I'll wager someone definitely did that at some point. Otherwise, to discover so many useful plants in one area would be surprising."

She reached out with a loving hand to touch one of the fiddleheads.

"Should we ignore her while she prattles and fondles fern fronds?" Teyla asked. "And set up a camp?"

"I've been informed in the past," Fel said, "that princesses don't prattle. They rhapsodize on their passions."

"That sounds like something Nyvia would have said." Syla smiled sadly as memories of her sister came to mind.

"I was her bodyguard for many years." Fel sounded sad too.

He was always so stoic and unflappable—other than complaints about his age, joints, and old injuries—that Syla hadn't considered that he probably missed her family too. After all, he'd served as a bodyguard, first for her parents and then for her sister for almost twenty years after his twenty years of service in the military.

"And she never prattled?" Teyla asked.

"Not that she would admit."

Syla touched the back of her hand. Other than the brief flare of silver her moon-mark had given when the bug had bitten her, it hadn't glowed since coming ashore, but she also hadn't attempted to use her magic. Since the preserved moss bulbs she sought were magical, might her power allow her to sense some in the area? She'd never tried to use her power to find anything, but maybe locating medicinal objects would be within her realm.

Actually, *Teyla's* power might be more suited for this. As a gods-gifted archaeologist, might she be able to sense ancient ruins? Especially if magic lay within?

Syla turned, about to ask when the quarter moon outlined itself on her hand. The mark warmed, but she had the sense that it was a warning, not an offer to guide her somewhere. When she peered into the dark rainforest again, something glinted yellow-orange in the distance.

Fel patted his pack. "I do want to move farther inland to set up camp. I wish I'd thought to bring netting to protect us from all these bugs."

"Maybe we could smother ourselves in fern fronds," Teyla said.

"The moss would be more helpful. Do you two see that?" Syla pointed toward the distant glint, wondering what in the rainforest would account for that. Something reflecting the light of the dragon fire? It seemed too far away for that.

Could Vorik be out there? Carrying something magical? She thought of his gargoyle-bone sword but hadn't seen it glow.

As Fel and Teyla looked after her pointing finger, a second yellow-orange glint appeared next to the first. Bloody daggers, were those *eyes*?

"I see them," Fel said.

The bespectacled Teyla took longer to pick it—*them*—out. "Yes. Eyes?"

"I'm not sure," Syla said. "They're not moving."

"If they're still there in the morning, we can check them out," Fel said.

"Sergeant," Syla said, "we have competition in this quest, and all of Harvest Island is threatened as we speak."

He glowered at her.

"We're not setting up camp if something inimical is over there *watching* us. Come with me, please." Syla picked her way toward the glinting eyes—or whatever they were. They didn't move. But one had appeared and then the other, as if they'd opened one at a time, so they might well belong to an animal. A *threat*.

Fel swatted an insect at his neck and continued glowering but came with her when she ventured deeper into the rainforest. Teyla hesitated, then walked behind them, wiping her sweaty palm so she could keep a good grip on her sword.

If there had ever been a trail leading from the river, it had long ago been swallowed by the rapid growth of the vegetation. Navigating the fern-, shrub-, and plant-covered ground would have been tricky during the day, but at night, with the firelight fading as they moved farther away, Syla tripped and banged her legs repeatedly. Only determination kept her going. And curiosity. Further, her moon-mark brightened, acting as a light to illuminate a small area around her. Repeatedly, she had to brush away insects, but as she crept closer to the glowing eyes, she could make out dark shapes that were straighter-edged, different from the natural curves of leaves and branches.

"Are those slabs of stone?" Syla asked.

"Covered with vines and leaves, yes," Fel said, his eyes keener despite his various age-related woes. *He* didn't need spectacles. "There are old buildings, I think, though there are trees growing up from some, and if there are roofs, half of them have collapsed."

"How did people find stone for building out here?" Teyla waved around them.

They hadn't seen a lot of boulders and definitely nothing like a quarry.

"Oh," Teyla said, coming up with the answer to her own question, "I bet they floated them downriver on rafts. Those ancient people were impressively resourceful considering how low a technology level they had."

Fel reached out and caught Syla's arm, distracting her from answering and halting her advance. He pointed his mace at something darker than the surrounding stone. The remains of a doorway? It wasn't far from the yellow dots gazing unsettlingly in their direction. On the other side of the doorway, another pair of dots— *eyes*—opened.

Syla's moon-mark glowed brighter. "Are those..."

"Gargoyles," Fel stated. "They blend in with the stone slabs. Except for the eyes."

Two huge creatures with armored stone-like skin, wings, and powerfully muscled arms and legs sprang away from the ruins. Their skin flared white-blue, and Syla abruptly sensed their magic. They'd come out of dormancy and were ready to hunt. Their eyes focused on Syla, and they charged.

18

Syla's moon-mark glowed, providing light by which to see, but she had no idea how to summon its power and employ it against gargoyles. Even if they came close enough for her touch—without them *killing* her in the process—they were magical beings. She doubted she could turn her healing power into an attack on creations that didn't have anatomy similar to humans or animals.

Fel pushed past Syla and Teyla, shouting, "Take cover in the ruins!" as he braced himself to meet the gargoyles.

He held his mace but managed to one-handedly fire his crossbow. A quarrel clinked off the stone-like chest of one enemy and ricocheted into a tree.

Not wounded even slightly, the gargoyles continued toward them. Their wings flapped, and they bounded, half-flying through the undergrowth toward the group.

Ignoring Fel's command, Teyla tried to come up to his side and join him.

"Get back!" he snarled at her, then swung as the first gargoyle reached them.

As tall as he was, it was taller, looming eight or nine feet, and it swung human-like arms with long claws on its fingers. Using his mace, Fel blocked a blow, but it staggered him, and he barely kept his feet.

Syla shook her head, agreeing with Fel's sentiment that Teyla wouldn't be a match for one. She was brave for fighting, but Syla rushed forward, hoping to grab her and pull her out of the way. The second gargoyle, however, targeted Teyla, swiping toward her head.

She ducked and swung her sword at the same time. Her blade clanged off, as useless against the gargoyle's armored skin as the quarrel, and the arm clipped her, knocking her back into Syla.

Syla stumbled, trying to keep her spectacles from falling down her nose while maintaining her balance and catching her cousin. Though she managed to stay on her feet, the gargoyle opened a mouth twice the size of a man's, and magical purple vapor wafted out.

"They spit acid!" Syla warned and tried to jumped to the side while pulling Teyla with her.

"The ruins," Fel yelled again, glancing at them, though he shouldn't have risked splitting his attention.

Clinks, clangs, and thuds rang out from his battle as he struck a gargoyle while parrying its powerful blows. Its arm slipped past his defenses, bashing him in the shoulder and knocking him several feet. He grunted as he crashed into a tree.

"Or run!" Fel added, voice pained as he fought to keep his balance. "Get away from here."

By the silver light of her moon-mark, Syla witnessed a wad of spittle—*acid*-filled spittle—from their gargoyle shoot past, missing her head by scant inches. Not pausing, the yellow-eyed creation stomped toward her. Syla tried to angle around the gargoyle so she could run into the ruins—better that than fleeing blindly into the rainforest and getting lost and eaten.

Teyla must have accepted that she couldn't hurt the beasts

because she tried to follow Syla, but their stone-skinned foe wouldn't let them escape. The gargoyle charged after them and blocked the doorway leading into the ruins.

Syla stepped forward and reached for it with her hand. Though her magic wouldn't likely affect the storm god's creations, she had to try.

The gargoyle lifted both arms and leaped toward her, wings flapping to carry it farther.

"Don't get close," Teyla warned and stepped past Syla, swinging her sword at its swinging arms, trying to knock them away.

Again, her blade did nothing but clang off. Syla ducked under one of the muscled limbs sweeping toward Teyla, then lunged in close. Though the maneuver felt suicidal, she planted her hand on the side of the gargoyle's cold stone torso, vainly hoping to sense how its innards worked and find a way to attack before it swung back at her again.

All she sensed was a wall of magic. Though she tried to send tendrils of power into it, the armored skin blocked her as surely as it blocked blades. There was no way for her power to enter the gargoyle, a creature not only imbued with magic but made *from* it.

It threw an elbow back into her. She tried to dodge, but it was too fast, and the blow thudded into her chest like a solid-stone battering ram. Only the padding of her breasts kept her ribs from crunching, but the attack hurt and sent her flying. She almost smashed into the wall of the ruins but clipped the edge of the doorway instead and tumbled through it.

Inside, she landed hard, dirt and decaying leaves that coated the ground doing nothing to soften her fall. Her momentum carried her into the dark interior, the sounds of battle following her.

Though her chest hurt so much she couldn't draw a breath,

she forced herself to her knees. Determined to figure out a way to help her comrades, she crawled back toward the doorway.

Syla patted her pocket, assuring herself that she hadn't lost the dragon figurine, but could Wreylith reach them through the dense canopy? She would have to light the forest on fire around the ruins to clear the way.

Syla was about to grip the figurine and call out, hoping the dragon would do exactly that, but something dark dropped down in front of the doorway. It spun, yellow eyes peering in at her. Another gargoyle. She cursed and scrambled to her feet.

Ducking to fit through the doorway, the new foe lunged for her, keeping her from delving into her pocket. She backpedaled and almost tripped over a rock but managed to make it to another doorway in the back of the room. The gargoyle stomped after her, forcing her deeper into the ruins.

More rubble on the floor nearly tripped her, and Syla turned to check her route. Her moon-mark continued to glow, the only brightness in the area, the only thing allowing her to see. She entered a room without a ceiling, the roof having collapsed long ago, and a hiss came from a pile of leaves. A snake reared up, and she sprinted around it and deeper into the room.

Behind her, the gargoyle stomped through the doorway, knocking a chunk of the stone frame free. The snake hissed again, its attention drawn from Syla, and attempted to bite it instead of her.

Thanking the gods, she made it through another doorway, but then the way was blocked. The back half of the next room had been buried by a rockfall, what had once been the ceiling and a level above crumbled. The front half of the room lay open to the elements, but, unless she could climb the moss-slick rubble, she was trapped.

Unbothered by the snake, the gargoyle strode after her.

"Fel!" Syla called, though she knew he couldn't help.

Shouts and clunks and cries of pain still came from the front of the ruins. He couldn't even win his own battle. Like Syla, he didn't have a weapon capable of hurting the gargoyles.

A thunderous boom came from somewhere outside, and the ground shook. Startled, Syla stared toward the hole in the ceiling, having caught a flash of light out there, but it was already gone. Only the sounds of trees and branches hitting the ground lingered.

"Fel?" she called uncertainly.

The gargoyle pursuing her had paused when the ground shook but only for a moment. Now, it continued toward her.

Syla tried to climb up the rock pile, but the moss and leaves littering it were damp and slick, and she struggled. Aware of the gargoyle's inexorable approach, she clawed her way up, her progress painfully slow.

Something *clinked* onto the stone roof, then bounced down the rock pile past her to land between the gargoyle's legs. The magical creation didn't slow, simply charging past whatever that had been, intent on reaching her. Its clawed hand reached for her, scraping her through her dress.

As she flattened herself and rolled to the side, trying to escape, a great boom came from behind the gargoyle, and white light flashed, blinding after the darkness. Raw power struck Syla, knocking her to the side and down the rock pile. Her head cracked against the stone wall, and debris tumbled down all around her, half-burying her.

Thuds sounded, the gargoyle stomping as it turned around. Still after her? Undeterred by that explosion? Or had that been a magical attack? Her head throbbed, pain stabbed her body from multiple directions, and Syla struggled to figure out what had happened.

Wings flapped as the gargoyle wobbled toward her, lopsided but still coming. Until someone jumped down through the hole in the ceiling. Fel? No, a shock of short white hair stood out on the man's head as he landed on the gargoyle's shoulders. With a bone blade that gleamed almost as whitely as his hair, he drove a great blow into its head.

Though dazed, Syla wanted to get up so that she wouldn't be helpless, but she struggled to push away the rocks that had tumbled down the pile with her.

Wings flapping erratically, the gargoyle reached up, slashing its claws at its attacker. The man—was that Vorik's comrade?—stood on its shoulders on either side of its head and jumped to evade the swipes. Again, he struck with his blade—his gargoyle-bone blade—and its magic damaged the creation in a way that Fel's mace and Teyla's sword had not.

The stormer slashed off the top of a wing, then slammed his sword into the gargoyle's head. Twice more, he had to leap to avoid its counterattacks, but he did so, then jumped free when it wobbled and finally toppled. The heavy gargoyle shook the ground when it landed on its side, wings crunching under its weight. It didn't rise again.

Sword in hand, the white-haired man looked at Syla. Her first thought was to slump in relief and be grateful, but something in his eyes told her that she wasn't safe.

"She's down, sir," the man called through the great hole in the ceiling.

He walked closer, looming into Syla's view, a view that was lopsided thanks to her crooked spectacles hanging halfway down her nose. She straightened them, but her arm hurt with the movement. *Everything* hurt.

"And the dragons aren't nearby," the man added, still calling to someone outside. Vorik. It had to be. "This is our chance to kidnap her."

Kidnap her?

Syla fought against the pain pulsing in her head to focus on the young man as he crept closer. He was bleeding, black riding leathers torn from the gargoyle claws, but he reached for her with determination in his eyes. Was *kidnapping* her part of Vorik's mission? His words from the ship rang in her mind. *Come with me.*

Maybe he'd wanted it to be voluntary, but, for some reason, his people—probably his odious *general*—wanted her. Could they know that a moon-mark was required to access the storm god's laboratory? Yes, of course. They had the same information that she did.

"Nobody's kidnapping me." Syla gritted her teeth against her pain and shoved a rock off her hip. As if to emphasize the sentiment, and certainly her feelings, her moon-mark flared.

Not answering, the white-haired stormer reached for her. If he'd meant to help her up, she would have allowed it, even thanked him, but the silver glow illuminated his features, and his set jaw and stance promised he meant to sling her over his shoulder and tote her off to his superiors. Her heart pounded at the thought, and she imagined General Jhiton somehow using her against her own people, turning her into a tool to harm the Kingdom.

He grabbed her wrist and started to pull her up. Setting her own jaw, Syla grabbed *his* wrist.

Unlike with the impervious gargoyle, he was a flesh-and-blood human, and she knew his anatomy intimately. When she sent her magic coursing into him, only the fact that he was Vorik's comrade—and her life wasn't in immediate danger—kept her from replicating the attack she'd made on the assassin. But she *did* wrap tendrils of power around his trachea, tightening his airway, as she'd done days before to another stormer. Like that enemy, this man didn't have the power of Vorik or Captain Lesva, no means with which to combat her magic and drive it away.

Syla squeezed his airway shut completely, and he dropped to

one knee. He tried to lift his sword, but with his limbs rapidly growing numb, he fumbled and almost dropped it.

The grip on her wrist loosened, and the man's eyes widened. He'd faced the gargoyle fearlessly, but this... This was different.

Syla wouldn't have loosened her own grip, not until he passed out, but a shadow dropped through the destroyed roof, startling her. Was that Vorik?

The white-haired man released Syla and pulled away from her. That broke her link to him, and he gasped, reaching for his throat, his eyes still bulging. He lifted his sword, as if he might strike her, but Vorik stepped between them, blocking his man from reaching her.

"Greetings, Your Highness." Vorik leaned over her, eyes scouring her with concern. "Given your current tenuous position, I do not mean to be overly critical, but you came into the rainforest without a dragon *or* explosives? Have you heard that this is a dangerous place?"

Vorik raised his eyebrows and smiled, the smile that always altered his appearance from fearsome enemy warrior to achingly handsome friend—*lover*. Someone she longed to have as a permanent part of her life. The blood and soot on his lean, angular face couldn't disguise his inherent appeal.

"I thought more of bringing along food, water, clothing, and first-aid supplies than explosives," Syla said. "Back at the temple, black powder isn't on the packing list they give to healers heading into the field to do their work."

"Goodness, your people are short-sighted."

Syla adjusted her spectacles. "Quite literally."

"Are you all right?" Vorik lowered a hand to her.

Though she was more wary than ever of him after his man had blurted out the kidnapping plan, her body reacted without the hesitation that her mind felt, and she clasped his hand. Vorik pulled her gently to her feet and folded her in a light embrace.

Maybe he knew she'd been close when that explosion went off and had been battered.

"My cousin," she said, "and Fel."

As much as she wanted to lean into Vorik and relax, they might yet be in danger.

"They're all right," Vorik said. "I started out there. I didn't *know* you'd invited your very own gargoyle inside."

"*Invited* isn't quite the word."

"I expect your allies will find a way back here soon, though the explosives made the roof fall in places. *More* places than it already had fallen. This is quite the treacherous jungle of broken rock. You should be grateful to Lieutenant Wise for finding you in it."

"I'd be more grateful to him if he hadn't said he was here to kidnap me."

As if he hadn't heard that comment, Vorik continued with, "He must have seen or heard something and come to investigate while I was with your bodyguard and, ah, the lady you brought out here, who's also moon-marked." He raised his eyebrows. "Is that the same girl who was in the tunnels?"

"Teyla, and yes. Your people *already* kidnapped her once, so don't even think about doing that again. To her *or* me."

Though her bruised and beleaguered body longed for support, Syla made herself step out of Vorik's embrace. Her heel caught on the edge of the rock pile, and he reached out to steady her.

"Damn it, Vorik," she caught herself blurting in frustration. "Stop helping me if you're my enemy."

He lowered his hand. "I would prefer not to be."

"But you are, aren't you? Unless you resign as an officer and leave your horrible general, I can't think of you as anything else."

"The horrible general is my brother."

"I hate him."

"You barely know him." Vorik had the gall to smile. "He likes you."

"So much he wants you to kidnap me?"

"He actually hasn't made that order." It sounded like a silent *yet* belonged at the end of that sentence. Vorik frowned at his lieutenant. What, because he'd voiced their plan aloud?

The man—was his name truly *Wise*?—stepped back, hands lifted. He looked like he wished he were anywhere else except here for this conversation.

"But you *do* have orders to find the components to a shielder to keep me from getting them, don't you?" Syla asked. "You stole our scrolls and know as much about where they are as we do, and you also know it takes a moon-mark to open the laboratory, right?"

She held up her hand. Its glow had faded, but it hadn't disappeared completely.

Vorik gazed sadly back at her. It was as much a confirmation as if he'd nodded or spoken an agreement, but it irritated her that he wouldn't admit it. Also that he thought his brother wasn't horrible. His brother who was probably even now on Harvest Island, rounding up her people for internment—or death—and directing the stealing of more crops.

"Wise," Vorik said, "search the rest of the ruins, and see if that moss thing is here."

The lieutenant opened his mouth, as if he might correct *moss thing* to a more accurate term, but maybe he read the grimness in Vorik's face because he didn't.

"You think there'll be something here? After centuries of abandonment?"

"*She* did." Vorik nodded to Syla.

She bared her teeth at him and didn't say that nothing but luck and seeking high ground had guided her here. Besides, was that true? Her moon-mark had first brightened when they'd reached the bank.

Wise headed for the doorway but halted. Fel stepped into view, his face slick with blood and his clothes torn. He held his crossbow, a quarrel loaded, and aimed it at Wise, who stopped and lifted his hands.

Vorik, who looked like he'd expected Fel at any moment, barely reacted, only flicking a finger for his lieutenant to go another way. There wasn't another doorway out of the room, but Wise climbed up the rock pile far more easily than Syla had, then disappeared onto the roof, a few shards of stone falling in the aftermath of his passing.

Fel shifted his crossbow to point at Vorik's chest.

Vorik snorted softly but didn't object. Unlike the rest of them —Teyla was just visible leaning against a wall behind Fel's shoulder—*he* wasn't injured, at least not that Syla could detect. And, unlike his lieutenant, he had the magic of his dragon bond, enhancing him far beyond normal human capabilities. He could likely have darted across the room and disarmed Fel without much trouble.

For several minutes, they stood in that position, nobody moving. Even though Fel had his crossbow pointed at Vorik, Syla was the one who felt like a prisoner.

Sooner than she expected, rocks shifted overhead, and Wise climbed back down. He carried a ceramic amphora so coated in cobwebs and dust that one couldn't have discerned if any designs or decorations marked the side except that the front had been wiped clean. Wise must have used his shirt. The clean spot revealed a painting of a tree with a cylindrical-shaped bulb growing out of a patch of moss. Further, Syla's hand warmed in its presence, and her moon-mark glowed again. Cheerfully.

"I think this is what we need, sir. I broke the seal to look inside." Wise shook his hand, as if some magic might have zapped him when he'd done so. "There's a gray-green powder, and it glows like..." Wise looked at Syla's moon-mark, then set down the amphora. He wiped dust off the lid and opened it. Silver moon-light flowed out, shining on all of their faces.

"Oh, brilliant," Teyla said, eyes alight as she leaned around Fel.

It would have been more *brilliant* if a stormer hadn't been holding it.

"Were there any more urns back there, Wise?" Vorik watched Syla's face as he asked.

She glared at him. "They're amphoras. Two handles, a narrow neck, and a tapered bottom."

"*Yes.*" Teyla sounded enthusiastic at the correction. "People designed them for transport of goods around the settled world in the era before the Gods War. They're usually for liquids but holding powder isn't unheard of. That one might be a thousand years old."

"There was a whole bunch of stuff back there." Wise tilted his head toward some part of the ruins behind the rock fall. "I think the room was actually sealed until we set off the explosives. As for amphoras, this was the only one with a mossy tree on the front and glowing powder inside."

Syla could hardly believe that ruins so old still held the contents of what sounded like an ancient apothecary. Had some power preserved it over the centuries? Before the storm god's mad tinkerings, magic had been scarce in the world and nothing that humans had known how to summon and manipulate. Only the gods themselves and that which they'd touched had possessed it.

"We'll take it and go," Vorik said.

"Yes, sir." Wise hesitated, looking at Syla's hand. "What about, uhm?" He pointed a finger in Teyla's direction.

To suggest kidnapping *her* if Vorik wouldn't take Syla?

Syla folded her arms over her chest. "Don't even think about it. Our dragon allies are waiting just above the canopy and will stop you if you try to kidnap either of us."

"They're hunting off in the distance, but I do believe Wreylith would come to your rescue." Vorik's smile was a touch bemused.

"Of *course* she would. I've proven myself to her." Syla was less confident that Wreylith would do anything more than she'd promised—carrying Syla around the world on her quest in exchange for livestock—but she doubted Vorik had any details on their arrangement.

His gaze shifted thoughtfully toward Teyla. She must have caught the gist of the stormers' contemplation because she frowned and lifted her sword. Fel growled and slapped his hand against the side of his crossbow stock to remind them of where it pointed, still straight at Vorik.

"We may have to wait for a more opportune moment," Vorik told Wise without taking his gaze from them.

Maybe he didn't truly *want* to kidnap Syla—or vex her by kidnapping her cousin. As she'd been thinking, he was so fast and agile that he could probably evade being shot and disarm Fel and Teyla without trouble.

"I do have another..." Wise's free hand strayed to a pouch on his belt.

What? Explosive?

"We'll get another opportunity," Vorik told him. "Or find another moon-marked person that we can borrow. One who isn't protected by a dragon that neither of our males would attack."

Wise's eyebrows rose, and he tilted his head in what might have been realization or agreement. "Yes, sir."

Vorik pointed his chin toward the sky, and Wise, the amphora again sealed and tucked under his arm, climbed up the rock pile.

"Your Highness." Vorik bowed. "As always, it was a delight to see you."

He walked toward the rock pile to follow his lieutenant.

Damn it, Syla and her moon-mark had found this place. He'd skulked around like a vulture, waiting to steal what she'd been on the verge of locating herself.

Frustration made Syla clench her fists, wishing she had something to throw at him. "I'm still pissed at you, Vorik."

"I know." As he turned back to bow again at her, he glanced down her body, his gaze lingering on her chest. For a moment there was longing and regret in his eyes, but he recovered and, ignoring the crossbow trained on him, started up the rock pile.

"This isn't *honorable*," she called.

He paused, frowning back, that word affecting him more than most. "I must follow my orders, not because the general or our chiefs are always right, but because our people need food, and your people weren't willing to let us back onto any of the islands to share what was meant for all of humanity. Your mother specifically didn't."

"*Your people* left the Kingdom because they didn't like the rules. They made that choice over generations. Don't pretend my family is at fault for their decisions. It's not our fault the climate has gotten harsher." Syla snapped her mouth shut, trying to rein in her temper. She was frustrated and letting her emotions speak. She didn't think she was wrong, but... as she'd implied to Captain Radmarik, she wouldn't be as opposed as the queen had been to a peace treaty that allowed the stormers some kind of access to the islands. But Vorik's leaders had scoffed at what she'd been willing to offer. They'd only come as part of a ruse, seeking again to destroy another shielder. She bared her teeth at Vorik, even if she didn't believe he'd been behind that scheme or even fully aware of it.

"Nor is it ours, but we must adapt and do what we have to in order to survive." With those words, Vorik climbed out of sight before calling back, "Thank you for not killing my man!"

Syla slumped against the wall, exhausted.

Teyla walked in, limping and gripping her side. Fel lowered his crossbow, and now he also slumped, probably more injured than any of them. Syla would have to stave off her exhaustion to heal everyone before they could continue on.

"I should have ordered you to shoot him," Syla said to Fel.

He hesitated. "Yes, Your Highness."

That hesitation surprised her. When they'd been on Harvest Island, Fel had tried to talk her into sharing Vorik's location because he'd wanted to slit the captain's throat while he'd been passed out.

"Would you have done it?" Syla wondered what had changed.

"If you'd ordered it, yes."

"But not if I hadn't? I thought you hated him, considered him a deadly enemy, and believed him an ongoing threat to the Kingdom." *Syla* felt those things... except the hate. It would be better if she *could* hate Vorik. Instead, she wished things were different and that she could have stayed in his embrace, letting him protect her so that she could rest.

"Oh, I do. But he also..." Fel looked at Teyla.

She grimaced and touched a bloody gash visible through a torn sleeve. "He saved us from the gargoyles, Syla. Why did he bother?"

"Because he likes to do that. Save your life while plotting against you and stealing your amphora. It confuses everything."

"Yeah." Teyla smiled wanly and sat down. "I hurt so much." She looked at Fel, as if wondering how he could still be upright. He'd taken the brunt of the gargoyles' blows.

"I always hurt," Fel said.

"I'll heal you both in a minute if you'll give me permission to use my magic." Syla reached into her pocket, feeling she should make one more attempt to get the amphora back. If they failed to return with any one of the three components, they would have failed entirely.

The figurine was cold to her touch. That usually meant Wreylith wasn't nearby, but Syla tried anyway to reach out. The dragon was her last hope of getting that amphora.

Wreylith? Can you hear me?

She had to call three times before a distant, *I can hear you through the link in the krendala, yes. You are interrupting my sleep. What do you want?*

Sorry, I thought you were hunting.

And that it would be acceptable for you to interrupt that?

Syla almost pointed out that Wreylith was a curmudgeon, but if she'd woken the dragon from sleep, grumpiness was understandable. Besides, she needed a favor. She would be polite.

Perhaps later, you can inform me as to the times of day when it's acceptable to presume to speak with you. All right, maybe that was more snide than polite. *In the meantime, is there any way I could talk you into waylaying the stormer dragons?* Remembering that the next component was magical ore in the mountains, she wondered if Vorik might fly past wherever Wreylith had chosen to hunt and rest. *They stole something from us. Technically, they stalked us here and swooped in and took something before we located it, so it wasn't precisely theft, but there was only one, and we need it.* She shared an image of the amphora.

Waylay? Wreylith still sounded sleepy.

Attack them, and take the amphora. Or maybe you could talk Agrevlari into bringing it to you. To demonstrate his adoration and devotion to you.

I doubt he *is the one carrying a ceramic pot.*

No, but he's carrying the person who has it. Or the other dragon is. Does that gray one feel adoration and devotion to you?

Not that he's mentioned. I am sleeping, human, and I am not here to fulfill your every whim. You will have to acquire your own pot.

Syla frowned. She couldn't truly expect Wreylith to do everything for her, but her failure left her frustrated. And unwise. Before she could stop herself, she asked, *Is the problem that you're sleeping or that you fear battling those two? With Igliana's help, wouldn't you be a match for them?*

I fear nothing! Despite the distance muting their communications, Wreylith still managed to boom the words into Syla's mind.

Then is it that the singing worked, and you've developed feelings for him?

Vex me no further, human.

The krendala heated in Syla's hand, almost shocking her into dropping it. She set it down, lest it burn her, and immediately regretted snipping at the dragon.

"Everything all right?" Teyla eyed the figurine.

"I may have pissed off our dragon allies."

"Does that mean they're not coming back and we're stuck out here?"

Fel glowered at the suggestion.

"I... hope not."

19

VORIK YAWNED, THE DARKNESS OF NIGHT DEEP AROUND THEM AS Agrevlari flew toward the mountains. On Tonasketal's back, Wise's chin was drooped to his chest. He might have been sleeping. Vorik would keep an eye on the urn—the *amphora*, Syla had called it—wrapped in his arms.

When will we stop to sleep? Agrevlari asked, his wingbeats languid—tired.

I feel like an ass, Vorik said.

Since dragons lack that human anatomical feature, I am uncertain how to interpret your emotion.

I feel like a cloaca, then. One afflicted with vent gleet.

That's dreadful.

Yes.

A camp of nocturnal fang bats flew up from the trees, disturbed by the dragons' passing. Vorik reached for his sword, aware that the creatures were territorial and usually attacked intruders that passed through their area, but they took off instead of confronting Agrevlari and Tonasketal. Being aligned with a dragon made life easier.

You were victorious in acquiring the component for the shielder, as required by your orders, Agrevlari said. *Why do you feel as if your elimination vent is infected with fungi or bacteria?*

Vorik didn't point out that the dragon was taking his simile too literally. *Because Syla was right. It wasn't honorable.*

Your lieutenant located the component first, and you rightfully took it.

We only located it because Syla led us to those ruins. I've hunted in this area before, and I had no idea they were there. I wonder how she knew.

Her magic was a gift from the gods. The shielders were also gifts from the gods. They may guide her in this endeavor.

If the gods were guiding Syla, that wouldn't bother Vorik, but the idea that he was working against their wishes would. Long ago, his people had started calling themselves stormers because they dared live among the storm god's creations, but few claimed any allegiance to him. He was the one who'd made the world so difficult for humans to survive in. Vorik had always felt affinity to the sun god, even if he rarely attended religious ceremonies or prayed on his own. What if he was, in obeying his brother's orders, going against the wishes of the deities his people shared with those from the Garden Kingdom?

Not only his brother's wishes, Vorik told himself. Those lush islands were also what the tribal leaders wanted. No, he amended, reminded of Wise's words. Some of them wanted more. They wanted to enslave the Kingdom subjects.

That didn't sit well with him, and he resolved to talk to Jhiton when he got back. Maybe Chief Tenilor too. It had sounded like he'd been a part of that discussion.

Vorik had always considered himself a soldier, defending and feeding his people, and nothing more, but he had a high enough rank that he should have a voice at tribal meetings if he wished it.

Maybe he would have to show up for more of those and argue for a future of honor. Of course, if his feelings for Syla became widely known, his words might be brushed aside. He might even be held in suspicion by his leaders.

Vorik looked toward Wise again, wondering what the lieutenant would have said—would have *reported*—if Vorik had voiced the words that had come to mind when he'd faced Syla in the ruins. He'd been tempted to ask if there was enough of the powder that they could each take half—if that would be sufficient for *two* shielders to be made. But, according to Wise, only one of the final components grew at a time, so it wouldn't have mattered if they'd shared the other two. Besides Jhiton didn't *want* the Kingdom to be able to replace its broken shielder.

I believe it likely that the gods are *guiding the princess*, Agrevlari added after a few quiet moments. *You recall your battle with Captain Lesva.*

And that lightning knocked her off that cliff, yes. In that moment, Vorik had been relieved the decision whether or not to push her off had been taken from him, but the thought that it might not have been chance had occurred to him. And disturbed him.

An act of one of the gods, one would think, Agrevlari said.

Or luck.

That is possible. Agrevlari didn't sound like he believed it. *But if she* has *been chosen by the gods, we should be wary in our interactions with her.*

Yes.

I would not care to be hit by lightning.

Unless you're a cloud striker, it sounds unpleasant.

Even to a dragon, yes. We are powerful but not impervious, especially to the magic of the gods.

Few are impervious to that.

When the dragons reached the foothills of the Everfrost

Mountains, they adjusted their course to follow the two-thousand-mile-long chain to the north.

We can camp when you see a good place. Vorik yawned again. *I just wanted to get far away with the amphora in case Syla talked Wreylith into attacking us to retrieve it. We're only guessing that she might be chosen by the gods; she's definitely chosen by that dragon.*

Oh, to be chosen by one as magnificent as she, Agrevlari said. *Do you think I should compose another song? She wasn't as wooed by my ballad as I'd hoped.*

Based on our encounters with her, I have a hunch she's more likely to be drawn by a dragon who does great deeds or bests many foes in battle rather than one who has a nice singing voice. Vorik didn't point out that the screeches he'd heard didn't suggest Agrevlari fell into that latter category.

I do believe you are correct. She was pleased when I drove Ozlemar away from her, but perhaps it was not a sufficient display of my battle prowess to make her swoon with admiration.

I doubt she's ever swooned. Do dragons know how to swoon?

Sometimes, when we are affected by strong emotions, we dip one wing and fly in a pleased circle. Or we dive and twirl. Agrevlari shared an image of a dragon doing so.

Interesting. I've not seen that often.

It is rarely done in the presence of outsiders, but I've had a female twirl so for me. And that young dragon with Wreylith gazed with interest at me when we passed.

Did she? I didn't notice that.

Humans aren't attentive when it comes to dragon interest.

A proven fact. A hint of daylight was lightening the horizon, and Vorik spotted something flying in the distance above the snow-capped mountains.

Agrevlari picked up his pace, either invigorated by the thought of sleep or of a female twirling for him.

Is that another dragon up there? Vorik asked.

I sense several in the direction we are heading. Scar Peak lies that way. It's a popular meeting place for dragons desiring to hunt in the desert on the other side of the mountains.

Stormer-allied dragons? Vorik thought of the wing that had been flying up the coast, but they would have reached the Sixteen Talons headquarters by now. *Or wild dragons?*

Neither.

What other dragons are there? Vorik asked dryly.

Ex-stormer-allied dragons.

A testament to his fatigue, it took Vorik a moment to decipher that.

Like the orange one, Igliana, Agrevlari added.

Dragons linked to stormers who left the tribes to start the Freeborn Faction?

Yes.

I hadn't realized... Well, I guess I'd heard some of their dragons remained with them, but I thought most came back to our people or went wild because they didn't approve of an alliance with humans who weren't actively trying to gain access to the Garden Kingdom.

That is true for many, Agrevlari said, *but some dragons have stayed. I believe we may have inadvertently located the hidden faction headquarters that your superiors have wondered about.*

Since the Freeborn Faction had nothing to do with his mission, Vorik wasn't concerned about their headquarters but asked, *How many dragons did you sense?*

He would report where and how many they'd seen when he returned home.

There are only two outside of the mountain, but... there is magic within Scar Peak that is muffling my ability to detect if there are more dragons in its caves or the old mines.

Mines? The dragon-meeting mountain took on more interest

for Vorik. Wise hadn't said the scroll gave a specific location for finding the teal ore that was the second shielder component, but might this be a spot? *Mines with magic?*

There is ore within that emanates power.

Would it be teal *ore?*

I believe it may be. I've not visited the mines myself to look for it before.

I'll consult Wise when he wakes up, but I think Scar Peak may be where we want to head next.

To the Freeborn Faction headquarters?

They're not camped out on top of the ore, are they?

It appears that they, or at least their dragons, are in the same locale.

Vorik frowned. That could be problematic. The Freeborn Faction not only *wouldn't* help him, but they might impede him. On the other hand, they might help Princess Syla.

We may have lost our advantage in this quest, Agrevlari.

Is your infected cloaca disturbed further?

Yes, it is.

Syla slept poorly. Disturbed by having lost the amphora and knowing Vorik was already flying toward the second component, thoughts of failure plagued her. Throughout the night, she second-guessed her choices. It didn't help that the rainforest didn't settle down, so roars, buzzes, hoots, and slithering sounds invaded her dreams—her nightmares.

During one fit of sleep, she'd dreamed of returning home, only to have the soldiers throw her in the dungeon and send a thousand carnivorous centipedes in to eat her alive. That latter had surely been inspired by the noises outside, but the former... was more prediction than dream.

Now, as dawn approached, exhaustion made her want to curl

on her side and sleep. If only rest weren't so elusive. She *ought* to have been so tired after healing Fel and Teyla that she'd collapsed. *They* had. Even Fel, who'd promised to stand watch, was snoring in the doorway, his crossbow in his lap. She didn't blame him. Being injured and healed was as exhausting as *doing* the healing.

As it grew lighter in the stand-alone chamber they'd found— the apothecary, as Syla had been thinking of it—in the remains of a courtyard in the center of the ruins, she was tempted to explore. A hint of magic permeated the place, and it hadn't been raided or disturbed by animals over the centuries. In stone niches in the walls, glass and ceramic jars and jugs remained, as if they'd been set down months or years earlier instead of in a long-distant past era. Many containers had fallen to the floor and broken, probably once supported by wooden shelves that had rotted away, but it was still a fascinating find.

Muscles stiff and aching, Syla rose to expand upon her brief investigation from the night before. When they'd found the place, with the lantern Fel had reluctantly allowed her to light, she'd looked around enough to see if another amphora of moss-bulb powder might be on a shelf. When she hadn't spotted one, she'd forced her attention to healing the others. Fel hadn't hesitated to accept her magical ministrations, grumbling only that he was still bound from the last time, so it hardly mattered. Teyla also hadn't been worried about it since she'd endured another healing only days earlier. Her willingness to accept Syla's ministrations was part of the reason Syla trusted her without reserve. Even though she'd never believed Teyla planned to betray her or spy on her on behalf of Relvin, Syla was glad to know Teyla didn't have secrets to hide. Not like Vorik, who'd insisted she *not* use her magic to heal him.

"Oh, Vorik," Syla said with a sigh, wishing any other dragon rider had been pitted against her on this quest. Another might not have hesitated to kidnap her, but she also wouldn't have been conflicted about battling him.

Unfortunately, her second, more careful perusal of the contents of the apothecary didn't reveal an amphora that Wise had missed. Syla wished she could take some of the other ancient items with her and was momentarily distracted by a discovery of well-preserved argondar root, a species she'd read had gone extinct, but Teyla waking up and joining her reminded her of their mission. They would have to eat breakfast, hope Wreylith came, and then... what?

Head to the mountains to seek the teal ore, even though no single component would work without the other two? Or maybe they should search the rainforest for the ruins of another civilization that might have preserved moss-bulb powder.

"I feel compelled to tell you something this morning," Teyla said quietly with a glance toward Fel, who remained asleep in the doorway. "Is it a magical compulsion created by a bond from your healing?" Teyla sounded more curious than distressed or disturbed by the notion. Whatever secret she wanted to blurt must not have been that condemning.

"It could be," Syla said, "but I healed you back in the castle too. Maybe you just woke up with a need to divulge deep dark truths as a result of your near-death experience last night."

"That's possible. The gargoyle *did* almost take me out."

"*Are* there deep dark truths?" Syla wondered.

"Nothing you couldn't have guessed at, but my father... Well, he did say to keep my mouth shut around you. My beak, as he calls it." Teyla smiled, but her eyes were concerned.

Eyes of the moon, maybe there *were* secrets.

"I wasn't supposed to overhear their conversation," Teyla added.

"Between your father and... Relvin?" Syla guessed.

"Yes. It was after your message arrived and before we left. I got a little distracted by everything that happened after that and forgot about it for a time." Teyla frowned toward the doorway, some animal skittering through the leaf litter in the ancient courtyard.

"I didn't heal you so that you would tell me secrets. You don't have to say anything." Syla walked over to the krendala. When she'd gone to sleep, she'd left it on the floor, not wanting to risk annoying Wreylith further, but she had to find out if the dragon would return.

"I know you didn't. You wouldn't. I actually wanted to tell you from the beginning, just to spite Relvin and Father. I just wasn't sure if there would be... consequences if they found out, but I decided I don't care." Teyla brushed off her hands. "Father said that he would back Relvin financially and work on getting some of the minor lords and ladies on his side if Relvin attempts to acquire the throne."

"Ah." Syla wasn't surprised. Their father, minor lord Abbingdar, didn't have a moon-mark or a claim to great familial power of his own, except through his deceased wife. He was someone else who would doubtless love to have a relative on the throne.

"Like I said, you could have guessed that Relvin wasn't acting alone. But in that conversation, I also heard Father suggest that Relvin would have to hurry because others were already putting plans in motion."

"Like General Dolok?"

"Father doesn't speak often with military officers. I'd guess he was thinking of other minor lords or ladies. And then he implied that some of the island lords might lay claims too. Sorry, I should have told you everything I knew before we left."

"There wasn't time before we left."

There wasn't time now either, but until Wreylith came, they were stuck. Syla gingerly picked up the figurine. It warmed her palm but didn't feel hot or dangerous, as it had the night before. She risked calling softly in her mind to the dragon.

"Probably not, but I'm not sure what it says about me that I didn't confess all this until after..." Teyla waved at her left shoulder, which had been dislocated the night before, one of several injuries that Syla had tended. "I didn't feel as compelled to spill everything to you when you healed the bump on my head. Does a greater healing instill greater feelings of loyalty?"

"It can, yes. You also might have secretly disapproved of me since I *don't* send letters listing historical errors to the authors of published texts."

Teyla managed a smile. "I can't believe you don't do that."

"My work has kept me busy."

"Everyone needs a hobby, Syla."

You are not on the high bank by the river, Wreylith boomed into Syla's mind, the thunderous telepathic voice promising she was not only nearby but annoyed to be kept waiting.

Sorry, we had to camp inland where the insects weren't as bad. We'll be there as soon as possible. Thank you for coming.

If you are not here by the time Igliana finishes preening her wing-pit, we will depart.

Your patience and continued support mean the world to me.

Are you being snarky with a dragon? Wreylith asked. *That is unwise.*

I would never do anything unwise. Syla patted Teyla on the shoulder. "Grab your gear. Two grumpy dragons are waiting." She strode over to wake Fel.

"Igliana is *grumpy*?"

"Well, probably not. She's tending her armpit. Her *wing*-pit."

"Good. I like her. I'm glad she's not grumpy. She magically held us on her back. I'd been wondering how riders stay on dragons without something like a saddle and reins."

"*Some* dragons offer magical assistance." Syla hurried to put away her belongings, though she couldn't help but grab the argondar root and a couple more small containers to take home to study. One was supposed to collect souvenirs when one traveled the world, right?

"What's the plan?" Fel asked after they'd grabbed their gear and were trekking toward the river.

Yes, what *was* the plan? Wreylith hadn't been willing to go after the stormer dragons. She wanted Syla to handle her own problems. But how? It wasn't as if she could seduce Vorik and knock him out with Candles of Serenity. Even if she'd brought some along, he wouldn't have fallen for that again.

Still, that gaze of longing he'd given her before leaving came to mind. Might *some* kind of seduction work? Giving her an opportunity to take the amphora from him? Maybe Fel could sneak in and snatch it while she distracted Vorik with a kiss. But she would have to get past the stormer dragons too. Maybe Wreylith could distract *them* with kisses. She would probably object to the idea. Of course, Agrevlari was self-distracting when it came to Wreylith. Maybe she would only need to fly around the area, throwing in a sexy dragon sashay or two.

Fel looked at her. Waiting for an answer to his question?

"We're going to the Everfrost Mountains to get the next component," Syla said.

"We don't have the *first* component."

"We will," Syla said.

"You're almost convincing when you say that."

"What would I have to do to erase the *almost* from your sentence?"

"Lift your arms skyward, like your mother always did when she addressed the people," Teyla suggested. "And cultivate a regal air."

Fel nodded in agreement.

Still mourning her mother's passing, Syla couldn't manage a smile at her cousin's attempt at humor.

Ahead, Syla spotted a red-scaled head through the trees. And an orange one peeked into view as well.

The two dragons had landed on the vertical side of the bank, finding the only perches in the area. The golden eyes that locked onto Syla didn't appear pleased. She could understand why Wreylith was impatient, but she could have *told* Syla that she was coming and requested that they be waiting.

As they reached the edge of the bank, Igliana's head disappeared. Syla peered over. She hung from her talons by a clump of roots and was twisting so that she could nip at her scales under her wing. It was closer to the belly area than the armpit that Syla had been imagining.

"Are you scratching an itch? Or are you injured?" Syla remembered the fanged fish or whatever had attacked the dragon in the river the day before.

These wounds are not deep, but they broke my scales, and the ones under my wing chafe terribly. Igliana growled at the offending area.

Do not complain to a healer, Wreylith said, *or she will smear a foul-smelling greasy concoction all over you.*

"You pirouetted and sashayed after I put that on your foot," Syla said. "It must have felt good."

When I landed, it squished between my toes like slug slime.

"Only because you were once again able to put weight on that foot. I bet your wound felt *wonderful.* Also, the salve would have been unctuous, not slimy."

My toes could not discern the difference.

The orange head rose above the cliff again, eyes level with Syla's, fangs parting slightly. Only a cobweb that must have been on the roots and now dangled from the dragon's horn kept her from looking entirely fearsome. *I would endure slime if it made the chafing go away.*

"I did bring some of that salve, but you'd probably be better served by..." Syla removed her pack, pulling out her recently acquired ancient apothecary containers so she could reach her first-aid kit.

"Where did all those come from?" Fel asked.

"She was shopping while you were sleeping," Teyla said. "I approve. Those look like wonderful finds. Look at the art on the side of the ceramic jar. Is it Vyonetian? I had thought their people only settled in the mountains, but they must have used the river as a passageway to facilitate trade. I hadn't realized their goods reached so far. How fascinating."

Fel gave her a dark look. "Even without the moon-marks, I would know you two are related."

Syla found a small jar of heliska paste and crawled to the edge to peer over the bank again. The river flowed past thirty feet below, with the roots Igliana perched upon more than ten feet down the vertical slope. What species of tree sent roots so deep down into the soil? She glared balefully at the nearby rainforest, not only because of the deep roots but because their trunks and branches grew too densely for the dragons to climb up onto the bank where Syla could more easily reach Igliana's injury.

"Catch me if I fall, please." Syla tried to map a route, including possible toe and handholds, before turning so she could lower a foot over the edge.

Fall? Igliana looked at her, then at Wreylith.

Unlike stormer humans, those from the Garden Kingdom are rarely dexterous and agile, Wreylith told her, kindly sharing the words with all.

Is it because of the strange glass circles that so many of them wear over their eyes?

That may be part of it.

"It's because I'm a *healer*, not a hunter." Syla decided she didn't like it when dragons spoke about her. "I read books; I don't practice climbing."

"I can go down there instead if you tell me where to rub what." Fel came to the bank and dropped to his knees.

"You're still recovering from your injuries that I wasn't able to fully heal." Syla put the small container in her mouth so she could use both hands and carefully picked her way down. Dropping into the water from twenty feet wouldn't kill her. And the predatory fish so fearless as to bite even *dragons*? She trusted one of her scaled allies would pluck her out before that happened. Hopefully.

Fel squinted at her, as if he would come down anyway, but Igliana shifted her head to watch, inadvertently blocking him.

Despite her myopia—and *strange glass circles*—Syla managed to climb level with Igliana's wounded belly. The fish—had *fish* truly done that much damage to dragon scales?—had left abrasions and punctures. They weren't that deep, but there were dozens of them. Considering how briefly Igliana had been in the water, the number was impressive.

Syla shifted with extreme care to keep her feet and one hand clamped to the bank while she pulled the lid off with her teeth and applied an antibacterial salve that soothed as well as lowering inflammation. It had an anti-itch property, too. She'd used it on some of her bug bites that morning.

Oh. It's so cool and refreshing. If dragons could have purred, Igliana might have. Instead, she issued pleased clucks.

Later, you will find it slimy, Wreylith warned her.

Why so crabby about everything, Auntie Wrey?

"Auntie?" Syla mouthed as she finished applying the salve. "Are you relatives?"

My sleep was interrupted during the night, and, yes, we are, but more distant than the term aunt *would imply. Igliana came from the clutch of one of my sister's offspring's offspring. My sister, were she still alive, would have been deeply upset to learn that one of her descendants yoked herself to humans.*

My parents love me and are proud of me, Igliana said.

They would have upset my sister too.

She was probably as crabby as you.

Wreylith growled, but it didn't sound that ominous. Syla finished her work, managed to return the cap to her container and pocket it, and was debating how best to climb up when a rock she perched on gave way. She squawked and flailed, trying to grab a root. Her fingers only brushed it, and she fell.

Her spectacles loosened and Syla smashed a hand to her face to keep them on. Images of plunging into a den of deadly fish came to mind, but Igliana caught her a foot above the surface, jaws wrapping around her. Fortunately, her fangs didn't penetrate. She even had a lighter touch than Wreylith.

Below the surface of the water, shadows stirred. Hungry fish that had been waiting for a meal?

Igliana lifted Syla and deposited her on Wreylith's back. *Climb aboard, human friends, and we shall depart.*

"Maybe you should get a little figurine of *her*." Fel tilted his head toward Igliana.

Wreylith's slitted golden eyes narrowed. *Even if crafters remained who knew how to make krendala, one would never link one to an unproven callow youth.*

Ignoring the insult, Igliana flexed her wings and swished her tail. *I feel* wonderful *now.*

"Are you going to pirouette?" Fel asked warily, lowering Syla's pack down to her from the bank.

Most certainly, but I'll use my magic to keep you from falling off.

"That's not *all* I'm worried about," Fel grumbled. Did his face look green already?

No pirouetting. Wreylith launched from the bank.

Startled, Syla grabbed her spectacles again to keep them on, then flattened her hand to Wreylith's scales to establish her tether of magic. Riding on a dragon was almost as alarming as falling twenty feet toward deadly fish.

Without waiting for the others, Wreylith took off, flying above the river and toward the mountains to the east. When Syla looked back, she spotted Fel and Teyla sliding down the bank to climb aboard Igliana's back. When the orange dragon took off, she didn't pirouette, but she did fly back and forth in a distinctive sashay.

Glad she felt better, Syla settled in to plan how she would steal the amphora from Vorik.

20

THE DRAGONS THEY'D SPOTTED IN THE DISTANCE HAD DISAPPEARED by the time Agrevlari and Tonasketal reached Scar Peak, one of several mountains rising high enough to have snow above the tree line, even this late in the summer. They circled it, looking for caves or mine entrances.

A few times in his life, Vorik had flown this far south over the Everfrost Mountains on the way to the great desert to the east, but he'd never come close to this peak, only noting from a distance the deep and jagged canyon that ran from its apex for miles down the bare, rocky side. It looked like a wound left by the gods hurling lightning bolts.

For their second lap around the mountain, Agrevlari flew at a lower altitude, the smell of pine trees wafting up when his belly brushed the tops. A squirrel chattered irately at them but only after they were safely past.

I am catching a few scents lingering in the foliage, Agrevlari said. *Scents of dragons.*

Since we saw dragons recently, that isn't surprising, is it?

But we see no sign of them now. I thought they may be headquartered here with their human allies.

They may have flown farther north. That's the way they were going when we spotted them. Vorik would prefer if they could slip in, find the teal ore, and continue on without dealing with the Freeborn Faction—or their dragons. He didn't want to deal with any of what he could only think of as deserters. Some of the faction members were elders or women who'd never joined the Sixteen Talons or Storm Guard, and he felt they had the right to leave the tribes whenever they wished, but he struggled not to resent those who'd sworn to serve in the military and then departed. *Look for caves or mines, will you? Any possible entrance that could take us to teal ore, ideally ore located close to the surface.*

General Jhiton hadn't sent mining picks along, and Vorik had used his explosives on the gargoyles. He didn't fancy hacking at solid rock with his sword.

If we locate the faction's headquarters, we can ask them if they've seen the ore, Agrevlari suggested. *If they have been in the southern end of the mountains for many moons, they may have encountered it.*

We can find it without them.

If we fly aimlessly, the princess may locate the ore first. She likely has no aversion to dealing with your faction.

They're not my *faction.* Vorik bristled at the idea of being linked to them in any way. They'd given intelligence to the Garden Kingdom military on numerous occasions. That was a betrayal to the stormer people.

You claimed to be a part of it when you sought to seduce her.

You know *that was a ruse. Didn't you say you sensed magic within the mountain? There have to be caves.* Vorik peered left and right and sniffed at the mountain air, as if it might offer clues to finding the second shielder component. It was much cooler and dryer than the humid tropical heat that had smothered the rainforest, but if the scents of magical ore lingered in it, he couldn't detect them.

"Sir!" Wise called, waving from where Tonasketal flew above the canyon. "There's a huge cavern entrance over here. Big enough to fly into, and I see evidence of mining equipment from the past."

"There we go." Vorik waved an acknowledgment and urged Agrevlari to fly in that direction. "Wait for us to go in!" he called to Wise, thinking of those dragons that had disappeared and that Agrevlari had smelled.

Though it was unlikely he and Wise would chance upon the precise spot where the Freedom Faction made their headquarters, he didn't want to stumble into them. Just as he didn't think kindly of them, he doubted they would welcome a loyal stormer officer into their abode. Especially if they were trying to keep that abode secret.

Wise nodded, but his dragon had a different idea. Tonasketal flapped his wings hard and flew out of view, descending into the canyon. Maybe he'd spotted a tasty-looking mountain goat.

"We'd better make sure they don't get themselves into trouble," Vorik said.

Already flying in that direction, Agrevlari picked up speed. His nostrils twitched as he flapped his wings. *The scents of dragons are wafting out of the canyon toward me now. They include... There is a female in her fertile time.*

"Is *that* why Tonasketal isn't waiting?"

Vorik and Agrevlari soared over the edge of the canyon in time to spot Wise's dragon carrying him toward the cavern he'd mentioned. With the entrance at least twenty feet high and the width even greater, it offered room for the outstretched wings of a dragon. Wise was gesticulating while clutching the amphora, but Tonasketal didn't slow down, and they disappeared into the cavern.

"Catch them." A premonition of danger came over Vorik, and he almost gave the opposite order, for Agrevlari to stop and wait.

But if Tonasketal got Wise into trouble—a fertile female might have a male mate nearby who wouldn't appreciate another male approaching—they would need help.

With wings spread to catch the currents, Agrevlari soared into the dark cavern. No, it wasn't as dark as one would expect. Ahead, a strange aquamarine light glowed from the depths. Or was that... a *teal* light? Did the teal ore glow?

I sense magic, Agrevlari said.

More than that possessed by a fertile dragon? Vorik's hopes rose that they would not only find that ore but that some lay exposed at the surface.

Yes. This is—

Abruptly, Agrevlari tilted sideways and into a dive, but he couldn't go far, not with the bottom of the cavern scant feet below. Motion to the right made Vorik duck low. At the same time, a startled oath sounded ahead, followed by the screech of a dragon. Tonasketal.

A huge blade swept in from the side of the cavern, like one of the scythes the gardeners used to reap wheat and rye, but ten times the size. And the blade was edged in gargoyle bone. It swept through the air above Vorik's head. A few inches lower, and it would have struck him and knocked him off his dragon—if not sliced through his skull.

The blade disappeared into a slit in the stone wall on the far side.

"Sir!" Wise blurted, the word drowned out by Tonasketal roaring again.

Had another scythe swung out to attack them? And struck the dragon?

Over Agrevlari's head, Vorik glimpsed Tonasketal, his gray wings beating erratically. On his back, Wise struggled to stay on and keep hold of the amphora.

The floor of the cavern dropped away like a waterfall, descending vertically for dozens of feet before leveling off again.

There were campfires at the bottom, burning between hides hung to denote sleeping areas. The teal glow—several teal glows—came from the back of the large cavern.

Agrevlari flew toward an open area, a possible landing spot, but men and women ran out from behind rock formations and the hide flaps. They carried bows and quivers full of arrows.

"Don't land," Vorik barked, though he looked longingly toward what had to be the ore he sought. "This was a trap."

Maybe it hadn't been a trap, simply defenses the inhabitants had set, but, either way, they didn't look to welcome visitors.

Above them, the wounded Tonasketal had been trying to recover from being hit by a blade, but his wing clipped a stalactite, and he pitched sideways. Wise managed to stay on but lurched as the dragon tilted. The amphora tumbled from his grip.

Vorik cursed and, even as Agrevlari started flying up again, obeying the order not to land, Vorik sprang off his back. He dropped fifteen feet, landed in a crouch, and sprinted to catch the amphora before it hit the ground. The memory of catching Syla by the Kingdom lighthouse popped into his mind. She had been heavier than the amphora but much more pleasing to hold. At least he kept the ancient container from breaking.

Aware of the archers striding toward him with their bows, Vorik set it down and drew his sword, turning to face them. Agrevlari landed nearby, but two big dragons surged forward to keep him from breathing fire at the archers. More dragons crouched in the back of the cavern near the glowing ore.

Outnumbered, Vorik and Agrevlari would have to step lightly here.

Tonasketal recovered and landed twenty feet away. Wise scrambled off his back and joined Vorik. Unfortunately, they were still outnumbered.

"Sorry, sir," Wise whispered, glancing at the amphora. "My dragon got an itch."

"When you ally with creatures as mercurial as dragons, you must expect that occasional chaos will be thrown into your battle plans." Vorik remembered his brother saying that after *their* dragons had attacked each other over Wreylith, and was fairly certain he'd been quoting a famous rider of the past.

"No kidding."

The archers moved to surround them. Vorik's instincts made him want to run and put his back to a rock wall, but these people already looked irked and twitchy, like any sudden movements would prompt them to loose arrows.

Agrevlari growled at the two dragons that had approached. They stopped advancing, but they didn't back away.

"It's rude to enter a cave claimed by others without requesting permission beforehand," came a woman's voice from behind the archers.

"It's also rude to try to slash the heads or wings off those flying into a cave that had no markings to indicate it was occupied," Vorik said.

"Surely, our presence here couldn't have been a complete surprise."

"It was fairly surprising until Tonasketal detected a female in her fertile time."

The archers parted to let the speaker through.

Vorik didn't sheathe his sword, but he did lower it. Even though more than two-thirds of the people—the Freeborn Faction —were women, some were bonded with dragons, so he dared not underestimate them. Further, in addition to the two nearby dragons, four more were in the back of the cavern, perched directly on the glowing teal ore. Wait, were they perched? Or *roosting*?

"Captain Vorik of the Wingborn Tribe," the speaker said. A handsome woman with weathered bronze skin and two gray braids hanging over her shoulders, she stepped in front of the archers, though she also carried a bow. Captain Atilya.

Vorik hadn't seen her in years, not since she'd departed to form the faction with others, but she'd been an officer in the Sixteen Talons when he'd first been inducted.

"You remember me, Atilya. I'm honored." Vorik bowed. "But what a dreadful way you greet visitors."

"We have to defend those who can no longer defend themselves." She tilted her head toward the hides. Some elders were visible, doing crafting work with their hands while they observed.

"I'll wager you don't get holiday visitors bringing savik-berry pemmican," Vorik said.

"A treat we've had to do without."

"Dreadful. Here, despite you trying to take my head off, I'll give you something."

"Pemmican?"

"Better. I have *pears*." Vorik smiled at her, hoping his charm would smooth the way for him to chisel some of that ore out from under a dragon.

"Some of the pears that you've stolen from the Garden Kingdom, I presume." Atilya looked disapproving rather than charmed.

"They're *delicious*. And I actually paid for my pears. Admittedly, the farmers who tended the orchard weren't around, there having recently been an invasion, but I did leave coin."

Watching but not showing concern for the archers pointing arrows at him, Vorik walked forward and held out a pear, somewhat bruised after being in his pack for two days. It wasn't one of the ones he'd picked at the farm on Castle Island—he'd consumed those long ago—but a couple he'd packed back at their headquarters cave.

Atilya looked at the amphora instead of the pear, her gaze flinty. The archers shifted their weight, ready to loose those arrows.

Though Vorik didn't *think* he'd ever given the leaders of the Freeborn Faction a reason to want him dead, he couldn't be certain he hadn't wronged someone, however inadvertently, along the way. It was also possible their ideology alone might lead them to believe he should be shot.

"What is in that vase," Atilya asked, "and why did you come here?"

"It's an amphora, I'm told."

The flinty gaze did not change.

"I've orders to acquire a few items for General Jhiton."

Atilya looked toward the back of the cavern, at the ore deposits glowing cheerfully, some beneath dragon butts. Was its magical energy pleasant to sit upon?

"Why does General Jhiton want an *amphora* and teal ore?" Atilya had to be guessing about the ore, but she sounded certain, maybe because there was nothing else here, except the faction itself, that might have drawn a rider on a quest. "His hobbies are slaying people and ensuring the Kingdom will never trust our kind enough to allow us on their shores, not gathering collectibles."

"It's possible he's changed since you knew him."

"He has not."

Vorik spread his arms. He had no intention of revealing Jhiton's plans to these people, not when they had a history of giving stormer information to the Kingdom. As far as he knew, the Kingdom had never come to trust them, but they'd doubtless enjoyed the tidbits they'd received.

"I'm just a lowly captain," he said. "I'm not privy to Jhiton's plans."

"He's your brother."

"And yet, he plots and schemes without me. It's rude, isn't it?" Vorik tried his smile again, though he doubted he would make headway with Atilya.

One of the archers, a woman in her twenties, giggled. Too bad she didn't look like she was in charge of anything except perforating intruders with arrows. Atilya turned a cool gaze on her, and the girl wiped the amusement from her face.

Vorik waved the pear at Atilya again. "Try it, Captain. There are no strings attached."

"It's Chieftess. We've formed a tribe of our own."

"And you're in charge?" Vorik looked around, hoping a few others might share equally in the leadership responsibilities, others who might be more inclined to negotiate with him.

"I've been elected by my fellow tribe mates."

"Elected? Goodness, that's quite democratic."

"I can prove my capability as a leader as necessary," Atilya said coolly.

"I don't doubt it." Vorik recalled that she'd had a lot of prowess and been bonded with her dragon. Despite her gray hair, she didn't appear to have lost her fitness.

"No? Captains Lormark and Negg had snide comments the last time we spoke."

"I am not either of them."

"No." Her hackles seemed to lower slightly. "Your only fault that I remember was being your brother's puppy."

"He *is* my superior officer."

The grunt she made didn't suggest approval, but she waved to the archers to lower their bows. "We'll invite Captain Vorik to have the evening meal with us and, if he wants our ore, tell us his brother's plans."

"I don't know them, Chieftess," Vorik said.

"Perhaps after a few glasses of wine, you'll remember hearing him mention them." Atilya smiled at him, then turned away, calling for the preparation of a meal.

Vorik scratched his jaw. *Agrevlari, do you think you can dig out some of that ore? Unless Atilya is more successful in getting me drunk than I think she'll be, we're going to have to find a way to take it without their help. I can't tell them the mission, lest they blather to the Kingdom.*

Doesn't the Kingdom *already know what you're up to?* Agrevlari shared an image of Syla with him.

That is true, I suppose, though she's not sending back reports to her military leaders. At least, I assume not, given that they chased her away from their island. Even if I could divulge Jhiton's intent, telling the truth wouldn't get me Atilya's help. She doesn't approve of our people's plans.

It does seem that way. I'll ask these dragons about the ore, but it may behoove you to see if there are other deposits around the mountain.

Can you sense any?

Only the ones in here. Others would be difficult to detect if they're deep within the rock.

In other words, it would be much easier to take a chunk from here.

There are dragons roosting on it. It might not be that *much easier.*

What is its appeal? Vorik asked.

I understand it's warm and tingles. The dragons especially enjoy this hideout in the winter.

I didn't realize dragons were like the lions sunning themselves on flat rocks.

Tingling magical ore sounds even better than sunny lion perches, Agrevlari said.

"Come, Vorik." Atilya waved for him and Wise to follow her. "We will treat you to a meal in the hope that you *will* send savik-berry pemmican this way during the holiday season."

Why don't I trust her, Agrevlari?

She's immune to your charm?

That must be it.

After her poor night's sleep, Syla dozed as Wreylith flew over the rainforest and toward the mountains. Her subconscious remained aware enough to keep the magical tendril in place that anchored her to the dragon's back, and, unlike their younger companion,

Wreylith did not sashay or tilt alarmingly, threatening to dislodge Syla.

When she wasn't dozing, she read the book on her great-great grandmother, the wind of dragon flight tugging at the corners of the pages.

"After sailing off to avoid an arranged marriage with Lord Gerringtor and being captured by pirates, Queen Erasbella had to find a way to cleverly escape while worrying about a further threat: dragons attacking the ship. *Dragons*, Wreylith. And *pirates*." Syla looked at the back of the red dragon's head. "These things were *not* mentioned in any of the other books. They all said Erasbella went dutifully to her arranged marriage without complaint."

History is recorded in such a way that it pleases the sensibilities of those doing the recording, and unpleasing accountings are sometimes made to disappear. It is so with dragons as well. I've lived long enough to observe supposedly accurate historical tales changing over time with the passing generations.

"I can't believe she was trying to avoid her marriage. The other texts all suggest she was very proper."

She properly and soundly seduced the pirate captain and battled the dragons attacking his ship.

"You were *there*?"

When Wreylith didn't answer, Syla read on. "It looks like she went off on adventures even after her marriage and was captured another time by a ship of stormer troops. Against her bodyguard's advice, Erasbella used the glass lenses of her spectacles— Wreylith, you didn't tell me she wore spectacles. Did she read a lot? Spend her youth hunkered in dark rooms in the castle while taxing her eyes? But she was a warrior. She learned sword-fighting."

She did enjoy books.

"But the *sword-fighting*."

Do your glass seeing circles preclude learning to wield a blade?

"Not *technically*, but a lack of athleticism in general makes it difficult, and poor vision doesn't help anything." Syla thought of Vorik's suggestion that she learn to juggle to improve her abilities. Maybe she would try when she had time.

Erasbella did not lack athleticism.

"I guess I knew we weren't that similar, but I'm excited to learn that she wore spectacles and was a little more like me than I would have guessed from the other history texts I've read. She even *seduced* an enemy to get out of a jam. I wonder if it was natural for her, or she was more like me, and a little..." Syla kept herself from saying *awkward*. Wreylith might judge her for that.

Eager to learn what had happened next, Syla continued reading, sharing some of the words aloud. "She used the glass lenses of her spectacles to capture a ray of sunlight through the porthole, directing it into straw and rat droppings that littered her cell. It started a small fire, which she encouraged to spread, though the act endangered the life of her and her bodyguard. The flames burned through the wall of the cell and into the armory on the other side, where black powder for the cannons caught fire and exploded. Though injured by the event, Erasbella and her bodyguard, who cursed the gods for placing her at the queen's side, escaped, recovered their swords, and fought their way to the deck, the entire ship now in flame. A great red dragon descended and plucked them up so that they might escape. It was not the first time that the dragon had been observed in the queen's presence, even after her marriage. Despite her various adventures over the years, Queen Erasbella did ultimately marry Lord Gerringtor, birth children, and rule the Kingdom with grace and poise."

It is possible that Lord Gerringtor *was convinced to act as a very humble and proper mate after witnessing Erasbella flying upon a dragon's back and wielding a sword,* Wreylith said dryly.

"You were there," Syla said. "*You* were the red dragon."

Certainly.

"Why were other dragons attacking that pirate ship in her first adventure? And why did you decide to help Erasbella?"

The pirate captain had earned the loathing of one dragon in particular. As to the rest, I saw Erasbella battle nobly against the pirates and outmaneuver them more than once. She did that with many enemies, including stormers and dragon riders. Over the years, she again and again proved herself worthy. Wreylith sounded pleased by the memories of the decades-gone queen. *Eventually, we bonded, though her duties mostly kept her on her island instead of flying about with me. There were, however, occasional adventures when she wasn't busy with queenly duties or birthing and raising offspring. She saw that pirate captain more than once.*

"Did she actually disappear at sea in a storm later in life?"

She might have, deciding she'd produced a capable heir, arranged to disappear and continue to have adventures until the eventual day of her demise.

"That's amazing."

For a puny human, yes.

"Is that when the krendala was made?"

Soon after I met her, yes, by one of the last human crafters with the knowledge and ability to make them.

Syla closed the book, pleased to learn the truth about her ancestor. If it would help her in her quest, she didn't know, but she was beginning to understand more about Wreylith—and what did and did not impress her. With luck, that might come in useful one day.

21

THE SMELLS OF SEASONED ROASTING MEAT WERE SCINTILLATING, AND the faction people even produced bottles of gin and cactus wine to share with their guests. The alcohol produced from items foraged from the desert gave Vorik an idea about where their *last* head-quarters had been.

As he watched the preparations, Vorik felt more like a *prisoner* than guest, and he tried to figure out which food or beverage Atilya's people would drug or poison. If not for the teal ore glowing from the back of the cavern, he wouldn't have stuck around.

Wise sat shoulder to shoulder with him around one of the campfires, the smoke wafting up to haze the air in the high ceiling of the cavern. Vorik hadn't yet gotten an opportunity to speak privately with him and suggest he might not want to eat much of the food. Or would it be the drink? With its strong flavor, wine could hide bitter substances.

Faction members loomed close though, too close for even whispered conversations. Since Captain Atilya was bonded to her dragon, she would have keen hearing, and others present might also have magical enhancements. He eyed everyone wearing the fingerless black gloves of riders, gloves like his that could hide a dragon tattoo. It surprised him that so many of the self-interested predators had stuck close to the stormer deserters, but maybe they'd convinced the dragons that their plans would one day result in them gaining access to the Garden Kingdom islands and the protected prey and livestock that they craved.

Will offerings be made to dragons? Agrevlari asked from the back of the cave where he was ostensibly socializing with the scaled locals.

Vorik had asked him to subtly investigate the ore and whether it might be extracted without special tools. His gargoyle-bone blade had the strength to cut through many substances that would be impervious to simple steel, but he couldn't imagine using the slender sword to gouge out pieces of ore. And how much did they need? Wise hadn't mentioned if the scrolls said that.

There are many former riders here. Vorik waved toward Atilya, who hadn't gone far, and a couple of others he recognized as previous members of the Sixteen Talons. *I'm certain they've learned to treat their dragons well.*

What about visiting *dragons?* Agrevlari flicked his tail toward his body, then also looked at Tonasketal, though Wise's dragon had chosen a spot close to one of the fertile females and was attempting to woo her.

More than once, Wise had sent exasperated looks in his dragon's direction, probably because of Tonasketal's distraction—and his having flown them into a trap that could have been deadly.

Do you want me to make a request? Vorik asked as older men and women brought over platters of meat. His nose twitched at the spices. Not because they were unappealing—quite the opposite—but because they, too, could hide bitter poisons.

Need you ask, Vorik? I'd enjoy some of the fang porcupine and bayrok. But not the wyvern rotating on the spit there. They're too close to relatives.

Almost everything being served is an offspring of the mad god's tinkering. As you well know, those creatures are far easier to find these days than the juicier and tastier herbivores.

Yes, but some of the mad god's creations were less dragon-ish than others. Are those rabbits on that spit? Do have some rabbits sent over.

I'll do my best.

"How long will we stay, sir?" Wise asked.

Atilya sat across the fire from them, easily close enough to hear.

"As long as our hosts wish to feed us and provide good company." Vorik offered her a seated bow.

It appeared more that the chieftess was interrogating you, Agrevlari said.

Yes, and I expect that to pick up again after she drugs us.

"The storm outside looks rough too," Vorik added when a flash of lightning briefly brightened everything in the cavern. A faint buzz emanated from all the visible ore, as if the nearby electricity charged it further. He half-expected the dragons to spring off if surges of power went through them, but they settled lower on the ore, as if it felt good. "Maybe Atilya will allow us to spend the night."

"You're welcome to sleep here, Captain." Something in Atilya's voice made him think that had been the plan before he'd spoken.

Because the drugged interrogation would take that long?

A woman in her forties that Vorik recognized as a former instructor for the Sixteen Talons sat down beside Wise. She elbowed him, asked if he'd managed to swing his sword without falling off his dragon yet, and he smiled, appearing relaxed.

Yes, these were all former stormers, so why not relax and trust them?

Vorik did not.

Atilya lifted a platter. "We thank the earth, sun, and moon gods for blessing us with the power to find sustenance."

"We thank the gods," Vorik joined the others gathered around fires in saying the response to the short prayer.

Two older men had sat to his right. One wore a faded black rider's tunic, the leather creased with age, and openly displayed a dragon tattoo on the back of his hand. Like the tunic, it was faded, which usually indicated the bond was no longer active, either because the dragon had died or had, upon deciding its aged rider wasn't an effective warrior anymore, chosen to depart. It happened often with riders who survived enough battles and hunts to live long enough to reach old age. Since dragons had much greater longevity, they could have many riders during their lifetimes.

I haven't gotten a chance to speak privately with Wise, Vorik told Agrevlari, wishing he had the power, as his brother did, to speak telepathically to other riders, not only dragons. *Will you tell him— or have Tonasketal tell him—to be wary of poison?*

One of the male dragons near a nesting dragon stood and growled at Tonasketal. Agrevlari rose to stand at his wing mate's side. Numerous dragon tails went rigid.

You're not picking a fight when you're outnumbered, are you? Vorik asked Agrevlari.

Other than to glance over, the faction members didn't appear that concerned. So far, none of the dragons had shown their fangs or breathed fire.

Tonasketal is flirting with a female that this oaf has decided has a link with him. Never mind that he decided that only in the last ten wingbeats.

I don't suppose I could convince you two to focus on the mission instead of wooing females.

I am not attempting to woo anyone.

How long has it been since you lost yourself in musing ways to seduce Wreylith?

I am not attempting to woo anyone in this cave *while we are outnumbered and possibly in danger.*

Good. The warning for Wise, please?

Tonasketal lowered his head and showed his fangs while growling. Agrevlari's tail went rigid. Was he promising he would help his comrade if necessary?

Vorik sighed.

As Atilya and the others around the fire opened the wine and gin flagons and ate from the platters, Vorik lifted a drumstick from one in front of the older men, opting for that instead of the offering directly in front of him. Atilya was watching him but didn't react in any way to suggest he was foiling her plans. He took a small bite while attempting to make it look hearty.

The former instructor handed a flagon to Wise while cracking another joke about his skills. He smiled and drank the wine. It wasn't a shallow sip but the drink of someone having a rough day and looking forward to some alcohol-induced relaxation.

Did Atilya's eyes sharpen with interest? Or... triumph?

Vorik took it from Wise and pretended to sip. Unlike the cactus wine, it was a rich purple berry wine and quite pungent, its scent easily able to mask lesser smells. After pretending to drink, Vorik set it to the side to keep Wise from imbibing more, at least out of that particular flagon. He hadn't seen anyone else's lips on it. Hopefully, whatever drug Atilya was using wasn't lethal. She wouldn't want to risk hurting her own people.

"You'll be even *more* welcome to spend the night," Atilya said, meeting Vorik's eyes, "if you tell us what use you have for the ore. And an old ceramic vase."

"As I explained," Vorik said, "I'm collecting the items for General Jhiton. For more information, you'll have to invite *him* for dinner."

The flagon he'd set aside was picked up, one of the men taking a drink—or *pretending* to take a drink?—and moved around the fire. Some people passed but others lifted it to their lips, including Atilya. Hm, maybe that one *wasn't* drugged.

"He's the last person I would invite here." Her eyes flared with distaste. Maybe loathing. "He's holding two of my people prisoner, and he killed another. Were you aware, Captain?"

"I remember a few spies being captured last month." Vorik decided to distance himself from his brother, at least while speaking with Atilya. She wasn't yet looking at *him* with hatred. Even so, he had a feeling he would have to find a way to sneak off with the ore in the middle of the night. She wasn't going to give him anything. "Were they not there to observe the tribes and try to gain military intelligence?"

The faction members had been spying for years. Usually, Jhiton merely chased them off when he caught them. Since many faction members had ties to family still in the tribes, he rarely used deadly force, but it had been different when the general had been planning the destruction of the shielders and invasion of Castle and now Harvest Island. He hadn't wanted advance word of that to reach the gardeners, so he'd been harsher with the spies. One person *had* been killed, but only because she'd fought instead of allowing herself to be imprisoned. The others, the last Vorik had heard, were bound and under guard with the Sunchaser Tribe.

"They are—and *were*—stormers," Atilya said, not answering his question. "They left over a disagreement about how to ensure the future of *our* people. They deserved neither death nor imprisonment. Some of the chiefs—and *officers*—have turned into warmongers." The look she pinned him with promised she put Jhiton in that category.

Vorik wouldn't consider his cool and calculating brother a warmonger but admitted Jhiton tended to see military solutions to problems rather than diplomatic ones. Being a lifetime officer in the Sixteen Talons could do that to a person. Though Vorik had always trained hard to make his brother and deceased father proud, he would be open to considering a peaceful solution with the Garden Kingdom, if one could be found. He admitted he'd only recently started thinking along those lines, perhaps because of his interest in a certain smart and sexy princess...

His only answer to Atilya's glare was to smile and say, "So they *were* spies, yes."

"Erivy didn't deserve to die."

"Maybe Erivy shouldn't have sneaked into one of our camps and tried to seduce a colonel's daughter to gain military information."

"I *knew* you knew more than you were suggesting." Atilya scowled at him and waved toward a woman who was currently holding the flagon of berry wine. Though there were others, that specific one kept getting handed around the fire. "And I think you know exactly what you need with that ore."

"What I need to know is if you'll trade anything for it." Vorik watched out of the corner of his eye as the flagon returned to Wise's hand, and nudged him with his elbow.

Wise started to lift it to his lips but halted. He looked toward the dragons. The kerfuffle that had been brewing had deescalated from growls and fang displays to glares, and Tonasketal was looking in Wise's direction. Had the telepathic warning about the flagon finally been delivered?

Atilya was watching them, and her eyes narrowed at Wise's pause. He noticed and lifted it to his lips. From his side, Vorik could tell that he didn't swallow, merely pretending to drink. Good. When Wise handed him the flagon with a slight eye widening, Vorik also feigned a sip before passing it on.

"We would trade as much ore as you like in return for our men —Brolikon and Jarr," Atilya said. "Trusting *they're* still alive."

"They're not being held at headquarters," Vorik said, "so I'm not up to date on their status, but I believe they're still alive. Your female spy wasn't killed in cold blood either, if it matters to you. She resisted capture, tried to take out one of our officers before dying, and then was herself killed in the heat of battle."

"That'll be so comforting to her mate."

Vorik spread his arms. "You sent her to spy. What do you want me to say? You've all but declared war on us."

"We want *peace*, not war."

"Betraying our people—*all* of our people—" Vorik waved to place everyone in the cavern into that category, "—isn't a path toward peace."

"We had to do *something*. Everyone knew the belligerent chiefs and their faithful officers were preparing for war. Now that you've killed thousands of gardeners and destroyed one of their shielders, we may never get the peace that humanity deserves. *All* of humanity."

As she spoke, Vorik glimpsed Wise yawning and swaying slightly. Bloody daggers, had the couple sips of that wine been enough to affect him?

"The gods intended for all humans to be protected on the Garden Kingdom islands from the wrath of the storm god's creations and from the worsening climate," Atilya added.

"Yes, but most of our people chose to leave over the centuries because rule there was too stifling. To think we should be able to go back now..."

"My ancestors were driven out," she snapped. "Not everyone left voluntarily. Some were exiled."

"Because they were criminals, and the exile was considered kinder than death." Vorik couldn't believe he was defending the gardeners of the past. He would have to watch his mouth among his brethren back home, lest he be called a sympathizer. There was, after all, really only *one* gardener that he sympathized with.

"Not *all* were criminals," Atilya said as Wise yawned again and swayed. "My family has passed along its history from generation to generation so I know it well. Some people, like my ancestor, merely spoke their minds, pointing out that the hierarchal system there wasn't fair, with the gods-blessed being treated almost like divinities themselves, and rarely having to do real work, while commoners farmed and fished and supplied all the food that those with magic enjoyed without getting dirt under their nails. Their system hasn't changed much over the years, either, you know."

"Yet you want to return." Vorik yawned, as Atilya watched him intently, save for glances at Wise, realizing he would have to pretend the drug was affecting him too. Before, he'd believed it might induce them to speak the truth, but it seemed it would knock them unconscious. To what end, he didn't know. Would she take their bodies and throw them into the depths of the canyon? Surely, not while their dragons watched. Agrevlari would fight for Vorik's life; he had no doubt.

"We don't want to live under the yoke of the Kingdom, no, but we *do* want access to the fertile lands and an opportunity to grow our own crops and tend our livestock, having enough to feed ourselves and our allies reliably." As she spread an arm toward the dragons, Wise's eyes closed, and he slumped against Vorik.

"Wise?" Vorik slurred his voice as he reached for his officer. He was tempted to turn accusingly toward Atilya and, while yawning, try to indignantly demand if she'd drugged them, but he didn't trust his acting abilities. Instead, he yawned and sagged as he asked, "Wise?" again. "Are you..."

With one final yawn, Vorik slumped against his comrade, trying to relax his muscles and appear unconscious, though being on the ground and surrounded by enemies made him tense. His sword was nearby, so he could grab it and spring up if need be, but he would find out more if Atilya believed she'd knocked *both* of them out.

Growls, talons clacking on rock, and the thump of a tail drifted over from the dragon area.

You are not truly unconscious, correct? Agrevlari asked. *We are taking part in a ruse?*

Yeah. Tell Tonasketal if he's done wooing females. Be indignant but acknowledge that you're outnumbered and shouldn't get in a fight over us.

As you wish. Were you truly in danger, I would fling myself upon our enemies, no matter what the odds.

You're a good dragon.

Yes, I am.

And I might yet be in danger, giving you the opportunity for flinging. We'll see. Vorik heard someone walking close and forced his body to remain relaxed and kept his eyes closed.

"Are they both out?" Atilya asked from halfway around the fire.

Someone shook Vorik's shoulder. One of the men. "Yes."

A snarl and growl sounded. That was Agrevlari putting on a show.

"Will their dragons attack?" the man asked warily.

"We won't kill them," Atilya called toward the dragons. "You may take your lieutenant back with you, and I've a message for him to deliver. You may relay it to him when he wakes up."

The irritated roar that sounded came from Tonasketal.

Dragons didn't care to be manipulated *or* act as messengers.

What message do you presume to give to one of our kind? Agrevlari boomed indignantly into the minds of all present.

"Tell General Jhiton," Atilya said, "that we will trade Captain Vorik for the prisoners of ours that he's been keeping. We won't harm Vorik as long as Jhiton promptly arranges the exchange."

Agrevlari and Tonasketal snarled again.

"Will you help your riders in this way?" Atilya didn't sound worried by the snarls. It wasn't easy to stand up to a couple of dragons, even when one had allies nearby. As mercurial as dragons were, one couldn't always predict their actions.

We will take Lieutenant Wise to the general and relay your message, Agrevlari said, *but if you harm Vorik, I will return and bring this mountain down on your heads.*

"Noted," Atilya said. "If our men are still alive and returned to us, there's no need for Vorik to be harmed. Knowing his reputation, I do plan to keep him drugged while we have him."

Remembering that he was supposedly unconscious, Vorik kept himself from grimacing, but he did not like the idea of someone trying to force wine down his throat. Or would they smear a powder right on his tongue? He wondered what it was. Syla would have known. Where was she now? On the way here? What would the faction do to *her*?

The clack of talons approaching sounded. Tonasketal coming to pick up Wise?

Human hands shifted Vorik away from his lieutenant. The warmth of dragon breath whispered past his cheek as Tonasketal grasped Wise and picked him up.

We go, Agrevlari stated.

Vorik heard the beating of wings and sensed the dragons departing. Unease settled into him, the knowledge that he was by himself among enemies.

A faint scrape sounded. Someone picking up his sword and moving it elsewhere? They would take the amphora too.

"Tie him up, and put him in one of the sleeping areas for now," Atilya said. "Keep his sword elsewhere so he can't grab it if he wakes up. Holok, see what's in that urn."

"How long will he be unconscious?" The male speaker sounded wary. "He's... formidable. I wouldn't want to fight with him, not even with our dragons present."

"I know he is, but that's a potent drug, and he hadn't eaten yet, so it will have hit on an empty stomach. He should be out until dawn. We'll check him later though and force some more into him."

"This is just a musty powder," came a puzzled voice from nearby. The man investigating the amphora. What if he dumped it out? Not only Jhiton but *Syla* would probably punch Vorik if he allowed that to happen.

"I sense... something magical about it." Was that the old man with the dragon tattoo? He might have some lingering power from his bond, especially if it hadn't been dissolved that far in the past.

"Yes." That was Atilya. *Her* bond was fine. One of the dragons roosting on the ore was her ally. "The powder is magical. Just like the ore. Who knows what they're doing with it. I wish he'd told us. Maybe I should have added that to the message, let the general know we'll also trade the items Vorik is hunting in exchange for our people back."

"You offered enough. Vorik is Jhiton's brother. He's valuable. Besides, we may not *want* the warmongers to have these things."

"True. Put that urn out of sight with him. And bind him *strongly*. I wish we had shackles made from that ore."

"I will."

Two men picked up Vorik, and he made his every muscle go limp. *Stay near, Agrevlari,* he called to his dragon. *I may need you when it's time to escape.*

I have no doubt that you will.

I have to figure out how to get a chunk of that ore first. His best bet would be in the middle of the night, while most slept, but chiseling ore from rocks wasn't a quiet endeavor.

That may prove difficult with two dragons roosting on it.

I'll be resourceful.

Will you seduce someone? Agrevlari asked.

Probably not unless one of the female dragons would be amenable.

Neither they nor the available females in their fertile time were interested in Tonasketal.

I'm a lot more charismatic than he is.

True, but you are not anatomically formed to satisfy a dragon.

Alas. I'll find another way.

As he was toted behind a hanging hide to a sleeping area, his wrists and ankles tugged together for binding, Vorik wondered how.

22

As the dragons flew above the forested foothills and angled upward, leaving a brilliant blue sky to soar under gray clouds that grew darker as they neared the Everfrost peaks, Igliana took the lead.

That surprised Syla, and she blinked and put away her book, sensing they had to be getting close to something. Until now, Wreylith had been in the lead and clearly in charge.

"You're letting someone young and perky fly ahead of you?" Syla looked at Teyla and Fel. His face had grown less green so Igliana must have calmed her early-morning exuberance.

She knows the way.

"To... the ore?" When Syla had described the components to Wreylith, the dragon had been indifferent. She certainly hadn't implied that she knew where any could be found.

The ore you seek lies in Scar Peak. She knows of an area where deposits are exposed.

"I've only seen that mountain on maps."

Maps. Wreylith grunted. Or maybe that was a scoff. *Our kind all know where that mountain lies. It has been a meeting point for centuries.*

"Does it or the ore inside have some significance to dragons?"

You will see. You are welcome.

"I'm sure I am."

I chose Igliana on purpose. Wreylith sounded smug.

"Not because you enjoy her youthful enthusiasm?"

I tolerate that.

Syla looked toward her comrades again, wondering if Igliana had told them anything, but they were flying too far away for her to ask. She wished Teyla were sharing Wreylith's back with her. Or even Fel.

Not only would she have liked to share what she was learning about her great-great grandmother, but she felt lonely riding by herself. No, she felt lonely in general. And not without reason. After losing her family and so many colleagues—*friends*—who'd worked at Moon Watch Temple with her, she had few people to confide in. Or just to chat with. Her missions had kept her busy but not so busy that she hadn't noticed the lack, and tears threatened whenever she let herself think about those who'd passed.

Since she still *had* a mission, Syla lifted her spectacles, wiped the moisture out of her eyes, and attempted to focus on it. But, as the dragons soared toward a snow-capped peak that rose higher than those around it, she thought of Vorik. Too bad she had to pit herself against him to get the amphora back—and, ideally, beat him to the ore. A part of her almost wished she'd let him kidnap her. It had been his officer who'd been about to toss her over his shoulder, but she trusted she would have ended up with Vorik. Maybe he could have shown her how to use the juggling balls he'd given her. She couldn't imagine figuring out how to toss them about on her own.

Unfortunately, if she *were* kidnapped, it would be because the stormers wanted to use her against her own people. She couldn't allow that.

Igliana led them around the peak of the mountain, slushy rain falling from dark clouds hanging over the range, and soared into a deep canyon that gouged the slope, running from the peak down its bare side and into the trees at a lower elevation. Presumably, it was the "scar" that had given the mountain its name.

Thunder rumbled as Igliana flew toward a cavern within the canyon. High up on one of the vertical sides, it was large enough for a dragon to fly through. Fel looked around and pulled his crossbow into his lap.

Probably glad to escape the storm, Wreylith followed without hesitation, wings outstretched to glide into the cavern behind Igliana. Though the entrance was high and wide enough for dragons to soar through, Syla ducked her head, the dense rock on all sides feeling as if it were closing in on them. Unless one counted the tunnels under the castle, she hadn't been in many caves in her life.

Surprisingly, the scents of roasting meat wafted to her nose, and they soon flew into illumination provided by campfires, lanterns, and a teal glow from the back of the cavern. Syla blinked. There were many people and several dragons inside.

The humans had claimed a portion of the cavern where the ground was relatively flat. Old mine carts and shovels in one corner suggested some of the area might have been intentionally carved out long ago. The humans living there now had used hanging hides to section off rooms against one wall. Many people sat or stood around the campfires, the scents of roasting meat originating there. With platters and flagons in use, the inhabitants were finishing off a communal meal.

Ignoring that area, Igliana flew straight toward the dragons roosting in the back, some curled on their sides and snoozing and others perched right atop the glowing teal spots.

"Is that..." Syla started.

The teal ore that you seek. Igliana landed, and a larger orange dragon stood, stretched, and ambled toward her. Though male, he looked much like her except for a horn that had been broken off in the past. *And my father,* she added.

Wreylith landed in the center of the cavern, neither getting close to the dragons nor the humans. Clad in leathers and furs, the men and women gazed without surprise toward the newcomers. Some of the fitter individuals gripped bows, but they didn't raise them. Syla spotted a gray-haired woman with black fingerless gloves and shifted uneasily.

We are invited, Wreylith said, *thanks to Igliana. Her parents live here.*

With the... stormers? Syla responded silently since she didn't know if she wanted these people to overhear. She trusted Wreylith would understand her.

I know and care little of humans and how they designate them-selves, Wreylith said, *but Igliana has informed me that these people broke away from the stormer tribes. Supposedly, they seek peace with your kingdom.*

Wait, are these people in the Freeborn Faction? Syla looked again at the gray-haired woman—she was walking toward them. *Or is this the entire faction?*

She estimated sixty or seventy people living in the cavern. She'd thought—or maybe hoped—that the faction was larger than that and had more resources they could bring to bear. Not that she'd managed to arrange a meeting with them to speak of alliances. The messenger she'd sent at the same time as she'd invited the stormer tribes to visit Castle Island for negotiations hadn't known where to start looking for the faction.

Since the gray-haired woman was heading toward them, Syla slid off Wreylith's back. The woman's keen gaze followed her movement, and she stopped and nodded respectfully toward the red dragon before giving Syla her full focus. She'd only glanced at Fel and Teyla as they'd eased off Igliana's back.

"You are Princess Syla," the woman said.

"Yes. Are you— Is this the Freeborn Faction?"

"Yes. I'm a former captain of the Sixteen Talons. Now, my people call me Chieftess, though I don't claim to be a ruler, just an organizer." Despite the words, she had the mien of a leader. "You can call me Atilya."

"Oh. You must be Captain Radmarik's, uhm." Syla almost said *wife*, since he'd used that term, but he'd also suggested their marriage wasn't legal, and when he'd spoken of the romantic encounters he enjoyed, she'd wondered if the stormer woman truly considered him a life partner. "Companion," she finished.

Atilya snorted.

Not sure how to interpret the sound, Syla added, "The one who gives him sugar cane."

"Yes, I like to reward him for enthusiasm under the furs."

"Er, yes."

Apparently, Atilya was going to be as open about discussing sex with a near stranger as Radmarik had been.

"I've heard that's a good idea," Syla added.

"It encourages good behavior and repeat performances." Atilya didn't wink, but she did smile slightly.

Syla had yelled at Vorik instead of rewarding him, but he'd arrived to steal her amphora and kidnap her. He'd deserved it.

"Are you also here for teal ore?" Atilya waved toward the large orange dragon, suggesting Igliana's father as her source.

"I am hoping to acquire some, yes. It's critical to repairing... something that was recently broken." Maybe Syla didn't need to be vague, but she'd just met this woman. She couldn't confide in her.

"Ah, is that what it's for? Repairing a shielder?" Atilya sounded certain of her guess.

"One of them, yes," Syla admitted.

She adjusted her spectacles and noticed Fel and Teyla standing nearby, probably wondering if this was a private chat or if·they should come over.

"You're not what I expected from one of the royal family." Atilya flicked two fingers toward her spectacles, then lowered her gesture to include the rest of Syla. "Your older siblings were all warriors, weren't they? Even your sisters?"

Syla's cheeks warmed at the insinuation that she was lesser. Captain Lesva's words—*insults*—came to mind. Did all female stormers think of Kingdom women as soft and weak? At least those who didn't study swordsmanship and keep themselves heroically fit?

"They were." Syla didn't want to talk about her deceased siblings. She wanted to negotiate for ore—and maybe the help of these people and especially their dragons.

Wreylith had been watching those dragons—maybe she was speaking telepathically with them—but now her head swung around, her eyes glowing golden as they locked onto Atilya. *The human princess has a magical gift greater than typical for your puny kind, and she's proven the ability to use her power to slay an enemy.*

Syla's cheeks flushed further. Normally, she would be delighted to have Wreylith come to her defense, but she didn't want her telling people that she'd *killed* that man. It had been self-defense.

"I'm a healer by training," Syla said as Atilya's eyebrows rose.

"I suppose that would give one the knowledge to kill by many means. Potions, poisons, and... magic?" Atilya's eyebrows climbed further, as if she hadn't contemplated it before, but she didn't scoff or suggest it wasn't possible.

"I've healed hundreds if not thousands of people. I've only... Well, if I have to defend myself, I've recently learned—"

It would be far more advantageous to be the ally of the princess than her enemy, Wreylith said. *She has potential to gain greater ability than her weak eyes and body suggest.*

"It's wonderful when you stand up for me," Syla murmured.

Maybe it had been better when Wreylith hadn't.

I am assisting you in gaining an alliance. The words didn't seem to reach Atilya. *Again, you are welcome. Feel free to add more sheep and horn hogs to what you've already promised me. Many more horn hogs.*

"But does she have the potential to become queen and lead her people?" Atilya's eyebrows had descended, and now she squinted thoughtfully at Syla. "And make decisions regarding who and who is not invited to visit their islands?"

"Right now, I'm on a mission to help my people by returning protection to the Kingdom—to *all* of our islands. After that, I'll deal with those at home who seek to usurp the throne for themselves. I've had to prioritize this mission." Syla winced, expecting Atilya to point out that this had been a bad time to leave, that it would be hard to wrest power back from someone who'd already claimed it.

"Understandable," Atilya said. "One stands a much better chance of surviving the winter if the entire tribe is kept fed and healthy, not only an individual."

"Yes. I do hope to return as soon as possible so that I can put an end to the scheming and plotting and..." And what? Had she decided that she *wanted* the throne? All along, she hadn't thought herself capable, but she'd already admitted that she also didn't want a power-hungry person taking over the Kingdom, someone who might care less about the welfare of the people and more about him or herself. "I'll ensure someone capable and good for the Kingdom is on the throne in the end."

Surprise flickered in Atilya's eyes. "Not you?"

"As I said, I trained to be a healer. And as my parents' youngest, I wasn't educated and groomed for a life in government."

The words felt dishonest when they came out, and she made herself adjust them. "I chose not to be educated and groomed for a life in politics, and, because I was the youngest, my parents allowed that."

"You're still young now. Plenty of time to learn. If you *want* to learn."

"I..." Syla did not but caught herself finishing with, "I'm going to have to consider it. The other options may force me to."

"I didn't even care for the *previous* option. Your queen had no interest in working with our people—or allowing any stormers at all to come ashore, whether we had a link to dragons or not. Those who tried were rounded up and kicked out." Atilya's voice chilled. "Or killed."

Syla wanted to balk at the idea. She'd never heard of stormers being killed unless they'd been there as spies or saboteurs. But she'd skipped as many family dinners as possible and had never asked about Kingdom relations with their people or anything else going on around the islands that hadn't been related to the temples or herbalism.

"King Blaylok was better," Atilya added. "He'd listen to us and wasn't opposed to trade with our people."

"I'm not opposed to that either. I tried to send a message to you to invite you to come for negotiations, but... I don't think my messenger knew where to find you."

"We don't publicize our camps. We don't trust that the tribes wouldn't destroy us if they could." Atilya looked toward the hide flaps forming rooms, acting as walls to hide the contents. "If you *were* to become queen, we would be open to negotiations."

"I don't suppose I could imply I have an alliance with you to assist me in solidifying my place on the throne."

Syla didn't expect Atilya to promise real assistance, but if she wouldn't mind Syla insinuating a link, it could help her. And if the woman truly wanted someone amenable to her cause to lead the Kingdom, maybe she would agree.

But Atilya's eyes narrowed again. "To be worthy of ruling your people, you should be able to claim your throne on your own. *Our* people don't grant leadership by birth. It must be taken through strength and cunning. That is what we respect."

Syla was tempted to point out that the Kingdom had hundreds of thousands of people in it and wasn't a small tribe where everyone knew everyone else's name. It took more than winning a duel to lead—and be allowed to lead. As Fel had pointed out, she needed allies. Cunning would only get her so far, and she didn't even *have* strength.

"I understand your position," she made herself say.

"Should you become the queen on your own, we would negotiate with you. We might even support you in keeping the tribes from hostile actions."

"That would be valuable."

"Yes."

Syla told herself that was at least something. She hadn't expected the faction to help, regardless. Though... "Will you allow me to mine some of your ore for my mission?"

"We have no claim on the ore. You are welcome to it, if you can convince one of the dragons to dismount." Atilya smirked and gestured toward the back of the cavern.

"Why are they roosting on it?"

"I understand it's warm and tingles pleasantly through their scales." Atilya shrugged. "When I put my hand on it, the buzz of magic is almost painful, but skin is thinner and more fragile than scales. It must take firmness to make a dragon tingle."

I am growing curious to sit on that ore, Wreylith said.

She wasn't the only curious one in their party. Teyla had left Fel's side to wander the cavern with a journal and pencil as she alternately looked at the stone walls and scribbled on the pages. Some of those walls had faded paintings from a long-past era.

More interested in the *ore* from a long-past era, Syla said silently to Wreylith, *Why don't you see if you can bump one of those males aside, claim a spot, and let me carve out a chunk while you're enjoying the tingle?*

I will consider that.

"Thank you for allowing us to mine some." Reminded of her competition, Syla said, "Someone else may arrive looking for ore. Captain Vorik." She was surprised he hadn't found the cavern first, but his dragon presumably wasn't related to any of the dragons here. "I would consider it a great favor if you *didn't* allow him to mine any."

"He's already been here." Atilya smiled tightly. "And he will *remain* here."

Syla stared, alarmed by the triumphant gleam in the woman's eyes. Was Atilya implying that she'd killed Vorik?

Atilya spread her arm, pointing to one of the rooms created by hides, the flaps on all sides down so that they couldn't see inside.

"He's not tied up back there." It wasn't a question. Syla was certain *ropes* couldn't bind Vorik. She'd seen him break metal shackles before. And rip iron bars out of windows.

"He's bound and unconscious."

"Unconscious?" Syla thought of Candles of Serenity but hadn't caught the scents of eucalyptus and dragonquell in the air along with the woodsmoke and meat smells. Of course, there were many substances that could act as a sedative on a human.

Or, might he have been knocked out in battle with a greater warrior? Or—more likely—a dragon? She hadn't seen many men or women who could best Vorik in battle.

"Yes, and he should remain so throughout the night. Dayvak buds are very potent."

"Oh, you fed him a drug." Familiar with the powder made

from the dried flowers, Syla looked toward the platters of meat. Had they invited him to share the dinner but tainted it?

Poor Vorik. People kept knocking him unconscious. Understandably, since he was exceedingly dangerous when alert.

"Normally, we prefer honorable means over treachery," Atilya said, "but I've seen him fight. It wouldn't have gone well if I'd pitted even my best warrior against him. I was also hoping he'd divulge more about what his people are up to if we pretended amiability and gave him food." Her shrug suggested that hadn't happened.

No, Vorik was good at keeping secrets.

"What about the rider who was with him?" Syla asked. "And their dragons?"

"We sent them back to their headquarters to let their general know we have Vorik as a hostage. The Sixteen Talons captured some of our people last month—the ones who were attempting to spy and would have, as it happens, learned about the attack on your kingdom ahead of time if they'd been successful. One of them was killed outright." Anger and fury flashed in Atilya's eyes. "Others yet live, or so we're told. I *hope* we can trust Vorik's word. If they're alive, we've proposed a trade. And, from what I gather, you wouldn't mind if Vorik were stuck here for a time while you complete your mission."

"I wouldn't mind that at all."

If they wanted to trade Vorik in a prisoner exchange, they shouldn't hurt him. Syla had no qualms about leaving him behind, though she would have to find that amphora. If she could get it and the ore and take off for the storm god's laboratory... By the gods' blessings, was it possible something was finally going her way? All she had to do was get the last component. If only she were sure that she and her allies had the power necessary to infiltrate that laboratory.

"It takes magic to extract the ore from the surrounding rock," Atilya said, "but it looks like your dragon might handle that."

Wreylith was stalking toward one of the males. His head came up, and he appeared more interested in her approach than threatened by it. Syla had no idea what allure Wreylith had, beyond the power that even she could sense, but she undeniably had a quality that intrigued the opposite sex.

"She's not *my* dragon, I assure you," Syla said. "She's deigning to work with me in exchange for a somewhat ridiculous amount of livestock that I've agreed to acquire for her."

"That's not why she verbally—telepathically—defended you and said you have potential." Atilya gazed thoughtfully at Syla.

Lightning flashed outside the cavern, brightening the interior for an instant, as Syla considered the words. "I think she's hoping I'll increase the horn-hog allotment."

"Dragons do work up a big appetite when they're flying riders around the world." Atilya extended a hand toward the campfires. "Will you have a meal with us? And rest here tonight? The weather is turning dark, and it takes time for even a dragon to cut teal ore away from its rock bed. What's exposed was like that when we arrived. We think human miners long ago excavated the stone around it, only to find that they lacked the magic necessary to remove it. The rock around it is hardened by the ore's magical presence, so it's not as easy as simply chiseling it out."

"A meal sounds wonderful as long as it's not drugged." Syla smiled at Atilya to make it a joke, but she wondered if it was one. She'd never wronged the woman, but she doubted Vorik had either. And Atilya had as much as admitted she'd held a grudge against Syla's mother.

"We'll give you a portion treated only with spices. Though we won't go to war with the Kingdom on your behalf to help you claim the throne, we also won't hinder you on your quest. We'd *prefer* that someone who will think kindly of our faction gain power there." Atilya nodded firmly to her.

Syla found herself wanting to believe the woman, especially after Captain Radmarik had helped her, but vowed to take only dainty portions from the platters—and only after she'd witnessed others eating from the same dishes.

More than eating, she wanted to figure out where the amphora had been stashed, and she looked around the camp. Her eye snagged on something familiar. A gargoyle-bone sword. Was that Vorik's weapon? It leaned against the rusty mining equipment, as if tossed aside as garbage—or something nobody would need in the future.

"Chieftess Atilya?" Syla asked. "What will you do with Captain Vorik if his people *won't* agree to a prisoner exchange?"

"Don't worry. We won't let him go to harry you on your quest."

"That's a relief," Syla said, though it wasn't why she'd asked.

"One way or another, we'll make sure he doesn't trouble you again." Face grim, Atilya walked away.

Dread sank into Syla's stomach. Would they kill him? Simply because he'd dared fly into their cave looking for ore? Or, more likely, because he was General Jhiton's brother and, as many others had said, his right-hand man?

Syla followed Atilya to the campfires, but she had lost her interest in eating.

23

As Vorik lay on his side, little light penetrating the hide flaps creating three walls of the room that he'd been placed in, he waited impatiently for voices and sounds of people moving about to die down. Not long ago, one of Atilya's warriors had come to check on him, and he'd continued to feign unconsciousness.

Hours earlier, Syla had arrived with her allies, and he'd done his best to listen to what she and Captain Atilya had been discussing, but without Agrevlari nearby to facilitate eavesdropping, he hadn't caught much of it. Only that she was being invited to take ore—he'd had no trouble sensing Wreylith breathing fire to incinerate the rock around the impervious stuff. The men who'd dragged Vorik into this room had brought the amphora with him, setting it and his pack near the rock wall. Only his sword had been taken elsewhere. He would have to find it before he left, then catch up with Syla.

Or would he need to catch up with her? He sensed Wreylith and that orange dragon here with the others of their kind, so Syla ought to still be here. Would she think to ask about the amphora?

If she came in to take it, what would he do? It would depend on whether she came alone or was accompanied by others.

Vorik flexed his shoulders. He'd already broken the bonds his Freeborn captor had tied around his wrists and ankles. They should have known that such wouldn't hold him, but they'd probably expected to keep him unconscious with that drug.

Are you still out there, Agrevlari? Vorik asked, trying to use his power to make his words travel farther to reach the dragon.

I am on the next mountain over, came Agrevlari's distant reply. *I'll fly over there when you're ready to escape, but I had to hide far enough away that I wouldn't be sensed. Dragons came out to check and see if we were lingering in the area.*

All right. I'm waiting for most of the camp to be asleep so I can sneak out with the shielder components.

You've acquired the ore?

Not yet, but I will. It occurred to him that stealing what Syla's dragon had excavated would be easier than acquiring a piece on his own. But his honor threatened to crumble at the thought of absconding with something else that she'd found. He touched the amphora. Already, he felt like a thief for taking that. Even if he was following orders, his actions were not honorable.

Vorik closed his eyes, wishing he could find another solution. There was a part of him that wanted to gather all three components and give them to Syla. He could even return to the Kingdom with her to help her claim the throne that was rightfully hers.

But what would he tell General Jhiton? And all their tribal leaders?

When the gardeners returned a working shielder to Harvest Island and, with their vastly superior numbers, were able to drive out his people, the stormers would lose all they'd fought for. Yes, they'd claimed some food that would help see them through the coming winter, but what about the winter after that? And the one after that?

The flap stirred, and Vorik sensed someone coming in. A soft tick sounded as something hard tapped the stone floor. He half-opened one eye. In the dim light, the person was a shadow, but he or she carried a long slender white object. That was his gargoyle-bone blade. Had someone come to ensure he didn't wake up in the morning?

A strange scent came in with the person, stirred by the flap as it closed. Something astringent. *Another* drug? Or a poison this time?

When the person stepped close, crouching down to reach for him, Vorik surged into action.

As he grabbed a wrist, yanking the intruder down to him and knocking the blade aside, the startled gasp of a woman reached his ears. Since more than half the faction people were female, that didn't stop him from wrapping an arm around the intruder and turning her so that her back was to his chest and he could flatten a hand over her mouth to keep her from crying out.

His hand bumped something on the woman's face. Only as he decided the curves pressed against him were familiar did he realize it was the frame of a pair of spectacles that had fallen down her nose.

"Syla?" he whispered, loosening his grip over her mouth. He didn't let her go completely, reminded that they were at cross-purposes. She must have come for the amphora. But why would she have brought his sword and whatever was making the astringent scent? "You smell funny," he added as she nodded.

"You're not a delight either," she whispered back. Most of the camp might be asleep, but the hides wouldn't do much, if anything, to muffle their voices. "Haven't you bathed at any point in this journey?"

His arms loosened of their own accord, and he caught himself smiling. "Sorry. The rainforest rivers are full of fanged fish that like the taste of human flesh."

"I've heard."

"Had I known you would sneak in and fling yourself upon me in the middle of the night, I would have scrubbed my armpits with the ropes my captors used to bind me."

"I'll wager those ropes are lying on the ground, far from your wrists and ankles where they belong. Also, I didn't *fling* myself. You yanked me down on top of you."

"Yes. That was rude of me."

"Very."

"You're still here." He'd loosened his grip enough that she could have squirmed free. Instead, once he'd removed his hand from her mouth, Syla had relaxed against him. Her weight and warmth made him want to tighten his grip again, this time in a snuggling embrace rather than a restraining one. "Perhaps my aroma isn't as distasteful as you implied it is."

"*You* aren't as distasteful as you should be." She sighed and leaned her head back against his shoulder, her soft hair brushing his cheek.

His nerves lit up, desire flaring to life, and he decided snuggling wasn't *exactly* what he wanted to turn his embrace toward. "I've never found you distasteful. You're quite lovely. Astringent scents notwithstanding."

"I brought something to wake you from the drugged stupor I was led to believe you'd be in until morning."

"You came to wake me? Not take the amphora?"

"I'd planned to do both. The latter should have been my only priority, but the chieftess said that if your general doesn't respond favorably to her proposed prisoner exchange, they might... do something else with you."

It touched him that she cared, that she'd come to save him, and he turned his face to rest it against her hair and kiss the side of her head. "If my enemies want to kill me, you should let them."

"Oh, I know."

He slid a hand along her side, wishing they were in a more private place so they could enjoy each other's company. Instead, he needed to grab the amphora, find and steal the ore she'd acquired, and depart. That would be a horrible way to reward her for her coming to save his life, and he didn't want to do any of it. He would much rather reward her in a way that made her cry out in pleasure.

"Don't get too relaxed and amorous," Syla warned, though she'd turned to facilitate his hands' explorations instead of moving away from him. "I've come with a plan that involves attempting to manipulate you."

"Do tell." Vorik trailed his fingers up her side to find the warm curve of her breast through her clothing.

"I was hoping you'd be grateful to me for waking you up and would agree to join forces with us and help us get into the storm god's laboratory. If the scrolls are correct, what we'll face in there may be more dangerous than gargoyles, and..." She paused before adding with audible reluctance, "we wouldn't have survived those if you hadn't shown up."

"The world is a dangerous place. My people have a lot more experience surviving in it."

"So you know that dragons and explosives are required."

"Absolutely." The idea of flying away from Scar Peak with Syla and working *with* her to complete this journey rather than against her had great appeal. He *wanted* to be her ally. But... "What would you propose to happen afterward, if we were successful and stood with all three shielder components between us?"

Vorik stroked her gently, following her curves, wishing they could remove their clothing and fully enjoy each other's company.

"Then..." Syla turned slightly, pressing her breast more fully into his hand, as if drawn by her yearning for him.

He smiled a little smugly at the knowledge that she wanted him as much as he wanted her. But it was leading his thoughts in a dangerous direction, and he needed to be careful here. If he made a deal, he would be honor-bound by it.

"Then, unless you come to your senses and *give* me the amphora so that my aunt can repair what your people appallingly and savagely destroyed, we would dissolve our alliance. At that point, we could each try to escape with the components, doing whatever is necessary to aid our people."

Since Vorik needed someone with a moon-mark to get into the laboratory, and there might be dangers inside that would threaten even a powerful rider, combining forces made sense. But it wouldn't be any easier to betray Syla after they'd worked together than it was now.

"Your proposal intrigues me," Vorik said when she lifted her face toward him and rested her hand on his chest. "Is there any chance that, in the end, you'd attempt to seduce me and knock me out with scented candles rather than commanding your dragon allies to attack me and mine?"

"I can't command Wreylith to do anything."

"And yet she is here helping you. And has recruited another dragon too. Since I've lost my lieutenant and his dragon, you'd have me outnumbered."

"Yes." She didn't sound bothered by that.

"In addition, you have your cousin and your bodyguard. He would happily leap on me with his mace."

"That's an idea that doesn't alarm you in the least."

"He's not a bad warrior, especially for someone of his age."

"But you've defeated him every time he's tried to get the best of you. When it comes to the *humans* in my party, you don't have a lot to worry about." Her fingers curled, kneading his chest through his clothing. A fresh tingle of heat ran through him, arousing him further, making him want to kiss her.

He lifted his own fingers to brush her hair, then rub the back of her neck, even as his other hand continued to stroke her breast.

The way she shifted into his grip, pressing closer, promised she was aroused too. If they escaped the cave and journeyed together, might they have an opportunity for a private encounter before reaching their final destination? Before having to battle each other for the shielder components?

"It's the dragons in your party that concern me most," Vorik murmured, "though I haven't managed to defeat *you* yet either."

"Because I'm such a strong and capable warrior," Syla said with a snort. "All the people I meet remark upon it."

"You *are* strong and capable." He kissed her, wanting... what he couldn't have. Not here. He *shouldn't* want it with her ever. Reluctantly, he drew back his lips.

"I did consider that maybe I could seduce you while Fel sneaked away with the components," she whispered.

The admission shouldn't have made him hard—*harder*—but it did. Oh, how he wanted to let that scenario play out. As long as those candles weren't involved.

"I might let you," he whispered.

"Seduce you? Or have my bodyguard steal away the components?"

Vorik hesitated, tempted to lie, to let her believe what she probably *wanted* to believe. But his honor forced his tongue to speak the truth. "As much as I want you to succeed and become the queen your people need, I can't let myself knowingly fail my mission. That battle over the whaling ship was... bad enough. I have to do my best to..."

"Prove yourself worthy?" There was a wryness in her tone.

Had someone suggested *she* needed to do that? Before becoming queen?

"I thought I'd done that long ago, but I *am* feeling the need to redeem myself in the eyes of my people. I also trust... I trust Jhiton with my life—and our people's future. Whenever I've doubted him in the past, it turned out that I was silly to do so. I regret that his plans are at odds with your plans and that you..." Vorik sighed and stroked her cheek, relieved that she didn't turn away from his touch. He wouldn't blame her if she did. She *should*.

He had a feeling she had a plan to ensure *she* walked away with the shielder components in the end. He knew it wasn't personal, but she would do anything for her people. No, that wasn't quite true. She wouldn't kill him or even stand aside and let another end his life for her.

"I understand that your brother raised you after your father died," Syla said, "but you may think more highly of him than you should."

"That's possible."

"Especially if he's the one who wants you to kidnap me." She rubbed his chest through his tunic as she spoke, as if her mind wanted to argue with him but her body wanted other things. *Him*.

"Maybe I shouldn't admit it, especially since I'm enjoying you fondling my chest and want you to fondle other certain parts, but I came upon the kidnapping thought myself after Wise figured out we'd need a moon-mark to get into the laboratory. I realized we'd either need you or your cousin, but you weren't amenable to us taking either."

"I was not, no. Your people *already* kidnapped Teyla and used her for her moon-mark, then left her unconscious on the ground."

Instead of her hand drifting lower, as he'd been fantasizing about, Syla drew away and shifted off him. She didn't retreat fully but lay on her back next to him.

"I wasn't a part of that decision," he said.

"I know."

"I will point out that they could have left her worse than unconscious."

Syla turned a sour look toward him. Maybe that hadn't been helpful to add on.

"Kidnapping aside," Vorik said, "if you feel you'll be in danger and that assassins will harry you and it's not safe for you to remain in the Kingdom—or if you simply pine for me whenever I'm gone and fantasize about being in my company—

Her snort wasn't that flattering.

"—the general said you could come back with me and join our people."

"With the shielder components?" Syla asked dryly.

"When he said that, we didn't yet know that you'd be sent to acquire them. I think even if you bested me and got them home, you could then join us after the fact."

Syla didn't snort again or scoff, but she only thought about the words for a moment. "Even if I believed that to be an earnest invitation, and it turned out I had to flee the Kingdom for my life, I wouldn't fit in among your people. I'm... Let's just say that your Captain Lesva's unflattering description of me has come to mind often."

Vorik winced. "That *wouldn't* be everyone's opinion. She's abrasive."

"A lot of your people seem to be."

"We've had to learn to be tough. It's hard to survive in our world if you're not. But *many* of our people would value a healer. Especially a gods-gifted healer who uses magic and can knit bones back together in minutes instead of weeks. The magic that a select few of us get from our dragon bonds doesn't turn us into healers. We're stuck with mundane bandages and potions and hope."

"Moon-marked people are rare in the Garden Kingdom too, and few of them become healers. The magic always works best when it's aligned with a person's interests and passions."

"Are you making a further argument for why my people would adore you?"

That prompted another snort.

"We're wounded *often*," Vorik said. "We need you."

"That I believe. Is that why your general said I could join you?" Syla sounded skeptical that the invitation had been in earnest.

"I know that's part of it, even if he didn't explicitly say so, but I also think... He knows I've developed feelings for you and am conflicted about these missions."

"You think he cares that much about your *feelings* toward a woman?"

"Syla, I'm amazing. *Many* people care for me that much."

"Many? Really?"

"My brother, my dragon, and you. At least three. That's *many*."

"I see."

His mood lightened by their banter, Vorik couldn't keep from turning onto his side and snuggling close to her again. Even beyond the wonderful sex they'd had in that cave, he enjoyed her company.

"I agree to your proposition," he said.

It wasn't wise—had he been there, Jhiton would have been the first to say she had tricks ready to deploy—but Vorik needed her to get into the laboratory anyway. Better to have her come of her own free will than to piss her off by kidnapping her or her cousin.

"Working together until we get the final component?" Syla asked. "And then battling it out with honor to determine who gets to take the pieces home?"

"The seduction scenario holds more appeal for me than you springing upon me with a dragon."

"You've suggested you wouldn't be lulled into letting my bodyguard sneak off with the components just because my mouth was on yours."

"I've said that." Vorik found her hand in the dark and drew it back to his chest, then kissed her, stroking her with his tongue, attempting to instill in her a longing for him that would keep her at his side without need for kidnapping. "Whether it proves true or not is questionable. As you saw once before, my *mind* isn't always the thing ruling my actions."

He guided her hand lower, wanting her to know what kind of effect she had on him. And, he admitted, simply wanting her to touch him. And she did, fingers lightly tracing him through his trousers, as she returned his kiss.

Maybe she was calculating the odds of successfully distracting him once they had all the components. He should have cared more about the possibility than he did. He caught himself shifting over to lie atop her, pressing his chest to hers and his groin into her hand as their kiss deepened.

They needed to slip out of here, not make noises that would alert the faction people camped all around to the fact that he was awake—*very* awake—but her touch electrified him. It filled him with passion—with lust—and she tasted so good, her lips erotic and eager against his. He'd been joking less than he wished about his body ruling over his mind at times, and he was so drawn to her. To the woman who kept proving her loyalty to him, trying to save his life, even though she had every reason not to. Why she cared, he didn't know, but everything about her made him want her.

Syla took her hand from him and pressed it against his shoulder. He growled, not wanting to stop kissing her, his lust threatening to knock wisdom completely on its ass, but she turned her lips away.

"Not here, Vorik," she whispered. No, she *panted*. She was as much into their touches and kisses as he, and that only made him want her more. "The faction doesn't know... I'm making deals with you... They want..."

"I know what they want," he said, his voice raspy with desire.

"It's dangerous for you to stay here, to be caught awake. I don't want to be the reason."

Gods, she was looking out for him again. He couldn't help

himself and slid his hand around her head, fingers pushing through her lush hair, and kissed her again. Her grip tightened on his shoulder, not pushing him away but keeping him close, and she rocked up into him, as conflicted as he. Wanting to be with him as much as he wanted her.

If only—

"Did you hear that?" someone asked groggily from a nearby room.

Vorik pulled back, his heart pounding.

Syla released him, pushing him away, and she rolled to her hands and knees. Taking a deep breath, he attempted to pull himself together, though the thought of springing upon her and grabbing her from behind swept into him. He shook his head. He wasn't a savage animal, damn it.

With that thought, he managed to grab his sword and stand up. He offered a hand to help her to her feet, but she reached for the amphora instead of him. If he hadn't heard voices murmuring nearby, he would have laughed at her determination. Maybe it was unwise, and he would be made a fool in the end, but he looked forward to completing this adventure with her.

24

DO YOU HAVE THE ORE, WREYLITH? SYLA ASKED IN HER MIND, HOPING the dragon was paying attention to her thoughts.

She was creeping away from the campfires with Vorik so close behind her that she imagined she could feel the heat of his body. She could certainly still feel the heat of her *own* body, her need lingering, longing to be satisfied. But she tried to quell those thoughts—and her desire—especially since Wreylith would have snarky comments.

Of course. It is my patience that I've almost lost, not the ore. Igliana and your comrades wait at the cave mouth, and I've had to endure the inept flirtations of horny male dragons who don't know that night is a time for sleeping.

I'm sorry. Thanks to the teal glow that emanated from the back of the cavern, Syla could make out Wreylith's form near the base of the cliff under the entrance tunnel.

A horny male of your own kind follows close behind you.

Yes, that's, uhm, part of my plan. Syla groped for a way to request that Wreylith carry Vorik out of the cavern with her. She hadn't asked—funny how she'd gotten distracted back there—but assumed Agrevlari had gone back with the other dragon and rider to report on Vorik's prisoner status.

Some prisoner. Every time she thought he'd been rendered helpless, he was simply lying in wait for an opportunity to spring.

When you spoke of retrieving the amphora, Wreylith said, *I did not know you would also return with him.*

He's agreed to help me in the storm god's laboratory. In case you dragons aren't able to enter it, I'll need a powerful ally.

It is likely to be well guarded by some of his eternal creations, yes. And your current allies were insufficient for warding off gargoyles, some of his more basic of minions.

Yes. Syla was glad Wreylith didn't point out that *she* had been even more insufficient at warding them off.

For a puny human, that one is powerful and a capable warrior. Bringing him is a wise decision, but since he desires what you desire, you must be ready for him to betray you after the goals have been achieved.

I'm going to betray him first. Syla hadn't figured out exactly how yet, especially since Vorik would be ready for any attempt at seduction—they'd discussed it openly, after all—but she would come up with something. She had to.

Excellent, Wreylith said.

Syla smiled sadly as she reached the dragon's side, wishing betrayal needn't be involved.

Vorik stopped close, touching her shoulder with his hand, as if he longed to continue what they'd started. She did, too, and caught herself stepping back into him, but that would have to wait. All it would take was one of the dragons noticing that a prisoner was leaving, and it could alert the whole camp.

As if to act as a further deterrent, Wreylith swung her big head down to look at them, her golden eyes glowing slightly.

"Will she carry me as well?" Vorik asked. "Or do I need to start climbing out of here?"

He sounded like he expected that, but he remained close. Or Syla did. Their bodies were both distracted by each other tonight.

Wreylith? Syla picked up her pack, which was waiting by the dragon's foreleg, a bundle of ore now wrapped and tied to it. *Will you carry both of us to the next destination?*

If I allow him to ride until his dragon can reclaim him, Wreylith said, *you will* not *fornicate on my back.*

Syla's cheeks heated, but the tingling magic of the ore seeped through the fabric, and that distracted her from her embarrassment. *Of course not. That would be... weird.*

And insulting to the dragon beneath you. Stormer riders have done it, and their domesticated pet dragons have allowed it. I cannot imagine the indignity. I would not mate with a male while a rider was attached to me.

I'm glad to hear that. I think I'd have a hard time staying on if you did.

Undoubtedly. Dragons mate very vigorously.

"Are you discussing whether she'll let me ride with you?" Vorik held out his arms, offering to hold the components for Syla.

"We're discussing... something." Syla didn't accept his offer, instead tying the amphora to her pack. Carrying everything would be awkward, especially if they had to walk later, but she wouldn't hand over the components unless it was an emergency. "I think you can climb up."

With his pack and sword secured, Vorik sprang atop Wreylith's back, as if leaping more than twice the height of a horse was an easy feat. Syla didn't know if she could even *climb* up there. It wasn't as if scales came with handholds. So far, dragons had grabbed her in their mouths and tossed her onto their backs, but that wasn't pleasant.

Could she use her power to turn tendrils of magic into foot and handholds? She wasn't certain she could pull her weight up even with that assistance.

Vorik, leg hooked over Wreylith's broad back, lowered himself to extend a hand. She could just reach it. He pulled her up effortlessly, as if she were the most slender of princesses. He turned, angling her so that she came down behind him, and moved his pack to rest in front of him.

"I'm afraid if we rode the other way, I wouldn't be able to keep my hands off you," he murmured.

"Did you hear Wreylith's comment about fornication?" Syla wondered how much Wreylith had shared with him.

"I did not. I suppose she wasn't in favor of it."

"Not on her back, no."

Wreylith sprang into the air, and Syla flattened a hand to her scales, sending her power into the dragon to secure her hold. She wrapped her other arm around Vorik.

"In other places?" he asked with amusement.

"I don't think she objects in general to us having relations." Her cheeks flushed again as she remembered Wreylith's approval that Syla had drawn a powerful mate to kneel and satisfy her needs.

"No?" Vorik asked. "I may be starting to like her."

They flew into the tunnel, Igliana's outline with her two riders visible in the entrance ahead of them.

"Even though her magnificence prompted Agrevlari to attack your general's dragon?" Syla asked.

"Even though." Vorik somewhat brazenly patted Wreylith on the shoulder.

She growled.

He laughed softly and lifted his hand. "She may not yet like me."

"She considers you less puny than most humans."

"I'm honored by her deep regard."

Syla also laughed, relief seeping into her as they flew into the canyon without any alerts going up in the camp. Her relief was short-lived, for when she looked back, a lookout stood on the cliff above the cavern entrance, someone silhouetted against the cloudy night sky.

Chieftess Atilya? Or someone she'd put out as a scout?

Maybe it didn't matter. They were flying away with Igliana. If she hadn't yet informed the other dragons of the situation, she surely would in the morning. Either way, Atilya would soon learn that Syla and Vorik had flown out of their camp on the same dragon. As allies.

Syla didn't know what the ramifications would be, but, at the least, Atilya would be irked that Syla had taken the prisoner she'd wanted to trade for her own people. Atilya hadn't promised assistance, regardless, so maybe it wouldn't matter, but Syla worried she might have alienated someone who could have been a powerful ally. The odds of her claiming the throne and leading her people to a better future seemed worse than ever.

If Syla ever got the chance, maybe she could explain to Atilya that Vorik could have left any time he'd wanted, something that became doubly evident when a familiar dragon flew out from behind the next mountain top. Agrevlari. He didn't get too close to Wreylith or Igliana, merely matching their pace as they flew east, toward the desert.

The air dried and warmed as the dragons spent the morning flying across the mountains. By afternoon, they soared over the desert, and bright sun blazed down upon them. Though Vorik had traveled over the mountains numerous times in his life, he didn't know where any abandoned laboratories were and was content to let Wreylith lead the way without input from him. Or was it the orange dragon who knew the location? They were flying side by side with Agrevlari remaining far enough back that he wouldn't risk irritating the females.

Had I known you would remain on Wreylith's back and did not need me, Agrevlari said, *I would have continued snoozing in the cave I found.*

We flew through the night, and you haven't ventured close enough for me to jump onto your back, Vorik replied, eyeing tall cactuses below, their arms stretched toward the sky, thorns lining their green and gray flesh. Among them were countless other varieties of shorter and squatter cactuses—everything from bush shapes to spiky grass-like clumps to a sprawling ground-cover species with prickly pads that formed meandering patches across the pale, dusty earth. The tall many-armed varieties were most distinctive.

Had I risked Wreylith's ire and done so, would you have jumped over to me? One of Agrevlari's eyes rotated toward Vorik—no, toward Syla who was riding behind him.

The last Vorik had peeked back, she'd been snoozing, her cheek against his back, her spectacles hanging on a strap around her neck. When they'd mounted the red dragon, it had been wise of him to arrange Syla *behind* him, instead of between his legs, a very intimate position that would have been on the excruciating side after their arousing kisses and touches in the camp. Since Wreylith wouldn't likely have humored them with a stop so they could get *more* intimate, he wouldn't have had a release. Of course, having Syla pressed up against him from behind hadn't been without stimulation, either, but after hours of riding and dozing, his body had settled down and accepted, however grudgingly, that a sexual encounter wasn't on the horizon.

I admit I haven't minded riding over here. The grin he directed at Agrevlari might have been lecherous, not that the dragon would recognize it as so.

To be so close to the magnificent Wreylith would be appealing.

Agrevlari sighed into his mind and turned his gaze toward her head.

Yes, your dragon *is the one I'm enjoying being in contact with.*

Wreylith was flying straight and not looking back at them. More often, she glanced over at the young orange dragon as they partook in some conversation or another. They seemed to know where they were going, which surprised Vorik, since Wise hadn't mentioned figuring out more than that the storm god's laboratory was in the Dire Desert.

On the orange dragon's back, Sergeant Fel was alternately eyeing the cactus fields below and the route ahead, red-rock formations rising in the distance. Surprisingly, he hadn't glared over at Vorik that often. The woman riding behind him, Syla's cousin, Teyla, was perusing an atlas while she rode, one hand gripping Fel for support and one attempting to keep the pages from flapping wildly in the wind. Maybe she was the one directing the dragons?

"Are you awake, Syla?" Teyla called over.

Behind Vorik, Syla stirred, affixing her spectacles above her nose. "Off and on."

"I've been chatting with our delightful dragons."

"Wreylith has been delightful?" Syla asked.

"I've mostly been chatting with Igliana. Apparently, the Freeborn Faction spent a lot of time in the desert last winter, and she's hunted all throughout this area. She's seen a rock formation in a canyon that has runes on it and thinks there *might* be a spot where someone with a moon-mark could touch it."

"Is that where we're going now?" Syla rested a hand on Vorik's shoulder and peered past him.

"Igliana hasn't heard anything about laboratories of the gods, but it seems like a good place to start the search."

I am aware of the area, Wreylith spoke into their minds. *I have been all over the world and seen many things.*

Vorik remembered Agrevlari suggesting that the red dragon was specifically not old but mature, having lived through many centuries.

Long ago, Wreylith continued, *the desert all around those rock formations ahead was known as the storm god's playground. To this day, some of his magic affects the nearby flora and fauna.*

"That sounds promising," Syla murmured.

Since her hand remained pleasantly on his shoulder, Vorik rested his own on it. For encouragement.

She shifted her grip to link her fingers with his.

"I forgot to thank you for wanting to rescue me from my captors," Vorik said.

"You did that with your lips."

"Not as thoroughly as I would have liked."

"I'd be open to more thoroughness later."

"Before or after you seduce me?" Vorik asked.

"*During* might be the logical time for lip play."

"True. But I had hoped..." He looked over his shoulder at her. "I would enjoy being with you when it's *not* part of our mission and neither of us is angling for something."

Syla smiled sadly and brushed the side of his neck with her fingers. "I would enjoy that too."

"Yes. I'd ensure you would."

"I'd call you cocky, but my experience thus far indicates..."

"Accuracy in my statement?"

Syla bit her lip, and were her cheeks a little pink? "Yeah."

Her gaze lowered to his mouth, and she leaned forward, as if drawn to kiss him. Anticipation thrummed through Vorik, but Wreylith tilted and flew sharply lower to the ground.

You'll note magical flora below, the dragon stated, inadvertently —or maybe *advertently*—stopping anything that might lead to fornication on her back.

They flew over a clump of spiky pink cactus with giant purple pods on the tips. From their height and distance, Vorik couldn't tell if they were magical, but they were like nothing else he'd seen in the desert and had an alien aspect to them. An animal that looked like a cross between an antelope and a wyvern ran off as the dragons flew overhead. He'd also never seen a creature like that before.

Few people or animals—or even dragons—are drawn to the storm god's playground, Wreylith continued. *The prey is stringy, tough, clawed, venom-possessing, and sometimes has a strange taint to its flesh that makes it unappealing.*

My parents always told me not to fly far into the rock formations, Igliana said. *There are no rivers and few oases where dragons might quench their thirst.*

Then how did you gain knowledge of the formation to which you lead us?

I didn't always obey my parents.

You can imagine how surprised I am.

I'm sure you disobeyed your elders once or twice, Auntie Wrey.

"Auntie?" Vorik asked.

"Apparently, they're related," Syla said, "though more distantly than that term would imply."

"Huh."

With Igliana leading the way, the dragons angled toward one of the red-rock formations, a fat pillar with a wide, flat platter at the top. Beyond it, the ground sloped down into a deep box canyon, with nearly vertical rock walls on three sides. A carpet of flowering bush-shaped cactuses stretched across the floor, save for a few animal paths that meandered through them. Maybe the dragons were wrong, and there was an oasis somewhere back there. Something had to provide water to the animals they'd seen.

Agrevlari's head lifted, and he turned enough to look back the way they'd come.

Vorik didn't think much of it until he spoke a few minutes

later. *Numerous Sixteen Talons dragons and riders are passing through the mountains. I heard from Zandelek.*

That was one of his wing mates who had a long telepathic range and could sense other dragons from farther off than typical, even for their powerful kind.

"Why are they passing through the mountains?" Vorik asked, then repeated the question telepathically, realizing Agrevlari was far enough away that he might not hear.

Syla stirred, looking curiously at Vorik. Had Agrevlari not sent the information to all of them?

I thought most of our warriors were heading to Harvest Island to help capture it, Vorik added silently to the dragon.

I believe many went across the sea to join Captain Lesva, but these are traveling to Scar Peak to rescue you.

"Oh." Vorik slumped and rubbed his face. He hadn't considered that Wise returning with Atilya's message about a prisoner exchange would prompt his people to respond with force. He'd assumed that Agrevlari would relay to Wise's dragon that Vorik had *let* himself be captured, but maybe he should have composed more of a message to send along. Not that relaying messages through dragons always worked well. They often only heard and remembered what mattered to them.

General Jhiton and Ozlemar are with them, Agrevlari said. *Tonasketal is leading them to the previously unknown Freeborn Faction hideout.*

The canyon on Scar Peak.

Yes.

Can you reach them telepathically from here? Vorik asked. *And tell them that I'm all right and that they don't need to... What are they planning to do?*

Annihilate the faction for their betrayals but mostly for presuming to capture you.

"Storm-cursed hells," Vorik couldn't keep from saying aloud.

"What's going on?" Syla asked. "Who's passing through the mountains?"

Vorik debated whether to answer her or not. He shouldn't have spoken aloud if he'd wanted this to be a secret.

After deciding she couldn't do anything from here—it wasn't as if Wreylith would turn around to help what she would consider inferior stormer-allied dragons—Vorik said, "My people got the message that I'm a prisoner and are flying to rescue me."

"That's... proper of them." Her tone suggested she didn't like the news. Probably because she hoped to turn the Freeborn Faction into allies.

"I guess I'm chuffed to know my brother cares," Vorik said.

"He probably wants an excuse to destroy people who dared leave your tribes."

"He hasn't acted against them in the past, except to punish spies we caught." It didn't bother Vorik that Syla hated Jhiton—given that he'd spearheaded the attack on her people, how not?—but it was a sad reminder of how much stood between them. His fantasy that she leave her people and join his... was probably only that. A fantasy. Even if assassins drove her out of the Garden Kingdom, she wouldn't go voluntarily into the stormers' arms. And he didn't want to wish assassins on her. He wanted to *protect* her from anyone who would try to kill her.

"I hope the faction was smart enough to pack up their camp and leave when they realized you'd escaped," Syla said. "They *should* have been making plans to do that as soon as they sent your lieutenant away with his message. They had to have known he could direct your people back to them."

"Yes." Vorik didn't know if Atilya would have expected such swift retaliation when his people were embroiled in their quest to take over the Kingdom islands, but agreeing with Syla's logic might set her mind at ease. And it might well be correct. He would hate for her to believe her choices had had anything to do with the killing of faction people.

I must go back and warn them, Igliana said to everyone. *And fight beside my parents if there's a battle.*

Wreylith, who was stretching out her wings and talons, about to land in the mouth of the box canyon, let out a fiery breath of irritation.

I must! Igliana said.

Vorik suspected he was only hearing half of their conversation. Still flying, Igliana started to bank around the rock pillar so she could return to the mountains. Fel and Teyla remained on her back.

"Uhm." Syla raised a finger.

Wreylith roared at Igliana.

At first, the orange dragon looked too determined to pay attention, but she hurried to fly to the canyon floor. She landed, and Fel and Teyla slid off her back. As soon as their feet hit the ground, puffs of pale desert dust wafting up under their boots, the dragon took off again.

"Come back after you warn them, please!" Syla called after Igliana.

Flying with urgency, the orange dragon didn't respond or even glance back.

Syla looked bleakly around, her gaze settling on Agrevlari. Her lips pinched together in disapproval. Not so much at the green dragon, Vorik was sure, but at the realization that it would be harder for her to seduce him while her bodyguard gathered the components. They wouldn't be able to escape Vorik with only *one* dragon on their side. One dragon who could carry only two riders. If Igliana didn't return, one of Syla's people would have to fly back with Vorik on Agrevlari. Or *she* would.

If he hadn't cared about her feelings, Vorik might have been glad that things were working out in his favor, but he felt more glum than triumphant. Whether he lost or was victorious in their competition for the shielder components, he couldn't help but feel he would lose in the grand scheme of things.

25

BUSHY CACTUSES SPREAD FROM RED-ROCK WALL TO RED-ROCK WALL of the dusty box canyon, growing without trouble out of the dry earth, even thriving there. A hint of magic permeating the area made Syla wonder if the storm god had found them useful for ingredients in his various creations and cultivated them. Something about the magic was comforting, even relaxing, which surprised her. Shouldn't a canyon near the storm god's laboratory reek of malevolence or at least unstable madness?

The air was fragrant with a heady scent wafting from orange flowers that grew from the edges of the cactus pads—the nopales, she corrected, thinking of diagrams she'd seen of varieties of cactus in her herbalism books. She wouldn't have guessed this was the time of year for anything to flower, but the climate was so different from that of her island home that she couldn't know if it was atypical or not.

Walking on foot now, with Vorik at her side, her pack on her back, and the amphora in her arms, Syla followed a path through the cactuses toward the pillar-shaped rock formation. Fel and Teyla trailed right behind them. Wreylith had already flown ahead and perched atop it. Agrevlari found a different perch, though he'd flown close to her, eyeing the wide platter at the top with speculation, as if he'd wanted to join her on it. She hadn't flicked a wingtip in invitation or even looked his way.

"I'm wary about this path." Fel's hand never strayed far from his mace.

"There's magic in it. And in that formation there. It's practically calling to me." Teyla waved her hand, showing him her moon-mark. "The whole canyon seems significant. And those flowers smell wonderful. I had no idea cactuses were so fragrant. Archaeology books never mention that."

"Do they mention cactuses at all?" Syla asked.

"More than you might think. Ancient peoples found a lot of uses for their parts."

"Modern people do too. I have salves that call for the fruits and flowers. Some of the farmers that work for the royal family have greenhouses and grow them, but I haven't seen this variety before. I'm not familiar with it at all." Syla would have been tempted to take a sample, maybe some of the flowers to dry, but bristly clumps of sharp thorns protruding from the nopales didn't invite one to stray from the path.

A screech came from above, a wyvern flying over the valley. It saw the dragons and veered away.

"The best sky watchers you can have." Vorik smiled and waved toward Wreylith and also Agrevlari, who'd found a perch along the rim of the canyon where he could observe without intruding upon the red dragon's space.

Surprisingly, she was looking in his direction now. She'd even shifted to gaze at him. Maybe there was something else interesting in that direction.

"Have you had an opportunity to practice your juggling yet?" Vorik gave Syla a sidelong look.

"Between being attacked by gargoyles and soldiers from my own kingdom, my schedule has been oddly busy."

"When you ride a dragon, there are many hours spent idly on his or her back."

"Are you suggesting I attempt to learn an entirely-new-to-me hobby involving throwing and catching balls while flying a thousand feet in the air? That sounds like a quick way to lose all the balls someone gave me as a gift."

"That is true. Starting on the ground is ideal since even the most dexterous and agile of people drop the balls a lot in the beginning. Or any time they're trying to learn a new trick."

"The words dexterous and agile do not describe me."

"Well, the juggling might help with that." Vorik winked at her.

"I thought it was to improve my peripheral vision."

"When you do that, it helps with the other things. Vision is a big part of balance and knowing where you are in the world."

Maybe Syla should have sighed and felt defeated by the idea, since she couldn't remember a time when she'd had sharp vision, but she found herself smiling and clasped Vorik's hand. This was a safe topic. It didn't involve being subtly interrogated for Kingdom intelligence. She enjoyed speaking with him about nothing of importance.

"Here's a tip," he offered, pantomiming juggling with his free hand. "Wait until you're home, and stand in front of your bed when you practice so you don't have to bend as far to pick up the balls."

"That sounds more practical than trying to learn from a dragon's back."

"Likely so. I can say from experience that if you drop a ball—if you drop *anything*—your dragon is unlikely to turn around and dive down to get it. I lost my water gourd once and asked Agrevlari to fetch it. He turned, dove, and incinerated it, then said dragons don't *fetch*."

"Wreylith's reaction would be similar." Syla recalled the newspaper she'd been attempting to read.

"She might incinerate you as well as the water bottle."

"A distinct possibility." Without conscious thought, Syla found herself walking more closely to Vorik, her hip brushing his. "I doubt I'd be able to learn to juggle, regardless, without an instructor."

He squeezed her hand, his clasp gentle and warm. "Are you inviting me to visit you at the castle to provide tutelage?"

"I wish I could."

"The flowers smell so good," Teyla said from behind them.

Reminded that they weren't alone—Fel, in particular, would have comments later about the hand clasp—Syla released Vorik and looked back.

Teyla had paused to lean close to smell one of the orange flowers, careful not to brush the thorns.

Movement among the cactuses to the left made Vorik and Fel start to lift their weapons. The oversized rabbits they spotted had huge ears and... were those fangs? Maybe everything out here had fangs or thorns. Nearly waist-high, the rabbits were moving together between a clump of cactus.

Despite their size, they didn't appear threatening. They were not only moving, Syla realized, but busy engaging in... erm. She looked away to give them their privacy, not that the furry creatures cared.

"That's a brave thing to partake in while surrounded by thorns," Vorik said with amusement.

"Maybe they find it adds stimulation," Syla waved that she would continue on to the pillar.

They'd drawn close enough that she could make out runes carved into the side, as Igliana had said. Was this the place where her moon-mark would be required? Would a secret door open in the floor of the canyon?

"Would *you* find thorns embedding themselves in your naked backside stimulating?" Vorik smiled, letting his gaze shift to *her* backside.

Warmth flushed Syla's body, and she had the urge to shift to give him a better view. But sex was *not* a priority now, especially not with Teyla and Fel right behind them on the path.

Actually, they'd fallen back, Teyla still considering that flower and Fel lingering as he gazed about for threats that might creep up on them.

"No," Syla said. "You'd have to pull them out for me."

Vorik's eyebrows rose, and a smile curved his lips. "With a gentle caress? While running my calloused hands lightly over your bare flesh?"

His eyes grew more heated, the smile fading as he likely imagined the scenario. Syla caught *herself* imagining the scenario, her libido coming to life, her body tingling in anticipation.

"While curling my fingers around the inside of your thigh," he continued, his voice husky now as his gaze grew molten, "I'd enjoy your tender warmth, stirring your pleasure with my touch, sliding my finger up into—"

"Vorik." Syla planted a hand on his chest, half embarrassed that he was speaking of such things and half turned on. Again, she glanced back, certain she would find Teyla and Fel gawking at them.

But neither was paying attention in the least. Though Fel still had his mace in hand, lest the randy rabbits turn threatening—or a more serious predator dared to sneak past the dragons and approach—he had shifted closer to Teyla, almost brushing *her* backside as she bent over. She'd opened her pack and pulled out a magnifying glass to further examine the flower. What could be *that* fascinating about it? She must have been wondering if she'd read about it in an archaeology book that covered ancient desert cultures.

LINDSAY BUROKER

Vorik rested his hand over Syla's, his warm palm as calloused as he'd described, thanks to all the hours of sword practice that he had to put in. She immediately imagined his fingers brushing over her bare skin, just as he'd said, and then sliding into her depths to stimulate her, to pleasure her as he had in the wheelhouse.

That moment—and Wreylith's commentary on it—made Syla look up, reminded that the dragons were also potential witnesses.

Wingbeats sounded as Agrevlari flew toward Wreylith's perch on the platform atop the pillar. She bared her fangs at him and growled, but he still dared land opposite her, a few pebbles falling over the edge as his weight settled. He growled back, but it didn't sound that threatening. It also didn't sound *threatened*, though the dragon had heretofore given her a wide berth when she'd glared at him.

"There's something about this canyon," Syla decided, her gaze shifting toward the rabbits and then the cactus flowers.

"Magic," Vorik said. "You can sense it too."

"Yes, but I don't know what it does. If it's dangerous or... I don't know."

"If this is the entrance to one of the storm god's laboratories, I would expect danger."

"Yes. We'd better figure out how to get in and out as quickly as possible." Syla tried to extract her hand from Vorik's grip.

For a moment, his fingers tightened, keeping her palm against his chest. His eyes flared with lust, as if he wanted to push her down onto the path and take her, the threat of thorns be damned.

But he swallowed, released her, and nodded tensely toward the pillar. When Syla walked in that direction, he stayed close, and she could feel the heat from his body even more than that from the sun. She eyed one of the orange cactus flowers. Was their heady scent growing stronger as they approached the pillar?

Her body remained aware of Vorik, and she envisioned pushing *him* against the ancient rock. She could tug off his tunic and trousers and climb atop him, legs spreading so that she could ride him as he held her up, roaring and plunging into her.

Syla gulped and pushed aside the sexual thoughts. She almost ran the last few steps to the pillar and the runes, stepping into the shadow from the overhanging platform above. A green dragon tail dangled over the edge, and growls—it sounded like a whole conversation of them—floated down.

She set her pack and the amphora down to study the pillar. Most of the runes carved into the rock meant nothing to her, and she didn't know if human hands had made them or if the storm god himself had marked the surface, but her gaze snagged on a dragon carving so similar to the one on the back of Vorik's hand that it was startling. At some point, a mark identical to the quarter moon on *her* hand had been engraved atop it. Or had it been there first? And then some blasphemous dragon rider had put his or her sign over it? No, the dragons had been some of the storm god's creations. It made more sense that a pillar outside his laboratory would have one of their kind on it. Maybe it had been one of *her* ancestors who'd come through and placed the moon-mark. Or could the gods themselves have done it? The earth, moon, or sun? After all, the scroll had described this place, promising that a moon-mark would be required to gain access.

Vorik stepped close behind Syla and wrapped an arm around her waist, pulling her into him as he nuzzled the back of her head. Delicious sensations swept through her body, her nipples tightening with eagerness, with the desire for him to pull off her clothes and stroke her with his fingers... his mouth... his tongue...

"It's the flowers," she blurted with abrupt enlightenment.

"I think so too," Vorik agreed, his voice even huskier than before.

He didn't sound surprised. Maybe he'd figured it out right away.

Even if he had, that didn't keep him from lowering his mouth to the side of her throat and inhaling deeply as he slid his tongue out to taste her. She caught herself leaning into him, her head falling back. One of his hands came up to cup her breast, stroking her deliciously.

"We shouldn't." Syla managed to keep her gaze on the runes carved into the stone. The quarter moon and the dragon.

"No," Vorik agreed, then slid his hand from her breast, down her abdomen, and between her legs.

She gasped, startled but instantly aroused. Pleasure ricocheted through her as he rubbed her evocatively through her clothes. Oh, how she wanted to yank those clothes off, but that would only make it easier to do something foolish. Instead, she leaned toward the pillar, as much as she could with Vorik's arms around her, and pressed her hand against the moon mark.

Maybe if her magic opened a secret passage and they slipped inside, they would escape the pervasive scent of the flowers. Then their libidos could calm down. Inasmuch as they ever did. Her body was always so eager for Vorik's touch. Even knowing they were being magically manipulated, she couldn't help but squirm, not trying to move her lower half from his touch as she planted her palm on the cool stone. A tingle of magic flowed from the pillar and into her hand.

Vorik stepped closer, pressing her against the rock formation as he pressed himself against her. She could feel his hard cock through their clothes, rigid with need for her. His expert fingers, far more deft at pleasuring her than she'd ever been with herself, kept rubbing her, stroking her, making her long for him. Even as she watched the moon-mark on the pillar for a reaction, she pushed and arched into Vorik, so aroused that she struggled to focus. And was she panting? Vorik's breathing was heavy, too, as he rocked into her from behind, excited by her movements, her eagerness for his touch. Would he bring her to a climax without taking any of her clothes off? Here with their comrades watching?

Despite the tingle against her palm, nothing happened. No trapdoors opened, nor did magic flare or promise that anything besides an old pillar was here in the middle of the desert canyon.

"Maybe *you* need to touch it," Syla whispered, marshaling all her self-control to keep some focus on the mission when all she wanted was to turn around and give Vorik full access to herself. She longed to kiss and rub him, inviting him to plunge into her, to satisfy her like only he could.

"Yes," Vorik agreed and pulled off his gloves, dropping them in the dust alongside his sword scabbard, but instead of reaching for the pillar, he slid her underwear down.

"Not *that*," Syla gasped as his fingers delved into her. She cried out at the heightened stimulation, the exquisite pleasure. "The dragon," she managed to get out.

"You like *this*." Vorik sounded smug and aroused all at once, pushing into her from behind as he stroked her from the front. His teeth grazed her throat, nipping and teasing her from another direction.

Syla groaned, driven to distraction, and struggled to articulate herself.

"Yes," she rasped even as he brought her closer and closer to a climax. "But I'm afraid it's a trap."

"If it is, I'll protect you. Always." Vorik almost snarled the words. "You're *mine*."

She wasn't, but she nodded eagerly. She *wanted* to be his. This was amazing. *He* was amazing.

Though she was panting and could barely form words, she gripped his hand. Not the one pleasuring her. She couldn't bring herself to push that away. She wanted him to continue, but she also wanted...

"Here," she rasped and turned his hand to press his tattoo against the dragon rune.

Another tingle of magic emanated from the pillar, and did a

slight blue light flare from that mark? It hadn't done that for her. But the scrolls hadn't said anything about a dragon tattoo being needed. Soon, the light faded, and she didn't know what else to try.

"Syla," Vorik said, drawing his fingers away from her needy core.

She moaned a protest. Even though she'd been struggling to complete their mission, to get them out of a possibly dangerous situation, her body didn't want him to stop. *She* didn't want him to stop.

"Look at me," Vorik commanded.

She turned, not wanting to disobey, not wanting to risk him leaving her unsatisfied.

A roar came from above, startling her, but not so much that she looked away from Vorik. He'd untied the strings fastening his tunic, leaving his chest bare, and he'd unfastened his trousers, leaving his cock free. It arrested her attention as it strained toward her, Vorik's eyes burning with fiery lust.

She forgot all about the dragons as she stared at him, her hungry gaze riveted. She couldn't look away from his sleek muscles, his beautiful taut flesh, and his penis, so huge and engorged and full of desire for her. He would never be able to fight with it hindering him. In case there *was* danger, she needed to sate him, to make sure he could move freely. For their safety. Yes. It made sense.

She dropped to her knees, pushing his trousers completely off his hips so she could grip him with her hands as she took his hard shaft into her mouth.

Vorik threw back his head and let out a triumphant roar, thrusting toward her, as his fists clenched at his sides. His response almost startled her, but she took him deep into her mouth, excited by how much her attention meant to him. It even stimulated her, and her core throbbed as she licked and sucked, relishing his taut texture, his scent. It was almost as arousing as when he'd been touching her, and she moved more quickly along his length, wanting to satisfy him but also eager for him to take her.

Another roar came from above, the platform creaking, a few pebbles sliding over the side. Vorik roared back.

Lost in her own desire, Syla forgot about everything but Vorik's lust and hers as she took him in and out, eager to please him, to return the ecstasy that he'd given to her.

For the briefest of moments, it crossed her mind to wonder what Wreylith would think. She'd approved that Vorik had knelt to pleasure her, but now Syla was on her knees before him. But she couldn't stop. She wanted to make him love being with her, to bring him such intense satisfaction that he wouldn't want to return to his people, wouldn't want a stormer woman. Or *any* other woman.

"Syla," Vorik groaned, his fingers threading into her hair.

Her spectacles shifted down her nose. She hurried to take them off so they wouldn't hinder her further and she could return her grip to him. But before they left her eyes, she caught movement down the path. Fel and Teyla. She'd forgotten about them and expected them to be gawking. But Fel had moved behind Teyla, wrapping his arm around her and pulling her trousers down, and she... she was rocking back into him, her magnifying glass in the dust as she moaned and matched his thrusts.

It *was* the flowers. They were making everyone—and everything—lose their minds with lust.

Even knowing that, Syla couldn't stop. If anything, the eroticism of having others mating around her made her more eager to give Vorik pleasure—and have him complete hers.

She took him in and out, fingers flexing around his ass, her own need building again. Roars came from above. *Human* roars came from the path behind.

Vorik gripped Syla's shoulders, lifting her from her knees and hiking up her dress. As they'd been in the cave for their first joining, he leaned her back against the rock. She wrapped her arms around his shoulders and kissed him, wanting to mold herself to him and for him to—yes. His fingers found her, checking to make sure she was still ready, still slick with need, still throbbing for him.

"Please, Vorik," she begged, wanting more than his fingers now, wanting that beautiful thick—

"You are *mine*," he said with lusty satisfaction, then plunged into her.

"Yes!" Syla arched into him as he thrust deep. "Vorik!" she cried as they rocked and rubbed, so aroused that their movements were frantic. The rock was hard against her back, but she didn't care. Every moment she was joined with him was so intensely pleasurable that no discomfort could take away from it.

They writhed and rocked against the stone pillar, sweat glistening on their bodies, breaths ragged, and the other roars faded from her awareness. Soon, Syla heard only their own groans and pants and pleas for release as need and pleasure built and built. When they finally came, climaxing and crying out at the same time, Syla flung her arms wide, baring her chest to Vorik, to the world. Her moon-mark landed on the runes, and Vorik caught her hand, his fingers twining with hers as their sweaty palms pressed together.

Blue light flared, much brighter than before. A brilliant flash came from beyond and all around the rock pillar, visible in Syla's peripheral vision. It disappeared before she could look squarely at it, but a faint *hum* sounded briefly in the canyon behind them.

Panting, she clung to Vorik and didn't want to part, but sanity crept back to her, and she worried again about traps.

"That... was unexpected." Vorik kissed her but also extricated himself from her and glanced at his sword scabbard in the dust.

He touched her shoulder and tugged up his trousers as he stepped aside to peer around the pillar.

Syla knelt and grabbed her spectacles. Creaks and thumps came from above, and more rocks tumbled over the edge of the platter.

Belatedly—very belatedly—Syla realized Agrevlari and Wreylith were mating. And Fel and Teyla... Syla almost didn't want to look, but they'd finished and lay spent on the dusty path, Fel atop her. Judging from the way Teyla was trying to look all around and also giving a nearby cactus a scandalized look, she was coming to her senses and perhaps bewildered as to what had happened.

And the dragons... Syla peered up again. Only a red tail was visible, twitching rhythmically over the edge. She and Vorik were lucky that platter was firmly attached to the pillar, and the ancient formation was sturdy, or they might have been crushed when the whole thing collapsed.

"You'll want to see this, Syla." Vorik held out a hand in invitation as he looked not toward the dragons but into the box canyon.

Spectacles back on, Syla joined him. Instead of the small trapdoor she'd expected, the path now led a few dozen yards through more cactus and to an entire laboratory that stretched from wall to wall of the canyon and hundreds of feet to the back. Sunlight beamed upon crystalline formations, strange pipes and vats, and ancient equipment that Syla couldn't name. At the same time, she seemed to see the cactuses and the dusty desert floor, the same as they had appeared before, but they were faded now, the laboratory more solid and real.

"Since we activated the runes or whatever made this appear," she said, glancing at the pillar and glowing dragon and quarter moon, "are we invited in?"

"I doubt the storm god ever intended for *humans* to enter his laboratory. He spent decades making creatures that like to eat our kind."

"Yeah. But we have to go in anyway." Syla gave him a significant look.

Vorik nodded, returning her look, his eyes sad but determined at the same time. Once they found the third component, they would be enemies again.

26

Vorik held his sword and resisted clasping Syla's hand as they walked down the desert path from the pillar to the now-exposed laboratory. They were, he reminded himself for the tenth time, at cross-purposes. Even if they'd just had glorious sex, it had been induced by the magic of those flowers, not something they'd engaged in because it had been a wise and opportune time for it.

All along, he'd been aware that the heady flowers had influenced him—all of them—but that hadn't made him stop. As usual, when he was with Syla, he hadn't *wanted* to stop. Even now, so recently sated, he found his gaze wanting to pause whenever she fell into it, to linger to admire the determined set of her jaw, the cuteness of her nose, the curve of her ear—and other lower curves as well.

Danger, he reminded himself, forcing his eyes to point in another direction. The scrolls had spoken of danger. He was surprised it hadn't arrived, like a stampede of man-eating moragothi, while everyone had been engaged. The dragons were *still* engaged. No, wait. When he looked back, he could see the upper part of their scaled bodies, now lying quiet atop the rock formation, red and green tails dangling over the edge, touching. Agrevlari would be delighted. Wreylith... might be less so.

If Teyla was any indication, her clothing disheveled and her cheeks red with embarrassment as she rushed to catch up with Syla and Vorik, not all of these pairings would have occurred if not for the magic. Fel strode behind her, looking more dazed. With his bald head, scars, and age, he probably didn't attract younger women that often.

A cool breeze swept toward them, seeming to flow over the laboratory and into their faces, wreathing their bodies. In contrast with the intense sun, it stirred goosebumps on Vorik's skin.

Syla paused. She must have felt it too.

Vorik also stopped. Still in the path, they were about ten feet from where the solid desert floor grew less substantial and turned into what he assumed was an illusion that usually hid the laboratory. Some magic, similar perhaps to the translucent shields that protected the islands, allowed sunlight into that space while keeping out dust and wind and animals. Many centuries had passed since the storm god had been driven away, all the gods disappearing soon after, but the laboratory appeared pristine and undisturbed, like he might have been working there earlier that morning.

Syla looked down at her hand. Her moon-mark was glowing silver.

Vorik's dragon tattoo didn't do that, but his goosebumps warned him of a threat.

"I don't see anything that looks like an orb growing in there," Syla said. "I hope, after all this, the scroll wasn't mistaken."

"There could be an orb in the back somewhere. It's hard to see through all the crystal... shapes. What would you call those?" Vorik waved to the blue, orange, yellow, and pink formations growing up from the dark marble floor of the laboratory, many waist-high, like tables, and others rising above his head. Aisles wound through the crystal formations and along walls lined with bookcases and nooks containing racks of flasks and beakers and strange equipment he couldn't name.

"Workstations?" Syla looked from crystal formation to formation until her gaze landed on a bookcase, numerous tomes inside preserved. Or was she looking at the huge white marble piece of furniture near it?

A rectangular platform framed by columns, it reminded Vorik of some of the lavish four-poster beds that gardeners crafted, complete with a canopy. Made from marble, it was out of place among the jagged crystals, dark floor, and natural red-rock walls of the box canyon. Though white rather than silver, the platform reminded him of the quarter-moon mark on Syla's hand. It seemed a strange thing to find in the storm god's laboratory.

"We'll have to go in and look around." Vorik stretched his sword outward, expecting to encounter resistance, an invisible barrier of some sort. "Let's see if we can."

"Yes." Syla didn't look like she wanted to but nodded and walked at his side again.

He was tempted to lift a hand and tell her to wait while he risked himself, but he knew she wanted to find the orb before he did. Even if she hadn't, she wasn't the sort to hide while someone else took on the brunt of the danger. He smiled at her.

"Do you know something I don't know?" she asked, catching his expression.

"Oh, many things."

"Besides how to juggle?"

"Hm, maybe not."

They reached a straight edge—the start of the flat black floor visible underneath—no, *through*—the illusion of the desert. Vorik blinked a few times, as if *that* might make the image clearer. Right above that edge, the tip of his sword sparked. The gargoyle bone didn't act as a conduit, instead absorbing the power so that he didn't feel it in his grip.

Not until they stepped over the line did electricity—no, *magic* —buzz over Vorik's skin. It didn't hurt, but he braced himself for a greater threat to appear.

An eerie moan came from the depths of the laboratory, and then another cold wind swept toward them, stirring their hair.

"Like a storm coming in," he murmured.

"That would be apt. I—"

"Syla?" came Teyla's concerned call.

Vorik and Syla turned. On the path halfway between the pillar and the laboratory, Teyla and Fel crouched, as if some threat had appeared. They'd faded, though, almost gone fuzzy to Vorik's eyes. The entire cactus-filled valley had faded, including the rock formation, both dragons now sitting up and gazing around.

Can you hear me, Agrevlari? Vorik expected an answer—he could *see* the dragon, after all. But he didn't get one.

He took a step back, intending to show them where they'd gone, but he bumped into an invisible wall. The barrier that had allowed them to enter without trouble had turned into something as solid as the rock walls of the canyon.

"Uhm," Syla said.

Vorik prodded the invisible barrier with his sword. Again, sparks came from the tip, but the invisible wall didn't give this time. He poked it harder. A great flash of light appeared as an invisible force hurled him backward.

Though startled, he managed to somersault in the air and land on his feet. "It looks like we're prisoners until we can find another way out."

"Or a way to turn this shield off." Syla touched the mark on the back of her hand to the barrier, but nothing happened. At least it didn't knock her back.

Warier now, Vorik eased back to her side and tried touching

his tattoo to the wall. Wouldn't something with power granted by a dragon be more likely to activate—or deactivate—magical items in this place? After all, their kind had been among the pinnacle of the storm god's creations.

The barrier didn't hurl him backward again, but it remained solid.

Vorik looked toward the vertical rock walls, thoughts of climbing out coming to mind. Though sunlight blazed down upon them, now that they were inside, the rims of the canyon were also fuzzy, and motes in the air arching over the laboratory like a ceiling made him think another barrier blocked escape in that direction.

"Don't come in!" Syla raised a hand.

Teyla and Fel were heading toward them and gave no indication of hearing her.

"Agrevlari also can't hear me." Vorik touched his temple to indicate telepathy.

Syla looked toward Wreylith. "She didn't respond to me either."

When they arrived, Syla tried to block Fel and Teyla from entering, but the barrier didn't remain completely flat. It shifted to keep her hands from reaching them. They stepped fully inside before she was able to touch them.

"Damn it," Syla said.

"That's not a very polite greeting." Teyla only looked at her for a second before gazing all around the laboratory, wonder on her face.

"We're trapped," Syla said. "And I'll wager you are now too."

Fel reached behind him and encountered the invisible barrier, but he only shrugged. "Bodyguards are supposed to be trapped with their charges, not without."

"Can the dragons get in?" Teyla wondered.

"Since we can't communicate with them, we'll have to see if they get concerned about our absence and try," Syla said.

"Agrevlari should try," Vorik said. "Now that he's... less distracted. And presumably sated."

An embarrassed or maybe *aghast* expression crossed Teyla's face.

"That was so weird," she whispered, glancing at Fel without looking at his eyes.

Fel reacted with a bleak expression. He'd doubtless been as out-of-control as the rest of them, but it probably disturbed him that the joining wasn't something Teyla would have chosen of her own volition.

Outside, Wreylith sprang into the air and started flying around the canyon. She soared overhead, her golden-eyed gaze toward the ground, but nothing indicated that she saw them.

"Does she not see the laboratory?" Syla watched the dragon circle the area. "It appeared to us after we pressed our hands to the mark."

Her explanation was for Teyla and Fel, who probably hadn't seen what had happened. Even though he'd been at the rock formation and a part of activating the mark, Vorik didn't know fully himself. Of course, he'd been distracted by *other* matters at the time.

"Maybe it doesn't appear to dragons," Fel said.

"Why would it appear to humans and not dragons though?" Teyla asked. "The storm god didn't have any fondness for us. Quite the opposite. It was the other gods who looked out for humanity."

"The moon-mark on that pillar might have been added later," Syla said. "I had that thought when I looked at it, that the dragon mark and moon-mark might not have been carved into the rock at the same time."

"Because the gods knew humans might need access one day?"

Teyla guessed. "The *friendly-to-humans* gods? After all, the scroll talks about getting the orb from here if it's needed. If that was an impossibility, they wouldn't have listed it in what was essentially their repair manual, right?"

Another cold and ominous wind swept through, and something clicked in the back of the laboratory. As if a magical device had been activated?

Once Wreylith reached the end of the canyon, she banked to come back in their direction, this time flying low. Her talons extended, and she swiped at the air twenty feet up, where those motes tickled Vorik's vision. Sparks appeared, and she jerked her limbs up to her chest, her wingbeats faltering. She recovered quickly but roared in irritation.

On top of the pillar, Agrevlari stood, as if he might fly over to investigate it himself, but then he turned, peering toward the distant mountains that they'd flown from that morning. Was the orange dragon returning? Agrevlari's tail went out straight, tense.

"We might have company of some kind coming." Vorik doubted the playful orange dragon would have made Agrevlari tense. Nor, if ally stormer dragons were on the way, would he be worried.

"Of some kind?" Syla watched his face.

Maybe she was thinking about stormer dragons too—and that they wouldn't be allies to her. It was the Freeborn Faction dragons that concerned Vorik, though he couldn't imagine why they would bother hunting him—them—down. Unless Jhiton had threatened harm to their prisoners if Chieftess Atilya couldn't produce Vorik.

Abruptly, Vorik wished he'd been able to send a message back with Wise. If Wise hadn't been *unconscious* when he'd departed...

Another cold wind gusted from the back of the laboratory. It felt like something out of the arctic rather than this southern desert. A few clicks and a faint rumble sounded, whatever made the noise not yet visible. The crystal formations blocked the view of the distant back wall.

"Our more immediate problems are likely to come from that direction," Vorik said.

Syla watched him for another moment, as if she were less certain of that, but then also faced that way.

"Let's look for the orb." Teyla brightened at the prospect of exploring.

Face grim, Syla pointed to Fel. "Stick with Teyla, Sergeant."

"I'm *your* bodyguard, Your Highness."

"I know, but I've got Vorik and his sword, and I need to keep an eye on him."

Fel bared his teeth but surprisingly didn't suggest that Vorik wouldn't sufficiently protect her.

"I think you're friends now," Syla whispered to Vorik.

"We've battled together against great enemies," Vorik murmured back.

"So, friends."

"I think he'd still like to brain me with his mace, but I have more relationships with people who feel that way than you'd think." He gave her a significant look.

"I don't want to brain you."

"No?"

"No. I wouldn't mind cracking your brother and commanding officer on the head, but he hasn't lingered in my orbit long enough for me to try."

"I don't think you would find that an easy thing to do. Even our best warriors don't cross him."

"There *are* times when I've wished you would fall off your dragon in the middle of the ocean and stop trying to thwart my plans."

"Ah."

"If you hit your head on a piece of driftwood when you landed, that might be all right."

"Your adoration warms my heart." It saddened Vorik that he had to keep vexing her. If only...

Apparently having no interest in their conversation, Teyla walked toward the marble bed without waiting to see if Fel accompanied her. Once again, she held her magnifying glass, and her pack, heavy with books inside, dangled off one shoulder.

"This looks like something the moon god would have made," she said.

Probably more concerned with finding the orb, Syla waved toward the other side of the laboratory. A few objects glowed from niches carved into the wall and also sat upon the crystalline workstations.

Vorik walked that way with her, but he kept peering past the crystal formations, trying to spot whatever had made those noises. Syla looked like she wanted to avoid it, but Vorik didn't know if that would be possible. Faint scratches floated out to them, like something scurrying across the hard floor. Were there animals in here, after all? Or were most deterred by the tremendous need to mate that the flowers had instilled?

Those cactuses were such an unlikely item for the storm god to have planted. Vorik wondered if—

"Oh."

Syla paused to look at him.

"We think that huge marble bed came later, right?" he asked.

"Yes," Teyla called to them from where she crouched at its head. "It's clearly the moon god's work. There are glowing silver runes all over the back. It's *wonderful*."

"Maybe when the gods added the moon-mark to the pillar," Syla said, "they brought that for... Well, we don't know what it does. I'm sure it's more than a spot to lie down and take a nap."

"I'm going to find out soon," Teyla declared. "I recognize some of these runes. You would too, Syla. There were some carved into the walls of your temple."

"Do you think the special cactuses came later too?" Vorik glimpsed movement above.

Wreylith and Agrevlari were circling the area. Looking for them, though Agrevlari glanced toward the mountains more than once.

"Are you asking if the gods planted them?" Syla asked.

"The gods who don't hate humans. Or animals or anyone. As a nonlethal way to keep them away from this place. For their own good."

"That might be more of an earth god kind of thing. Prompting people to have orgies in order to save them."

"People and rabbits."

"Yes. It's possible." Syla gazed toward the back of the laboratory as another cold wind swept in from that direction. "Are we going to need saving soon?"

Vorik looked up again as the dragons stopped circling and flew at top speed back toward the pillar. Something was agitating them.

He flexed his hand around the hilt of his sword. "We might."

Following the various glows of artifacts, Syla trod deeper into the laboratory. Objects in niches looked like magical versions of the kinds of medical tools she would have enjoyed having in her collection, but she resisted the urge to touch things, suspecting booby-traps. Given the warning on the scroll, she was surprised nothing deadly had yet sprung out at them. The crystalline formations they passed glowed and hummed, emitting energy. *Magic.*

She didn't yet see an orb, but it had to be here. She hoped.

Carrying the teal ore and the amphora was tiring, especially since the container wouldn't fit in Syla's pack. When more scratching noises came from deeper in the laboratory and Vorik held up a finger, indicating she should wait while he checked on it, she decided to risk setting her belongings down by the bed. Busy studying it and murmuring to herself, Teyla didn't look like she would leave the area anytime soon. And the dragons couldn't get it, so it wasn't as if Agrevlari would swoop down and take the items. Vorik... She only had to worry about Vorik. And he was busy doing—

"Stay back," Vorik barked as he sprang onto a chest-high crystal formation.

At first, Syla thought him yelling at whatever he'd spotted, but his glance in her direction promised the words were for her. Hisses responded to him, then clacks, like claws or talons on the floor. Many sets of them.

As Vorik crouched, sword poised, six-legged thigh-high creatures that looked like a cross between a cockroach and a Gila monster rushed into view down various aisles. Antennae wavered, long-slitted tongues darted out, and saliva—or was that *venom?*—glistened on sharp fangs.

Jaws snapped as the giant bug-lizards ran first toward Vorik. But some rushed toward the bed too.

"Climb up on the canopy," Fel ordered Syla and Teyla, placing himself to block the creatures as Vorik sprang from his perch to land on the back of one of them.

The giant bug-lizard didn't buckle under his weight, not even close. It swished a long, thick tail while using its antennae like whips to attempt to knock him off. He plunged his gargoyle-blade sword into its back, crunching through its scaled carapace.

Several creatures scurried toward the bed from different aisles. Fel met the foremost one with his mace, slamming it down onto their foe's broad head before it could bite him. Syla pushed her pack up ahead of her and climbed a marble post. What she'd been thinking of as a canopy was rock-solid—*marble*-solid—but would it be high enough to keep them from the creatures' reach? Both lizards and insects could climb vertical objects...

As if to answer her question, one scurried up onto a wall to avoid Fel as it continued forward. Like a spider, it wasn't disturbed by gravity. Its tongue flicked out, and it hissed as its beady black eyes locked onto Syla.

The unnerving steadiness of its gaze as it looked at her was disturbing. A *lot* of them were looking at her. Even a pair that Vorik had intercepted, forcing them to deal with him, darted glances toward Syla.

At the base of the bed, Fel's mundane mace smashed into more creatures, knocking them back if he hit hard enough, but it didn't break through their scales or stop them.

Atop the sturdy marble canopy, Syla and Teyla crouched, not certain how to help. From their elevated perch, they could see past the crystalline formations and tell that dozens of the bug-lizards were heading in their direction. Syla wished she had explosives she could throw at them.

A huge gust of wind battered at her, stronger than any that had yet blown through the laboratory. Syla would have tumbled off the bed if she hadn't grabbed onto one of the columns. It rose a couple of feet above the canopy, the top open to reveal it was hollow, like the barrel of a canon.

An eerie moan wafted from the back wall, and the lighting in the laboratory dimmed, as if dark clouds had gone over the sun. It still blazed in the blue sky above the canyon, but something affected its brilliance.

Another gust of wind tore at Syla's hair and clothing and almost knocked her spectacles off her nose. Beside her, Teyla cursed and flattened her hand to her face, afflicted with the same problem.

Syla considered climbing down to be more protected from the

wind, but the creatures swarmed the area now, and the lower part of the bed wasn't that high off the ground. Though still on his feet and swinging his mace, Fel had been pushed back against it.

Several yards away, Vorik plunged his sword into the head of another bug-lizard and looked toward them. He'd already downed four, his raw power and magical blade effective on the storm god's creations, but there were so many. *Dozens.* Even though they'd come down different aisles, they were all angling toward the bed. Toward *Syla*. She couldn't tell if they were focused on the moon-marked Teyla as well.

One started up what Syla thought of as the headboard of the bed. Teyla dropped her magnifying glass, picked up her sword, and leaned off the canopy to whack it. Though the creatures didn't dodge or parry, they could take a beating. Like Fel's mace, Teyla's blade couldn't pierce their armored scales. It kept climbing, and she had to draw back to avoid its long darting tongue. Another blast of wind gusted through the laboratory, and Teyla fell against Syla.

Syla grabbed her pack and pulled out the hunk of ore. As the bug-lizard crested the canopy, she took the glowing teal lump in both hands and cracked the thing on the head. Beside her, Teyla leaned in to jab at the creature's eye with her blade.

That proved a more vulnerable target, and the sword tip pierced it, thick fluid spattering them as the orb burst. Syla struck the creature again with the ore, the teal glow reflecting off the polished white marble of the bed. The bug-lizard didn't go flying, but it did fall back to the ground, head and tail flexing as it hissed its displeasure at them.

More creatures appeared in the aisles. How many *were* there?

Vorik must have realized they were specifically after those with moon-marks because he ran and sprang past several, bypassing them to reach the bed.

As another great wind threatened to knock Syla flying, the

darkness grew even more pronounced, the sun now blocked out completely. A black cloud formed in the center of the laboratory. Unaffected by the wind, it spread, stretching twenty feet high and equally wide. Something amorphous and vague but undeniably ugly formed in the center, with a pair of glowing red eyes appearing in the middle. The figure made Syla's stomach twist, and she couldn't resist the urge to look away.

Who dares intrude upon the storm god's chamber? came a booming telepathic voice from the center of the cloud. *All who are uninvited shall be destroyed.*

Was that the storm god himself? Or a magical version of him that had been left behind? It matched what the religious texts said of the gods, that they weren't themselves human and were difficult to look upon.

"The pillar responded to my touch," Syla called over the wind that whipped about as she held up the back of her hand. "We thought that was an invitation."

More creatures started climbing the bed, tongues flicking as they hissed and tried to reach Syla and Teyla. But Vorik had made it to the base and joined Fel. One by one, he knocked away the climbing creatures.

Syla caught him glancing at the amphora that she'd been forced to leave below. Maybe it crossed his mind that he might snatch it while she was distracted, but he might only have been worried that it would be destroyed in the battle. Either way, he put his back to the bed and focused on defending Syla and Teyla.

Who dares intrude upon the storm god's chamber? the voice from the cloud repeated. *All who are uninvited shall be destroyed.*

"I don't think whatever that is has the ability to chitchat," Teyla said.

"Darn." A creature coming up a post opposite Vorik and Fel made it to the canopy, and Syla bashed it on the head with the ore. "I was so hoping for a witty conversation with a mad god."

Though she struck true, the bug-lizard hung on to the bed, and its tongue flicked out, slapping her wrist with burning pain. And the antennae—she'd forgotten about them. One snapped like a whip, and its flexible tip caught her in the jaw.

As she jerked back, fearing the creature would climb onto the canopy and do more damage, Vorik ran around the bed and leaped for it. He ripped it free, and it dropped to land beside him, tongue flicking. Not hesitating, he drove his sword into it.

"Thank you!" Syla wiped warm blood from her jaw and grimaced at her wrist. The tongue hadn't broken the skin, but an angry red welt stung, and she believed the venom she'd worried about was a real threat.

"You're most welcome, Your Highness." Vorik spun to help Fel, knocking aside one of three creatures rushing him at once, trying to take him down so they could climb the bed.

All who are uninvited shall be destroyed, the ugly shape in the cloud said for the third time.

The wind picked up, swirling around like a cyclone, and a force like a battering ram struck Syla in the chest. She hadn't been holding on, and it sent her flying across the laboratory, over creatures and crystals, and far away from her comrades.

When she struck a wall, she hit hard enough to knock the air out of her lungs, dazing her. Even the strap attached to her spectacles wasn't enough to keep them from flying off. They struck the ground and skidded away as more wind blew.

Cursing, Syla scrambled after them on hands and knees as her stunned diaphragm made it hard to breathe, terrifying her. But losing her vision would be almost as bad.

As she rushed after the skidding spectacles, the dreadful wind kept knocking them farther from her grasping fingers. It was as if an intelligence guided it.

The world around her was nothing but a dark blur, save for movement. The movement of many things. More of those creatures. Were they heading toward her? Disoriented, she didn't know if she was going toward the bed or away from it. And what of her allies? Had they also been knocked across the laboratory?

Her knuckles brushed the lenses, and she snatched them up. Something pulsed near her head, and she twitched, lifting an arm in case an enemy meant to attack. No, it was a small crystal, growing up like a flower out of the floor. Other crystals glowed in niches carved into the nearby rock wall. And in that large niche, was that...

Syla reached for the spherical silver orb growing on a slender crystal stalk before catching herself. It was as the scroll had described, the third component, identical to the large outer spheres of the shielders themselves, with two divots on its surface to represent the eyes of the moon.

If the orb was alive, as the text had suggested, might it defend itself? Or offer some magical backlash to whoever tried to pick it from its stem? Glowing drops of water like dew coated its surface and seemed to run up from the base of the stalk, from within a fuzzy blue substrate growing atop the stone in the niche.

An itch from the back of her hand signaled her that those droplets were more dangerous than dew. Everything the mad god had touched was. To brush one might hurt her. Or *kill* her.

In the laboratory behind her, battle noises continued, and the storm god's likeness railed against invaders. Scurrying sounds suggested some of the creatures had located her new position and were heading her way.

"Syla?" came a call from the front of the laboratory near the bed. Vorik.

She opened her mouth, almost calling her position, but now that she had located the orb, should she reveal herself? What if Vorik leaped over, sliced through the stalk, which could be vulnerable to his powerful magical sword, and snatched the third component before she could?

One of the bug-lizards came around a counter and into view, tongue flicking out, beady black eyes focusing on her. With eager hisses, it headed straight toward her.

With the orb on its stalk less than two feet away, Syla wrestled with indecision.

27

VORIK HAD BEEN KNOCKED AWAY FROM THE MARBLE BED WHEN THE cyclone struck—they *all* had been—and now he sprang from crystal workstation to table to unidentifiable object, trying to avoid the creatures swarming the floor so that he could find Syla. Though they were difficult to kill with their solid bodies and scaled carapaces, they weren't the speediest of foes, and he'd only suffered a couple of lashes from the antennae. Those wounds burned though. More than that, his muscles felt heavy and sluggish, and he worried some venom had flowed into his bloodstream.

"Syla?" Vorik called again, worried because she hadn't responded.

Might she have struck her head and blacked out? He'd only glimpsed her flying toward the back of the cavern. The powerful swirling wind had hurled him in another direction.

It was the creatures that made him realize Syla's location. Some were still after Teyla—fortunately, Fel had found her quickly and was defending her, helping her return to the bed and whatever she believed it could help them with. But the other bug-lizards...

Drawn by—he assumed—moon-marks, they scurried toward the back of the laboratory. Vorik sprang past more of them, hoping to find Syla before they did. Especially if she'd been knocked out. His gut tightened at the thought of losing her to the creatures. He wanted to get the components but not that way.

"I could use a hand, Vorik," came her call from the direction he was heading.

"Coming!" Relief renewed his strength, and he leaped from a workstation to what looked like a huge crystal pin cushion. "I have two excellent hands. Very skilled."

That was assuming his muscles didn't grow more sluggish. He hoped to finish this as quickly as possible so they could find a way out of here before they triggered any more of the storm god's defenses.

"I can't argue with that assessment," Syla called back, the words light, but there was a tense—or scared?—warble to her voice.

"No, you cannot."

A gust of wind blasted into Vorik when he was in midair, jumping to the next platform. It knocked him off course, and he landed on a creature heading toward Syla.

Antennae slapped him before he could spring free. He received another painful welt—another brush with whatever cilia delivered the venom. Irritated, he slashed his sword through *both* antennae, then twisted his grip and drove the blade into the back of the creature's broad skull.

Leaving it to die, he rushed toward numerous glowing crystals and artifacts along the side wall of the canyon. Panting by the time he arrived, with the ichor of the creatures dripping from his sword, Vorik found Syla kneeling on the floor. With her tongue tucked into the corner of her mouth and her surgical kit spread before her, she lifted a small tool to pluck glowing droplets of who knew what from a sphere a little smaller than one's head.

Vorik gaped. Was that the orb he was supposed to find?

"Thank you for killing those things," Syla said mid-pluck.

Was that the same tool she'd used around the fang embedded in Wreylith's foot? To extract venom from the wound?

After removing enough droplets to fill the tool's small reservoir, she moved it aside and dumped it out. The glowing liquid hissed and flashed and smoked when it spattered down, and Vorik jumped.

"Is that poison?" he asked. "Venom? Something else?"

Something *worse*?

"It's acting like an acid on the floor, but it hasn't eaten through my tool, so that's fortunate." Drop by drop, Syla filled the reservoir again—removing more of the liquid from the orb—and dribbling it into the smoking hole left by the first deposit. "I first tried to wipe them off with my sleeve, and the fabric not only disintegrated but went up with a burst of flame and smoke."

The sounds of battle came from the other side of the laboratory, and Vorik glimpsed more creatures heading toward them. He strode forward to see if he could help Syla. The sooner they figured out how to remove the orb, the sooner they could escape. Or try. He well remembered that they couldn't walk out the way they'd come in.

"We have to stay by the weapons platform," Teyla called, an exhausted pant.

Weapons platform? She wasn't talking about the big marble bed, was she?

"Those *things* are staying by it," Fel snarled back.

"They're going wherever I am."

"Which makes it cursed hard to defend you. Princess Syla, where are you? Can you make it back to us?"

"In a moment!" Syla called. "I'm otherwise engaged."

"Eyes of the moon, what does *that* mean?"

"Funny he should mention the moon," she murmured.

Yes, the orb, like the shielders themselves, not only glowed with silvery moonlike light, but the craters in the real moon were replicated on its surface.

A creature scurried out of an aisle between Syla and Vorik. Ignoring him, it rushed toward her. She squawked in surprise but grabbed a small vial from her first-aid kit and threw it between the thing's eyes. When Vorik reached it a heartbeat later, the glass vial had shattered, spattering liquid onto its face. Halting, the creature shook its head, antennae quivering.

Vorik drove his blade twice into its back, the scaled carapace crunching as the weapon sank in. To ensure its death, he also plunged his sword into its head. The creature shuddered and collapsed.

"Do you carry magical venoms around too?" Vorik stepped around the dead creature to Syla's side so he could more easily defend her.

"No, that was margroth tree oil. It's an astringent."

"That's a weapon?"

"It stings a lot if it gets in your eyes."

Vorik laughed, more out of relief from having reached Syla's side than because it was a joke, but movement overhead made him pause.

Above the canyon, an orange dragon flew into view—Igliana. Her maw opened in what looked like a roar, but no sound penetrated the laboratory's barrier to reach them.

"Healers don't usually carry *weapons* in their first-aid kits." Syla glanced up but returned to the orb.

Maybe all that magical liquid had to be removed before they could take the thing with them. She'd also withdrawn scissors and a scalpel from her kit, as if she intended to do surgery on it. Maybe she did. It seemed to be *growing*, like a plant—or a crystal—so maybe it would require a delicate touch to remove it without damaging it.

Overhead, more dragons flew into view. Vorik recognized several of them from the cavern. Igliana's faction-allied kin.

Storm god's wrath, had Igliana led them here? *Why?* Had they come all the way across the desert to try to recapture Vorik? He couldn't be *that* important of a prisoner.

Oh, but wait. Earlier, Agrevlari had said Sixteen Talon dragons —Vorik's allies—were flying down the mountain range to retrieve him. To possibly invade the now-revealed faction camp?

Even as Vorik wondered if his comrades had found Chieftess Atilya and her people, Agrevlari flew into view with Wise's Tonasketal beside him. Were Vorik's allies chasing the faction dragons? Because Atilya had imprisoned him? Soldiers were caught and imprisoned all the time, if not killed, and a single person wasn't that important, but... Ah.

The black dragon Ozlemar flew into view with General Jhiton on his back, grim-faced with his twin longswords in his hands, ready to slay someone. Maybe Chieftess Atilya specifically.

Vorik spotted her flying on a green dragon near the far end of the canyon. She was trying to evade Jhiton at the same time as she followed Igliana. The orange dragon must have led them here, to where she'd last seen Vorik and the others. Now, Igliana flew in a circle, her gaze scouring the ground. Searching for them. For Vorik? In the hope that finding him would keep the Sixteen Talons from killing the faction dragons and riders? They *did* appear to be outnumbered.

"My brother came for me," Vorik said, touched but also worried. When he'd allowed himself to be taken prisoner, he'd only been thinking of completing his mission. He hadn't intended to start a war. "He brought a whole wing of dragons. Maybe two."

Syla glanced up but not for long. Face intent, she set aside the venom extractor and grabbed the scalpel. All the magical droplets had been removed from the orb's surface and the top of its stalk, but a couple of new ones—did the liquid seep up out of that fuzzy blue substrate?—were starting slowly upward, defying gravity to infuse the orb with magical nutrients or who knew what.

"Should I try...?" Vorik extended his sword toward the stalk, assuming the orb needed to be cut free. Might the magic of his blade be sufficient for the task?

"I wondered if that would work, but I'm considering a more delicate touch." Syla nodded that he could try if he wanted.

Gingerly, Vorik tapped his sword tip to the crystal stem, not risking an attempt to slice the orb free until he tested it.

Silver white flashed, burning his eyes as a great jolt of power ran up his blade and into his arm. He couldn't keep from dropping his sword as he stumbled away, his back slamming into a crystalline formation. Earlier, the gargoyle-bone blade hadn't conducted magic, but this burst had been a lot more powerful. Blinking, he shook out his numb hand.

"Maybe you should carry on with your delicate touch." Aware of more creatures nearby, Vorik picked up his sword again.

"I'm going to try to soothe it with my healing power while cutting it free."

"It *needs* soothing."

"All of the storm god's creations do."

"Tell me about it."

Wreylith cruised over the canyon, but she was neither chasing anyone nor being chased. She landed on the rim opposite Syla and Vorik and scratched at the edge, her talons strong enough to rip rocks free. They fell through the barrier, clunking down on the far side of the laboratory. A creature that had been wandering over there hissed loudly. Vorik hoped it had been crushed.

Wreylith's golden eyes sharpened as she looked down. From her perspective, had the rocks disappeared?

She dove off the top of the cliff and toward the laboratory but encountered the invisible barrier. Her wings wobbled, then corrected as her belly bounced off.

With smoke wafting from her nostrils and her eyes glowing with irritation, she flew to the opposite side of the canyon, turned, and perched at the edge, peering down. Not more than twenty feet from where Syla and Vorik were, she tore more rocks away. A boulder the size of a cow slammed down onto a crystalline formation, breaking it and sending shards flying everywhere. Several hit the walls and flashed, exploding like holiday fireworks.

Syla lifted a protective arm as one struck five feet away. "She'll kill us by accident."

A yellow dragon from the Sixteen Talons flew toward Wreylith, interrupting her investigation of the barrier. Vorik recognized the rider and wished he could shout to wave him away. The red dragon wasn't an ally of the Freeborn Faction, and his people had enough foes without picking a fight with her.

Wreylith abandoned her perch and flew to meet the oncoming threat. The two dragons collided, biting and scratching, but their flight took them out of Vorik's view.

"I don't know whether to be relieved she won't crush us or worried for her." Syla returned to her surgical maneuvering.

Wind whipped through the laboratory again. Syla cursed as it tugged at her first-aid kit, and some of her small tools skidded away.

As Vorik bent to catch them and pluck them up for her, the telepathic voice in the cloud spoke again.

Enemies have turned my children away from their purpose, and they would now invade the laboratory of the storm god.

"That's a different message," Syla said.

"Yes." After the several repeats of the other words, Vorik had thought the apparition a mindless part of the security defenses the storm god had long ago left, but this indicated it had awareness of what was going on. "His children? Does he mean the dragons?"

"He did create them." Syla accepted her tools and returned to work, using her sleeve—a hole singed in it, as she'd said—to wipe sweat from her forehead.

Scalpel in hand, she risked leaning close and resting her fingers on the orb. Vorik readied himself to catch her if it hurled her away. It flared a brighter silver, as if it was thinking about it. But he sensed magic flowing from Syla's moon-mark and into her fingers and then the orb, even running down the stalk to its base and the substrate.

One of my children remains true. It will defend against the wayward ones and the uninvited.

A thunderous grinding came from the back wall of the canyon, and a hidden door in the red rock opened. A *huge* hidden door.

A black dragon stomped out, its eyes glowing red, and it spread its wings. It looked like a bigger and even crabbier version of Ozlemar, and it glared up at the sky, at the dragons and riders engaging with each other, the vengeful Sixteen Talons descending upon the faction. Though she wore an expression of frustration, Atilya turned with determination to face Jhiton and the others. Blood would soon spatter the desert floor and the magical cactus flowers. If their potent scent had reached the dragons and riders flying about, it hadn't done anything yet to change them from aggressive to amorous.

"Probably too windy," Vorik muttered, though he didn't know if the continuing gusts affected the canyon outside.

Inside the laboratory, the black dragon crouched, maw opening to reveal eager fangs. Since its gaze had focused skyward, Vorik thought it would fly up to battle the aerial intruders. Then, a soft *snick* sounded. Syla had cut the orb from its stalk. As she hurried to wrap it in protective bandages, the dragon's head swung toward her, its red eyes glowing brighter.

"We may get a visitor." Vorik jumped to put himself between Syla and the storm god's defender, but his heart pounded. Facing a *dragon,* especially one with enough power to make its *eyes* glow, would be a lot more difficult than battling the bug-lizards. "Any chance you can take your scalpel and find something to cut that will bring the barrier down so our people can help us?"

"Those aren't *my* people," Syla said, "but I'll look."

The dragon bunched its muscles and sprang. Wings flapping, it flew straight toward them, and there wasn't time to speak further.

Not toward *them,* Vorik realized. Just like with the creatures, Syla was its target.

"Run back to the bed," he urged, shifting to block it. "Or try to find a way out. Or both."

"I will, but you need to run too."

With crystal formations all over, the dragon couldn't fly as directly as in the open sky, but it came quickly, nevertheless. There wasn't time for Vorik to run.

Syla hated to abandon Vorik to the wrath of a dragon—surely, even with his enhanced abilities, he couldn't defeat one of their kind—but he was right. If they couldn't figure out how to escape the laboratory, they might all die here. Now that she had the orb, they had no reason to linger.

With the dark cloud and hideous visage of the storm god roiling in the center, she worried for all their lives. Especially when the red-eyed black dragon roared and breathed fire, the fluctuating orange light reflecting off the crystalline formations in the dark laboratory.

As she ran down the crooked aisles, trying to avoid creatures and find a way back to the others, she risked glancing back. She couldn't see Vorik but, from the way the dragon leaped atop a workstation, one wing snapping the top off a crystal formation in its haste to move, it had to be chasing him.

He must have dared stab it to draw its attention away from her. The moon god bless him.

Vorik jumped onto a formation behind the dragon and came into her view, swinging his blade at its tail. He must have dived under the great creature to come up in that position. He managed to clip its tail, but the dragon was fast for such a huge foe. It whirled and flung fire at Vorik while slashing its deadly talons toward him.

Vorik ducked in time to avoid the flames, but they nearly caught him. The fire might have singed off some of his wild black hair.

Amazingly, Vorik rushed *closer* to the dragon, diving below its slashing talons to reach its belly. He sliced into its scaled flesh, but right away, its fangs whipped down toward his head. He dove between two crystalline formations, and Syla lost sight of him again.

Terrified for him, she almost turned to run back to help, but what could she do? Throw an astringent at its eyes? No, she had to find a way out. For all of their sakes.

Overhead, Wreylith returned to the edge of the canyon. Syla couldn't hear her—couldn't hear anything of the battle raging overhead—but the dragon's maw opened in what had to be a frustrated roar. She'd escaped—or slain—the yellow dragon that had been after her, and now she returned to tearing pieces of rock from the canyon rim.

Was it possible she would claw her way inside by destroying the area *around* the barrier?

As Syla patted her way along the wall, hoping to find a glowing crystal or switch that would open the barrier or turn off the defenses, Vorik came into her view again. He flew, somersaulting through the air, more than ten feet. The dragon must have struck him, knocking him flying.

He twisted in the air and landed on one of the workstations. His sword remained in his hand, but blood dripped from the side of his face, and the uncharacteristically concerned look in his eyes said he was in over his head.

The black dragon glanced at Wreylith and roared, but Vorik must have annoyed it sufficiently, because it returned its focus to him.

A crossbow twanged, and a quarrel flew across the laboratory. Fel and Teyla were back at the bed, Teyla poking at something on the platform while Fel stood beside her, firing at an enemy he shouldn't have wanted to attract. Maybe he felt compelled to help Vorik? Regardless, the quarrel bounced off the dragon's scaled flank without harming it. It didn't even *notice*, instead flying again for Vorik.

"Syla, these are ancient temple runes," Teyla called. "I can read them and tell there's magic to them, but I think they'd mean more to you."

"Not now," Syla yelled, forcing herself to continue searching for a switch. Unless the marble bed held the secret to escaping, she wasn't interested.

More boulders slammed down, landing near the wall under Wreylith. She kept tearing them free, determined to get inside.

As Syla worked her way down the wall, patting and searching, a bug-lizard appeared out of a side aisle. She managed to escape it but had to jump over a workstation and scramble to the other side to avoid a second creature.

The bed came into view again, and she ran toward it. Since they believed it had been added after the storm god departed, she doubted it had anything to do with deactivating the defenses, but more creatures were coming after her. She had little choice but to rejoin Fel. With Vorik in deep trouble of his own, she needed her bodyguard's protection.

Before she reached the bed, a boulder slammed to the floor scant feet in front of her. She flailed, almost dropping the orb.

"You're going to *kill* us, Wreylith!" Syla yelled, though she hadn't seen if the dragon had knocked that piece free.

The creatures she'd escaped seconds earlier followed her across the floor. She sprinted for the bed but, even with Fel and his weapons there, she didn't know how much safety it offered.

"Here." Teyla waved for her to hurry.

As if she wasn't already.

The orb warm and glowing under her armpit, Syla rounded two dead bug-lizards and skidded across the floor in her haste to take cover behind the headboard. Sweat and blood ran down Fel's red face, but he remained their stalwart defender. He'd switched back to his mace, probably having no more luck firing the quarrels at the scaled creatures than he'd had with the dragon.

A roar boomed from the back of the canyon. One of frustration? Syla couldn't tell but hoped there were too many obstacles for Vorik to hide behind for the dragon to reach him.

Something crashed after the roar. Another chunk of the canyon wall falling down?

Above, the Sixteen Talons and Freeborn Faction dragons flew in and out of view, none aware of the chaos below, but they had chaos of their own. Riders that had once all been allies loosed arrows and crossbow quarrels at each other as their dragons dove and wheeled, biting and launching streams of flame. One rider screamed in pain as an arrow pierced her shoulder, and she lost her sword.

The gargoyle-bone blade startled Syla by falling and clattered onto the floor ten feet away. Like boulders, it appeared weapons could pass through the barrier. If only Syla knew how to use that to their advantage.

If any of the aerial combatants noticed that the sword had disappeared instead of landing on what they perceived as the desert floor of the canyon, Syla couldn't tell. They seemed too busy battling each other. Wreylith arrowed across the canyon with a black dragon and a gray dragon chasing her.

Syla stiffened. The black dragon was familiar, and so was its rider. General Jhiton.

Why was the bastard chasing *Wreylith*? Wasn't his vexation with the faction riders? Those he believed had taken Vorik as a hostage?

"Here are the old runes." Teyla touched a glowing silver mark, and it throbbed. In the temple tongue, it read: *Defender.*

Though Syla wasn't the one poking at things, the mark on the back of her hand also throbbed, pulsing in time with the rune.

She was too busy clenching a fist and glowering at General Jhiton to wonder at the significance. She wished she could get rid of the stormer officer, not only because he was chasing Wreylith, but because...

Her gaze shifted to Vorik, magnificent Vorik fighting with all his speed, stamina, and skill to keep that dragon from reaching them, to protect *her*. If not for the commanding officer of the Sixteen Talons being his brother, would Vorik even be her enemy? He was loyal to his people, but they were the general's orders that he was obeying. If Jhiton were gone, maybe—

"Pay attention, Syla." Teyla gripped her shoulder as another eerie wind gusted through the laboratory. "I've translated enough to determine that this is a weapons platform."

The new information pulled Syla from her thoughts. "What? The bed?"

"These runes say that one blessed by the gods and sworn to protect her people might call upon its power. That's you."

Syla peered at the runes.

"Unfortunately, it's not me." Teyla waved to the platform under the canopy. "I already tried standing up there and putting my palms on the marks on the columns."

"Marks?" Syla rose and climbed onto the platform to look.

The two columns framing what she'd been thinking of as the headboard had faint handprints etched into the marble, as if one was meant to stand between them and rest one's palms there. Another set marked the columns on the foot-end of the bed. Or, if Teyla was right, of the *weapons platform*.

"I think that's how to activate it," Teyla said. "Give it a try."

The black dragon roared again as the battle continued above, the combatants unaware of the other threats below.

"I'm not a protector either," Syla said but tucked the orb into her pack with the ore and set it next to the amphora, then stood between the headboard columns. Arms stretched wide, she could just reach two of the handprints, the marble cool beneath her palms.

Fel cracked a creature on the head and jumped off the platform to drive it back and give Syla more room.

"You're a healer," Teyla said. "What more protection could a person give?"

"I'm sure it means warrior."

Even if it did, as Syla flattened her palms to the marks, power surged into her. At first, she thought it an attack and willed the magic within her to drive it back, but it was warm and invigorating, not painful.

Protect humanity, a soft ethereal voice whispered into her mind. *We never meant for this to be, for our children to be threatened by his creations. Use this power to defeat him.*

The bed—the weapons platform—thrummed with power that reverberated through Syla.

Teyla and Fel must have felt something too because they backed away, eyeing it warily.

Deeper in the canyon, more rocks tumbled free as Wreylith

gouged another chunk from the rim. For the first time, as boulders crashed down the wall to hit the floor, a beam of unadulterated sunlight flowed in. With it came the sounds of dragons roaring, riders shouting, and swords clashing—the battle above.

Wreylith, talons gripping the canyon rim, lowered her neck far enough to peer through the hole in the still-translucent-but-damaged barrier.

The red-eyed black dragon spun away from Vorik to look at this new intruder. It roared. An instant before it flew toward Wreylith, Vorik ran up its waving tail and jumped onto its back. The black dragon shook itself, trying to knock him free, but it kept going toward Wreylith.

Did she see the threat? She'd withdrawn her head to claw at the edges of the barrier, trying to widen the hole so she could fit through. Wings folded to her body, she dropped into the laboratory where she was vulnerable to the oncoming dragon.

"Look out!" Syla cried as Vorik, kneeling atop the black dragon's back, drove his sword into its neck.

Power surged within the weapons platform, and two glowing silver balls of energy shot out from the hollow tops of the columns. Instead of going straight up, they hooked sideways and blasted toward the black dragon, the creature screeching when Vorik's sword plunged into it. It shook like a dog and knocked him flying, but the silver balls smashed into its flank, and magical energy and light enveloped it.

The attacks derailed the dragon's flight toward Wreylith, and it struck the wall instead. She lifted her talons and slashed at their foe, then bit for its neck.

An angry roar came from the center of the laboratory, not from a dragon but from the apparition of the storm god. Great power radiated from that cloud of ugly energy. Darkness pushed out the beam of sunlight, and a horizontal line of circular orifices opened on the rock walls on both sides of the laboratory. Black balls of energy similar to the silver ones that the weapons platform had emitted shot out. Dozens of them.

Several slammed into Wreylith, and she screeched in sheer pain and pitched to the ground.

"No!" Syla cried.

The other balls blasted through the barrier, knocking holes into it as they flew upward. Sunlight streamed through the holes, but it didn't help anything. Those destructive balls of energy flew toward the dragons and riders who'd been too lost in their own battle to notice Wreylith finding a way into the laboratory.

Unlike cannonballs that could only fly along their trajectory, the storm god's defenses twisted and turned to follow their targets. Several struck dragons. One slammed into the chest of a faction rider. Yet another ball shot across the laboratory to blast Wreylith.

"No!" Syla shouted again, trying to figure out how to make the marble weapons platform fire again.

With nothing targeting the black dragon, it recovered and leaped for the wounded Wreylith. Too dazed by the storm god's projectiles to recover in time, she only managed to get one wing up, a feeble defense from the usually mighty dragon. Her foe lowered its jaws, fangs ready to crush her neck.

The columns thrummed under Syla's touch, and she willed the gods' magic to come to the defense of Wreylith, to kill the cursed black dragon.

This time, not two but *ten* silver balls of energy shot out. They sapped her of her strength, but she didn't care. One after the other, they slammed into the black dragon with tremendous power.

Their enemy flew away from Wreylith, silver energy crackling all over its black scales. Tail rigid and its back arching unnaturally, the storm god's creation screeched in pain until it crashed to the floor and didn't move again. The red glow of its eyes disappeared in death.

28

As Syla stood between the columns on the marble structure, bathed in silver light and somehow shooting great balls of pure magical energy from it, Vorik made sure the black dragon was indeed dead, then headed toward her. On the way, he skirted Wreylith, who was on her feet again but panting and recovering from the ordeal. She exuded irritation and would likely kill anything—or anyone—that wandered close.

Syla continued commanding energy balls from... Teyla had called it a *weapons platform,* hadn't she? They slammed into the rock walls, hurling shards everywhere as they destroyed the cannon-like weapons that had appeared there, also blasting balls of energy. Vorik approved.

Out of the corner of his eye, he spotted someone in black half-falling and half-climbing down the canyon wall to enter the laboratory—what remained of it. The barrier appeared to be down now, and sunlight shone upon everything.

"Wise," Vorik called softly, recognizing his lieutenant.

Judging by his wobbly landing, Wise was injured, but when he spun and spotted Vorik, relief made him smile.

"Sir, you're alive!"

"Yes." Vorik gripped the lieutenant to steady him, and blood dampened his hand.

A sword slash had opened Wise's tunic—and his abdomen.

"One of those things knocked me off Tonasketal." Wise waved toward the sky, but then spotted Syla and gaped. "Is *she* doing that? Sending those things? One killed Vagnoran."

"She's casting the silver ones. The black ones are the storm god's defenses."

"Oh, the silver are helping."

"Yes." Vorik watched the moonlight-colored balls streaking from the platform and the concentration on Syla's face. One by one, she was blasting them into the orifices in the canyon walls, destroying the storm god's weapons.

Fel and Teyla, both slumping against a rock wall some yards from the platform, watched it warily as they gripped wounds. The bodyguard didn't look like he had the energy to lift his mace again. Even Teyla's face was bruised and bloodied, and she appeared on the verge of collapse.

Vorik noticed the amphora resting on the floor beside the weapons platform, and Syla's pack with the other components had fallen down beside it. Maybe he could have darted over there to snatch them, but the thought of stealing them from Syla, whether it was his mission or not, turned his stomach. Besides, it might be suicidal to approach that platform while it was shooting out such powerful blasts.

In the sky above, the battle had faltered as the combatants realized that what they'd thought was the desert floor of the canyon was a huge strange laboratory. One with weapons that could kill them.

Most of the dragons soon flew out of sight—if they were wise, they would fly all the way back to the mountains. But Vorik spotted a familiar black dragon, one *without* red eyes. Ozlemar.

At the same time, Jhiton saw him. Vorik smiled and lifted a hand.

"Sir." Wise pointed at the weapons platform.

Syla had launched another silver ball out, slamming it into the last of the storm god's defenses. No more black balls hurled up toward the dragons in the sky. Vorik started to nod in relief but was watching Syla's face when she noticed Jhiton.

Her eyes tracked him, and an unsettling premonition filled Vorik. She was a healer and had a gentle soul—he believed that— but the gods had given her the opportunity to slay the man who'd ordered the invasion of her kingdom—the assassinations of all of her close family.

Before her eyes hardened with resolve, Vorik was sprinting across the laboratory toward the platform.

Her fingers twitched on the columns, the moon-mark on her hand glowing silver. Terrified that he would be too late, Vorik dropped his sword and summoned all of his strength to leap at her.

An instant before more deadly magical blasts would have shot out, he slammed into Syla. He struck so hard that they tumbled off the platform, hitting the ground on the far side and rolling away. Syla cried out in pain, and Vorik regretted that he'd hurt her, but he couldn't regret saving his brother.

When they came to a stop, he made sure to come down on top of her, pinning her so she couldn't return to the platform. She slumped under him, her face bathed in sweat and exhaustion seeping from her. She might have wanted to curse his name for stopping her, but she didn't have the energy to do more than groan in disappointment.

Overhead, Ozlemar flew over the rim of the canyon and out of view, but not before Jhiton lifted a hand again, acknowledging what Vorik had done.

A snarl came from nearby. "Traitor!"

Fel half-ran and half-limped toward them, his mace raised.

Vorik rolled off Syla and got to his feet. He'd dropped his sword, not wanting to risk striking Syla with it, but he wasn't afraid to face Fel unarmed.

"I am not that, my friend," Vorik said.

Fel stopped when he reached Syla's side and stood protectively over her. He surprised Vorik by not attacking, but they'd fought together numerous times now. It was hard to try to kill a battle brother, even one who remained an enemy.

Teyla didn't move from the wall but watched, her gaze locked on them. Syla seemed dazed, her unfocused eyes toward the sky, her spectacles askew.

"Get out of here, Captain," Fel growled.

From his position, Fel couldn't see behind the platform, but in his peripheral vision, Vorik could. So he saw Wise sneaking toward it to grab the shielder components. Though Vorik hadn't been willing to take them himself, and he almost moved to stop his lieutenant, he didn't. In the end, this was their mission.

"If that's what you wish." Vorik shifted to keep Fel's and Teyla's attention on him.

Behind the platform, Wise gave him a sky-is-clear gesture and slipped away with the shielder components.

A green dragon soared into view overhead. Agrevlari.

"It is." Fel knelt to touch Syla's shoulder. Her eyes remained open, but she barely reacted. "We'll deal with you no more," Fel added.

Though he wished he were the one who could kneel by Syla's side and make sure she was all right, Vorik bowed, retrieved his sword, and walked out of the laboratory. It was time to meet Agrevlari and go home.

～

Vorik was gone. All the stormers and their dragons were. The Freeborn Faction had left as well. Syla hoped Wreylith hadn't abandoned her. After her encounter with the black dragon—and the storm god's weapons—she'd left the canyon to recover—or because she'd had enough of dealing with Syla and humans.

She frowned at the thought. If all the dragons had departed, how would she and her allies get home?

Glum and full of despair over the choice she'd made—and the *loss* it had resulted in—Syla searched the laboratory, hoping vainly that the scrolls had been wrong, that she would find another orb. But she didn't. The blue substrate remained, but it would take another ten years before another orb would grow. Or, after so much damage being inflicted on the laboratory, would another one *ever* grow?

She sank to her knees, aware of Fel and Teyla elsewhere in the laboratory but too numb to be more than vaguely aware that Fel was standing guard, as always, while Teyla poked around, braver now that the storm god's magic seemed to have faded. Piles of rocks lay all along the walls and covered workstations, the remains of Wreylith's fury.

Syla needed to dig out the figurine and call to the dragon, but she was afraid to do so, that she would receive nothing but silence in return.

"Look at all these artifacts," Teyla said from a row of wall niches. "I'd *love* to take some to the museum back home. Do you think it's safe to touch them? We shouldn't abandon them here. What if scavengers destroy them? I don't think this place is hidden and protected anymore. Is there any way we could take that weapons platform back with us? That would be amazing. You could put it on top of one of the castle towers, Syla, and zap any dragons that dared approach our island. Maybe you could zap Relvin and General Dolok too. Anyone trying to take the Kingdom from you."

Syla rose to her feet and walked over to contemplate the marble platform. A boulder rested atop what she'd thought of as the canopy. She didn't remember the huge rock landing but supposed Wreylith or one of the other dragons had hurled it toward the end of the battle.

Though Syla believed Vorik had knocked her off the platform to keep her from killing his brother, he might also have thought he was saving her from flying boulders. Despite its weight, the platform didn't appear damaged, and it still emanated magical power.

"It's huge and has to weigh tons," Syla said. "I doubt a dragon could carry it."

"You'd have to send a cart with a team of horses. A *big* team. At the same time, you could send a team of archeologists to study this place." Teyla's eyes gleamed as she spun toward Syla. *She* wasn't distressed about the loss of the orb. Maybe she hadn't yet realized they'd lost everything they'd gone on this quest to retrieve. "I could head the team. As queen, you could appoint me." Teyla almost bounced as she touched her chest. "Would that be nepotism?"

"Yes."

"Would you do it anyway?"

"Probably. I doubt any *sane* archaeologists would want to come to a desert full of man-eating animals, lizards, and probably even cactuses. You'd have to bribe people to join your team."

Fel nodded.

"I could do that. I'm good at wheedling people into things." Teyla lovingly stroked a crystal with a rune carved in it.

"It wouldn't be safe to come back here without any dragons."

"Well, *you'd* have to wheedle them into helping. That's your forte."

If only.

"I'm not even sure," Syla started but trailed off when Wreylith glided into view in the mouth of the canyon.

Not too gravely injured to fly, the red dragon soared over the pillar and toward the laboratory. Was it Syla's imagination or did Wreylith give the place where she'd mated with Agrevlari a scathing look?

No longer denied by a barrier, Wreylith landed in the middle of the laboratory. She showed her fangs as she glowered around the place, then growled at the destroyed weapons along the rock wall. And was that also a hiss of displeasure? Did dragons *hiss*?

Too bad Vorik was gone so Syla couldn't discuss their peculiarities with him.

"I'm glad you're well," she said when Wreylith finished glowering and growling and looked at her.

Never had she thought that her quest would endanger the mighty dragon. Had Syla the ability to hiss with suitable vitriol, she might also have directed such venom at the remains of the weapons.

This day has been abysmal, Wreylith boomed into their minds.

"Because of, uhm..." Syla looked but did not point to the top of the pillar. She imagined Agrevlari was chuffed about his encounter, but he'd wisely not stuck around to sing ballads to Wreylith.

For many *reasons.* Wreylith bared her fangs again, giving the laboratory a second sound glowering.

Finally, her gaze settled on the weapons platform. Did she know it had ultimately helped her?

"It didn't turn out how I was hoping either." Syla slumped back against a clump of crystals.

Discussing dragon peculiarities wasn't the only reason she wished Vorik were around. Since he'd flown off surrounded by his allies, she wouldn't get another chance to retrieve the components from him.

My fault, she thought glumly.

You proved apt and capable, Wreylith surprised her by saying.

"I got caught up in trying to slay my enemies and let their minions skulk off with the shielder components." Syla didn't know if the dragon had figured that out yet—or even cared—but she hated to admit it.

The drive to slay one's enemies is very difficult to overcome.

"I usually don't have a problem. I'm a healer. I'm not supposed to want to slay anyone." Syla looked bleakly at the ground, ashamed.

What had happened to her? She wanted to help her people but not by becoming a killer. That was everything she stood against.

Queen Erasbella slew more than a few enemies. You are not so unlike her as I first believed.

"Thanks," Syla murmured, trying to be heartened.

Coming from Wreylith, it was quite the compliment.

You also assisted me today in escaping the mad god's wrath. Wreylith would probably never admit that she'd been in true peril or that Syla—technically, the platform—had saved her life. *Who would have thought such power could linger so many centuries after he left this realm?*

"I knew there would be dangers here but not that they would threaten dragons."

Few things do, but even our kind haven't the power to stave off the wrath of the gods.

Syla didn't know if the storm god had been wrathful or simply, as her mythology taught, mad.

You have proven yourself today. Before, I never would have considered bonding with one with no martial prowess and who thought to sit astride a dragon's tail instead of her back.

"That was an emergency situation, and I was clutching it, not sitting on it."

You are interrupting me.

"Sorry. Go on."

Wreylith gazed at her, perhaps deciding if she *should* continue. What had she intended to say? Was she debating something?

To the side, Teyla had paused in examining everything to raise her eyebrows with curiosity. Overhead, an orange-scaled dragon flew into view. Igliana had returned. She settled on the pillar, probably not knowing it had been used as a dragon rendezvous point an hour before, and watched from afar.

If you are willing to continue to improve your abilities to fight and defend yourself so that you will not be a hindrance in battle, I am willing to bond with you and assist you with protecting your kingdom.

"Bond?" Syla mouthed, stunned.

All she'd hoped for was that Wreylith would help with this quest and, now that it was over and Syla had failed, take her home.

You are familiar with the word and what it entails when related to dragons and riders?

"I know something of the relationship that Agrevlari and Vorik have." In truth, she knew very little and wished she'd asked him more. How had he met Agrevlari? What had made the green dragon decide to link magically with him instead of only allowing him to ride?

Agrevlari! Smoke wafted out of Wreylith's nostrils as she growled.

Maybe Syla shouldn't have mentioned him.

"Will you, ah, not be seeing him again?"

He took advantage of the magical randiness flung about by those flowers.

"He was probably as much under their influence as you were. As we *all* were." Syla didn't look at Fel and Teyla, not wanting to embarrass them, and only touched her own chest.

You are randy all the time with the rider captain. You must have enjoyed your encounter.

"Er, it wasn't... unpleasant." Speaking of embarrassment, Syla's cheeks warmed. She'd thought the dragons too distracted with their own joining to be aware of what went on below. "I'm sorry if your encounter was less pleasant. At least he didn't sing during it."

Wreylith issued a noise close to a *harumph*. Dragons were proving to have a greater vocal range than Syla had realized.

It wasn't loathsome, Wreylith said. *But I did not initiate it. I contemplated biting off his head afterward, but you'd disappeared into the laboratory by then.*

"And you were worried about me?" Syla asked, catching Fel mouthing, "Biting off his head?"

I was concerned that if you died, nobody would arrange the delivery of the agreed-upon livestock.

"That would be terrible. You've worked hard and deserve those horn hogs."

Yes. Step forward and raise your hand. We will bond.

"Now? Is there a ceremony? Anything I have to do?"

The domesticated dragons allow the humans to get naked and chant and sing and paint themselves while their wing mates watch. What a cacophony. It is not necessary. More, it is foolish, since the stormer riders then wear gloves to hide the mark of the dragon, lest others know of their enhanced powers. Wreylith squinted at Syla as she stepped forward, stopping a few feet in front of the dragon. *You will not hide your mark. All will know that you have bonded with me, and, if they are wise, they will bring me offerings.*

As Syla raised her hand, nerves fluttered in her belly. "Will I have to do anything? Besides mentioning to my people that you are agreeable to accepting offerings?"

The bond will allow me to pass through the sky shield on whatever island you stand upon, and I may hunt while you go about your day.

"And that's all you want out of the deal?"

Should I need it, you will assist me, just as I will assist you. Wreylith lifted her forelimb, showing the faint scar that remained in her foot from her encounter with a basilisk fang.

"That's fair."

Yes. The other hand. The mark of a dragon may not supersede the mark of a god.

"Oh." The nerves returned as Syla lifted her birthmark-free hand.

It didn't help that more smoke wafted from Wreylith's nostrils. She told herself that Vorik's mark was a tattoo, not a burn scar. Wreylith wasn't about to light her on fire.

She'd no sooner had the thought than the red dragon's maw parted, and flames appeared in the back of her throat. Syla's instincts told her to leap away, but she rooted her feet into the ground. She didn't turn her face away or close her eyes though that fang-filled maw was a terrifying sight. Something told her she had to be brave right now and show that she trusted Wreylith.

Yes, the dragon said as if reading her thoughts. Did she sound amused?

Before Syla could contemplate it further, blue-tinged yellow fire flowed out from between Wreylith's jaws.

"Syla!" Teyla blurted in alarm. From the side, she must not have seen the building flames.

Surprisingly, they were only warm, not inferno-hot, as dragon fire usually was. The coloring was strange, almost a rainbow as the flames danced all around Syla. The heat grew warmer, especially on the back of her left hand, and magic tingled and made her skin itch, almost burning it. She gritted her teeth.

"Syla?" came Fel's uncertain voice.

Through the flames, he was visible with his trusty mace.

"It's all right," she said. "I'm still alive."

"You're *smoking*."

"It doesn't hurt."

Much. Long seconds passed with her hand burning, but Syla didn't step back, for she also felt power flowing into her, the power of the dragon. It coursed through her veins, mingling with the magic of her gods-gift, making her feel vital and alive.

Now you will not need a tool to reach out to me, Wreylith said. *You may use your power to speak into my mind across many miles when you wish to barter for assistance that takes me from an engaging hunt.*

That'll be handy.

Wreylith snorted and lifted her head, the flames dying out.

"Her clothes," Teyla blurted.

"Are you *sure* you're not injured?" Fel said with a glower toward the dragon.

Wreylith bared her fangs at him.

Fel bared his teeth at *her*.

Unconcerned, Wreylith made a chuffing sound that might have been a laugh. *You will ride back with Igliana, bodyguard. Her youth makes her more tolerant of your human quirks.*

Feeling a warm desert breeze whispering through the canyon and across her chest, Syla looked down. She was nude. Wreylith *had* incinerated her clothes.

"This must be why the stormers get naked for their ceremonies," she murmured and lifted her hand.

The skin was warm and inflamed, as if she'd received a wound, but the pain had lessened with the disappearance of the flames. And a bright red dragon tattoo now marked the back of her hand. There was no mistaking that it was Wreylith.

"It's beautiful," Syla said.

Yes, Wreylith said. *Are you ready to fly to your home? My stomach craves horn-hog meat.*

Syla dreaded returning empty-handed to the mess on Castle Island, where the ambitious souls vying for the throne might already have established a hold, and she especially regretted not acquiring the shielder components. What would she tell her aunt? Or the lord of Harvest Island? She would have to find a way to get those components back from the stormers. One way or another.

You will not return empty-handed. Wreylith looked at the tattoo. *You will have a dragon to help you.*

Syla smiled. That would be exciting. "Can you incinerate my enemies for me?"

Certainly. Just point them out.

Syla doubted it would be that easy, but maybe...

"Are you counting Relvin as an enemy?" Teyla asked.

"It depends on how many gossipy and insulting newspaper articles he's published in my absence."

"Well, we've only been gone a few days, so probably not that many."

It felt like it had been much longer.

"Let's just see what's happening when we return," Syla asked. "I'm ready, Wreylith."

Excellent. Fresh meat awaits.

29

THEY FLEW THROUGH MOST OF THE NIGHT, STOPPING TO SLEEP FOR A few hours along the coast before heading across the ocean. In the morning, a soft mist fell, the sky a hazy gray, but it wasn't enough to truly dampen them or make the journey unpleasant. That was good since Syla was down to one set of clothing, due to the unexpected incineration of her other garments. She wished she had something luxurious and regal to arrive home in, not rumpled travel clothes that smelled of sweat, but at least she wasn't naked. And she didn't let her bedraggled state keep her from mulling while they flew. By the time Castle Island came into view on the horizon, Syla had a few dozen ideas about how to get the shielder components back. She would find a way.

As if he could guess her thoughts, Fel patted her on the shoulder. Despite Wreylith's suggestion that he go with Igliana, he'd ridden back with Syla, saying he would be ready in case anyone presumed to attack when they arrived. When Syla recalled the events around her departure, she deemed that possible but thought her new dragon ally would deter overt attacks. More subtle ones... like assassins creeping into her bedroom in the night? She shivered at the thought. Threats like that were more likely. And unless Wreylith slept on the roof of the castle, they weren't something the dragon could help her with.

I will not be able to enter the barrier, Igliana pointed out. *I am not bonded to my rider.*

Maybe you should consider it. Across the way, Syla had learned that she could now speak telepathically with the dragons, whether they instigated the communication or not. She didn't know how great of a distance she would be able to do it across, but it was easy to reach out to Igliana, who flew to the side of Wreylith. *Teyla would be ecstatic.*

That's a big decision, the orange dragon said. *I would have to ask my parents.*

Teyla wore a wistful expression.

In the sea below, a familiar whaling ship as well as a couple of military ships were approaching Castle Island. The whaling ship wasn't under attack, but it was sailing at a wary distance from the war vessels, even though they were both angling for Sky Torn Harbor.

Drop Teyla there, please, Igliana. Syla waved toward the whaling ship. *We'll find a way to get your portion of the livestock reward out to you.*

A single sheep, Wreylith said. *A small one.*

You're a generous dragon, Syla told her.

I worked up hunger during my... during the adventure.

Agrevlari was that engaging, was he?

Certainly not.

I did notice that your joining lasted longer than mine, and Vorik tends to have... stamina.

Humans are puny. Dragons have far greater stamina.

That must be true. We were lucky that rock formation didn't collapse on us.

Yes. Did Wreylith sound slightly smug? Maybe that encounter hadn't been as unpleasant as she'd claimed. *It was reinforced by the magic of the gods.*

And that's the only reason it didn't collapse under your vigor?

Yes.

Syla patted the dragon, wishing they could keep flying and bantering all day. She didn't want to deal with the mess at home.

The crew of the whaling ship had spotted the dragons and was rushing to the cannons and grabbing crossbows, but Captain Radmarik stepped out of the wheelhouse. He recognized them and ordered his men to stand down.

Syla had only intended to drop off Teyla, assuming it would be more dramatic if she herself arrived on the back of a dragon, but a second person walked out of the wheelhouse, and she blinked. It was Chieftess Atilya, her gray hair down and stirring in the sea breeze.

Will you land for a moment, please, Wreylith?

The red dragon did so, perching atop the wheelhouse, where a tarp covered the hole that the dragons had made earlier in the week. As she'd done before, Igliana alighted on the harpoon launcher in the back, letting Teyla climb off with her pack stuffed with items she'd gathered from the laboratory.

"Morning, Princess," Radmarik drawled as Atilya came to stand beside him. "Or should we say Queen?"

He glanced at his mate.

"We're betting on that." Atilya nodded toward Syla and Wreylith, not appearing surprised by the new tattoo on Syla's hand. "You've bonded with a great wild dragon, something few have ever done. After our sour clash with the Sixteen Talons, we're ready to more drastically cut our ties with them. Should you need our assistance in getting your other island back or dealing with the stormers, you will have it."

"I... thank you," Syla said when she realized this wasn't a negotiation, that Atilya wasn't asking for anything in return.

Atilya had to hope that her people would be allowed access to the islands one day, but that was reasonable. From the beginning, Syla had been willing to negotiate with them. If only the stormers, the tribal leaders and their generals, were more reasonable.

"I trust you won't help Captain Vorik sneak away from us again though," Atilya added, her tone dry.

"He knew you were trying to drug him and was never unconscious. He would have sneaked away on his own."

"Oh? He may be brighter than I suspected. His brother has always overshadowed him, and he tends to be irreverent and insouciant, so one doesn't get a sense of a mastermind."

Syla almost said that Vorik wasn't a mastermind, but he'd just gotten the best of *her*. Even if she blamed herself for that, he'd placed himself in a position where he could win the day.

"He's not dull," she decided on for an answer.

"No."

"I suggest you make a grand appearance at your castle—and tell your people not to attack Radmarik again. He's a simple whaler, nothing more."

"That's right," Radmarik said with an agreeable wink.

"I will tell them." Even if they hadn't been aboard, Atilya promising an alliance, Syla would have done her best to protect the ship. Her cousin was on it, now, after all.

Wreylith bunched her powerful muscles and sprang into the air, turning for the harbor.

"I'm nervous, Fel," Syla said as they flew through the barrier and toward the capital, the mist not enough to keep people indoors.

Bangs and thuds sounded as repairs went on near the docks, in the city, and also in the castle. The flag of her family, a quarter-moon on a starry blue background, flapped in the breeze. That didn't entirely assure her that General Dolok or another outsider hadn't claimed the castle, but at least it hadn't been ripped down and replaced with another family's flag.

Unlike with the stormers, people weren't trained to look up often here—thanks to the shield, their lives didn't depend on it— so Wreylith was close to shore before anyone noticed her.

"Dragon!" someone cried, pointing up.

More shouts followed, calls for weapons or to get inside.

Syla waved, and Wreylith flew lower so people would be able to see her and Fel on the dragon's back.

"That's the princess!" a child called, fearless as she pointed. She was a little older than the girl who'd finagled healing for her mother but reminded Syla of her. "Princess Syla is *riding* the dragon."

Instead of heading straight for the castle, Wreylith banked and flew around the city, staying low, showing everyone that Syla rode her.

I'm not sure if this is a good idea or not. Syla smiled and waved but also watched for potential enemies.

Your people must see you—and that you've earned a powerful new ally. They will wonder and be eager to hear tales of how this was done.

Shall I mention how I first proved myself to you with Vorik in the wheelhouse?

Certainly. Sexual prowess is not as great to achieve as battle prowess, but it signals the worthiness and power of a female.

I'll be sure to have the Kingdom Journal *write an article on it.* Syla imagined Relvin's reaction at being asked to print such a thing.

When people realized they weren't in danger, they flooded the city streets, coming outside to look up at Syla and Wreylith. Many peered toward the harbor and beyond, probably wondering if the barrier had failed and more dragons were coming, but the misty sky was free of other winged beings.

"Princess Syla has tamed a dragon!" someone with a booming voice that traveled far claimed.

Tamed? Wreylith exhaled smoke. *Really.*

Don't incinerate anyone, please. Claiming the throne will be easier with the support of the populace.

Hm. Wreylith did another lap of the city.

"Princess Syla!" a chant went up. "Princess Syla!"

The introvert in her wanted to shrink away from all the eyes turned in her direction, beg Wreylith to fly to the castle, and put an end to the show. But she needed the people to see her, didn't she? And her new ally.

"Queen Syla!" the man with the booming voice called.

"She rides a dragon, just like Queen Erasbella did!" an older woman yelled.

Huh. Someone else who'd read the less public version of her great-great grandmother's tale. Or maybe the woman was old enough that she'd been a girl when people who'd been alive to witness it had told stories.

"This is a good plan," Fel said. "The dragon has a surprising flair for the dramatic."

"I think dragons are all dramatic by nature."

We cause awe in those we encounter, Wreylith stated.

"I won't argue with that," Fel muttered.

Wreylith turned for a final flight over the city and angled toward the bluff that held the castle. Syla adjusted her spectacles and could make out Royal Protectors in blue uniforms lining the courtyard walls and standing atop the towers. It looked like every soldier in the castle, if not the city, was up there. Some of those men had fired at Wreylith before, when she'd first taken Syla from her room in the castle, but the dragon flew toward them without fear.

Two men in the black uniforms of the Royal Fleet appeared on the flat rooftop of an industrial building at the base of the bluff. They pointed crossbows toward Syla.

She swore and flattened herself to Wreylith's back, hoping their quarrels would fly over her.

"Assassins!" someone cried from the rooftop of a residential building with a view of them.

Only one of the men got a crossbow quarrel off before Wreylith flapped her powerful wings and sped toward them, her jaws parting. Terror widened their eyes, and they turned to run for the edge of the building. But Wreylith roared, smoke rose from her nostrils, and fire boiled up from within her.

Don't kill them, please, Syla said. *They're...*

They were what? Kingdom subjects? Yes, but they were trying to kill her.

Fire blasted onto the rooftop, a huge wave of it that engulfed both men before they could leap off. They screamed, but the fire was so hot and intense that it charred them to death within seconds.

Stomach twisting, Syla looked away. She would have preferred capturing them and trying to talk them into switching sides, but... she supposed she'd known that wasn't how a dragon handled enemies.

"Is this still a good plan?" she whispered, catching Fel gawking toward the flaming rooftop.

"Yes," he said without hesitation.

None shall harm Queen Syla while the great dragon Wreylith is near. The booming telepathic voice went out to everyone in the area, and people gasped and stared, as if they hadn't known dragons could speak in any way.

Syla admitted her own knowledge of them had been limited before all this had started.

Queen Syla is the rightful heir of your throne, and I am here to defend her. Before, Wreylith had been heading toward the castle, but she took another lap of the city, her powerful wingbeats carrying her about, an impressive display to those below.

At first, in the aftermath of the men's deaths, there was silence, but then the chant started up again. "Queen Syla! Queen Syla!"

"She who tamed a dragon!"

Are all your people so vapid? Wreylith grumbled into Syla's mind.

No. Let's go to the castle, please. Better to arrive before those who oppose my rule have time to react and come up with a plan.

Agreed. Wreylith flew swiftly to the bluff and over the walls of the courtyard.

Though most of the uniformed men remained, all staring at her, nobody lit a cannon or fired a crossbow. When the dragon's glowing golden-eyed gaze skimmed over them, several men lifted their hands and stepped *away* from their weapons. Syla didn't know if they'd been able to see the burning of the assassins below, but they must have gotten the gist.

As Wreylith landed in the courtyard, Syla spotted the white-haired General Dolok walking out with two armed officers at his side. His familiar scowl marked his face.

Though Syla would have preferred to avoid him, she slid off, straightened her back, lifted her chin, and strode forward. Fel grunted, his knee threatening to buckle when he jumped off, but he caught up with Syla by the time she stood before Dolok. He stopped at her side and looked sternly at the general and his men.

"Good morning, General Dolok," Syla said, hurrying to speak before he did. "I thank you for guarding the castle and overseeing the military and island while I was away." She assumed he'd done those things, even if it had been while he was maneuvering to claim the throne. "During my journey, I gathered intelligence and allies, and I'm eager to tell you more about everything so that you may prepare the military for what lies ahead. I am also ready for my coronation as queen."

She lifted her chin.

Dolok sputtered at her audacity. "You're not being coronated for anything except queen of the dungeon. You—

Make way in the courtyard, Wreylith boomed, looking toward the sky.

Dolok followed her gaze. Every soldier in the courtyard and on the walls did.

Directly above them, flying just over the translucent barrier, four dragons flapped their wings, maneuvering in a tight circle. They were carrying something large and white. It looked heavy. It was—

"The weapons platform," Syla blurted, gaping.

Make way in the courtyard lest you be crushed, Wreylith clarified.

"They're not going to *drop* it, are they?" Syla lifted a hand, though it wasn't as if she could do anything to stop the dragons. "That's a priceless powerful artifact, not a haunch of meat."

As soldiers scattered, Fel gripped Syla's shoulder and pulled her to the courtyard wall. At first, General Dolok wore a defiant expression and didn't move, and she imagined him being crushed. Fortunately, or perhaps *unfortunately*, he realized the threat just before the dragons dropped the marble platform, and he backed away.

Sparks flew from the barrier as it passed through, but it didn't keep the ancient artifact from descending. Since it had been made by the same gods who'd created the shielders, maybe that made sense.

Syla winced as the weapons platform whistled toward the center of the courtyard, imagining it shattering into a thousand pieces. But it was the flagstones underneath it that shattered, shards flying as the platform crashed down. Surprisingly, it landed and stayed upright, just as it had been in the laboratory.

You are welcome, Wreylith said smugly into Syla's mind as the four dragons flew away.

I... thank you for arranging that.

Yes. And you will arrange my horn hogs and sheep soon.

I should be able to, yes. You deserve all that I promised and more.

Clearly.

"What *is* it?" General Dolok stared.

"A powerful weapons platform created by the gods themselves. It is capable of slaying dragons but responds only to one who is moon-marked and destined to protect *her* people." Syla held up her hand, the birthmark glowing cheerfully to emphasize her words.

His jaw sagged open. For the first time that she'd observed, Dolok was speechless.

Chants of, "Queen Syla! Queen Syla!" drifted up from the city below.

"We'd best arrange my coronation soon," Syla said. "The people demand it."

A long moment passed as Dolok looked toward an open doorway in the keep where someone lurked in the shadows. Cousin Relvin. And was that another man behind him? Syla didn't recognize him. Dolok's and Relvin's gazes held for a moment.

Wreylith growled deep in her throat, and a single tendril of smoke wafted from one of her nostrils.

Dolok swallowed, returned his focus to Syla, and bowed stiffly. "We'll start the preparations, Your Highness."

After a long look at the weapons platform, Dolok turned and walked toward the military barracks and offices, waving for his men to follow him.

None of the troops on the wall clapped or cheered—alas—but they didn't glower down at Syla either. Mostly, they looked stunned. Stunned or nervous as they shot looks at Wreylith and the weapons platform. A few men, however, smiled and nodded when Syla's gaze skimmed across them. The military might not be as easy to win over as the civilians in the city, but at least it didn't look like *all* the troops would oppose her. Of course, what mattered most with soldiers was if their superior officers opposed her, and she highly doubted she'd won Dolok over.

"I don't think this will be easy, Fel," Syla said quietly, glad her bodyguard remained at her side.

"No, but you've declared your intentions. That will clear up a lot of people's murky thoughts on the matter. And you've acquired new allies." Fel nodded. "*Powerful* allies."

Yes, Wreylith stated, though the word had been plural and probably meant to apply to the Freeborn Faction as well as the dragon.

Doubtless, Wreylith believed that she was the most powerful and could be paramount in Syla securing the throne and returning peace to the Kingdom.

Yes, Wreylith stated and swished her tail.

EPILOGUE

VORIK CLIMBED TO THE TOP OF THE CLIFF ABOVE THE HEADQUARTERS cave to where Jhiton gazed out across the sea, the salty breeze stirring his cloak and short black hair. Their quasi victory hadn't delighted the general enough to change his usually pensive expression to one of ebullience—not that Jhiton had ever in his life experienced ebullience—but he didn't look as forbidding as he sometimes did. Still, Vorik couldn't resist teasing him.

"You look like the villain from one of the Vengeful Dragon legends."

Jhiton slanted him a sidelong look.

"It's the cloak," Vorik explained. "Remember how the Wrathful Rider wore one? And it always flapped dramatically and villainously as he and his marauding dragon attacked stormer and gardener alike, ravishing women and pillaging food stores."

"How does a cloak flap villainously?" The wind kicked up, lifting his hem so that it snapped.

"Precisely like that," Vorik said.

"It's my cloak of office for the leadership of the Sixteen Talons."

"I know, but as the commanding officer and general, perhaps you could suggest a uniform change. A crown? Nobody finds crowns villainous, even though plenty of the Garden Kingdom monarchs were of dubious morality. And those rulers from kingdoms that pre-dated the Gods War and the fall of so many civilizations? They were *always* doing nefarious things, at least in the legends."

"Speaking of kingdoms and rulers," Jhiton said, ignoring the rest of Vorik's chatter, "our spies say it's all but assured that Syla Moonmark will be crowned queen. It seems you were correct about her."

"Oh? The last I spoke with her, it sounded like a lot of other people were vying for that position. There were, in fact, assassins after her when she departed on her quest."

"Yes, I heard about how you delayed the mission I assigned you to detour hours across the ocean to help her." There was that sidelong look again.

"That was Agrevlari's fault. He'd composed a ballad for Wreylith and wanted to croon it at her."

"Dragons." Jhiton shook his head.

"Ever whimsical. It's good that we caught up with Syla though. We needed her moon-mark to get into the storm god's laboratory, just as the scroll promised." Vorik looked in the direction of Castle Island, though it lay far too many miles across the sea for even keen eyes to see.

He wished he could speak with Syla, though she wouldn't want to see him again, not after he and Wise had taken the components. Still, he couldn't help that his feelings for her remained and likely would for a long time. He was curious about how she'd gotten her people to agree to crown her. Would Jhiton know?

"I figured she could find a way to take the crown if she was determined to do so," Vorik said, "but I don't think she fully believed she was the right person for the job. Did our spies say how she wrested control?"

"She flew into the harbor and right up to the castle on a red dragon who apparently breathed fire to incinerate snipers, then arranged the delivery of an ancient tool of the gods capable of slaying dragons."

Vorik laughed. "How'd she get that thing there?"

"It was delivered by dragons."

"They delivered a weapon capable of slaying their kind?"

"Apparently."

"Impressive." Vorik couldn't help but smile.

His brother's expression was more sour. Since he'd seen that weapon in action, he would think twice about ordering another attack on the Kingdom capital.

"Wait, the Castle Island barrier is still up, isn't it?" Vorik asked. "You said Wreylith flew *through* it with Syla?"

"According to multiple spies who witnessed it, yes."

"That could only happen if... They're not *bonded* now, are they?"

Jhiton looked at him through narrowed eyes. "You tell me."

"I didn't see anything like that happen. Not while I was there. And with Wreylith being a wild dragon to the core, I'm surprised. I couldn't believe she was even carrying Syla about. From what I gathered, there was a promise of livestock. A *lot* of livestock."

Jhiton clasped his hands behind his back and gazed out to sea again. "Originally, I underestimated the princess. I won't do so again."

"No, she's got a lot of determination."

"And power."

Vorik remembered Syla, wreathed in magical silver moonlight as she used the weapons platform. He also remembered that she could kill a man by touching him.

"She does," Vorik said.

"I'm fortunate that she didn't succeed in killing me." Jhiton gripped Vorik's shoulder to acknowledge the role he'd played in keeping that from happening.

Glad his brother was aware of that, Vorik nodded. "You *are* fortunate. She thinks you're loathsome."

"Really," Jhiton said dryly. "We've never even spoken."

"She's seen your villainous cloak." Vorik smiled, making it a joke, but it saddened him that Syla felt so strongly that Jhiton should be killed. He understood perfectly—as he'd acknowledged before, the general had been behind the invasion and assassinations of her family members—but Vorik wished things could be different. He *liked* her, damn it. Maybe he even loved her.

Uncharacteristic tears moistened his eyes. He blinked them away, not wanting his brother to see him be anything but strong, physically *and* emotionally.

When Jhiton glanced over, Vorik looked seaward and hurried to lightly say, "Does her trying to kill you again change your mind about inviting her to the tribe? If I can convince her to do so, may she come live with us?"

"*Queens* don't leave their kingdoms to live with nomadic dragon riders."

"No, probably not." Vorik almost wished that Syla hadn't been able to establish leadership over her people, that she'd been forced into exile and walked into his arms. But that wouldn't have been best for her or her kingdom, and he couldn't truly wish that she were an exile, possibly with assassins trailing after her. He wanted her but he also wanted the best for her, and he knew he was not that.

"I wouldn't rescind my invitation, though, no," Jhiton said. "You and she would have strong children who would be a boon to our people."

"Which is more important than her trying to kill you."

"I might get a little vexed if she *kept* trying."

"She'll probably be too busy as queen to think about assassinating you or even leaving her castle for a while."

"I don't know about that. She's going to try to get the components back, I'm certain." Jhiton waved toward their headquarters, as if he expected Syla to skulk in during the night to do so. "It's possible she'll send someone else—it would be much safer for her if she did—but... she's the one with a dragon at her beck and call."

Vorik thought about pointing out that Wreylith, even if she *had* bonded with Syla, wouldn't be at anyone's beck and call, but Jhiton patted him on the shoulder again and headed down toward the cave. Before he descended, he looked back and said, "I suspect you'll see her again."

Even though Syla would come as an enemy if she came, Vorik couldn't help but hope his brother was right.

THE END

www.ingramcontent.com/pod-product-compliance
Lightning Source LLC
Chambersburg PA
CBHW020925020726
47495CB00002B/352